The Joyful Delaneys

HUGH WALPOLE

The Joyful Delaneys

A NOVEL

DOUBLEDAY, DORAN & COMPANY, INC.

NEW YORK   1940

PRINTED AT THE *Country Life Press*, GARDEN CITY, N. Y., U. S. A.

For
ELLIE and GEORGE BLAKE
Not Forgetting
SALLY
With Love

*When the Stranger says: 'What is the meaning of
  this city?*
*Do you huddle close together because you love each
  other?'*
What will you answer? 'We all dwell together
*To make money from each other'? or 'This is a com-
  munity'?*
*And the Stranger will depart and return to the
  desert.*
*O my soul, be prepared for the coming of the
  Stranger,*
*Be prepared for him who knows how to ask ques-
  tions.*

T. S. Eliot.

Contents

ix

PART II
CHARLES STREET

PART III
THE GREEN PARK

PART I

Curzon Street

CHAPTER I

How Fred Delaney Talked to Mr. Munden, a Poet—and Then Had Breakfast with His Family

---

'HAPPY New Year!' Fred Delaney said, standing in the doorway and smiling at the in-no-way beautiful person of Mr. Munden.

He had switched on the electric light, and the illumination revealed Patrick Munden lying half in, half out of the bedclothes. No, he was not beautiful, his thin pointed face unshaven, his black hair spread about the pillow, his lean body protected from the cold by pyjamas, grey with blood-red stripes, by no means so fresh as they should be. The light pressed on Munden's eyes and he opened them, stared wildly about him, then, cursing, buried his face in the pillow.

'Happy New Year!' Delaney said again.

'What the hell——'

'Eight-thirty. You asked me as a special favour to call you.'

Munden raised his head and stared at Delaney. It was not a bad-looking face. The blue eyes were good, the forehead broad and clear, the chin finely pointed. He looked clever and peevish and hungry. He stretched himself, his open pyjama jacket showing a chest skeletonic and hairy. He rubbed his eyes with a hairy wrist.

'Oh, it's you, is it? Let me sleep, can't you?'

3

Delaney watched him with genial good temper.

'I'm doing you a favour. You said last night it would be the greatest of your life. You have to see the editor of something or other at ten sharp.'

'He can go to hell. Turn the light off and let me sleep.'

'You said I was to drag you out of bed if necessary— that your whole life depended on your getting there at ten.'

'Well, it doesn't. Let me sleep, can't you?'

'All right. But I'll leave the light on . . .'

'No, don't go.' Munden sat up, blinking. 'How damnably fresh you look! It's revolting. You were up till three, I don't doubt——'

'I was,' Delaney said cheerfully. 'I don't need a lot of sleep.'

'Well, I do. . . . Oh, blast! Why did I ever tell you anything about it?'

'You were very serious. Most earnest. You said you must begin the New Year properly.'

'Speaking of which, can you lend me a fiver?' Munden asked. 'Only for a week.'

'Afraid I haven't got such a thing,' Delaney said, laughing.

'Hang it all, I paid you the rent only a week ago——'

'Thanks very much. But those are the terms, you know. If you don't pay you go. Although we'd hate to lose you.'

Munden sighed.

'Look in the trousers, old man, will you? They're hanging over the chair. See if there's anything there.'

Delaney looked in the trousers and found half a crown, some coppers, a lipstick and a half-filled packet of cigarettes. He laid these things on the dressing-table.

'You don't use lipstick, I hope, Patrick?'

'No, of course not. What do you think I am? How much is there?'

'Two and ninepence halfpenny.'

'I'll make them advance something on the two articles. You wouldn't like to buy a Chrysler, would you?'

'A Chrysler? Whatever for?'

'It's a marvellous bargain. Ponsonby's only had it a year and simply not used it at all. He'd let you have it for one-fifty and I'd get a commission.'

Delaney laughed. 'We go round in our Morris—just as we always have—same old family, same old Morris.

Munden looked at him with curiosity. 'I don't understand you, Fred. You own this house; every bit of it is let to people who pay their rent. You're none of you what I'd call extravagant and yet you never have any cash.' He stared resentfully. He went on: 'You're a horrid sight—so cheerful and clean and bright. You're all like that. I ought to hate the lot of you. So unintellectual too. You never read a book, have horrible bourgeois politics, believe in things, in England, beautiful virginal girls, Dickens, cricket, football. . . . Oh, God! You're vile! I don't know why I go on living here.'

'You live here, Patrick,' Delaney said, 'because you get this room damn cheap, it's a first-class address, and you like us—you can have breakfast with us if you want to.'

'I don't need your charity,' Munden said. 'What I really want to know is why you look so disgustingly happy, all of you? What is there to be happy about?'

'Oh, the usual things. Little things mostly. For instance, I'm hungry and I'm going down to a good breakfast.'

'No. Wait a minute. I really want to know . . .'

'Want to know what?'

'Why you Delaneys are so cheerful and why I don't hate you for it.'

'Why should you hate us for being cheerful?'

'How *can* you be cheerful with the state the world's in?'

Delaney turned to the door. 'Here, I've really got to

go. You're properly awake now. I've done my job. Anyway,' he went on, 'the world's been in a mess plenty of
times before and will be again. As a family we're just
like anybody else. I've got the hell of a temper, and you
should see Meg when I come back at three in the morning,
and Kitty can raise the deuce——'

'Kitty's a darling,' Munden said morosely. 'Whenever
I make love to her she laughs.'

'Yes, Kitty can look after herself,' Delaney said,
smiling.

'No. But don't you understand?' Munden began to get
excited. 'You're going against the whole trend of the
world. We shall all be Communists soon. Those of us
who are left. The next war——'

'All right,' Delaney said. 'You go on talking to yourself. I've heard all this so many times. Meanwhile there's
my breakfast . . .'

Munden got up and leaned his long bony legs over the
bed. He stretched his long bony arms and yawned. His
hair stood up on end. Some of it tickled his eyes.

'You're wonderful for your years,' he said to Delaney.

'I'm only fifty-two.'

'You look about forty.'

He was right. Delaney was fine for his years. He still
had plenty of hair, brown and curly. His eyes were bright
blue, his cheeks ruddy, his body tall, straight, muscular,
non-corpulent. He had beautiful hands, and when he
smiled he wrinkled at the corners of his eyes. His nose
was straight and his mouth soft-lined but not weak. His
clothes were excellent—easy, well-fitting, fresh as flowers
in the spring, but, beyond all things, comfortable. He
looked what he was, an active, care-free, good-natured,
Irish gentleman, who might have the devil of a temper,
whose heart was good, conscience easy, sentimental a bit,
quarrelsome a bit, honest, careless, and of an excellent
digestion.

'It's a funny thing,' Munden said peevishly. 'I might get my clothes from your tailor, be shaved by the best barber in London, have a bath twice a day, walk for miles. I'd never look straight from the canvas as you do. . . . Not that I want to,' he added. 'You're the type—good healthy Englishman—that to-day is an absurd anachronism. In another fifty years your type will be extinct, thank God. You're loathed by the whole world. Americans detest you, Germans spit on you, Italians despise you——'

'I'm not English. I'm Irish,' Delaney said mildly.

'You were born in London, your father was born in London, your grandfather was born in London.'

'Yes, London's my city, thank God. And this house is my house. One more year of battle, beginning this minute. Do you know, Patrick, we never thought we'd keep her this last year, Meg and I?'

'Keep her—keep who?'

'Why, the house. Everyone wants her. Dollinger and Druitt are just aching to tear her down and build filthy flats over her corpse. Margraves would give us almost anything for her. Wunder and Thompson are at us every week——'

'Well, why don't you sell her? You and Meg torture yourselves making both ends meet, so you tell me. Get a nice fat cheque for her and live in the country where you belong. She's bound to go sooner or later. Everything's going. Nothing but shops here soon. You can hear Shepherd Market's dying groans now if you listen.'

'We'll keep her, we'll keep her!' Delaney cried. 'Do you know Delaneys have lived in this house for two hundred and fifty years? Do you know the William and Mary clock in our dining-room has been on that same Adam fireplace for nearly two hundred years?'

'Well, what of it?' said Munden contemptuously. 'Isn't that just what's wrong with you? You and your clocks! Your William and Mary world is done for, completely finished, and the sooner it's buried the better. There's no British aristocracy any more, thank God. There's no leisure, no money, no old culture, no beautiful England. There's a new raw world, with every man for himself and all of us living under the shadow of imminent death. That tickles a man's vitals, *that's* something to watch and share in—the whole of civilization going down together with a crash-bang. That's truth, that's reality, *that's poetry!*'

Munden was quite excited now and was walking about the room, tossing his head and hugging his meagre body with his long arms.

'I've got you out of bed anyway,' said Delaney. He turned at the door for one last word. 'As to the end of civilization, what rot you poor fellows talk! Civilization doesn't end like that. There are changes, of course, but nothing that's ever happened in a place dies. The history in this house is deathless. Anyway Meg and I are going to keep it, save it for another year of its lovely life if we ourselves die in the process.'

'Yes, you stuff it with decaying bodies and call that life. "Going, going, gone, gentlemen!" The British aristocracy! Who wants to watch the last agonies, catch the final groan, the wheezy whimper, the faint whistle through the air as the life expires! By God, that's good!'

Munden wheeled round. 'There's stuff for a poem there!'

'There's stuff for a poem,' Delaney said, 'in every inch of the ground from Piccadilly Circus to Hyde Park Corner. Isn't it pleasant to think, Patrick, of how, not very long ago as time is, the Anglo-Saxons knew this very place where we are as Bulinga-Fen, a horrible marshy swamp? Do you know that round Buckingham Palace the ground is still water-logged?' As Delaney worked himself up a faint touch of brogue could be caught. Munden had moved into the bathroom, and Delaney came to the other side of the bed and began to shout. 'Yes, and think of Hay Hill where the Prince Regent was robbed once—Aye Hill it is really—the Aye Bourne, and so you get Tyburn. Well, there was a stream ran all the way down from Hampstead through Marylebone, across Oxford Street, Stratford Place, lower part of Brook Street, Bruton Mews to the foot of Hay Hill. It ran through May Fair and entered the Green Park in the hollow of Piccadilly (there was a stone bridge over it). Then on, under Buckingham Palace to the Thames. All the way from Hampstead heights to the Thames. It's still running. The Early Britons bathed in it and you can still see a trickle of it under the ventilators of Green Park. The Aye Bourne, the meadowlands of Mayfair, the milkmaids' song where the Ritz is, the reaper whistling in Half Moon Street, hares coursed down Bond Street——'

'Oh, damn and blast!' Munden said. 'What did I use a new razor blade for?'

'And then,' continued Delaney, who, his bright eyes shining, had advanced to the bathroom door (he must raise his voice now against the running bath-water). 'What about Old Q? He would sit with his muffs and his stockings from Paris and his three-cornered hat in his Piccadilly window ogling the women, his head shaded by a parasol, held by a powdered footman—or old General Blücher, sitting in an armchair on the top of a flight of steps at the hall door, smoking a pipe and acknowledging the salutations of the passer-by? Or the crowd breaking the windows of Apsley House and learning that Wellington's Duchess lay dead inside and going quietly away, or Palmerston riding his horse every morning down Piccadilly to the House of Commons . . . and who started it all? Do you know that, Pat? Ever heard of Robert Baker? He was a tailor, my lad, who in 1615 was rated at twenty pence for ten acres of agricultural land behind the King's Mews at the Town's End. That started it all

round here, for the King's Mews went from Trafalgar
Square to the Haymarket, and Mr. Baker, tailor, built
many houses and one of them was called "Piccadilly."
There his residence was at the corner of Windmill Street,
and perhaps they were mocking the tailor for setting himself up in the world and his house was a nickname after
a ruff or collar called "Pickadel" . . .'

Munden raised his face from the bath in which he was
now lying. 'My dear Fred, you may be my landlord, but
that's no reason at all why you should also be my school-
master. . . .'

'And then there's Baroness Burdett-Coutts' white cock-
atoo which my father used to see hanging every day inside
the window overlooking Green Park. A mob of rioters
stopped in the street once to argue whether it was real
or sham and, having stopped, they raised a cheer for the
Baroness and forgot the riot.'

'And was it real?' asked Munden.

'No. It was sham.'

'Well, that's enough. If you won't lend me five quid,
clear out. Only a week, mind.'

'Afraid not,' Delaney sighed. 'Meg will be thinking
I've overslept. Cheer up, Patrick. The editor will take
your articles, I don't doubt. I read one of them somewhere
last week saying that any writers to-day who are not
Communists should be ashamed of themselves. Why
shouldn't writers be what they happen to be? Why this
sheep and goat division by politics?'

'Don't you begin to talk about literature, Fred. I suppose there's no one in London knows less about it than
you do.'

'Well, I can't read your poetry if that's what you
mean,' said Delaney.

'It isn't written for you.'

'Who is it written for?'

Munden grinned. 'Damned if I know,' he said.

Fred Delaney went on down to his breakfast.

Patrick Munden's attic rooms were at the top of the house, then came the flat of Lady Helen Pake and Lady Millie Pake, then the flat of the Honourable 'Smoke' Pullet and 'Dodie' Pullet, his wife. Lastly, on the ground floor, was the abiding-place of the Delaneys themselves.

So he must, to reach his breakfast, descend from the top to the bottom of the house—must descend, after leaving Munden's attic, by the great staircase itself. It always amused them to call it that, although in fact it was not so very large—only 'quite, quite too beautiful,' as Millie Pake, sighing gently, used to murmur. They had cleverly—when, in 1930, the great 'conversion' had taken place—managed without disturbing the staircase. 'Like a piece of music,' their friend Connie Beaminster always said it was. Perhaps it was. As, from below, you looked upwards and saw it turn the corner the rhythm of its movement was musical, and the dark deep patina of the wood, exquisitely simple, profoundly right, was like a Palestrina tune that repeats itself and repeats, but never too often. 'Rather rot,' Fred Delaney thought, 'comparing all these things with one another. A staircase is a staircase.'

But, although he was almost running down, he yet had time to reflect that he was glad (and proud too) that they had been able to keep it as it was. That 'conversion' time had been terrible, dividing the big rooms into little ones without destroying too fearfully their character, putting in the baths, the kitchenettes. Poor house, poor house! It had seemed when the work was in progress, as though a blow had been struck at its very heart; but that young architect, Mortimer, how clever he had been! and how tremendous his bill had been too! Well, no matter—it was all paid for by now, and so long as Munden and the dear old Pakes and the Pullets paid up at the proper time ends were just met and the house was saved.

The day would come when, his ship sailing into port, he would turn them out and restore the house to its own true life again; then Bullock should be master, and to his sons in their turn the house should be handed on. . . .

Whistling, he had reached the door of his own particular dining-room.

Before we go inside with him a word ought to be said about the Delaneys; Margaret—Meg—Mrs. Delaney, her son Bullock, her daughter Kitty.

Meg Delaney was at this time a tall, rather stout, magnificent middle-aged lady who looked, in her more dishevelled moments, like a gipsy fortune-teller at the Derby. Sometimes her raven-black hair was beautifully dressed and her clothes superb. Because of her black hair and high colouring she could wear clothes of gold and orange and crimson. When, altogether at her grandest, she entered a ballroom or was a late guest at a fine party (she was always unpunctual) everyone gasped. She was better than the Queen of Sheba. Her uncle, Lord Renys, a little horsy man, full of oaths, had, when alive, been so proud of her that, if he had had any money, he would have showered her with gifts. But most people adored her even when they were most enraged with her.

She had always had in her a burning fire of happiness —happiness often enough without rhyme or reason. Sometimes this fire died down very low and then she would cry: 'My God, why, oh, why was I ever born!' Her tempers were as prodigious as evanescent, her generosities absurdly lavish and sometimes disastrous. She was altogether honest, loyal, courageous and indiscreet. Her behaviour was extravagant and vexing.

But this happiness that she felt and was quite unable to account for, gave her a kind of radiance; it was a happiness entirely without selfishness. She made friends on the instant with anybody—on buses, trains, in shops.

Beggars in the street always caught her. You might tell her again and again that they were rolling in riches and anyway drank what she gave them—it made no difference. She had always been as poor as a rat herself: her father, Captain Wendover, 'Mumps' Wendover, had lived by precarious gambling on the Continent, attended by a succession of beautiful ladies. Her mother having died when Meg Wendover was six, Meg Wendover had kicked herself up into life rather than grown into it. She adored Delaney her husband and her two children, but preserved, with all her impetuosity, warmth of heart, friendliness, a curious, unstained independence.

They were perhaps rather naïve and unsophisticated, these Delaneys; many people thought so and patronized them heartily. Kitty and Bullock had something of this same *naïveté*.

Kitty, nineteen years of age, was, everyone said, 'very sweet.' She disliked intensely this description of herself. What she wanted to be was strange, austere, remote, but gaiety would keep breaking in. She was tall and slight, dark in colouring like her mother, with very bright eyes, but not really beautiful because her nose was snub. Unlike her mother, she was neat and quietly dressed. She was not clever, read but little, cared nothing for music or painting or (the craze at this time in her set) current politics or social economy. She was neither Communist nor Fascist, but tried to listen seriously when her friends ardently discussed these things. She had hosts of friends and was constantly made love to. She was as free in speech and knowledge sexually as were all her friends, but remained virginal, apart, in such matters. One thing about her that her friends thought odd was that she was rigidly teetotal, not from any principles but because she detested the taste of liquor. When a man kissed her she did not resist, but, in some fashion, conveyed to him that he would find someone else more amusing.

She had, of course, very little money but managed cleverly. At present the strongest instinct developed in her was the maternal. She was passionately interested in people, and anyone who was in trouble came to her chiefly because she was never bored and had a practical mind. She was always on the side of the underdog, often very unwisely. She could be impetuous like her mother and then, quite unexpectedly, calm, practical, reserved. She supposed she would have to find a job, but *which* job was the question. Her only real gifts lay in her relations with people. Some of her friends thought that she would be excellent at Girls' Clubs and such. But she knew that she would not be good because as soon as anything was organized she lost her interest in it.

Behind her gaiety, love of life, busy days, devotion to her family, was a private never-expressed wonder and expectation—something was coming, something *must* be coming, a great event that would, in one instant, change everything. What this event would be she had no idea.

Her brother, Bullock, was in one particular a great disappointment. He had been a small stocky boy, a useful scrum-half at King's School, Canterbury, where he had received his nickname of Bullock. (His real name was Stephen.) He had then gone to Oxford, been cox in his College's first boat, and, to everyone's surprise, had not grown an inch. He had never grown any more and was so short that it would have been ludicrous had he not been broad-shouldered and sturdy-legged. He had a round merry face and was immaculate in his appearance. He had a deep voice rather like his mother's and the blue eyes of his father.

He made a very small and precarious income by writing 'funny bits' for *Punch* and other publications. He had two gods at whose shrine he worshipped: Surtees and Mr. P. G. Wodehouse. He liked almost every girl in sight but no girl in particular. He would sit, with his short legs

crossed, thinking, then suddenly slap his knee, cry aloud
'By Jove, that's good!' whip out a pocket-book and write
something down. He worshipped his sister, owned a
dachshund called Endless to whom he confided many of
his best witticisms; he found most people extraordinarily
funny. Especially poets like Munden seemed to him excruciating, but he had learned that to laugh in people's
faces hurt their feelings, so he would stare, his face very
grave, his eyes puckered up, struggling to be polite. He
had beautiful manners. To old ladies especially he was
quite old-world in his courtesy. Like all the Delaneys he
was very happy-go-lucky and refused to be excited when
Mussolini was rude to his country or Hitler talked about
gun-fodder. He kept his small bedroom as neat as a pin
and was apt to be indignant if anyone touched his possessions. He was always busy from morning to night and
would comment in an exaggerated way on quite ordinary
things like the state of the weather, an accident with the
Morris or an incident at his Club.

When Delaney stood inside the room and looked at
his family he felt, as he always did on such occasions, a
deep affection. The room itself with its cream-coloured
walls, the fireplace, the William and Mary clock, the
pictures, two Rowlandsons, a large portrait over the fireplace of his grandfather, a fine merry gentleman in a very
decorative uniform, his grandmother, an old lady with
twinkling eyes, her black corkscrew curls hanging from
under a lace cap, a Wilson landscape, the very good Chip-
pendale chairs, the sideboard with the silver breakfast
dishes, the dark plum-coloured window curtains, the fire
leaping with a kind of eagerness as though it had never
been a fire before and had had no idea what an amusing
thing it would prove to be, Endless the dachshund, his
black beady eyes fixed in a kind of trance on his master;
his family—Kitty, as always officiating, pouring out the
coffee, laughing at something her mother had just said,

Bullock at the sideboard lifting up the silver covers to
see what was there; and Meg—Meg herself—in a loose
morning-gown of some dark purple with gold braid at the
neck and wrists, a costume that would have seemed tawdry
on most women but looked exactly right on her, her black
hair piled high on her head (she would not dream of cutting, clipping, bobbing, waving, cropping), her long white
hands with the rings that she loved, examining her letters,
talking, laughing, swearing, reminiscing, despairing, exulting. . . . He looked at her and thought how, early
that same morning, she had lain in his arms and been like
a little child, rubbing her cheek against his, enchanting
him with those long slow kisses that were so peculiarly
hers. For he had known many, many women in his time
and there had never been any one like Meg—no one
like Meg for comradeship, gaiety, sensuality, honesty,
humour, and that final necessity in life, freedom of soul
both given and taken when life demanded it.

She heard the door close and looked up. 'You're late,
disgracefully late. We are all finished. Here's a letter
from Barty Perrin and he has the cheek to ask for a
meal next Friday. He doesn't like us, but he'd go anywhere rather than pay for his own food. . . .'

Delaney went over and kissed his daughter. 'Darling,
how are you? Did you sleep beautifully? . . . Oh, Barty
isn't a bad sort but he hasn't a bean. He worships you,
but you're so unkind to him. Yes, I'm late. I went up to
get Patrick out of bed and he kept me talking. . . .'

'And,' Meg went on, 'here's a letter from old Alice
Pomery. Why, she must be ninety if she's a day! I can
remember her perfectly well at Nice, that time Father
won such a lot at the tables and rented that absurd house
in the Rue de—Rue de *what* was its name? Never mind.
It was a house like a pair of pink stays set up on end—
all ribs. We had the most enormous parties. I used to
come down for dessert and old men covered with scent

used to pinch my legs. I remember Alice perfectly well. She was a little woman with a face like a pretty pig and she had a French poodle that I adored. She was married then to old Lord Worgan and when he tried to kiss her she'd hold her head back and say "Non. Non. Pas aujourd'hui." She liked to talk the most excruciating French and no one knew why, and he ran away with a Salvation Army girl from Liverpool or somewhere. Extraordinary how I remember that house. I was supposed to share a room right at the top with a French governess whom Father had engaged, but she was always sleeping with some man or other, so I'd be alone and—terrified! My God, but I was terrified! The house used to shake as though it had an ague, and there were rats. I saw one once, nibbling at the wood of one of the chairs. You didn't know rats did that, did you, darling? And the whole place smelt of patchouli. There was dust everywhere and plants in pots, dead as anything. . . .'

She stopped quite suddenly and stared at her husband. 'How beautiful you are, Fred! So fresh and cool. Give me a kiss, darling.'

Fred kissed her. Her warm arm lay against his cheek.

Then he remarked: 'It's New Year's Day.' No one said anything, so he repeated it: 'It's New Year's Day.'

Kitty smiled at him over the coffee. 'Of course, darling, we know that. I was with the Whartons at Quaglino's and we drank the New Year in over and over again.' She wrinkled her forehead. 'Nice place. Nice people— but I don't know. I agree with Endless. Breakfast's better than supper.'

'Why, if that's *all* you've got to say about the New Year! Don't you realize? We've kept the house for another year—and now we've got to keep it for a year more! Caesar asked for a rise last night—I'm afraid he'll have to go.'

Bullock lifted his face from his plate. 'Caesar *go*,

Father? Oh, impossible! We'll never get anyone as good again! Why, I'd rather give him what I make out of my writing. I would really.'

Delaney shook his head. 'It's all very well. Give Caesar more and then the General will want more and then everything topples over!'

Meg tore off her two diamond rings and pushed them beside Delaney's plate.

'Sell these, darling,' she said in her richest contralto. This was a gesture she'd often made before. They all laughed, and Endless, who realized that excitement was in the air, gave a series of short staccato barks.

'No, it's all very well,' Fred Delaney went on. 'Patrick says we're fools to hold on to the house as we do when we could get a nice fat sum and live comfortably in Sussex or somewhere. But he doesn't understand. He knows nothing about the past. He's no feeling for London or any place. He's as detached as a bird in the air. All he thinks of is his beastly unintelligible poetry. . . .'

Meg caught her husband's hand and held it fast.

'It's all right, darling. You shall have your London. You shall have your house—even though I have to sell my body to keep it for you. That's what Bridget is always saying: "I'd sell my body to give Harry what he wants." So silly—no one would give her a penny for her old body. But what *I* want to know'—here she leaned her firm bosom right over the table, her purple robe floating about her—'is—what does Caesar want a rise for? We pay him nobly—nobly! *Don't* we pay him nobly, Fred? You have all those things in your head. *What* do we pay him and why does he want a rise?'

'We pay him,' Delaney said, 'well, I don't know about nobly. But quite enough. Of course he says he will stay with us even if we pay him nothing at all. But it's his mother. She can't ever forget she was lodge-keeper at Wintersmoon. She's the greatest old boor the world has

ever known, and Caesar says she has neuritis and he has
to buy a lot of things for her.'

'Pay him! Pay him!' Meg cried. 'Raise his wages.
We'll raise the rent on the Pullets.'

'You know we can't, darling. It's a miracle they pay
us as it is. *How* they live I can't imagine.'

'They were at Quaglino's last night,' Kitty remarked.
'Looking as swell as anything. Dodie was as near nude
as not to matter, but what she *did* have on was lovely.
Must have cost her a fortune. Two wisps of something
and a silver band. They danced together all the evening.'

'Raise their rent,' Meg said. 'Then they'll go and we'll
get somebody else. "Smoke" Pullet always frightens me.
One day he'll be desperate. I can see it growing behind
his eyes. They're nice. I like them. But I don't want their
climax here. You know, children, this is a happy house.
It is really. There isn't a soul inside it's got a farthing—
all the same it's a *darling* house, a *darling* house. I never
was so happy anywhere.'

Bullock, who had finished his breakfast, came from the
fire and laid his cheek for a moment against his mother's.

'Sweetheart, it isn't the house that's happy, it's you.
You really are a radiant woman.'

'I know.' Delaney looked at them all. 'Patrick says
we're revolting. He says we're selfish, self-centred, behind the times. The world is falling, falling. Civilization
is going out with a bang. And here we are happy, contented.'

'And what did *you* say?' Kitty asked.

'*I* said that yes, we *were* happy. We had small minds
and were pleased with small things. I said, too, that the
world has often fallen to pieces before but nevertheless
the seasons returned punctually and were charming at
each return, that our digestions were good, and we
couldn't be called the rich mocking the poor because
there was probably no one in all London poorer than

we were. All the same, perhaps we're smug.' He looked
at Meg and laughed. 'Darling, are you smug?'

She was slipping her diamond rings on and off her
fingers. She looked up aimlessly.

'Am I? I don't know what I am. Who knows what
they are anyway?'

And then the door opened.

First there was Caesar. Caesar's real name was Rudge
and he was butler, footman, messenger boy, shoe-cleaner,
gossip and friend to the Delaney family. He was known
also as the Dickens character, being a remarkable combination of Weller, Pickwick, Poor Joe, Traddles, Mark
Tapley and now and again (Delaney said) Silas Wegg,
all these raised on a basis of Cockney. He had been in
service from birth, his mother being lodge-keeper at
Wintersmoon in the days of the old Duke of Romney.
He had been simply no age at all when he had helped in
the pantry, and then in cocked hat and gaiters sat in the
back of the trap that went to the station for luggage, and
then (wonderful promotion) had been the Duke's own
body-servant under Sellars (how deeply he had loathed
Sellars! how truly he had worshipped the old white-haired
Duke!).

Then had come changed times and Wildherne Poole
had married, the old Duke had died, hard days had followed. Wintersmoon had been closed for a long while
and was only open again in part. Then *that* Duke had died
and his son, still a boy, reigned in his stead, or rather his
mother, the Duchess (a fine good woman surely), reigned
in his stead.

All this Caesar had constantly from his old mother
with whom he lived in two rooms above the news-vendor's
in Shepherd Market. Caesar was short, bony, but very
cheerful-featured. No beauty with his large mouth and
sharp little Cockney eyes, but he was a faithful devoted
soul, feeling proud—even in these days—of his place as

a family servant. There were still many of his kind in
London, born into service and proud of it, thinking it no
degradation, hating more than anything else 'the bloody
Bolshies.' *'What* nonsense!' Caesar would say to Mrs.
Ganter, the cook, known as The General. 'Men's born
to be different. Start 'em all level, and in no time at all
one's up, one's down. Share and share alike! I'd like to
see Ma share anything she's got with anyone else.'

He liked all four Delaneys and would work himself
to the bone for them, but finances were a terrible problem
with him. His old mother was always 'fancying something'—food, drink, a book or a trinket. And if she didn't
get it she'd cry and say that no one loved her any more
and it would be better if she'd died long before. Her
whims and fancies cost money. Moreover Caesar wasn't
sure, but he fancied that for the first time in his life he
was really in love . . . no, he couldn't be sure, but it
looked a little like it.

Dressed in his official black suit, his funny ugly grinning
face glitteringly shaved, he looked a respectable retainer.
He introduced the visitors without a word, as well he
might, for they were part of the family. There were three
of them—Larry Delaney, Fred's brother, Phyllis his
wife, and an exceedingly pretty, slim, shy-looking girl.
Larry Delaney resembled his brother in his fair curly
hair, rosy countenance, general freshness, but he was
stouter and coarser. You could see at once, however,
that he had all his elder brother's cheerful indifference
to the dangers of to-morrow and enjoyment of the present
hour. He looked a little less of a person than Fred, shal-
lower, less important. He earned a precarious living by
acting as a sort of middle-man in Society. That is he went,
with Phyllis his wife, everywhere, discovered that someone wanted to sell something, persuaded someone else
that that was exactly what he or she wanted to purchase,
and then brought buyer and seller together. He then re-

ceived a commission. Practically *everything* in Mayfair
was for sale—pictures, furniture, silver—you could enter
no house or flat in Mayfair nowadays without someone
saying to you, 'Don't you love that Turner water-colour?
I happen to know you could have it for almost a song.
It's a damned shame, but Dodo's being forced to sell
almost *all* her lovely old things.' So that it was positively
dangerous now in any house or flat to look at anything
with too personal an appreciation because *at once* someone said, 'Do you like that? Rather lovely, don't you
think? I'll have a word with Doris after lunch and see
if I can't persuade her. . . .'

Things being as they are, Larry Delaney's job should
have been a lucrative one. There were, however, a number of drawbacks to it as a career, one of the principal
being that people were curious about payment. Also a
sort of Exchange and Mart went on, so that he would
receive a note:

DARLING LARRY—I'm sure Sophy won't mind if I delay in
paying for the bit of tapestry which really isn't as nice as I first
thought it. I have by the way a really *lovely* Charles II musical
box which has been in the family ever since Charles gave it *himself*
to my great-great (ever so many greats) Aunt who was his Mistress
you know for quite a while. Don't you think Sophy would like the
musical box? I'm sure it's worth a lot more than the tapestry. After
all, it was a *gift* from a King! Do see what you can do about it,
darling Larry.

And then, of course, he was as likely as not to get no
commission at all. However, Phyllis and he worked very
hard and went about everywhere and, perhaps, didn't do
so badly.

Lastly there was the exquisite silent girl with the white
face, red lips and wide-open startled eyes. She was a Miss
Alice Van Renn, whose old mother was an energetic silly
snobbish widow. Mother and daughter had two rooms

in Half Moon Street. The old lady was aristocratic and
poor. The girl Alice had a kind aunt who had paid for her
'finishing' in Paris. Thence she had but lately returned.
Fred Delaney, in fact, had never seen her before, and
now he stared at this lovely thing in his doorway as
though he had been struck from heaven.

Alice Van Renn had such perfect features that she was
almost unreal. Although her colouring was pale, yet it
was exquisite. To stroke her cheek was the first natural
desire of any natural male, and Delaney was a very
natural male indeed. No one knew whether Alice was
brilliantly clever or exquisitely stupid, for she spoke but
little. What was heavenly, maddening, to every man was
that she appeared to be in a kind of trance; she was as
yet unawakened. To be the first to achieve that awaken-
ing, there was an ambition!

In any case at this particular moment Fred Delaney
stood with his mouth a little open, staring, and Meg
Delaney saw that it was so.

'Happy New Year!' said everybody.

And so, with that ancient greeting, new events in the
Delaney family began.

CHAPTER II

Brocket's

ON that same New Year morning, not very far from the Delaneys' breakfast table, at the precise moment when Fred Delaney gazed for the first time, open-mouthed, at Miss Alice Van Renn, Mr. Claude St. John Willoughby woke up in his bed at Number Twenty-three White Horse Street, Shepherd Market, to find Brocket standing in his doorway looking at him, even as Patrick Munden had found Fred Delaney.

A very different greeting this, however, from the other: not at all friendly—quite the contrary.

Claude St. John Willoughby sat up and rubbed his eyes.

Mr. Brocket in his shirt-sleeves and only-too-familiar brown apron said in a voice intended to be elegantly and even classically ironic, but, in reality, thick, beery and brutal:

'I was only wondering *when* your lordship intended to rise and allow 'is room to be done—no offence, but it's past nine o'clock.'

These last words were said with a tang like the slap of a wave on a rock. Mr. Willoughby looked at Brocket and thought how loathsome he was. Brocket had the

24

build of a prize-fighter, but instead of the jolly purple countenance set about with a crooked nose and a cauliflower ear that you might expect, his skin had the thick grey-white consistency of dough, and his head was especially unpleasant, being bald like a tonsured priest's, with a fringe of grey hair round a faintly yellow poll, grey hair that appeared, unless you looked at it very steadily, to be always a trifle on the move.

He was clean-shaven, and the end of his wide-nostrilled nose, his lips, and his hands were always damp. He appeared during most of the day in his shirt-sleeves and a grey waistcoat on which there were yellow stains. His sleeves were rolled up and revealed brawny but unhealthy-pallored arms. On these also grey hairs crawled. His vast middle was always bound around with a faded brown apron. He wore in the morning slippers that gave him the appearance of webbed-feet, for they were sliced at the toes because of his corns. His slippers could be heard flap-flapping all over the house.

He was a bachelor but was reputed a devil with the women and immensely rich. This last was, in all probability, untrue, but he did own Number Twenty-three and let it out to bachelor gentlemen. Within Number Twenty-three he ruled like the God of the Israelites. Everyone trembled at his approach, more especially if he had had a drop or two. The bachelor gentlemen at present his tenants were: on the ground floor, Colonel Badget; on the second floor, Mr. Best; on the third floor, Major Pierson; and on the top floor, Mr. Willoughby.

Brocket behaved like a self-indulgent sensualist to his tenants. Of some he made favourites, others he tortured. At this present time Mr. Best was his favourite and Mr. Willoughby he tortured.

You may ask then—Why did Mr. Willoughby remain there? He remained because, in the first place, he was growing old (he had passed his seventieth birthday) and to change quarters now was an alarming business; secondly, because he was poor and his room was cheap; thirdly, because Brocket had a sort of terrible fascination for him; fourthly, because he could not conceive of saying: 'Mr. Brocket, I think I will go away now.'

His room was cheap, but it was not very pleasant. It possessed only one small window and, being immediately under the roof, was very hot in summer, very cold in winter. He had to share the bath with Major Pierson on the third floor, and although Major Pierson had known this when he engaged his rooms, he was sometimes unagreeable about it.

There was not a great deal of space. There was a wash-stand, a table, an easy chair, two straight chairs, a glass cabinet behind which Claude Willoughby kept his treasures, and a wardrobe. On the mantelpiece were photographs of his mother, a girl to whom he had once been engaged, and a setter dog that he had once loved. Over the mantelpiece was an old engraving of Longton Hall in Derbyshire, once the family place, the house where he had been born. Everything was extremely neat and tidy. He himself sitting up in bed, his Adam's-apple moving nervously within his bony neck, his few grey hairs still tidy on his head, his faint brown eyes anxious and concerned, was very neat and orderly. His thin bony hands were almost bloodless against the dark rug with which he covered the bed on cold nights. He raised one hand now to stroke nervously his short grey brush-moustache.

'I'm sorry,' he said. 'Something must have happened to the alarm-clock.'

'Something *must*,' said Brocket bitterly. 'Didn't you 'ear the girl come in? There's your breakfast been on the table a hour if a minute—and stone cold by now.'

'No, I didn't hear the girl,' Mr. Willoughby said with dignity. 'Happy New Year!' he added courteously.

Brocket studied him. 'Marvellous how these old boys go on living,' he thought. 'You'd have thought *he'd* have been dead long ago.'

However, he didn't want Mr. Willoughby to die. He paid the rent regularly; moreover Brocket felt a kind of sadistic affection for the old boy. He loved to see the look of timorous uncertainty creep into those brown eyes, he liked to raise his voice suddenly so that the old boy jumped, he liked to begin a complaint slowly, cumulatively, and then listen, with a glowering brow, to Mr. Willoughby's slow, stammering explanations. Yes, he almost loved him. Mr. Willoughby was one of his principal daily entertainments.

However, this morning he had work to do, so with a grunt he departed and his slippers flip-flappered down the stairs.

Claude was delighted when he was gone. He raised his thin arms and yawned. Then, very carefully, for he had always, when he woke in the morning, a touch of lumbago, he got out of bed, felt for his brown dressing-gown, his faded green slippers, brushed his few grey locks with his old silver brushes, washed his face and hands and brushed his teeth, and then, humming a little tune (as though in pleasure at the departure of Brocket) sat down to his breakfast. It was not, of course, very agreeable: the tea was lukewarm, the toast was tough, and the two pieces of bacon had congealed round the one egg so that the dish looked like a very unappetizing surrealist painting. Nevertheless he was hungry and there was the Oxford Marmalade which oversleeping could not affect.

All the same how very odd that he had *not* heard the girl enter! She made always such a clatter! The way that she breathed through her nose was enough alone to waken him. And, being an old man, he was wide awake and staring at six o'clock as a rule. He had, however, gone to bed rather late last night. He had found at the newsvendor's in Shepherd Market (they maintained a Lending Library; so obliging and kind they always were!) the reminiscences of old Colonel Blake called *Random Shots and Tender Memories,* and had sat up reading the book. It had brought the old delightful past so vividly back to him that his eyes had filled with tears as he read. He had known so many of the places and people that Reggie Blake had known. He remembered, as though it were yesterday, Ernest Cassell calling Reggie 'a Tom Cat with a Hundred Tails,' because Reggie had been an indefatigable raconteur—bit of a bore that way!

But there it was. He had sat up remembering old times, and so his breakfast was cold! There were, however, many pleasant things and one of the pleasantest was his *Daily Telegraph.* An extravagance, perhaps; but if so, his only one.

He drew to the fire the old armchair with the tear in the right arm that always greatly distressed him because he thought that it must distress the chair who had been for so long a good and faithful friend to him. He said 'the fire,' but that was a title by courtesy, for the girl who had lit it an hour and a half ago had used the coal extravagantly, and now, when there were but embers and a piece of vexed-looking charred stick, he did not wish to put on more coal because in that case his allowance for the day would soon be exhausted.

So he drew his dressing-gown about him and, smiling at one winking coal as though it were his best friend, stretched out his legs and read his paper. He read about how terrible had been the fog and darkness over most of England, how the *Codex Sinaiticus* had arrived from Russia in charge of a special courier, of a terrible railway accident in France on the Paris-Strasbourg line, and of New Year's Honours conferred on a number of gentlemen whose names were quite unknown to him. He read, too, with a rather twisted smile under his little moustache, of distressed areas and starving multitudes. They can't be really starving, he thought, because there is always the dole; I wonder if any of them are quite as poor as I am. Obviously if you were living at Number Twenty-three White Horse Street, Mayfair, you couldn't be quite as poor as if you were living at Number Twenty-three Fish Street, Old Kent Road. And yet not quite so obviously!

He put down his *Telegraph* and got out from the drawer under the cabinet the dark red book where he with extremely neat accuracy kept his accounts. For once they were on the cheerful side, for the dividends he had received last week had gone up a little. As a rule when he had paid Brocket the rent and the bill for breakfasts and extras, there was almost nothing left at all. Still, so long as he kept well, he could manage.

It was the thought of possible sickness that truly terrified him. You might say (and Claude said it to himself sometimes) that he had no right to live under so high a rent. But Brocket's was as cheap as he would find in Mayfair, and the whole happiness and colour of his life came from these streets around him. From Piccadilly Circus to Hyde Park Corner had been, from the beginning of conscious things, his world. For sixty years he had known it, loved it, cherished it, consoled it, thanked it, congratulated it. For thirty years he had had rooms, very fine ones too, in Berkeley Street. When Devonshire House had gone it was as though he himself had lost a rib or a kidney. Nevertheless he had accommodated himself to the changes. He had not been foolish about that, for he had known that changes must occur as they had always occurred. And, at this very moment of time, January 1st, 1934, the changes at the south end of Berkeley Square in course of construction were devastating, frightful, appalling; but he intended, on this very afternoon or possibly to-morrow afternoon, to walk along there and sur-

vey them, bravely, with his head up as though, in the
process of nature, they were inevitable.

Take him their way, remove his little feet (his feet
and hands were remarkably small) from this piece of
ground and he would die. Simply die. Not that it mattered
to anyone but himself whether he lived or died, but to
himself it still mattered a great deal. He loved to be alive
and the little things, the very, very little things, were quite
enough to make his days exciting and sometimes even
melodramatic. . . .

A door, in the dim distance, banged. His bath! Unless
he took it soon, Pierson would be indignant at his having
one so late in the morning and would bark at him like a
seal. He hoped that, by taking one now, he might avoid
Pierson altogether.

So he gathered his soap in its talc case, his sponge-bag
and his bath-towel together and proceeded forth. At the
bottom of the short flight of stairs was a long shivering
passage, and down this he must go, passing the doors of
Pierson's bedroom and sitting-room. He always walked
tiptoe, tiptoe, and if he reached the bathroom without
arousing anyone he would close the door behind him and
then stand for a moment, smiling, his hand pressed on his
heart.

To-day he was not so fortunate. He was almost in
safety when a door opened and Pierson's voice was heard.

'Hullo, Willoughby! You're late, aren't you?'

Claude turned and felt, as always, that he was taken at
a disadvantage with his old dressing-gown and faded
slippers. However, he answered gallantly.

'Hullo, Pierson! Happy New Year!'

Major Pierson was short, stout, and red of face. He
wore a toupee and was always dressed as though about
to lead a charge against the enemy. His clothes were in
themselves ordinary, but tingling with a kind of com-
bativeness. He was, however, in reality an amiable man so

CURZON STREET
31

long as one wasn't a foreigner and had nothing to say
against the British Army, the virtue of English woman-
hood and the English climate. A familiar type made plain
to us in many a work of fiction. His *individuality* (for we
all have souls) lay perhaps in his extreme prudery. He
could not endure a bawdy story nor any light allusion to
sex. In spite of a varied life in India, China and Africa,
he still believed that women were angels, and if an angel
strayed, then it was some vile man's intolerable fault.
He had never married, perhaps because he had never
dared to test his beliefs too severely. He regarded Claude
Willoughby as an old woman and therefore pure of heart
and conduct. But he felt a vast superiority to him and
treated him rather as the Squire in the good old days
treated a faithful village dependent. Willoughby never
interfered with Pierson's bathing plans and was scrupu-
lously neat in his behaviour; nevertheless the sight of Willoughby on the way to the bath always annoyed him.

'Don't expect you'll find the bath water very hot.'

'Oh, that doesn't matter in the least, thank you.'

'What happened—oversleep yourself?'

'Well, as a matter of fact I did; most unusual—sat up
late reading.'

'Reading, eh? Seen in the paper about these damned
Bolshies?'

'No, as a matter of fact . . . what have they been
doing?'

'What have they been doing? What are they always
doing? Plotting against the peace of the world. That's
what *they're* doing.'

'Yes, I suppose so. It's really terrible.'

'You'd better get in there. Damned draughty this
passage.'

'Yes, I suppose so. Thanks very much.'

Lying flat in the bath, Claude was happy. The water
was *not* very warm, but warmer than it might have been.

He reflected: 'Why am I always so nervous when Pierson speaks to me? He's a very kind man and means nothing but good. He looks down on me, of course, because he's an Army man and I'm not. All Army men look down on civilians. But he's nearly as poor as I am. He has only his Army pension and has to support, I believe, a very aged mother and an invalid sister. He is also, I fancy, extremely lonely. He has a Club, which I haven't, but from what I hear, he's not at all popular. Why, then, be nervous when he speaks to me? We ought to be friends. I ought to go down and visit him of an evening. But the mere thought of visiting him fills me with terror. Besides we should have nothing to say to one another. He's more agreeable than Badget, who has money and lets you know it, and less of a bore than Best, who never stops talking. How charming it would be if someone lodged in this house who was a real friend and companion! But you must not, I suppose, expect friends after seventy. I've had a lot of friends in my time.' And that made him think of Helen and Millie Pake, very old friends of his. What a good idea! He would go and have tea with them this afternoon and wish them a Happy New Year. They were always at home at tea-time and enjoyed a chat. What an *excellent* idea! Filled with pleasure, he finished his bath, dried his little shivering body, and hurried up to his room again.

He clung to his intention although the scruples, now so constant with him, that he might bore them, that they would have other visitors, that he might suffer once more that unpleasant experience of people looking right through him as though he didn't exist, crowded about him. He *must* go out, he *must* pay visits. He had noticed in himself lately a tendency to stay in his room as though there only was to be really safe. That was dangerous. That way madness lay.

At length in his blue suit with the dark tie and grey gloves and cane with the ivory head of a dog, and his

soft black hat, he was ready to venture. All he hoped was
that he would not encounter Brocket. One moment's experience of Brocket scowling at him and the dangers of
facing the outside world were greatly increased. But there
was no Brocket to-day and, as he walked into Shepherd
Market, happiness returned to him as it so easily did at
the slightest excuse in the world. Although it was half-past
three in the afternoon there was still a faint sun-stained
fog about. He liked that sun-stained fog almost beyond
any other weather that London provided, and it seemed
especially kindly and reassuring now, for London had
been so very dark of late. Lights were burning in the news-
vendor's and, as always, he stopped to look at the rows of
books behind the glass on the opposite side of the narrow
passage. How very many books there were in the world
to be sure! It must take so much energy and trouble to
write a book! He admired authors greatly so long as no
one forced him to read their works.

In Curzon Street there was an orange light in the air
and the Christian Science Church loomed behind the fog
almost like a mystic temple, and the steel and chromium
of the new cinema up the street gleamed like the silver
lines of a ship. How greatly vexed and hurt he had been
at the first appearance of that cinema. It had seemed to
him not only an insult to all the past history and characters of this sacred ground, but a personal insult to himself as well. He had become, however, not only accustomed to it but he even liked it. He wished it well. He enjoyed the photographs of the pictures, the uniformed
figure on guard, the cars that assembled outside it. This
after all was life; it meant happiness to many people, and,
because he could not himself possibly afford to enter it,
there was a quality of mystery there that stirred and excited him.

So, through the orange fog he walked to the home of
his friends.

Outside the door of the handsome house were the names of the tenants and under each name a little bell: Patrick Munden, Lady Helen Pake, the Hon. Mark Pullet, Frederick Delaney. He touched the Pake bell, gave the big door a push and was inside the hall, then up the beautiful staircase, past the Pullets', challenging the Pake door. Now, while he waited, once more fears attacked him. The house was so *very* silent; everyone within it might be dead. Suppose they *were* dead, those two old ladies, the young girl who looked after them during the day out on her shopping; dead, the two poor old things, and nobody knew it! Or suppose, on the other hand, they were entertaining their friends, as they well might be on New Year's Day, and he would find himself in a circle of cold, indifferent strangers. *That* he would not be able to endure, and so, after a quarter of an hour, he would depart and return to his lonely room with nothing to do for the rest of the day but sit and miserably reflect on his wretched isolation? Or Helen might be in one of her grand tantrums and sit there, like a tragedy queen, making life horrible for everybody? Oh, it were better that he had not come, far, far better, and he was about to turn away and slip down the stairs again when the door opened and the little maid was there and, yes, Lady Helen and Lady Mildred were at home and would he come in, please?

Inside the little hall he listened and was comforted because there were no gay and raucous voices. There was no New Year's party at least. And then when he saw his old friends sitting one on each side of the fire as he had so often seen them before, his heart beat with happiness. Here was sanctuary, here safety!

The sitting-room was small, as it was bound to be when you considered that out of the two original rooms there had been created two bedrooms, a bathroom, a kitchenette and a sitting-room. But the ceilings were high, the fireplace noble, there were flowers and old family silver, an oil painting of Twyden Hall, the family place, now in the possession of Lord Rocklyn their brother, and a very fine portrait of Helen and Mildred painted in the 'Nineties by Sargent. The room was a little over-full perhaps and you had to walk carefully to avoid tables and chairs, but it was of a warm and cosy friendliness.

The ladies themselves were exactly what Claude considered that ladies ought to be.

Helen was now seventy-five years of age, Millie some five years younger. Helen was sitting up in her chair, stiff as a poker, her body thin as a divining-rod. She was pale of cheek, hawk-like nose, pouches of dark under her eyes, her silver-grey hair tight about her head. She had long thin hands, so thin that the light seemed to shine through them. She had a long bony neck like a hen's and held her head so high that you watched to see the neckbones crack. Her magnificent flashing, tempestuous eyes were her finest feature. This she knew very well, for they had been called flashing and tempestuous often enough. She had never been beautiful, but always regal, and now at seventy-five was more regal than ever. All her life she had been the victim of fits of imperious temper, but now those fires were dying and she was slipping into the dusk of evening. She had always behaved like a queen, for no very adequate reason save that she had been the eldest daughter of the Earl of Rocklyn. That had mattered once; alas, it mattered nothing now. That she should be sister of the present Earl, who, poor Tommy, had wasted and rioted away in earlier days all the family patrimony and was now a withered skeleton living in a semi-closed Twyden with a housekeeper and a pack of dogs, martyred by gout and rheumatism. No, Helen had no longer any reason for grandeur, but that did not mean that she was not grand. Although her faculties were still sharp and acute, she lived in a kind of dream-world, not the Past only, the Past shot through with the Present (which she loathed and despised), then finally transmuted into a place of colours, rhythms, voices that had little relation to the reality of other people.

Millie, her sister, had worshipped and served her all her life long. In appearance Millie was short, plump, with snow-white hair and a most amiable behaviour. She too had her dignities and could rebuke a presumer most effectively, but she loved gossip and the small transactions of human nature and could not therefore hate the modern world as her sister did. She was the practical one, managed the small income of herself and her sister; it was the great business of her life to save her sister every possible discomfort and inconvenience. She worshipped her, was sometimes terrified of her, loved her and spoilt her. In spite of their smallness of means, confined existence and occasional aches and pains, Millie got much pleasure from life, although she considered that the way the world was going was appalling. Appalling and exciting. At the back of her mind was always the fear that they would wake up one morning and discover that they had no money. The investments, once so fat and satisfying, appeared with every year to dwindle. Of course, come the worst, they could always go to Twyden and make their home with Tommy, the dogs, and Mrs. Hardcastle, the housekeeper. Anything more appalling Millie could not conceive.

They were both delighted to welcome dear Claude Willoughby. He was exactly their contemporary, and though, in younger days, they had patronized him and thought him a good little man to run messages for them, he was now one of the few holders of the fort remaining. Moreover he had known everyone they had known and was an excellent gossip: he held identically their views about the present disgraceful state of the world; and, best of all, he had even less money than they had.

Helen received him as Queen Elizabeth might have greeted an ambassador from a foreign country, but her beautiful eyes mellowed nevertheless. Millie showed her pleasure without any dignity and told him to draw his chair to the fire and that tea would be there in a minute. They had rung for it just before he came in. Then Millie began at once, without a moment's pause, to ask him whether he had heard of the latest horrible behaviour of Princess Corleone.

Very briefly, Princess Corleone was the villain of the piece in the lives of the members of the Pake world. Princess Corleone was an American, and there was nothing against being that, because some of the most charming women in the Edwardian world had been American. She had arrived in London before the War as a Mrs. Peter Twine, the wife of an American steel man. She had attempted then a little social advancement. She had been at once checked on all sides. There had been nothing whatever to recommend her as she had been ugly, vulgar, with a voice like a pea-hen, and had never stopped talking. However, Mr. Peter Twine had died, leaving her a large fortune, and she had married an Italian, Prince Corleone. He had been killed at Caporetto and she had returned to London, finding in the new post-war world all that she had needed. To her house in Grosvenor Street she had gradually lured politicians, painters, authors, younger nobilities, and finally Royalty itself.

Paula Corleone haunted the Pakes and their friends and fascinated them as well. In the old days they would not have considered her at all, and would have scorned to gossip about her. But now from their little fastness, with the wild savage new world roaring about them, they saw her as a kind of witch directing the storm. They saw her with her little restless body, her sharp eyes, they heard her shrill never-ceasing monotone, they could not learn sufficient detail of her personal life, her 'affairs,' her parties, her social indiscretions. They thought of her continually because they were baffled by her power. In the only world that they had actively realized she would not have been permitted for a moment. But she had money, and money now was everything. Birth, tradition, taste, morals, decent behaviour, charming manners, all these counted for nothing now beside money. They had been brought up never to consider money, never to mention it, never to think of it. In the old days there had been plenty. The parties at Twyden had been famous, and when there had not been parties at Twyden there had been parties everywhere else: house-parties in enormous houses, with vast rooms, icy passages, lawns dripping under the rain, the shrill cry of peacocks, frosty mornings and the Hunt assembled before the drawing-room windows, beautiful September mornings on Scottish moors and the ladies at luncheon-time driving out to join the gentlemen, endless, endless dinner parties, endless, endless balls—and always plenty of money.

Now no one stayed a minute over anything; off they went in a motor-car or an aeroplane. No one goes to church, no one goes to bed, no one goes to stay with anyone for more than a night. The noise about one's ears is a frenzy; all the world is preparing for the last War that is to exterminate everything—and, above all this horror, riding her broomstick, directing proceedings in her shrill vulgar accents, is Paula Corleone.

Very quiet, though, is it now in this little room, the lights shaded, the tea in front of the fire, Helen sitting bolt upright, half in a reality that applauds the little macaroons (she has always loved sweet things) and enjoying the detail of Paula Corleone poking the Minister for War (or was it Agriculture?) in the ribs and screaming at him like a parrot about a new laxative that she had been trying. Yes, and watching, as Helen loved to do, the

Chinese cabinet with the red dragons that had been among her very earliest perceptions at Twyden, there near the great stone fireplace in the Twyden drawing-room, when as a small infant she had been brought down for an hour with her mother and, on some especial occasion, like a birthday, had been permitted to turn back the panels and open the musk-scented little drawers, black with gold carvings of trees and pagodas. . . .

The Chinese cabinet was theirs now—Tommy had allowed them to keep it—and Helen had but to gaze at it and all the past came swimming up, the great country-houses, the gardens, the long line of the downs, the tinkling Sunday reiteration of the bell in the village church. So, nibbling her macaroon, she heard but little of what Millie and Claude were saying.

Claude was happy and thankful too. For really this visit had turned out delightfully and he would have plenty, in his room at evening, to think over. They were talking about the new Duchess of Wrexe, who, only eighteen, had just married the Duke, a bachelor of forty. She was, they said, exceedingly beautiful and the daughter of a Devonshire farmer.

'What the old Duchess would have said!' Millie exclaimed. 'You remember her of course?'

'I should think I do,' said Claude. 'Time of the Boer War—Rossiter's portrait of her is in the Tate. Did you know that? I went with Connie Beaminster the other day to see it. A silly woman, Connie, don't you think? But she means well.'

'She's a great friend of the Delaneys. . . . Dear, dear! What an autocrat the old Duchess was! And now see what her grandson is doing!'

'There are some farmers of quite good family,' Claude said reflectively. 'But I hear that this girl's mother's father had a shop in Taunton or somewhere. . . .'

'Oh, well,' said Millie briskly. 'No one cares any more

about such things. They'd call us dreadful snobs, Claude, if they heard us, and so I suppose——'

'Snobs!' Helen suddenly broke in, to their astonishment. 'If you tell me, Millie, that good blood doesn't matter and decent manners and bringing children up to know their betters——'

'I'm not sure,' said Millie, shaking her head. 'After all, Helen, our childhood wasn't *really* very happy. You know we were terrified of Papa and never dared open our mouths and always had chilblains and had to wear boards down our backs at lessons and could never read an interesting book on Sundays. I *do* think children are much happier nowadays, and as to birth, Charles the Second made an orange-girl a Duchess, and look at the way the Prince Regent used to go on! It was only Queen Victoria who altered everything, and although I wouldn't say a word against her, she did fill England with hypocrites, and no one can say that we're *that* any more. After all, in the light of history sixty years is a very short time. Until Victoria, England was quite a *rough* country, and now she's gone back to being *rough* again!'

Helen said: 'You've been *reading* something, Millie.'

'Not particularly. Only Lytton Strachey, and Mrs. Pullet tells me he's *quite* old-fashioned now.'

'You'd better go to one of Paula Corleone's luncheon-parties.'

'Oh no, of course not. I should be *most* uncomfortable! But of course we *are* very old-fashioned, living all by ourselves shut up in here, and we may as well recognize it. Why, do you know, Claude, there's one of the most modern young poets living at the top of this house now. I passed him on the stairs the other day—such a wild-looking young man, but he gave me quite a nice frightened sort of smile. Fancy *my* frightening a modern young poet!'

Millie laughed. 'Now if it had been *Helen* . . . !'

Helen smiled a grim smile. 'Millie's getting so light-headed, Claude, that I don't know what'll become of her!'

'Oh no, I'm not, but after all it isn't any use to pretend we're living in the old world. Two old ladies, buried away and forgotten—that's what we are!'

Her voice shook a little. She moved over and gave her sister a kiss.

'Put some coal on the fire, Claude, will you?'

Claude did so—not too much, for he could not help thinking of the economy that his own coal demanded.

The flames leapt up, they talked on cosily, as though Claude were their brother. The watcher on the threshold, looking at the figures, bent like ghosts about the fire, might have thought that they were seeking one another's protection and comfort. . . .

'And what about you, Claude? How are things going with you?'

'Very well indeed, thank you . . . oh, very well.'

'No more of that lumbago? I remember you were bothered . . .'

'Oh, ever so slight. There's a new embrocation I've been recommended . . .'

'And that horrible man, your landlord? He hasn't been offensive? If you have any trouble I'll come along and tell him what I think of him.'

'Oh no. I don't *like* him, you know—couldn't possibly *like* him. It's only his manner. I can't believe that he means to be as rude as he seems. But he can't *do* anything, you know. Only make it a little uncomfortable.'

Helen is half asleep. Her back is as straight as ever, but she is young, *so* young, and although not beautiful still striking. Even Aunt Milchester allows that she is *striking*. She is kneeling in front of the Chinese cabinet. She is old enough now; she need not ask permission any longer. She turns back the crimson panels, fingers with her thumb the raised gold on the smooth black surface of the drawers. Someone is practising the piano—Millie in the schoolroom. She hears the voice of Bannister, the butler —'I will go and see, my lady'—and then her mother's thin, rather languid voice: 'Ah, there you are, Helen! We are going down to the Lodge. I have to speak to Gummery about something'—and that sudden glorious vista through the window as you raise your head from the cabinet, of the sun behind the great oak and every leaf glittering. A baby moon just fading from the pale blue-white sky, and the thick bark-like scent of chrysanthemums. Millie playing 'The Carnival of Venice' in the schoolroom. Bannister, so fat, so unctuous, so devoted. 'I'll remember, my lady. Certainly, my lady. . . .'

'I must be going now.' Claude is going, going, gone. . . .

'Come again soon and see us.'

'I will. I will.'

But in the hall downstairs there was still a little adventure. As he moved to the hall door another door opened and a young girl stood there, all in dark red with a little fur cap on her very dark hair.

She smiled. What could he do but bow? He knew her, of course—Miss Delaney. He felt that he must account for himself lest she should think that he had been robbing the house.

'A little foggy, isn't it?'

Kitty Delaney came close to him. There was a faint scent of—what? Violets? Who was this little man, so small, so dapper, but his neat blue suit rather shiny? Her heart was moved by the anxious brown eyes, the mouth that trembled ever so slightly.

'I have been paying a New Year call on Lady Helen Pake.'

'Oh yes. Aren't they darlings? We are so glad they live here.'

Claude felt from her, as he felt from the girl's father

and mother when he met them in the hall or on the stairs, a renewal of his ebbing vitality. How charming a girl! Something pleasant for him to think over alone in his room that evening. . . .

'I live quite close by.'

'Oh, do you? . . .' She took him, as it were, under her care and protection. 'I'm so glad you do. All of us here—just in these few streets. It's like living in a village, don't you think? We all ought to know one another.'

'My name's Willoughby. Claude Willoughby. The Pakes will tell you all about me. They've known me all my life.'

'How do you do, Mr. Willoughby?'

Kitty held out her hand. Claude held it a moment. How warm it was beneath the glove! And was not the scent lilac? At any rate he could smell lilac, his favourite flower, white or purple, clusters of it—against the old dark wood of the stair.

'Well, I must be going on. Good afternoon, Miss Delaney.'

'Good-bye, Mr. Willoughby. You must come and visit *us* one day as you know the house so well.'

'Indeed I will, Miss Delaney. Thank you so very much.'

He went tripping out into the fog, which by now had thickened. But he hummed a little tune as he felt his way.

CHAPTER III

Mother and Daughter: Two Meetings

MEG DELANEY's nature was often childlike and even childish. Indeed, as I have already said, the Delaneys *were* on occasion childish and were sometimes patronized by persons who considered themselves more mature.

Meg herself was never aware of being patronized; too many things were always happening for her to notice patronage. Certain people alarmed her a little, like a friend of Kitty's called Joe Cardinal who wrote for the paper *Life and Leisure*—a journal owned, edited and written for by ladies who despised men and womenly women—but then Meg was always alarmed by writers. When Joe Cardinal came to a meal in Charles Street, Meg talked a little too much, laughed a little too gaily and agreed rather too eagerly that popular writers like Messrs. Adrian and Rose were too awful for words; not that she had ever read them. She didn't read books, partly because there seemed no time, but also because, as soon as she began to read, things, people, memories, flashes of sun, a cry, a whirr of the clock, the colour of a flower, a stiffness in the leg, a laugh, a bell *would* break in. She was a little of a coward with all women who did things for a living, because she thought they must despise her who did nothing at all. Also there was no doubt but

44

that as soon as a woman did something for a living she
was changed a little. Something was added to her personality, something detracted from it. Add two waistcoat-
buttons, subtract one blush of the cheek. Meg, like her
daughter, was preoccupied almost entirely with individuals. She saw the world as peopled with individuals and
therefore she could never understand politics or world
causes. She saw Mussolini as Mussolini—*Mr.* Mussolini
having a bath, asking why his egg at breakfast wasn't
fresh, chucking his ferocious-looking daughter under the
chin. When she learned that Hitler had been a house-
painter, when she realized that he really intended to keep
that ridiculous-looking moustache, she could never take
him seriously again and thought of him as someone who
needed poultices, Kruschen salts and warm underclothing.
She learnt that her views on politics seemed to her friends
very silly, so she kept silent about them as well as she
could. There were other things about which she said as
little as possible. For example, that she liked to go to
church. This seemed to all her friends a sign of imbe-
cility—because if she went to church she could have no
brains at all. Queerly enough, had she been a Roman
Catholic her intelligence would not have been accused.
This she did not even begin to try and understand. The
fact was that she liked to go to church and so she went.
She did all the things that made her happy and interfered
with other people's happiness as little as possible, but she
did not think about anything very consciously. She moved
and acted by instinct.

Now on this lovely afternoon, very early in the
adventure-seeking New Year, she was going with her
daughter Kitty as far as Hanover Square where Kitty
had a dressmaker. After this she would probably walk
in the Park.

She delighted to walk out with her daughter because
she was so very proud of her. She knew of mothers, like

Jessie Pinot for instance, who would rather die than be seen out with their daughters because of the age that it made them. But she, Meg Delaney, did not care of what age anything made her, and indeed looked forward quite eagerly to being a very old lady still able to enjoy a theatre. Herself and Kitty had almost exactly the same appreciation of small events and unexpected persons, and this made a walk delightful. Meg, of course, attracted attention in the streets because of her gay colours and large size, but for some reason she was never absurd. She wore large hats, flowing cloaks of dark red, dull gold, purple, and with her fine carriage, dark eyes and high colouring looked what Princess Corleone ought to look —that 'miserable little scratching hen of a thing' as Millie Pake called her. Kitty was tall also, and the pair of them floating down Bond Street was a fine sight.

Just at Agnew's door they encountered Marjorie Blandin. Lady Marjorie Blandin, related to all the best families and descended on every side from Ethelred the Unready, was a stout, mottle-faced lady whose work in life was to take out obscure girls in the 'Season' and be paid for it. She hadn't herself a penny, but she knew everybody and was physically indefatigable, so her prices were high. It was, however, a 'dog's life,' as she explained now outside Agnew's, where there was very little room on the pavement.

'A dog's life, darling—how sweet you're looking, Kitty! Well, I think I've got those two Glowrie girls and a fat price too. Mama was all right. She'd pay anything to get her little ones through the hoops. But Papa —what a man! And the girls. Plain! Quite frightful— and he insists on *everything*—Ascot, Cowes, the Beaminster Dance. However, money's no object and—well, dear, I must be moving. Tell Larry when you see him that Gladys Dorington has some Tang horses that are real treasures. Hoopy would have a fit if he knew she was selling them, but she's counting on his not noticing they're gone. Bring anyone to lunch any day, she says. Just ring up. Well, darling——'

'That reminds me,' Kitty said as they moved forward. 'I met the dearest little man in our hall two or three days ago. He'd been visiting Millie and Helen.'

'Yes, dear.'

'*Why* did Marjorie Blandin remind me? . . . Oh yes, I know—because she looks so very well fed. This little man looked as though he was half-starved. His clothes were shabby too. But he might have been King of England, the dignity he had. A very old friend of Millie and Helen. He lives in Shepherd Market.'

Her mother interrupted unexpectedly.

'Do you like Alice Van Renn, darling?'

'No, I don't.'

'Nor do I. I was quite vexed with Larry for bringing her in on New Year's morning. I can't see with the best will in the world *why* she appeals to men.'

They negotiated the traffic and turned aside up Conduit Street.

'It's because she never says anything.'

'Oh, do men like that?'

'Some men do.'

'Well, I've talked too much all my life and I've been liked by a good many men one way and another. Darling, are you going to be *extravagant* at the dressmaker's?'

'Certainly not.' Kitty laughed. 'But I'd *love* to be.'

'I hope you're not, because I *believe* we're very poor at the moment. Your father woke up in the middle of last night and laughed like anything. When I asked what it was, he said that he saw us engaging a barrel-organ and a monkey very shortly and wouldn't we do it well? I said I wouldn't mind in the least, and neither I would. I don't mind anything so long as we're all well. But what I want to know'—Meg stopped for a while and gazed at the shops—'is *who* has all the money? Because a lot of money there is somewhere. Now, for instance, that woman Marjorie Blandin was talking about will pay anything to get her daughters on, while we——'

'It's changed hands, I suppose,' Kitty said. 'It's always changing.'

'I've never had any,' Meg said cheerfully. 'Never my whole life long. And I must say I haven't minded.'

As they turned into Hanover Square they were both conscious of the sky. In the life of any Londoner the sky plays little part, but, on occasion, it is as though the houses retire, as rocks draw back when the ship moves out into the open sea. Then buildings and streets dwindle into nothingness, or a kind of wreckage that the sky has flung down. If clouds are flying, the surface of the earth, with its scattering of bricks, mortar, and pigmy figures, is scaled and bared as saucers and cups are tumbled off a table by the dragging of a cloth. Light flashes between clouds contemptuously on to the huddle of rubbish men have gathered here.

But now, above the Square, although the wind drove the clouds there was no anger nor contempt. The clouds were small and light, misted with an orange glow because there was fog about on this early January afternoon; the mist was in the small fleecy rounded clouds that drove forward like tufts blowing in the breeze from some divine daisy. But the fog did not touch the pale limpid blue of the real sky-flood, which was clear and infinitely pure.

The orange light touched the chimney-pots and roofs with a spreading thin gauze of shadow. The light fell in ladders to the street as it does when the sun shines on a dusty room. The sky was so alive with colour and movement that the town itself seemed to crouch, as though watching on its knees, eyes staring upward at the life and splendour.

Already dark shadows were clutching the knees of the buildings, so that in the heavens all was glowing and on earth there was half-obscurity. The orange light became with every moment more intense as the little clouds began to be hustled by the wind into a gathered company as a shepherd hustles sheep.

Kitty, gazing for a moment upwards, felt, once more, that beating excitement of expectation. 'Something is going to happen to me. . . . I have been waiting for years. . . .'

'What a lovely sky!' Meg said. 'I think I'll have an hour in the Park. It will be light there for a long time yet.'

'All right, darling. Don't be picked up by a strange man. And be back for tea. Connie Beaminster's bringing a friend.'

Meg laughed. 'You know, still, old as I am, I never take a walk anywhere without thinking something *may* happen. . . .'

She started off, a ship in full sail.

Kitty looked round for her dressmaker. As always the Church dominated the Square. So many absurd, wicked, greedy, snobbish, idle, wasteful marriages! And perhaps some good ones. But now all was very still there. Some sparrows were hopping from one step to another. Light had been falling on the pillars, but even as Kitty looked it was switched away as though by an impatient hand. Her dressmaker's was below the Church on the same side, near an Art Gallery. She stayed for a moment to look in the little window of this, for there was a picture of the kind that she didn't understand at all—a white curling thing with black edges in the middle, two purple blobs that might be fruit or mightn't, something brown that looked like a broken violin, and squares and slabs of colour, silver, dark brown and black. Fastened to the picture was a label with the word 'Braque,' whether the title of the picture or the name of the painter she didn't know. 'Now *what*,' she thought, 'is the use of *that?* Why shouldn't you paint fruit like fruit and violins like violins?' —and yet as she looked she was aware that the colours formed a pattern and that they were exquisitely painted. Such deep and glowing silver she had never seen, and, in a mysterious fashion beyond her understanding, the picture bore a closer relation to the shining sky and the dark walls of the Church than it would have done had it been an exact reproduction. Then she saw, next to the little Gallery, an Art-shop over whose window was painted in big silver letters: 'ZANTI LTD.' She had been to her dressmaker's often enough but had never before seen this name. It was as though, in these moments, extra vision was given to her, she was seeing everything with redoubled intensity, colours were twice-times rich and the dusk was deep, like forest-dark, about her.

Set in the middle of Zanti's window was a rose-coloured bowl. There were also some ivory-coloured figures, a triptych of Limoges enamel and a piece of old rose and gold embroidered cloth. She stared at the bowl: its design was simple and the colour wavered like sunset on water. Of course it was absurd. She could not remotely afford such a thing. But it would be pleasant to enquire. She entered the shop. The full glow of the sky, streaming in over the short buildings on the other side of the street, illuminated it. It was a small shop but held, as Kitty perceived, a number of beautiful things.

There was a young man behind the counter.

'I beg your pardon——' He looked at her gravely. He was a pale young man with black hair, dark eyes.

Kitty, feeling very tall and as though she had no right to be there when she knew that she could afford no purchase, said:

'No. It's nothing. I shouldn't trouble you. But the rose-coloured bowl in the window. Might I look at it?'

'Of course, madam. No trouble at all.' He drew back the curtain of the window, and while he leant forward she realized that he was very thin and little more than a boy. He returned with the bowl in his hands. 'Do you mean this, madam?'

'Oh no. It was—yes, I suppose I do.' She was examining it. All the colour seemed to have gone from it. 'Why—now—it isn't rose-coloured. I thought——'

'Probably the sun was shining on it. Things often look different in the window. It is a very old bowl. We have had it in the shop a great many years. It is Italian fifteenth-century—Mr. Zanti was very proud of it, I believe. I don't know because I never saw Mr. Zanti.'

Kitty put down the bowl very carefully.

'Thank you very much. I had no right to bother you, because I knew I couldn't begin to afford anything so beautiful.'

She smiled and the young man smiled. He had a smile so attractive, so friendly, intelligent and shy, that Kitty herself continued to smile.

'If you would only wait a minute or two, Mr. Zimmerman will be back. If there were anything else——'

'Mr. Zimmerman?'

'Yes. Mr. Zimmerman owns the shop. Mr. Zimmerman and his son. They bought it from Mr. Zanti and kept the name because he was well known. I am only the assistant,' he added. He was so very thin: did he have enough to eat? she wondered. 'I haven't been here very long,' he went on, 'and I always prefer it when Mr. Zimmerman is in. I might make a mistake.'

'You won't with me,' Kitty said cheerfully. 'Because I can't afford to buy anything.'

They were staring into one another's faces as though they were asking one another questions. The Italian bowl lay between them.

'Then you haven't been doing this always?'

'Oh no. I've been many different things.'

'Do you like this?'

'Mr. Zimmerman is very kind, but I'm so afraid of breaking something or mistaking values. Of course all the prices are marked, but everything here is so precious.'

'Do you like beautiful things?' she asked.

'Oh, I *like* things. Anybody would. But the world being what it is! If you only knew how much some of these cost! And so many people haven't enough to live on.'

'You'd rather do something else?'

'I'd like to be out of doors. I'd rather garden than anything. I love flowers.'

'Yes, so do I.'

'And the mountains and the sea,' he added.

'Can't you go away, then? Are you married? Does anything prevent you?'

It was nothing unusual for one of the Delaneys to enter into conversation with a stranger; ask questions and be asked them. At the same time Kitty thought the young man's voice, eyes and smile so very oddly personal to herself, as though she had asked for someone with just that delicacy and friendliness to be found for her. And lo, he was there!

'I am tied rather,' he said, his eyes on her face. 'My father is paralysed. I have a sister who looks after him, but I have to make what I can for us all.'

'Paralysed! How terrible!'

'It isn't really. My father is very happy, although moving his head is about all he can do. He was a builder and fell from a roof and injured his spine. But he's like no one else in the world—no one anywhere.'

'Wouldn't it be better for him if you lived in the country?'

'Perhaps it would.'

'Would you think me impertinent?' She paused, but, looking him in the eyes again, realized that he would think nothing impertinent from her. 'If you were to give me your name and address I might hear of something. One does sometimes.' She felt in her case. 'Here is *my* card.'

He said nothing, but out of a drawer produced one of the firm's cards, wrote on it and gave it to her.

'That's my name—Alton Foster. And my address.' He took her card and put it in his pocket without looking at it. He was suddenly formal. But she held out her hand. She felt the thin warm texture of his hand through her glove. She smiled.

'Good evening.'

'Good evening, madam. And thank you.'

She turned near the door. He was standing there staring at her.

'Please forgive me . . . if my questions . . .'

He went to the door and opened it for her.

'Don't lose the card,' he said in an urgent, trembling whisper.

Meg Delaney engaged a taxi. This was wrong of her when only last night Fred had told her how poor they were. She knew that it was wrong, but she wanted to have all her time in that light, under that sky, in the open freedom of Regent's Park.

She told the man to drive to the Botanical Gardens and then sat straight up, looking out at the sky and feeling very happy.

She should *not* be happy, because in the first place she should have walked to Oxford Street, only a step, and taken an omnibus (although she could walk it *all* in *no* time!), and secondly, Fred had, she knew perfectly well, begun a flirtation with Alice Van Renn. However, poverty and Fred's flirtations were no new things, which was possibly the reason why she did not feel as unhappy as she should. Hundreds and hundreds of times Fred had flirted, and possibly hundreds and hundreds of times Fred had been unfaithful. But *how* young had Meg been when for the first time she had learnt that there was one law for the woman, quite another for the man! About six years old, perhaps. She had at least been very young indeed when that hateful Mrs. Delias came and stayed so often in that little Clarges Street house and gave her sweets and took her into her bed with her.

She knew that she had with Fred a bond so strong and deep that no woman born of man could disturb it. And she wanted Fred to be happy, as indeed she wanted everyone to be happy. And healthy strong men in their middle years had certain problems to solve. She knew all this and allowed for it. But she must be honest with herself and would confess then that Alice Van Renn and her greedy old mother gave her the creeps.

It was this creepiness that ought to cause Meg uneasiness, because there was altogether something wrong in a fine healthy man like Fred flirting with a beautiful young corpse like Alice. Meg now unexpectedly burst out laughing inside the cab because, in the very middle of Oxford Street traffic, a Sealyham puppy on the end of a lead had sat down four-square, refusing the urgent solicitations of a stout man who held in the other hand a tissue-paper carton containing flowers. The man looked exquisitely absurd, being of all things in the world the most ridiculous, an Englishman who hated to be made a fool of in public. Such a very small puppy, such a very stout man! It was always thus: at the moment when you should be seriously upset about something life provided an irresistible incongruity. It was like dear Graham Pender, slipping on the icy path at Strathpeffer and falling on his behind, just when he was bending forward to kiss her. Dear Graham! How adorable he had been all those years ago when she, nineteen and divinely beautiful, had stayed that winter with Aunt Grace Linklater in Scotland! They had been engaged, Graham and she, for four whole months, and no one had known it, and then off to China he had gone, years had passed, she had married, *he* had married. . . . Well, well . . . to think of it, and that night after the dance at the Wotherspoons' they had so nearly, so very, very nearly . . . Only a miracle had saved her, a miracle and Graham's untimely sense of the incongruous. Meg's eyes were misted. The Queen's Hall swam in a vague of tenderness. Dear Graham! She had never loved anyone in quite the same way again: Fred *more,* perhaps, but not in *quite* the same way. And if she had married Graham there would not have been either Kitty or Bullock. Where would *they* have been? And what would Graham's children have been like? Tall and spare with high cheekbones and very, very intelligent.

The taxi stopped at the entrance to the Botanical Gardens and Meg got out, stepping at once into a blaze of light and colour made personal and poignant by a touch of frosty air.

'Thank you very much,' she said to the driver.

He was an old man with a white powder-coloured nose, rheumy eyes and a large grey woollen comforter.

'What a lovely afternoon!' she said.

'Yes, ma'am.' He leaned towards her as though he would confide an important secret. 'I've got a shocking cold,' he said.

'I'm so sorry. What are you doing for it?'

'Five o'clock my time's up. I'm going straight 'ome and put my feet in mustard and water.'

'Yes, you do,' she said, nodding her head confidentially. 'That's an excellent thing.' As she walked along the Inner Circle she wondered as to his home, his family and his general comforts. Was he as poor as they, the Delaneys, were? He was sure, in all probability, of his food and his bed.

In positive fact the Delaneys were sure of neither.

Forced out of Charles Street, where would they go? Oh!
there were plenty who would take them in! But it wouldn't
be their own beds or their own food. Fred would of course
get work. But what would he do, what *could* he do in this
new world where, if you were not efficient at something,
you were lost? Why was the world so over-full of people
now? It hadn't been in her younger days. Ever since the
Great War, in which millions of people had been killed,
the world have been overcrowded. How very odd! She
was walking on grass now and before her rose a sloping
green hill canopied with a sky of rose and blue that the
increasing cold seemed to crystallize. Children were running, dogs were barking, the bare tree-trunks gave off,
as it seemed to her, a kind of smoke, of faintly amber
shadow. Yes, the sun was sinking. She climbed the little
hill, found two small children crying because they refused
to go home, and stood face to face with Graham Pender.

She knew him at once. Year melting into year had not
changed him. She could see him at this moment, here on
this hill, bending forward to kiss her, his feet slipping,
his little cry of dismay. . . . He was standing very still,
looking at the rosy sky.

'Well, Graham,' she said.

He turned as though he had been shot. He stared.

'I beg your pardon.'

'I'm Meg Wendover.'

Colour flashed into his brown, thin and *very* distinguished face.

'Meg!'

'Yes, I'm Meg. I recognized you at once.'

He shot out his hand, caught hers, and then held it,
staring and staring. His hand was trembling.

'Meg! Meg! Meg!' he said over and over.

She was herself so greatly excited that she put her
other hand on his shoulder.

'Dear Graham! How enchanting! Although I should

of course really be angry. I wrote last—over twenty years
ago. Not a word since.' She took both her hands back
to herself and tried to be dignified.

'Often and often I've wanted to,' he began eagerly.
(His eyes were as bright and blue as they had ever been,
his height as commanding, his forehead as noble!) 'But
I saw in the paper that you married, and I seemed destined for the East for ever and ever, and I . . . I married too and—and——'

'Don't explain anything.' They began to walk down
the hill. 'Of course you married. What woman could
resist you? And I saw that you had been knighted. And
your books are famous and so clever that no one can
understand them. And you are just the same. Years
haven't made the slightest difference to you.'

'My hair's white,' taking off his bowler hat. Yes, it was,
and with his blue eyes, brown colour, tall, slim, erect body,
made him more beautiful than ever!

'Put on your hat. You'll catch cold. Tell me everything.'

He laughed. It was plain that he was delighted indeed
to see her.

'My wife and I have come to England to live. Surbiton.
I'm up for two days. I want to see the English pictures
at Burlington House. We are going to Marie Tempest
to-night—*Old Folks At Home.*'

He told her everything in exactly the direct boyish way
that he had done—when?—was it only yesterday?

'Oh dear, I'm so glad we met! And I felt that something would happen—I knew it! I knew it!'

'And you?'

'I'm Mrs. Delaney. We live in Charles Street and have
two children. And I've got fat.'

'No. No, you haven't. You look superb—and somehow
a child still.'

A thin little woman wearing an ugly hat so that she

reminded Meg of a penwiper was coming across the grass toward them.

'This is my wife,' he said. 'I walked up the hill to look at the sky. Evie, this is an old friend of mine, Meg Delaney. We knew each other in Scotland when we were very, very young.'

(Evie, thought Meg. What a ridiculous name for her!)

'How do you do, Lady Pender?' Meg said.

'How do you do? An old friend. How very agreeable!'

They walked to the Inner Circle, talking about Marie Tempest.

'I don't care for the theatre,' Lady Pender said. 'But my husband enjoys it. It makes it so very late returning to Surbiton.'

'What does it matter! We only live once!' said Graham.

'We do indeed,' said Meg joyfully, 'and must make the most of every minute.' She stopped a taxi. 'Now that is my address and—wait a moment—that is our telephone number, although it *is* in the book.'

'I think I have a card.' He felt for his pocket-book. 'Yes, here it is.'

They looked one another for an instant in the eyes. Then he took off his hat, gave a little bow and led Lady Pender away.

CHAPTER IV

Figures in Rain

HALF MOON STREET on a rainy afternoon in January has little aspect of beauty. It is true that to-day it has respectability—more than could be claimed for it even twenty years ago. Mr. Dare and Mr. Dolphin blaze and shimmer at the entrance as much as to say: 'Here are shirts, ties and dressing-gowns so superb that, try as it may, Half Moon Street won't, after you've looked into our window, be able to disappoint you.' And the tobacconist, opposite Mr. Dare and Mr. Dolphin, shows you pipes so beautiful that, slender of purse as you are, you wish that Sir Walter Raleigh had never been born. There are gay bachelors, too, in 90 Piccadilly—gay and at the same time serious, responsible, knowing as they do that they are under the benevolent but autocratic supervision of John Jones, master of all gentlemen's servants; morals and patriotism go, at this address, hand in hand with the rent.

Abutting on Number 90, moreover, there is a staid but elegant Club whose members constantly place their cars at the very portals of Number 90 to the aggravation of the aforesaid moral bachelors. All this is very well, and so far Half Moon Street has nothing to be ashamed of. Nor is there any very evident change as you advance. Excellent landlords, admirable landladies, bright fires seen between the curtains, cats, sleeker than the common or garden, rubbing their backs against area railings, a geranium or so, a glimpse of 'The Stag at Bay' above the friendly bookcase, a gentleman's gentleman, bareheaded, wearing a stiff white collar and side-whiskers as though he were even now in the service of Major Pendennis, two bottles of milk, twin innocents, still on the doorstep, two young men delivering a table, a bassinet and a rocking-horse, a window high in the sky suddenly opening and a gentleman with a teapot in his hand calling out 'Paper!', a stout man in a bowler hat leading two Pekinese, authority, disgust, and a simple touching kind of loneliness fighting for victory on his pale and very unintelligent countenance; here is the life of Half Moon Street on any afternoon in the week. 'On tiptoe for flight,' you might imitate Mr. Keats by calling it, for it will not remain as it is much longer. There is ghostly scaffolding about the houses and the smoky-dusty-carpet-geranium-smelling-iron-bedstead-basement-toastmaking-damp-washing period is nearly over and ended. It doesn't matter in the least, the number of the house where Mrs. Van Renn and her daughter Alice had their abode. Their rooms were on the middle floor—two bedrooms, bath- and sitting-room, meals sent up to order, service and electric light and coal extra.

The house must not be numbered here because, to tell the truth, it was a very poor, frowsty and uncomfortable house. Mrs. Van Renn took the rooms last year because the rent was low and the address good. It was one of her final desperate moves to get Alice off her hands, because if Alice didn't marry money soon they'd be in the poor-house. Mrs. Van Renn, it must be confessed, was very ugly, being more like a monkey than most monkeys manage to be, nor was she in any way an attractive character, but she adored her only child, although she was desperately afraid of her. If she *did* marry her off she would be so lonely an old woman that suicide would be the only way out; on the other hand, if she *didn't* marry her off, why, then they would die in the gutter. So there you were!

Alice herself expressed no opinion in the matter. She didn't care in the least what happened to her. That men were fascinated by her, her mother knew; that they never proposed marriage to her was also a fact.

'Why don't they, Alice?'

'I've no idea, Mama.'

'You give in to them too readily.'

'I don't give in to them at all.'

'Well, perhaps you ought to.'

'I don't want to be married, Mama.'

'Then we starve. That's all. We positively starve.'

'I'd rather starve than be married.'

'Then what about me?'

'I'm sorry, Mama, but you should never have allowed Papa to put our money in those mines.'

'I didn't know. I never knew *what* your father was doing.'

On an afternoon of driving rain Half Moon Street is really on the shabby side. Its resentment at bad weather is to be felt in all its bones: rheumatism, a sentimental melancholy for the past, and a waterproof that has known better days. Half Moon Street aches from head to toe; Mr. Dare and Mr. Dolphin give one look out of the window and for that afternoon at least decide that their residence is in Piccadilly.

Fred Delaney, seated on an uncomfortable chair in the Van Renn sitting-room, wished that he had not come. He had intended *not* to. He would write some letters, go and talk to the Pakes, wait finally for Meg to return from her visit to some old friends she had discovered who lived, of all inaccessible rainy-day places, in Surbiton.

Then the flesh had pricked as it is given to doing on a rainy day in London. A vision of Alice Van Renn's exquisite white neck hung, like a materialization of ectoplasm, right in front of the William and Mary clock. He didn't *want* it to be there. He turned his eyes away from it, but it followed him and in some mysterious way affected his stomach. It was exactly the same sensation as when, a small boy with no pocket-money, he had gazed in at a pastry-cook's window. Not a very worthy reason for visiting Miss Van Renn; and, through the rain, stopping to buy an evening paper from the newsman who stood beside Miss Bonda's archway, he cursed himself for a weak self-indulgent Irishman.

Inside the Van Renn castle, he decided, as he had already several times decided, that the girl was a complete fool. He tried her with the theatre. Did she like pantomimes? Had she seen *Babes in the Wood* and George Mozart?

'Oh, I never go to pantomimes.'

'No . . . well, not by yourself of course. But it's fun to take children.'

'Oh, do you think so? Children always behave so badly when they are with me.'

Yes, they would, of course. They'd *hate* her. He was aware then, as tea was being brought in by a girl who had plucked eyebrows and was heavily powdered, he was aware, for the first time, that Mrs. Van Renn didn't like him. Fred was not vain, but he did think that he was a big, jolly Irish gentleman and agreeable to most people. He had set out from the beginning to be charming to Mrs. Van Renn because of her beautiful daughter, and now all his efforts were wasted.

He didn't know, of course, that Mrs. Van Renn looked now on any male admirer of Alice's who was unable to offer her marriage as a danger. He didn't realize either that Mrs. Van Renn found him physically most attractive and that when she thought that of any man a sense of isolation and misery attacked her; for she was an ugly

brown-faced old woman and she knew it. Thirdly, he did
not know that Mrs. Van Renn realized that her daughter
was attracted also by this man, and that that was a rare
and alarming portent.

He did know, however, that the tea was stewed, the
madeira cake something only fit for the laundry, and the
bread and butter faded and weary.

Alice got up and stood by the window, staring out at
the rain. Then she turned and looked at Delaney. The
faintest hint of colour touched her cheek. She was dressed
in a very simple black frock. She was so thin and so pale
and her features were so lovely and her body was so
remote that he lowered his head and gazed at the carpet.
For a wonder she spoke.

'On a day like this in a street like this, Mr. Delaney,
don't you long for a gas-oven?'

'Really, Alice!'

'Well, of course, Mama. . . . It's the sensible thing.
Only I haven't the courage.'

'No, I can't say that I do.' Fred looked at her hands.
'After all it won't rain for ever.'

The impulse to get up and take her in his arms, there,
in front of her old mother, was insane and almost irresistible. It was then that he was aware of the danger that
he was in. It was a sharp warning, coming from within
himself. 'Get up and go! Go and never come back.' He
did get up.

'I must be going, I'm afraid.'

He held out his hand and it enclosed Alice's. She was
drawn a little closer to him. Her hand was warm when
he had expected it to be cold.

Mrs. Van Renn said: 'Oh, must you go? It's early
yet.' She had a habit of bending and twisting her thin
brown fingers together.

He said to Alice: 'You must come to a theatre some
night.'

'Thanks. I'd love to.'

The room was stifling and his heart was hammering. Mrs. Van Renn said: 'So nice to have seen you.'

As he went downstairs he was aware that he was carry-ing the scent of the room with him. There must have been, he thought, gas escaping somewhere; there was a smell of airlessness and as though a trap had been set baited with cheese and a mouse had been caught in it some while back.

He must walk. He must clear his head of the mouse-trap, Alice's white neck. He must investigate this new and unaccustomed sense of danger.

He started down the Green Park. Just a short round to the Palace, Hyde Park Corner and back. The rain curled and coiled about him like a great spider's-web. On an afternoon like this the London that he loved disap-peared and became as indistinct as the blurred film in a cinematograph. It had no character, no place, no past nor present.

In and out of the rain figures were constantly moving, but figures like germs in a medical chart. This was because, he often thought (for he studied London and all its moods with constant delight), under storm and rain London was not a city, but rather gladly returned to its original marsh-world. He had noticed how a bird flying through the air on a rainy day in London seemed gigantic, portentous, masterful, how men and women shrank to non-identity, and the long stretch of Piccadilly covered with the motion-less wet-gleaming cars and omnibuses was like a river of mud and slime between rocky barriers. When the rain, as to-day, was clinging and web-like, and the chill air wrapped you in damp underclothing, he rushed to some interior, for once be within walls on a London wet day and you were twice as comforted, consoled and reassured as you would be in any other place. It was as though on every side of you fortresses had been planted against the enemy. Once inside, you could, from the warmth, light, security, look out and mock the marshes and the gleaming dark-running river, the gigantic birds, the quagmires and the prehistoric beasts.

To-day, however, he realized that his attraction to Alice Van Renn belonged to the marshes and the gigantic bird. There is a world of physical passion which has no contact anywhere with common sense, morality, thought for others, friendship, nobility of character. All that you can say to a man is that he must keep out of it, for once he has crossed the border and breathed its unnatural air he will not listen to any warning voices, any threats of public disgrace or private hell, any stern implication of the law. That is why one is so often astonished by bizarre, macabre, abnormal occurrences revealed suddenly, planted there in the normal, colourless life of man like bright exotic poisonous flowers.

Delaney's attraction to Alice Van Renn was not as yet mature enough to seem so portentous, but, walking now in the rain, he realized quite clearly that it might become so, that it belonged to that crazy, dangerous world, that it was a sort of fever in the blood that led to deliriums, sleep-walkings, and acts that were destructive, without reward, comfortless.

This was not the first time that he had been beguiled by the flesh, but he had hoped that these mad, inevitably disappointing episodes were beginning to fade from his life. For he liked to be kind, jolly, generous and honest, and he loved Meg with all his heart and soul.

Then, with a flash, he realized that he was attracted to Alice Van Renn partly because she was, in physical type, the exact opposite of his wife. He was attracted sensually by the spare, the delicate, the remote, the silent. He had loved Meg passionately, he had passion for her still, but for some reason women of her type had always been easy of conquest for him. They had liked his health and sturdiness and joyfulness as he had liked theirs. He looked on Alice Van Renn as a collector of Chinese pottery sees a splendid horse in the Eumorfopoulos Collection. Her power over him lay in her remoteness from possession. That was why this obsession was so essentially foolish. If he didn't get her he would be exasperated, and if he did get her he would be disappointed. To all the other Figures in the Rain he cried out: 'There is nothing in this but folly, bitterness and unhappiness to others. Let's run from the marshes to dry ground.' He shook his shoulders with relief when he found himself safely once again within the walls of the Charles Street house.

There was a message that Captain Pullet would like to see him when he came in. He ran up the stairs, humming, feeling all the old buoyancy, his physical fitness, his freedom from alarm.

'Well, Smoke, what's the trouble?'

'Have a drink.'

'Thanks, I will. Not too much whisky.'

'What a filthy day!'

'Yes, isn't it? I had a walk but it was nasty. Not the right sort of rain. Glad to get in.'

'Smoke' Pullet was very trim, his face hollowed and sharp. He looked an Army officer and a discontented one. Or rather the puckered lines in his forehead stood for trouble more than discontent. He had lost a leg in the War. The sitting-room of the Pullets was furnished in the best modern fashion; the chairs had arms of steel, the carpet had a design of black and white squares, there was a Marie Laurencin lady in silver and pink over the fireplace, the walls were white and the curtains black. Fred Delaney thought the place hideous, but that was not his business. He liked Smoke and Dodie immensely. He felt for them like a father. He thought Smoke one of the bravest and least intelligent men he had ever known. Dodie was clever, but Smoke had no brains at all, only instincts. He had therefore been a great success in the War and had been awarded both the D.S.O. and the M.C.

He was so honest, so courageous and so stupid that he was not at all fitted for the economic storms that he was trying to weather.

He looked at Delaney with great affection and said: 'I'm sorry, old boy, but I'm afraid I have some bad news for you.'

'What's that?'

'It seems that Dodie and I will have to move. We are planning to sleep on the Embankment. Dodie's out now seeing about a pitch.'

This was what Fred had feared, but he showed no disturbance. His cheerful countenance beamed on his friend.

'Stuff! Leave here? I should think not!'

'Oh, but it's so, old boy. You know that Dodie's been helping Hazel Groom in her dressmaking place. Well, she's left. They had an awful row. There's only my pension and we're up to our eyes in debt. We simply can't afford even this rent.'

Delaney said nothing. He couldn't offer a lesser rent because one penny less and the whole place went under.

'I think,' Smoke said slowly, 'that the best thing I can do is to get out of this altogether.'

'Get out of it?'

'Yes. Bung off. Visit another world. Make a call on old Saint Peter.'

'My dear chap——'

'Yes, I know all about it. I'm not very bright, you know, and ideas move slowly. All the same, I get there in the end. Anyway, lots of chaps are doing it. You read about one or other of them every morning in the paper . . . and Dodie would be a lot better without me. She'd marry again. She's darned attractive and some smart feller would want her. Sure to.'

'You blithering fool,' Delaney said. 'She adores you.'

'Yes, she's fond of me. She's a good girl. She'd miss
me a bit at first and then she'd see what a good thing it
was. This isn't a world, old boy, for a chap with a wooden
leg, no cash and no brains.' Then he added slowly, staring
in front of him: 'I've tried for every sort of thing. Nobody wants me.'

Delaney was silent. He had a lot to think about.

'You've no idea, old boy, of the kind of life that Dodie
and I've been leading in the last year. We've cadged
deliberately on everybody we know. We've angled for
meals, been everywhere and anywhere with the chance
of getting something for nothing. We've spent days and
nights with the most awful people to be safe for food
and drink. It can't go on for ever. For one thing, *we* can't
stand it. For another, I bore nearly everybody. There are
only a few old stupids like yourself can stand me. Almost
all the people we really like are as poor as we are. And
that's another reason I'd be better away. Dodie amuses
them. She's bright and gay. Without me she would have
no end of a time. If I ever did have any ideas they are
gone now because my brain goes round and round about
the Bank worrying us and the debts and the rent and the
debts and the Bank. . . . So we must move out, old boy.
Sorry, but there's nothing else for it.'

Fred stretched his thick legs out, patted his stomach,
pulled at his tie, looked in front of him. Here was another
Figure in the Rain. Unless something happened Smoke
would do just as he said. And perhaps it would be the
best thing for him. That was the real problem at the
heart of the trouble. There was no place in this present
world for the Smoke Pullets unless there was a World
War again—then they would be admirable.

Before 1914 they had played a very necessary part;
they were a real need in English life and had been so for
centuries. They had been the Squire and the Squire's son;
some property, possibly a seat in Parliament, beneficent,

tyrannical, understanding in their country community, conforming, traditional, safe and sound. So it had been since the Wars of the Roses; from Agincourt 1415, say, until Serajevo 1914. And now, within the space of twenty years, they had become only a burden, and a wearisome burden at that. There was no future of any kind for Smoke and he without a leg which he had lost in the service of his country. Probably a nice gas-oven (who had been talking of gas-ovens that very afternoon?—oh yes! Miss Alice Van Renn!) *would* be the best thing.

And yet Delaney had only to look at Smoke to know that he would do anything in his power to help him—save only to lower the rent. That he must not do for the sake of the house. The house! The house! And then he heard Smoke saying:

'And the Pakes may have to do the same thing. Their income's gone down like anything.'

So there it was! The battle had been joined! Nineteen-thirty-four was already showing what she could do, and January not ended! He realized from the start, however, that it was Smoke with whom he had immediately to deal. Let him think of the house afterwards! Over Smoke's thin obstinate face there was a strange shadow as though he were half-way towards Saint Peter already!

'Look here, Smoke—don't be a bloody fool. No, I mean it. Killing yourself doesn't help anything. I'll speak to Rex Bennet, in the War Office. He'll think of something. Great friend of mine. And we'll manage about the rent. I've got to get it in somehow because we're running on a narrow margin as it is. There are so many things want doing to a house like this. You're right, though, in one thing. Fellows like you and me who haven't been brought up to doing anything particular aren't much use in this new world. You've got to be *efficient* at something these days if you're to get a job, and the public schools are still turning out heaps of young chaps who aren't any more efficient than we are. There are more young men hanging round London doing nothing to their parents' despair than ever before, and they don't want to do anything either. They've been to Eton or Harrow or Winchester and think they're swell. They look down on everybody, their parents first of all—and yet they're quite incompetent. They don't give a damn for their country. Patriotism is bunk, and so is religion and so is hard work. I don't like the Fascists and the Nazis, but I will say they give their young men something to be keen about. . . .'

The door opened and Dodie Pullet stood there, as smart and thin and straight as a wand cut from the willow. Delaney, looking at her, thought as he often thought: 'Where *do* they put all their figure to? Nothing either in front or behind. It must all be *somewhere.*'

But he was extremely fond of Dodie. She came and kissed him, ruffled his hair a little, and, in her mouse-grey frock with carnation at the neck and wrist, stood, with her arm around her husband's waist, looking very beautiful.

'Well, darling, have you told him?'

'Yes, I have.'

'And what does he say?'

'Oh, that it's all nonsense of course.'

'It isn't. Fred, sweet, we've got to go. That is unless I become a woman of sin and spend a week-end with—oh, never mind who! But I've had a very good offer.'

She was joking, she was talking nonsense, and yet the trouble in Smoke's eyes ever so slightly deepened.

'Now, you two children,' said Delaney, getting up and straddling on his strong legs. 'Leave it all to your uncle. He'll think of something.'

'I don't know what it is about you Delaneys,' Dodie said. 'You haven't any money yourselves and you none of you do anything for a living and you aren't very intelligent and yet you *are* a comfort. There's no denying it.

You *are* a comfort. Someone was calling you ironically the other night "the joyful Delaneys" and saying they detested your good spirits. But I don't know. It's as though you saw farther than the rest of us and knew there was a good place *somewhere*. I like you. I must honestly confess I like you. But you're getting fat, Fred. You must watch out for it. The Hay Diet. That's the thing.'

Later in the evening, in the middle of his happiness, he thought of the Pullets. But they were different now. Figures in the Rain, but the rain was shut out, and all that marsh-world was unreal. For, by an extraordinary piece of good fortune, all the Delaneys were in that evening— Fred, Meg, Kitty and Bullock. Not only did they all have dinner together, but they stayed together *after* dinner, all of them, until they went up to bed. Of how many families of their class in London that evening could that be said? They had one of Fred's favourite dinners, as Meg knew well—petite marmite, sole, mutton with currant jelly and baked potatoes, and apple pudding.

'Americans shudder at our food,' Fred said. 'And yet, how beautiful, how natural, how full of flavour. . . . Dodie Pullet says I'm getting fat.'

He reflected that it was strange that they always seemed to gather this happiness from one another. Trouble was brewing for himself, Meg had something on her mind, and Kitty—hadn't, in the last few days, something been happening to Kitty? but inside this room, close together, loving one another, they were conscious, perhaps, as Dodie said, of a happiness not dependent on the events of the day or material things. . . . He didn't know. Food and wine made him sentimental.

'And how was Surbiton?' he asked Meg.

For an instant—so swift that no one but he in the whole world would have noticed it—she pulled up her guard. She looked at him over the top of it with her large black eyes, as though she would say: 'Are we moving into a

new episode? Have I got to be careful?' for no marriage,
however long-lived, however intimately enjoyed, is ever
static. It changes colour, shape, balance of strength and
weakness with every striking of the hour. No one knows
anyone else sufficiently ever to be *certain* of safety.

'Surbiton? . . . Oh dear, such a wet day! I walked
up an endless road. Just imagine! The house was called
"Happy Nook".'

'Called *what?*'

' "Happy Nook." Really. Of course my friend hadn't
named it. It was like that when they took it.'

'Did you like them?'

'Of course it's funny after so long. The wife's a dowdy.
He's so very clever.'

'Ah, that must be a change after your own dear family.'

'And what have you been doing on this very wet day?'

'Oh, nothing . . . had a little walk in the rain . . .
waited for you to come back.'

Afterwards they sat in extreme comfort round the fire.
Once Kitty said:

"Anyone ever heard of a painter called Braque?"

'*Who,* darling?'

'Braque—B-r-a-q-u-e.'

'Lord, no! What a funny name!'

'I have,' Bullock said. 'Play you at backgammon, Kitty.'

'All right. What do you know about him?'

'Oh, he paints squares and cubes and nonsense like
that. You aren't going highbrow, my darling sister, are
you?'

'Of course not. Why should I be highbrow just because
I ask an intelligent question?'

Bullock kissed her.

'You look very beautiful to-night, as though you were
in love or something.'

Meg tried to read a novel for a brief while. She put
the book down. 'I know I'm not clever,' she said, 'but I

can't read modern novels. If they're intelligent they're about the nastiest people and take the gloomiest view of everything. If they're about nice people and end well, they're stupid. What I want is an *intelligent* happy novel. It's not much to ask.'

Later, from his very small dressing-room off their bedroom, he called out:

'Meg!'

'Yes, dear.'

'What stage are you at?'

'I'm in bed.'

He came in, in a superb dressing-gown of black silk with a purple collar and cuffs—a birthday present from Larry after he'd made a lucky deal in some Waterford glass. Fred called it his Waterford. He sprawled over his bed and drew her into his arms.

'Meg, dear.'

'Yes. What is it?'

'I think I'm a little in love with the Van Renn girl.'

'I know you are.'

'And the Pullets and the Pakes may be leaving.'

'Oh dear, oh dear!'

'Yes—altogether I feel as though things are going to happen. You're not quite yourself either.'

'Of course I am, darling.'

'Not quite. . . . Not quite.' He leaned his cheek against hers. 'What I want to say is—dearest, are you listening?'

'Of course I'm listening.'

'Whatever happens, *whatever* happens, we'll see one another through everything. We know, don't we, that no one, nothing, ever and ever can mean to us what we mean to one another?'

'Yes, we do.'

'That's why we're happy if we have to beg in the streets.'

'I shan't mind begging in the least if we're together.'

He drew back from her a little. He put his hand under her chin.

'Even your old flame—who's very very clever, isn't he?—won't take you from me?'

Meg laughed quite hysterically.

'Fred, what an absurd idea! Why, he's got white hair.'

'And you love me, love me, love me?'

'I adore you.'

Meg looked at him, smiling. Then she said slowly:

'If—for a day, a night, a minute, a second I *were* unfaithful—how would it be?'

'It would be as we said at the beginning it was to be. We agreed then that we should both be free—absolutely.'

'Yes, but you would love me less?'

'I don't know how it would feel.'

'People would think it disgusting if you didn't.'

'We've nothing to do with people,' Fred said, 'or any-one else's rules.'

But Meg was thinking:

'Yes—but I've a kind of wildness in me—always have had, and one day perhaps before I'm an old woman and everything's over I might—just to be kind, to smell a whiff of adventure—I might be *too* kind.'

'That would be up to you,' Fred answered. 'What I couldn't be responsible for would be my own feelings. But we'd be honest with one another and *I* think we'd go on loving one another whatever happened.'

'Yes,' Meg said. 'But not in the same way. I think there's nothing more horrible than for people to have *rights* over one another. Horrible, horrible! We're free, as you say, you and I! But, put laws and religion and tradition and what conventional people think *all* aside, love between husband and wife follows the same instincts as it did ten thousand years ago. Love can be damaged.'

'Has ours,' he asked quickly, 'by my—well—weaknesses?'

'Yes, I think it has—a little. I love you just as much, but a little differently and not quite so finely. Of course,' she went on rapidly, 'we aren't very fine people—not as fine people go. We're *happy* people, which is quite another thing. If we were finer we wouldn't be quite so happy maybe. There's a little bit of the guttersnipe in both of us, Fred. In Larry, too. In Kitty a little. But *not* in Bullock, I think.'

She got up, looking at him.

'All the same our love for one another is grand. And it would be silly—for some little quick sensation—to spoil it. People do—often. But I'm not to be trusted—not for another while or so. No other man but you has made love to me for years and it *is* so agreeable!'

He looked at her and then beyond her. 'We're free. Our love's based on that.'

'Perhaps we shouldn't *be* free. Maybe we're going to find that out.'

But he was never any good at serious discussion.

'Wait a minute,' he said. 'I'll be back.'

He went into the dressing-room to clean his teeth.

CHAPTER V

The Ground Trembles under His Feet

SHEPHERD MARKET about ten of the morning when the sun has not, as yet, broken through the wispy fog-mist, is like a little miniature town under water. Nothing is quite clear, yet nothing is really indistinct. If you enter under Miss Bonda's archway, with only a step or two, you drop the whole of London behind you, or rather you enter into the very nutshell of London, having within a few feet of you everything that London can provide.

In Carrington House you can see the backside of all London's present splendour: you may, by ringing a bell and murmuring a sentence or two, be the possessor of a regal apartment at a regal price and call the Green Park your own. Indeed one of the qualities of Shepherd Market is that it is not only a fortressed town in itself, but from its windows you can look out on to the whole campaign of the outer world. You are, in fact, here and now, the *very centre* of the world and well does every citizen of Shepherd Market know it. It is the last stronghold of mediaevalism, the supreme remaining quintessence of Victorian Dickens England as the very sign of 'Ye Grapes' reminds you; in its glistening blood-brown leather of boot and shoe there is the soul of the English Squirearchy; the

shops of fish and game smell of rivers running turbulently
to sea, and green meadows fading before the evening
star; the window of old books and prints offers you culture. Beer and kippers and varnished leather and fresh
spring flowers, the evening newspaper, a cut off the joint
and two veg. for a shilling, Apartments for Gentlemen,
strings of glass beads, Chinese boxes, Elizabethan ivory
in Philo's window, the butcher's red harvest, two canaries
in a cage for half a crown, 'All the Winners' and sweet
cakes and coffee at Café No. I—you can live within these
walls for ever, need never step outside, and can have all
your mental, bodily, spiritual wants supplied till the coffin
is ready for you.

In this rose-mist cold-snap morning light this little
square of ground has more of the spiritual sense of London than any other spot on this cinder of a star. Be
dropped here blindfold and you'll smell in a second where
you are. It is not only the fish and the leather and the
fresh spring flowers, it is rather the way that London
has of living with intense quiet, its finger on its nose,
plunged so deep into the past that you cannot, if you are
a foreigner, conceive that there is any present life at all
—a mistake that foreigners have been given to making
through all England's past history. If, dropped from an
aeroplane, you stood there blindfold, say in the very
centre of Market Street, you would hear people moving
on every side of you and almost no sound coming from
them. A dog would brush against your leg, you would
scent the rough fur of the cat as it moved toward the
fish-and-game Paradise, somewhere from a far distance
beyond the walls there would be the humming whirr of
traffic. You might fancy that you caught the echo of Sam
Weller's ghostly greeting or the ponderous dogmatism
of Samuel Johnson, Mrs. Gamp's husky endearments,
the shrill cry, like a call from the battlements, of King
James' apprentice, the ghostly song of Piers Plowman

himself finding this soil still stream-watered. Time marches on, and yet there is no Time here.

And then, your bandage removed, you would stand there blinking, for the thin fog has not cleared yet and it is as though under water the figures are moving and it is under water that the voices are hushed. Nevertheless wait a little and you will find the life as practical and workaday as in any one of the blessed Five Towns themselves.

Mr. Brocket is very practical indeed. There is no poetry-nonsense for him as he moves, hither and thither, engaged on his morning shopping. Mr. Brocket, in a decent dark suit and a bowler hat, moved very cheerfully among his fellow-men. Brocket was in no kind of way a bad human being. The only trouble with him was that he was, like many thousands of others, still a child. He wished everyone well so long as his greed, his animal desires, his sense of power were sufficiently fed. He had not reached that stage of maturity that demands consideration of others equal with goodwill to oneself. He was the type of whom all tyrants, and men who work gladly for and under tyrants, are made. But this was no sin in him. He had simply never developed from the stage when he seized his little sister's liquorice-stick because he was stronger than she, and twisted the arm of a boy smaller and more nervous than himself. He thought himself a very good man, as all tyrants think themselves good men. He had the utmost contempt for those who are foolish enough to give anything away without hope of practical return, who turn the other cheek or who believe in the virtues of their friends. He trusted, as he often said, 'in the strength of his good right arm,' although if a right arm stronger than his own appeared he was most polite, even sycophantic towards it.

He lied when there was no likelihood of being found out and called it 'good business.' He was often drunk and called it 'making merry with his pals.' He seduced any woman whom he could persuade or force, and called it 'a weak spot for the fairer sex.' He considered, without thinking about it, that the whole universe swung round himself. There had been moments—of illness, of plain speaking from someone too strong for him to defy, of money difficulties—when it had seemed to him as though this might not be so. Then he had been very frightened indeed. Under his jollity, good comradeship, and fun with those weaker than himself, there ran a tremor of apprehension. If, for half an hour, he knew indigestion he was certain that it was cancer. If one of his little financial adjustments were in danger of discovery he saw prison gates opening in front of him; if a girl threatened trouble he considered, for a moment, the gas-oven. All this was because he was still a child—a dirty-minded, ignorant, bullying child. Not his fault. Only, in parenthesis, one may remark that it is astonishing when you consider how long civilization has been at work that there should still be so many children about. Astonishing and a little disappointing perhaps.

Brocket was well liked, on the whole, in Shepherd Market. He was considered a big, jolly, friendly man. He had but few intimates and they knew well that, at heart, he was neither jolly nor friendly. Women liked him until they became intimate. After that, they were often too unpleasantly frightened to talk.

He moved about the Market, buying a thing here, a thing there. He knew the just price of everything. He knew also the characters of his fellow-citizens. Some he threatened a little (for he was a great repository of dirty and mean secrets), some he placated, with a few he had a kind of secret understanding. There was a young girl, a servant in one of the flats near by, whose person he considered favourably. She was very young, rosy-faced, and, he believed, ignorant of the world. He had, as yet, only passed with her the time of day; he hoped soon to know her better. He watched now, as he moved about, to see whether she too might not be engaged on a bit of shopping. She was nowhere to be seen. Then he remembered that he must have a word or two with his tenant, Mr. Willoughby, and so he moved homeward.

Claude was in his room considering a far from agreeable post. His post that morning consisted of one letter only and that was from Mr. Clive Markham, his solicitor, who managed his affairs.

Clive Markham also managed the affairs of the Pake ladies. They had introduced Claude to him, and very kind Mr. Markham had been, for he managed Claude's few investments with all the care possible and never charged him a penny for the service. Being a man of good heart he hated to have to write Claude this kind of letter —a letter which informed him that the Toddington Waterworks were unable to pay any dividend just now but hoped to be a little more generous next time. That meant that the twenty pounds upon which Claude had calculated would not be forthcoming. He had paid, happily, his last quarter's rent, but on what would he live during the present quarter?

He sat there, shivering, in his old dressing-gown, but the blood of the Willoughbys which had often assisted him before came to his rescue again. He was not defeated. He had no intention of being defeated. He must sell something. So he went to the cabinet, opened it and surveyed his treasures. There they were—his silver christening mug, a Jacobean dagger of chased silver, two gold snuff-boxes, the miniature of his mother as a child in a thin gold frame, a small, very ancient Toby jug in black and brown, a gold brooch with pearls that had belonged to his mother, and an exquisite little cup and saucer out of which, his mother used to tell him, Marie Antoinette had once drunk her morning coffee.

He looked at these, his thin little body shaking with cold, his head shaking with sentiment. He *could* not sell these things, not one of them! Something else must be done. He must consult Millie and Helen who, very nearly in his own condition, must have many brilliant ideas. He sat down again, picking up his *Telegraph* to read about the dreadful hardships of the South Wales miners, when the door quietly opened and Brocket, in his shirt-sleeves and brown apron, presented himself.

'Mr. Willoughby, it isn't an agreeable thing to bring forward, as I told Major Pierson, but the plain fact is that he's missing a bottle of bath salts bought at Fortnum and Mason's only two days back and he's wondering if you happen to have seen them when you was down there 'aving your bath.'

Claude put by his paper.

'Is Major Pierson suggesting I stole them?' he asked.

The hairs on Brocket's head seemed, like the stars of God, to sing together in glory. How greatly he enjoyed a little scene like this! It was meat and drink and more to him. Having been deprived of a little conversation that morning with the rosy-cheeked servant, he must take his pleasure some other way. It was true that Major Pierson had lost a bottle of bath salts or *said* he had (silly old fool, what was *he* wanting with bath salts!), but he had certainly never suggested that Mr. Willoughby had taken them. That was all Brocket's bright idea.

'Why no, Mr. Willoughby, in course not, most certainly not. Major Pierson's a gentleman, and between gentlemen such things aren't done, I *do* 'ope. He only suggested I might enquire about the 'ouse, the bottle being missing and being just new, practically unopened, one might say.'

'Please search my room, Brocket, if that gives you any pleasure.'

Claude was trembling with rage at the insult, and he knew that Brocket knew that he was trembling and was

pleased thereat. He was trembling with rage and also with
a kind of nausea at Brocket's close physical presence. This
nausea had in it anger, disgust, and also fear. Fear, lest
on some sudden occasion, Brocket should touch him. The
thought of that touch haunted him. It seemed to him fan-
tastically as though, at one touch from Brocket's horrible
hand, he, Claude, would crumble into dust as from the
touch of death itself. These are tall words but they were
not at all exaggerated in Claude's consciousness. He was
old, not in very good health, had never sufficient food;
under such conditions the walls of the physical material
world are thinned, physical contacts are more imminent
and more deeply charged with significance. Brocket had
never, in real life, touched him, but Claude had known
dreams in which Brocket's hairy arms were around him
and he was drawn closer and closer to the thick breath,
the evil panting heart, to the very horrors of anticipated
obscene death. . . .

Nevertheless he remarked very quietly: 'You know
very well, Brocket, that Major Pierson never even suggested that I took his bath salts. I have not seen them in
the bathroom. I'm afraid you must look elsewhere.'

Brocket stepped further into the room, scratching one
pale-grey arm meditatively with a dirty fingernail.

'Now, Mr. Willoughby, that isn't very polite, if I may
say. That is as much as suggesting that I'm a liar. You're
a gentleman, Mr. Willoughby, and I'm sure don't wish to
make such a suggestion.'

'I don't say you're a liar, Brocket. I only repeat that
I haven't seen Major Pierson's bath salts. That's what
you came about, I think.'

Brocket looked at him. What a miserable, half-fed
little weed this was! Had the Soviet Union been in command in London and Brocket a Commissar (a job he
would have discharged with a thorough and genuine enthusiasm), the fun that he might have had with little Mr.

Willoughby. As it was he continued broodingly to scratch his arm, and suddenly Claude gave a jump in his chair and cried: 'Don't do that! Stop scratching your arm!' There was a silence. The two men stared at one another. Then Claude, his heart beating as though it would strangle his words, said: 'I beg your pardon. I don't know what led me . . . I beg your pardon.'

Brocket coughed, rather as a delicately-minded lady might after she had been affronted by some unexpected coarseness. Then, his slippers flip-flapping under him, he left the room.

Claude dressed and thought that he would take a little air. The sun was out by now, and in Market Street he recovered some of his self-control. He was known to numbers of persons who respected and liked him. 'A proper old gentleman.' 'One of the old sort.' 'You don't see many of his sort nowadays.'

So he walked delicately, swinging his cane which he always carried in fine weather, and thinking how greatly he would enjoy breaking it over Brocket's rump had he but the opportunity and a strong arm. In reality, he was trying to force himself into the determination to give Brocket notice. He must find a room somewhere else in a more modest quarter of London. He must not any longer afford the grandeur of the Market.

But that removal seemed to him like a sentence of death. Once in a dreadful little room in Bloomsbury or possibly even in Camden Town (not that he had anything against either of those admirable districts) he would be so utterly lost that he would die. Lost. Forgotten. That's what he would be. So long as he was citizen of the Market and might walk about, as he did on this sunny morning, with his head up and his friends around him, he lived, he had a reason for living. He was afraid of Brocket; he hated, even detested him, but he would find a way to win a victory there. Banished from the world that he had al-

ways known, whose air he had always breathed, he would
be strangled and die. . . .

'Good morning, Mr. Willoughby. Nice day, isn't it?'

Claude turned, and there was young Bullock Delaney.
They had met, once, twice, for brief moments in the Pake
sitting-room. And what a nice young man young Delaney
was! He had such charming manners, listened to what you
had to say, smiled so often, was so anxious to be kind.

This, alas, was what all lame dogs thought of young
Bullock, and a dreadful curse in young Bullock's life it
was. He was dedicated, in the modern drama, to the rôle
of 'Charles, His Friend.'

He was invited to advise and arrange more domestic
troubles than he cared to count; not at all because he was
especially wise, but because his heart was kind and he was,
above all, a good listener. He differed from his sister
Kitty in that he possessed a wider sympathy than she. Like
all women she preferred to have all her eggs in one basket,
and once the basket was filled she concentrated on it
entirely. But Bullock, having, in spite of his literary in-
tentions, not a great deal to do, being happy himself and
very trustful of others, believed the stories that were
told him and guilelessly tried to assist. He was considered,
therefore, a fool by nine-tenths of his acquaintances, and
a deep Machiavellian plotter by the other tenth. He was
neither a fool nor a saint, possessing good brains in certain directions, and all the regular weaknesses. He was
for ever falling in love and had known one or two suc-
cesses in spite of his small stature. A little drink made him
so heady and gay that he looked and behaved foolishly.
When he played cards he played badly and lost more than
he could afford. Almost any scoundrel could take him in
with a tall story. He believed in his friends quite foolishly.
He was exasperatingly stupid at times. But his heart was
warm and generous, his sense of honour immaculate, his
courage undefeatable.

At the first sight of Claude he had been touched just as his sister was, but this morning, in the Market, he caught before Claude veiled it a look of troubled embarrassment, of a frightened anxiety, that moved him deeply. Brocket, looking out of the first-floor window, thought them a comic little pair. 'They'd go well in a midget show,' he commented to Mrs. Schneider, the cook, with whom he was having a kind of rogues' interview.

'Can't all 'ave *your* 'ight, Mr. Brocket,' said Mrs. Schneider, deeply brooding over the best way to cheat Brocket without his discovering it.

'Yes, it *is* a nice day, isn't it?' said Claude cheerfully.

'Out for a stroll?' asked Bullock, wondering what the old boy's trouble was.

'Only a little constitutional. We don't get the sun such a lot this time of year.'

'No, we don't, and that's a fact.'

'I live just here. Rooms in White Horse Street.'

'Oh, do you?' said Bullock. 'Most romantic spot in London I always think this is.'

'It *is* romantic, isn't it? I do hope they won't pull it down. They're always threatening to.'

'We'll have to fight for it if they do. You and I, Mr. Willoughby—side by side.'

Then Bullock had an idea. He had been considering. He could not bear to leave the man without some suggestion of friendliness.

'Doing anything to-night, Mr. Willoughby?'

Claude tried to look as though he *could* be doing a hundred different things and had the greatest difficulty in choosing between them.

Bullock went on. 'I'm going round to a little party in a friend's rooms this evening. Quite near here. Back of Berkeley Square. Care to come?'

'Oh, I—well, I think I *could* arrange . . .'

'That's fine. A pal of mine is coming with me. Has

rooms in our house. A poet he is, named Munden. Ever heard of him?'

'No. I can't say I have. But then I don't——'

'Don't suppose anyone else has ever heard of him, either, only *he* doesn't know it.' Bullock became very businesslike. 'Right. Meet you outside the Christian Science Church this evening at eight-thirty. That suit you?'

'Oh, perfectly—perfectly.'

Claude took a great deal of trouble to be smart and handsome for the occasion. He had been invited once more to a party, not merely to tea with the Pakes or a drink in somebody's Club, but a *real* party. Who knew what might come of it? He realized, as he stroked the creases out of his blue-and-white tie and examined the sleeves of his blue coat with anxiety to see whether they were too shiny or no, that, in his secret heart, he had been, during these last hard years, hungering for a little of his old social life. He loved a party. He had enjoyed, once, so many of them.

And now, through that kind young Delaney, he would enjoy another. He saw the beautiful girls with their kind attention to himself. He saw himself wagging his head with a roguish smile and heard himself saying: 'Oh, but I'm an old buffer! You won't find it any fun dancing with me!' and then, almost as though it were in a play by Barrie, the lovely young creature murmured: 'Mother has told me that in her younger day you were the life and soul of the Town. I see you as that now. To me you are not old, etc. etc.' Nor was he, for even as the lovely young creature spoke, at the word 'Mother' he was transformed, etc. etc. Well, who knows? This might be, after all, his Indian Summer.

He was a trifle disconcerted when he saw young Delaney's friend. He scarcely, in his appearance, promised the kind of party for which Claude had been spiritually

arranging. A tall gaunt hungry-looking young man in a
pair of not overclean flannel trousers and a waterproof.
But then, Claude remembered, Delaney had said that he
was a poet, and young poets were seldom clean or well-
dressed—although why that had to be so, Claude could
not imagine.

As they walked along Claude wished that he had never
left home, because Mr. Munden pushed along, talking at
the top of his voice and striding so fast that Claude almost
had to run to keep pace with him. Mr. Munden used many
oaths and strong words and was, once or twice, most distinctly indecent. He inveighed against the Nazis, which
Claude was glad of because he didn't like the Nazis himself, but, on the other hand, he seemed to be blood-brother
to Stalin, which Claude didn't at all approve of. The
main burden of his song, however, was that 'money should
be taken from those who had it and given to those who
hadn't.' He suddenly turned quite fiercely to Claude.

'You're nothing but a bloody plutocrat, I suppose?'

'I don't quite understand,' said Claude stiffly. His Willoughby blood was always up when anyone spoke to him
rudely.

'Well, you're rolling in money, I fancy. Don't you
think that you should give some of it to the workers?
Why should *you* have it? What have *you* done to deserve
comfort and luxury?'

Then Claude laughed. He laughed very heartily indeed
for an old gentleman of seventy. He laughed and laughed
and laughed. Then he remembered his manners.

'I'm very sorry. I'm afraid you'll think I'm extremely
rude, but the fact is—the fact is—well, to tell you the
truth, I've got no money at all. I can't even afford a new
suit.'

Bullock laughed too, as he always did at anything
Munden had, politically or economically, to say.

'That's one on you, old boy.'

Munden, who wouldn't hurt a fly if he could help it, was most apologetic.

'Well, I say—no, but I didn't mean to intrude on your private affairs—I thought from what Bullock said—I really am extremely sorry.'

The laugh had done Claude a lot of good, although he thought it a lapse of taste on his part to have spoken about money in public.

'Quite. No harm done, I assure you. Only that anyone should think me well off . . . ah, here we are!'

And there they were, outside a forbidding-looking building with some shabby steps and a very worm-eaten door. Bullock pushed a bell, the door opened, they climbed dark stairs. Another bell was pushed and at once they were in a room, filled with tobacco-smoke, faces, arms, legs. A voice was crying: 'Blood! Blood! Who ever got anywhere without bloodshed? You people all sit there so comfortably when, at your very side, men and women are starving. And *aren't* the rich men clever! How do they keep the poor man quiet? By giving him just enough to keep alive on, but *not* enough to have strength to fight. Scarecrows! Half-alive corpses! That's what we're breeding in England! If I had my way I'd hang all the Baldwins, Edens, Duff Coopers, Nuffields and the rest down Piccadilly! Piccadilly should swim in the blood of the rich if that means the poor are going to have fairer lives!'

'Bravo, Benny!' 'First class!' 'First blood to you, Benny!' Applause, some of it derisive, echoed.

Claude was surprised to realize that the orator was a tall handsome young man with a pullover and beautifully creased flannel trousers. He had a charming voice and one of the mildest, most amiable faces ever seen. He looked at his gold wrist-watch as soon as he had finished speaking. 'Time for food!' he cried.

Then he saw his new guests.

'Hullo, Patrick! Why, Bullock, you young bastard, I haven't seen you for weeks.'

'Hullo, Benny. . . . *This* is a friend of mine, Claude Willoughby.'

'How do you do, Mr. Willoughby? Come and have something to eat.'

Easy said. There was a table at the end of the long, low room, and everyone was pressing around it. There were a great many people. It seemed to Claude, with his old-fashioned eyes, that the women looked like boys and the men like women. Had he read any lighter literature of the last ten years he would not have dared to think anything so trite. It was clear enough, however, that this was a very different party from any that he had ever attended. No one was going to remember her mother here. There was a terrible noise. Everyone talked at once.

'Benny's right. Sweep everything away. That's what we've got to do,' a plump young man near Claude was saying.

A plain girl in enormous spectacles replied in a steady voice, as though she were breaking stones in the road: 'Well, I don't know. It's easy to talk like that, but a friend of mine's just had three months in Russia and she says it's *most* uncomfortable. You can't buy a thing and the streets are always up. But the worst part of it is it's so damned dull.'

The plump young man was most indignant. 'Oh, God! I suppose you'd rather have the bloody Nazis!'

'Not at all,' said the plain girl steadily. 'I don't see why we need have either. I think England's pretty good myself. Anyway, it's better than anywhere else except Scandinavia. What do you want to make a change for?'

'I see,' said the plump young man, and his voice rose into a shrill treble. 'It means nothing to you that in the Distressed Areas families haven't enough to eat, children are skeletons. Why, I heard the other day of a man in South Wales who had the same suit for five years!'

'All the same,' said the plain girl, 'things are improving. I lived in Durham as a small child. There were plenty of people starving, but nobody bothered. Sixty years ago half of England was starving and nobody cared.'

'Yes,' said the plump young man, almost spitting in his scorn. 'And you won't mind if in another two years England is Fascist.'

'Fascism,' said the plain young woman, 'is a joke in England and always will be.'

Claude listened to all this with a great deal of interest and considered how very different it was from the conversation at pre-War parties in London.

However, the real truth of the matter was that he was terrifically hungry. No one in the room knew it, but he had had nothing at all to eat since breakfast, feeling that he had better lose no time in starting new economies. Munden and Bullock had discovered friends, so he must fight for himself. This he did most gallantly. He was a little man and wormed his way first here and then there, until at last he found himself before the best-spread table he'd seen for months. There were sandwiches of every kind—foie gras, salmon, tongue. There were little sausages, and hot biscuits with cheese, and salads, enormous cakes, and as fine a bowl of some extremely intoxicating liquor as he'd ever tasted.

'They'd like this in South Wales,' he thought as he began to gobble.

Bullock had, for a moment, forgotten his friend, because, within five minutes of entering the room, he had fallen in love. This had often happened to him before and as quickly, but this time he had fallen in love with a child. Or was she a child?

He had seen her almost directly after entering the room. She was sitting on a chair and holding a plate

with a piece of cake on it. She was, however, not eating
the cake but looking gravely in front of her. She was dark,
slight, a child perhaps of fourteen or fifteen years, but
what touched at once Bullock's tender heart was that she
appeared to be quite alone in this gay and noisy company.
She was speaking to no one, and no one was speaking to
her. He touched a friend's arm.

'Look at that child. What on earth is *she* doing here?'
His friend followed his gaze.
'Oh, that . . . that's Lizzie Coventry.'
'Lizzie Coventry?'
'Oh, she comes to parties quite often. She's not a
child really. In years, yes. She's going on sixteen, I believe.
But she knows a lot about life. You'd be surprised.'
'How very extraordinary!' Bullock stared and stared.
'But *who* is she?'
'*Who* is she? The daughter of Captain Nicholas Cov-
entry. He's that good-looking, dissipated chap talking to
Mona.'
'Well, who's *he,* then?'
'Coventry? Watch your step, my lad. He's dangerous.'
'Dangerous? Why?'
'He's charming—very charming—and most certainly
will end in gaol. He lives on his wits. At present, I believe,
he's running a little friendly gambling establishment off
Coventry Street somewhere.'
'My God! And that child lives with him?'
'Certainly she does—and has always done. But she can
look after herself, I fancy. She's a nice kid really and has
the hell of a life.'
'Will you introduce me, Bellamy?'
'Why, of course, old chap.'
They threaded their way across.
'Lizzie, this is a friend of mine—Bullock Delaney.
He wants to know you. Miss Coventry—Mr. Delaney.'

She looked at him gravely and held out her hand. There was a chair vacant beside her and he sat down.

Bullock smiled and she smiled.

'Excuse my butting in like this. I've no excuse.'

Miss Coventry gave him her plate.

'Would you put that away somewhere, please? I'm not hungry.'

He took the plate and quickly returned.

'Awful noise they're all making, aren't they?'

'Yes. There's always a noise at parties, isn't there?'

She was entirely at her ease, but not, he thought, in the least interested. He wanted to take her in his arms and comfort her—and yet she did not appear to be at all in need of comfort.

'Do you go to parties often?'

'If my father takes me.'

'Do you like them?'

'Not very much. But I don't care——'

'Aren't you——? I mean——'

She laughed.

'You mean—I ought to be at school? Not at parties?'

'Oh no—that is, if you liked parties. But as you don't——'

'I've never been at school anywhere very long. You see, we're always moving about.'

'You travel a lot?'

'We *have* travelled a lot, but we've been in England now for nearly three years. First we stayed with my aunt, Mrs. Carlisle, in Westminster, and since then we've been with friends of my father's, and now we live alone together.'

'Oh yes.' He had never seen such dignity, such perfect poise in anybody. What would she say, he wondered, if he were to say to her: 'I only saw you a moment ago, but I'd like already to take you away and look after you. I'm sure you're frightened often, that you're unhappy . . .'

Instead he said: 'I suppose you've got heaps of friends in England?'

'My father knows many people. But one doesn't make friends often, does one?'

'I'm afraid I do. I'm very impulsive.'

She looked at him as though she were many years older than he.

'I don't think that's wise—to be very impulsive, I mean. I love my aunt and uncle and they have a nice boy, Edward. Although I never see them,' she added, and then, against her will it seemed, a small sigh escaped her and she did appear, in that instant, a real child. He obeyed, torrentially, his impulse.

'Look here. Tell me where you live, will you? I'm perfectly harmless. Everyone will tell you that. I'd like to see you again.'

She gave him a grave look. She was considering him.

'What did Mr. Bellamy say your name was?'

'Delaney. They call me Bullock because I'm so short and, oh, well, bullocky.' He laughed and she laughed too.

'Yes. If you like. Our address is thirty-five Borden Street, off Coventry Street.'

'I'll telephone. Could I meet your father?'

'Of course.' She got up, went a few paces, pulled at her father's arm and said something to him. Bullock got up.

'Father, this is Mr. Delaney. He'd like to meet you.'

Captain Coventry was extremely friendly. Bullock could see that he had been very good-looking, but that now there was too coarse a red, too stout a body, too thick a voice. Nevertheless the Captain was charming, and, although he had undoubtedly been drinking, could command all the courtesies and amenities of social intercourse.

'Come and see us, old boy. Ring up. Name's in the book. Any time.'

'Thank you,' said Bullock. 'I will.'

The Captain turned away.

'You'll forgive me,' Bullock said, 'for being so abrupt? Forcing myself on you?'

She stood up. They were exactly of a height.

'It was very agreeable,' she said. 'I am glad to know you,' and dismissed him as though she had been royalty.

For Claude there came a horrible ten minutes. A strange business. He never afterwards could remember it quite clearly. In truth, he had drunk a number of glasses of the delicious liquor and, having had but little to eat that day, and having also a certain weakness in the head under spirituous potencies, he found that the floor rocked ever so slightly under him, that he was very happy, ready to talk to anybody, and that people moved in tantalizing rhythms. Then, quite suddenly, his happiness was gone and his heart was filled with fear. For out of the confusion, the bright light, the crush and murmur of sound, there came a cold, dominating voice. He could see the speaker quite clearly—a short, broad-shouldered man who was addressing the party. The other voices died. This man spoke, it seemed, into a listening waiting world. Here, Claude knew at once, was the real thing. The man spoke politely, but it was obvious that he was scornful of every-one present. He spoke with a certainty and a freezing assurance that chilled Claude's blood. He spoke of the new world that was most positively coming. It was a world that would, it was clear, have no use at all for any-one present in that room, a world in which the rulers would be relentless, unsparing. A world without tender-ness or sentiment. A world without God, because God was a fable and belief in Him an ancient exploded superstition. A world in which everyone would work for the State, in which there would be neither individuality nor personal property. A world in which no human being would own anything, certainly not their own souls. Not entirely an ugly world—there were strong, shining, selfless qualities around and through it like rods of shining steel. . . .

But, for Claude, a world from which his life would be snuffed out as you snuff out a candle. It seemed to him as though this little man were speaking especially to him, as though the contempt in the man's eyes were directed solely against him. Claude felt himself die. The rocking floor caught him, swallowed him, buried him. The awful final thing was that in the man's voice there was a negation of all personal life. As Claude listened he ceased to be Claude.

The man stopped.

'Thanks for letting me say a word or two,' he ended.

'Let's dance!' someone cried. 'Come on, let's dance.'

CHAPTER VI

Family Foster

KITTY, as she saw her mother bend over the crying child, lift her up, brush her shabby little frock, give her a piece of money out of her bag, thought that there could be no one, surely, in the world, more charming. Her charm lay, at the moment, in her complete unself-consciousness, for although they were in Curzon Street on this gusty, gritty, unpleasant afternoon, with everyone in the world to observe them, although Meg was in her best clothes (for she was going ultimately with Larry to a grand cocktail party), she had knelt down on the pavement and been as completely absorbed in the dirty infant as though she were her own offspring. The child, running out of Shepherd Market, had slipped and fallen. She howled but was not damaged. Then she had stood staring at this tall lady in dark purple and a large hat; after that, with the piece of money in her hand, joyfully she had run on.

Meg started forward with her daughter again, continuing her conversation just where she had left off.

'. . . and so I think, darling, that Bullock's in love once again. He's such a sweet boy, but knows nothing about women, I'm afraid—nothing at all. But then, I say to myself, who does? Certainly not writers. Not politicians either, or they'd *never* let women have anything to do with politics. Fred doesn't either, and *I* don't and

96

Larry doesn't. The point about women is, can you ever be sure that they won't do something on the spur of the moment?'

'Can you be sure that men won't either?' asked Kitty.

'Yes, I think you can, dear, because they're so much more selfish. Once they're after something they want, *nothing* will change them or turn them. Although when they *have* got it they usually don't want it.'

But Kitty was thinking. She seldom read novels, but by her bed there had been a book, by a very clever young man, called *Mud in Your Eye,* and, being awake from three to seven (most unusual for her), she had read it. Very clever the young man was, springing from character to character like an acrobat, but very unpleasant too. Kitty didn't complain of that, because facts were facts, but she was thinking now how very out-of-place her mother and father would seem in such a book. And yet they were surely quite as real as the charwoman with the erysipelas (minutely described) or the shop-girl who went to bed with so many different gentlemen. The end of the book had been occupied with a brilliant description of a man spitting blood into a basin while his old mother, whose head was scrofulous, alternately smacked and petted him. Now if, instead of this, there had been a description of Meg, picking up a child and giving it six-pence, Meg a lady, happy, contented and handsome, *how* unreal the book would appear! How scornful the brilliant young man was of happiness! No one was happy in his book, not a single soul. No one was physically clean. But wasn't, even in these days, one part of life as true as the other? There *were* people who used soap and water, there *were* families happy and devoted, there *was* beauty to be found . . . Kitty pulled herself up. She was becoming platitudinous and complacent.

'But why do you think Bullock is in love, Mother?'

They were passing the bookshop whose window was

always filled with coloured illustrations of flowers and old maps with whales spouting water in the corners. Seen at a distance this window looked like a page from an old missal (neither Meg nor Kitty had this thought: old missals meant, I'm afraid, very little in their lives).

But the bookshop suggested something to Meg.

'What charming pictures of flowers! I often go this way instead of Piccadilly simply to see them. I think dear Bullock is so like those nasturtiums—aren't they beautiful, look at the colour!—and now he's in love again all his tendrils are twisting. Oh dear, what nonsense I'm talking! Just like that man who writes those charming books about his country cottage. But Bullock is very strange. He's asked whether I mind his bringing to tea one day a little girl and her scoundrelly father.'

'A little girl and her scoundrelly father?'

'Yes—and when I said of course, but why did he want to, he said because he was in love with the little girl, and when I said that that was nasty and unnatural he became quite excited and cried out that he wouldn't harm a hair of her head, but that she needed protecting. . . . And now I come to think of it, Kitty, you've been odd yourself the last week or two. I wish you'd tell me where you are going now this afternoon. At least no, I don't. A mother must never force a daughter's confidences. And yet all the same I *do* want to know. Do tell me, Kitty.'

And then Meg performed one of her more tiresome tricks. She stopped in the street where she was—just outside Cook's offices. This she sometimes did when she was very serious about something. She was altogether regardless of people, and there is nothing in life more irritating to sensible and busy men than to find two women planted in the middle of the pavement talking to one another. Meg looked with her large and lovely eyes at her daughter.

'On my side, Mother,' Kitty said, laughing, 'I want

to know why within the last fortnight you have been twice
to Surbiton.'

'Oh,' said Meg grandly, 'there's no secret about that
—no secret at all. They are old friends of mine—at least
he is.'

'Yes, he is,' said Kitty. 'But Surbiton—it's unlike you
to go to Surbiton. And twice in a fortnight.'

At this point an impatient gentleman, planning undoubtedly to go on a World Cruise straight from Cook's
door, gave Meg's arm a very impolite knock. She was
not at all disturbed but smiled at his angry face, wondering whether she'd met him perhaps at some friend's house.

'We're blocking the pavement, Mother.'

'Oh, are we? Well, if you won't tell me, darling, I
won't ask you—only will you be in to dinner?'

'Yes, I will—and Bullock and I will take you to a picture after.'

Meg was looking at her daughter as though for the
first time. She could not bear to let her go. She always
felt about the people she loved when she parted from
them as though they were just off to the South of France,
and all she would get now would be letters and possibly
a telegram.

Kitty hailed a taxi, gave an address and was off. Meg
walked into Piccadilly, smiling, although Fred had often
told her not to smile in the street when she was alone lest
people should think her insane. But she could not help it.
She was really so very fortunate to have so beautiful and
charming a daughter.

'This is undoubtedly the house,' thought Kitty. 'Ah,
yes. Here's his father's name—Albert Foster—on this
dirty card above the little bell.'

She paused before pushing the bell, looking up and
down the sordid paper-blown street. It was indeed a very
bold and probably foolish thing that she had done. She

had simply written to the young man and said that she had something to tell him about a job, and she would, if he thought it sensible, speak to his father and himself concerning it. The awful thing was that what she had to tell him about a job was that Lady Millie Temple, who had the big place Rathesay in Rutlandshire, wanted an under-gardener. The young man had said that he loved flowers and liked to live in the country—but did he know anything about gardening? Almost certainly not. Moreover he seemed altogether superior to the post of under-gardener, except that in these days anyone took anything that he could get. Why was she doing this insane and foolish thing? Even for a Delaney it was insane and foolish. She had put on her very quietest frock, but the sight of this dirty street made her visit officious, interfering and snobbish. But she could not help it. Her impulses always seemed to her like laws. She was not sentimental as Bullock was, that is, if sentimentality means spreading your feelings loosely and lightly over a great many things and people. She had never done anything like this in her life before. She was amazed, even horrified, at herself, but she never dreamed of turning back.

Alton Foster, in his answer to her letter, had said that she was very kind, that he would have an afternoon off on such-and-such a day and that his father would be proud. Well, she was in for it and would carry it out as handsomely as she could.

The door opened and she climbed some forlorn stairs. There, in a narrow grimy passage, was Alton Foster waiting for her. He was exceedingly nervous. His hand was trembling.

'There are a great many stairs,' he said.

His nervousness moved her kindliness and made her perfectly at home.

'Will you come in, please?'

She entered and found it one of the most surprising

rooms in her experience; for unexpectedness it ranked
with the bedroom of Rose Colthorpe's which was filled
with little tanks containing coloured fish, and Joe Cardinal's bathroom which was all glass, black tiles and scented
soap. For it was a broad room in shape like the large
waiting-room of a railway station. It had a little that
air of ancient disrupted newspapers and a heavy grumbling fire that refused to burn. Nevertheless, in spite of
a sense of almost religious discomfort, the walls were
painted with pictures in the most lovely colours. Well
painted too. Some of the paint had flaked away, much
of it was faded, but one could see clearly enough a kind
of Hoffmann world with witches, ghosts peering in at
windows, lovely battlements, forest glades and long
stretches of blue sea. Beautiful sensitive feeling this
artist had had, the colours, soft rose, gold and amber,
peacock purple, the silver-grey of the bark of a birch-
tree, the dead white of a vellum page—all these colours,
faint, still, toneless. . . .

But upon these painted walls were hung pictures in
cheap gilt frames, and pictures of a frantic and almost
obscene crudity. They were in rude oils—valleys with
autumn leaves, seas with sunsets, streets with timbered
buildings. The drawing was crude, the colour dreadfully
bright.

The room itself was kitchen, bedroom, sitting-room.
There was a cooking-stove; in the corner by the window
a bed partly behind a screen; there was a table spread
with a cloth on which was laid one of those teas provided
by the hospitably eager for the unhungry reluctant—
cakes and cakes, scones and scones, dishes of jam and
dishes of jam, and all of it looking, through no fault of
its own, as though it had been exactly thus on this table
for a month or two.

On a sofa near the fire was lying a man with an almost
cherubic face and snow-white hair—quite cherubic it

would have been had the nostrils not been unexpectedly pinched as though they had been held tight with a pair of nippers while someone had carefully spread out the rest of the face. Under the rugs there lay what was clearly a big and possibly corpulent body.

Standing with a nervous uncertain smile on her face was a stout woman whose hair was waved so smartly that the rest of her looked oddly old-fashioned. She was, of course, the daughter of Mr. Foster, the sister of Alton. It was with her that Kitty first shook hands.

'I'm afraid you'll think this a most impertinent visit on my part.'

'Why, no . . . *such* a thing. . . . Tee-hee-hee. . . . This is my father—Alton told you, I'm sure. . . .'

Whether Alton's sister had an impediment of speech, or ill-fitting teeth, or was merely nervous, Kitty did not know and never would know. Lucy Foster was a repository of sounds that were always a little different from your expectations. When, for instance, you were sure that she was about to sneeze, she surprisingly laughed, and when you were preparing sympathy for a choking cough, she merely yawned—very politely with her hand in front of her mouth. She seemed herself often astonished at the sounds her body arranged for her. Otherwise she laughed, giggled, tee-heed extensively. She was also in a perpetual state of surprise. All this Kitty discovered in the first ten minutes while she fought a determined battle against eating more than a piece of bread and butter.

She never, she explained, ate anything at tea. She was going on to say something about slimming necessities when she realized just in time that this might seem an affront to Lucy, whose figure was ample.

'Well, I never! Do you hear that, Dad? . . . Miss Delaney never eats with her tea. Fancy that now! What! Not a piece of this plum-cake? It's ever so good. Do try now, Miss Delaney. Miss Delaney should, shouldn't she,

Dad? She should really. And so you don't eat with your tea, Miss Delaney?'

Mr. Foster was Kitty's chief preoccupation. *What* a noble head, what a cheery smiling face, what rosy cheeks, what beautiful shining white hair! How smart, how spotless he was, and there was even a small Christmas-rose in his buttonhole. He must, once on a time, have been a magnificent man. His neck and shoulders were superb. His bright blue eyes had so courageous and friendly a gleam!

'Well, Miss Delaney, I call it kind indeed for you to have taken all this trouble to visit a poor helpless creature like myself—not that I'm so helpless as you'd think with my good Lucy here and Alton working for us as he does. Ah! Miss Delaney, how much one has to be thankful for! To have such good children, to be near the window here and see the clouds go by and think one's own thoughts, simple as they are, but all moving Godward, Miss Delaney. *He* understands. He understands. And the hours pass swiftly. There is the painting and the reading and the cup of tea now and again. When one thinks of the many poor homeless souls in the world, how fortunate, how very fortunate one is!'

He was making a most magnificent tea, Kitty was pleased to see. Except for his paralysis he was evidently in excellent health, and even his paralysis could not be as bad as Alton had described it, for he moved his arms quite freely.

Kitty, sitting opposite to him, very straight-backed in her chair, nibbling her piece of bread and butter, wondered at his serenity, his happiness, and yet was not completely reassured by it.

For this room was not really a happy room. She knew what a happy room was, having lived in one all her life long. This place was as clean as though it had been sterilized. On the walls these lovely soft colours, this romantic

world, with a long-ago touching cadence, a Conder-Pater
world of dim but exquisite beauty, was severed, interrupted again and again by the monstrous glaring oils.
And below these walls it was a bare and empty world, in
spite of the potted hyacinth on the window-sill, the glowing fire, the heated stove, the fine recumbent figure, the
loaded tea-table.

'Ah, yes,' said Lucy Foster. 'You are looking at our
walls, Miss Delaney. Everyone does, don't they, Dad?
Oh yes, indeed. . . . The walls were painted by two
young men years and years ago—weren't they, Dad? Oh
yes, Miss Delaney, they were. Isn't it astonishing? That's
why Dad took the rooms, isn't it, Dad? There's a little
one as well—my bedroom, Miss Delaney. Oh yes, and a
bathroom. They painted them all, didn't they, Dad? And
Dad thought they weren't half bad, so he took the rooms.
Most astonishing they are, and of course they're fading,
and most of our friends think they're silly, don't they,
Dad, and of course Dad's paintings are much finer
—brighter and all that. People have said he should show
in the Academy, haven't they, Dad? Try a bit of this
cake, Dad. It's got cherries in.'

'Thank you, my dear, I think I will. You mustn't listen
to my daughter about my painting, Miss Delaney. She's
partial of course. And I'm self-taught. God's hand guided
me. That's what I always say. God, seeing my helplessness,
revealed to me a fragment of His great beauty. Thank
you, my dear—I don't mind if I do have another cup.'

Through all of this Alton had been busy looking after
everyone. He had not said a word and Kitty at once suspected that, in the company of his father and sister, he
was very quiet and that they dominated him. He seemed
very slight and even foreign beside their hearty vitality.
He was like a bright-eyed bird hopping from twig to twig,
some alarm behind the flash of the eyes, on the watch,
on guard—against what?

But again, after a certain time, Kitty was conscious
that Mr. Foster and his daughter were vibrating with
wonder and excitement at her visit. *What* was she doing
there? *Why* had she come? Without any snobbery on her
own part she was aware that she must seem to them a
creature from altogether another world, and she knew
that Lucy was taking in every detail of her little hat, her
hair, her simple frock, her shoes. This led her to a further
discovery, namely that Alton had been quite other from
these two in this, that he had, from the first, had no sense
of social differences, that he was of her world, of anybody's world, that his mind and imagination were busied
with scenes, figures, surmises very different from those
of his father and sister.

Mr. Foster indeed could contain his curiosity no longer.

'My boy tells me, Miss Delaney, that you have most
kindly interested yourself in his welfare. He is a good
boy and his father is proud of him. My misfortune, Miss
Delaney, has hampered me so sadly, and the pension I
received after my accident is so meagre, that his sister
and myself are dependent largely upon Alton's earnings.
He works hard and I am proud of him.'

Nevertheless there was a tinge, Kitty thought, of
patronage in his mellow agreeable tones, and she was
reminded for an instant of a character in one of her
favourite novels, one of the few that she had read many
times, Mr. Turveydrop in *Bleak House*. She dismissed
the comparison as swiftly as it came because Mr. Foster
was clearly a person of generous and courageous goodness. Nevertheless he was *not* paralysed. Of that she was
certain. Could Alton really believe that he was?

'You see, Mr. Foster' (and, as she began her explanation, the soft rather floating eyes of Lucy Foster seemed
to swim towards hers with an almost indecent curiosity),
'I went into Zanti's to enquire about something I saw in
the window and there was your son! We began to talk

and I found that he loved the open air and gardens. It was a strange coincidence that two days later I heard that a friend of mine, Lady Millicent Temple, wanted an under-gardener at her place in Rutlandshire.' Kitty smiled. 'It would be an insult in ordinary times to suggest such a thing to your son—but these aren't ordinary times, are they? A cousin of mine as a matter of fact is working as a sort of under-gardener at a place in Devonshire.' (Isn't this, she suddenly thought, a very snobbish thing to say?) 'And so, as it wouldn't be very good policy to talk about this in the shop, and as writing about such things is always so unsatisfactory, I thought I would come myself and see you.'

She realized at once that this innocent proposal horri-fied both Mr. Foster and Lucy. Why? She looked at Alton. For the first time on that afternoon their eyes met. With that exchanged glance they were friends as they had not been before—quietly, but with a new and hopeful assurance.

Mr. Foster took another and fat piece of cherry-cake, cleared his throat, and with one of the cheeriest and brightest smiles Kitty had ever seen, addressed her.

'If that isn't good of you, Miss Delaney! I think that's one of the kindest things I've ever known. And I know Alton feels the same. He must answer you for himself, of course, but I am afraid, I'm seriously afraid, that his experience of gardening is scarcely sufficient.' He looked quite unconsciously at a large cherry embedded in his cake. 'What do you say, my son?'

Alton answered very quietly.

'It's extremely good of you, Miss Delaney, but I'm afraid Father's right. It's true that I do love the open air, but I don't know enough to take a gardener's job. I'm afraid I misled you by talking about flowers as I did.'

'I'm afraid you did,' said Mr. Foster, licking one of his strong brown fingers and speaking quite sharply. 'The truth is, Miss Delaney, that Alton here is really a town boy. He's seen very little of the country and so fancies it a Paradise. But in reality . . . Well, well, God places us where we can be most useful, I don't doubt, and Alton *is* must useful in town, I am certain.'

They don't want him to leave London at any cost, Kitty thought. He's too valuable to them. He's their prisoner.

'No, I see,' Kitty said. 'The idea won't do. But I thought I ought to tell you.'

'That really *is* kind of you,' Lucy broke in. 'It's astonishing really—that you should take all that trouble, I mean.'

'Oh, but I've taken no trouble at all,' Kitty said.

Mr. Foster raised his hand almost as though in blessing.

'If everyone showed the spirit of kindness there wouldn't be the trouble in the world there is to-day, nor all those starving who oughtn't to be. When I think, Miss Delaney, of all those poor fellows with not a rag to cover their back and no one doing a thing to help them my blood boils. It does indeed. But your goodness . . .'

There were all too many compliments flying about, Kitty thought, and she rose to go.

Her small hand was held for too long a time in the strong firm one of Mr. Foster, and she fancied that his eye was bold, gay and enterprising.

She said good-bye to Lucy who, she was sure, disliked her extremely.

Alton went with her down to the street. Standing there they regarded one another once again as friends. She knew now that, as far as herself was concerned, she liked him, trusted him and quite certainly would see him again. On his side he was timid, chivalrous, and clearly listening for some sound.

'When Father needs me, Lucy comes to the door and calls.'

'Oh, I see.'

'He's very helpless and is a big heavy man for Lucy to turn over and so on.'

'I'm pleased, though,' said Kitty, 'to find that he isn't as bad as I had expected. He isn't altogether paralysed, is he?'

'No, not exactly. Not physically, I mean. His spine *was* damaged, but I'm glad to say he can do a number of things for himself. Only it isn't good for him—to do too much, I mean.'

Then urgently, as though his whole life depended upon it:

'You'll let me see you again one day?'

'But of course,' Kitty said. 'We've made friends, haven't we? Friendship isn't broken as soon as it's made.'

'Friends—you and I?'

'Why not? I don't make a new friend so often. Can I telephone to the shop?'

'Yes, of course.'

'We might go for a walk in the Park or somewhere.'

'Oh yes . . . this is wonderful, miraculous for me. I've been so lonely. If I may just talk to you sometimes. . . . I've had no one to whom I can talk. I have ideas. I'm greatly interested in the theatre. I'm trying to write a play, only I have so little time. If I could speak to you sometimes about my ideas. . . . I know they are all weak and immature. I'm so inexperienced. I've seen so little of life. . . .'

'I'll tell you frankly,' said Kitty, laughing, 'that I'm anything but clever. I'm a perfect fool in fact. But if you'll take me as I am——'

'Take you as you are!'

Through the open door came the shrill cry of Lucy. 'Alton! Alton! Father wants you!'

He turned, caught her hand, pressed it.

'I must go. Good-bye! Good-bye!'

The door closed and, smiling to herself as her mother sometimes did, Kitty walked on.

She climbed on to a bus and, during a stoppage in Shaftesbury Avenue, she saw her father coming out of a shop, and with him was Miss Van Renn.

Inside the house, within their own room, they forgot altogether these disturbances from outside that were beginning to colour their imaginations. For now their imaginations were only for themselves. There was a kind of mysticism in their relationship when they were alone and unself-consciously loving one another. Perhaps there is always more than one world created by love, which is why immortality depends on love rather than faith.

'Oh, hell!' Bullock cried, looking in at them from the door. 'Someone's been in my room. Everything's messed up on the table.'

'I did,' said Kitty. 'I wondered if you'd have a safety-pin.'

'Oh, damn you, Kitty! *Can't* you leave me alone? It's all I've got. . . .'

And: '*If* you call this coffee, darling . . .' from Fred.

But their security was terrific. They would love one another perhaps more here in the heart of London than anywhere else, for their love had elements in it of all that London indifferently was creating—smoke like bats' wings, like torn paper, like the flutter of a scarf, but seen through the smoke an animal of sluggish, self-satisfied immortality. The consciousness of that never-dying, tower-topped, mud-based, smoke-veiled, conceited energy gives strength to lovers because, although the moment in which they are then believing may fail them, there is something here so real and so strong that their moment has in it the fibre of stone and the skeleton of iron. Fred Delaney felt that. He smelt the whiff of coal-smoke in the air, saw the sun-filled cloud spill its colours on Piccadilly, heard

Big Ben strike across the Park, and knew that the four of them, himself, Meg, Kitty and Bullock, were enclosed, protected, as though in a magic circle.

'Come on! Come on!' Bullock cried. 'The last programme begins at nine-five.' Then he went over and kissed his mother. They all knew that their strength, their unity radiated from Meg.

'It's one of those Viennese pictures,' she said delightedly. 'I *do* like them. All waltzes and uniforms and great four-posters.'

They sallied forth, Meg with Bullock, Kitty with her father.

'And where have *you* been all the afternoon?' she asked him.

'In the Club, darling; played bridge and lost three shillings!'

'In the Club *all* the afternoon?'

'*All* the afternoon, darling.'

CHAPTER VII

Portrait of a Lady

LADY MILLIE PAKE is, without question, an impossible
figure in any story of modern life. Did you begin anywhere, at any time in these foreboding 'Thirties, a story
introducing a perfect old gentlewoman, you would soon
be pausing, then clearing your throat, then at last apolo-
gizing, for your audience would be restless, their eyes
cynical and sarcastic.

Nevertheless Lady Millie did and does exist, and she
was, and is, a lady against whom no fault can be found,
in whom there is no blemish. How impossible it would be
for any novelist then to make her interesting were he to
attempt the task! He would be forced back into her past.
She had had once the devil of a temper, had been vain
perhaps, and certainly proud of her family. But time and
the long years had washed all these impurities out of her
and she was now clean and shining like a fine sea-shell—
although that is a poor simile indeed, because she had
a great deal of life in her, quite a grim humour at times,
and a real intolerance of fools. She was anything but the
'sweet old lady' you might have supposed from this pre-
liminary. She hadn't an atom of sentimentality in her and
bore down heavily on weak idealists. Nor, astonishingly

enough, did she deprecate these modern times. She saw
that the world was in disorder, but she could not remember a time when it was otherwise. In her old age she had
been gifted with a sense of Time. The immediate moment
had, it appeared to her, been always a moment of alarms,
and she was aware that present inventions had provided
every morning's breakfast-table with a full knowledge of
every single event that the world had created yesterday.
She was not an optimist in the sense of things being right
because God was in His Heaven. She was sure that God
was there, and she thought that if she were on God's level
she would be able to argue with Him on a number of
things. But she was not. She had not been on her dear
father's level when, at the age of seven, she had ques-
tioned him as to why the gardener had drowned a batch
of kittens.

But, taking Time as a very large order, she did feel
that things in general improved. She remembered when,
as a little girl, she had paid visits to her Aunt Horsborough, in the great rambling house in Templeton, where
two of the maids had slept under the back-stairs in what
was little more than a cupboard. She remembered her visits
with her aunt to Templeton village and the beautiful
thatched cottages down whose walls the wet dripped, and
the icy cold of the kitchen at the Vicarage had made her
shiver. She remembered the sycophantic greetings of the
postman's wife, crippled with rheumatism, and the beneficent magnificence of Aunt Horsborough.

Instead of railing at young Communists like Patrick
Munden, she thought their anxiety for the poor, the helpless, and the downtrodden very fine indeed.

For herself the constant anxiety about money meant
very little. She would be happy anywhere and she thought
that she could manage very nicely on almost nothing. It
was only for her sister that she was anxious. She disliked
nobody except the Corleone woman. She considered that

she and the set around her were hard, selfish and empty-headed. But she suspected that if she knew the Corleone intimately she would find many things to like in her. She felt that all the hatred that there was in the world came from lack of intimacy. You would not, of course, like *everybody* even though you knew them well, but you would in all probability understand why they behaved as they did.

At the same time she had a keen eye for foibles, including her own. She knew, for instance, that her hatred of 'litter' was almost a disease, that she was given to speaking her mind too frankly, that she was absurdly irritated by her friends' unpunctuality, and that she disliked young women who made up their faces during meals, told coarse stories, and bullied their husbands in public. On the whole she liked men better than women. She was modern enough to feel that the inequalities between rich and poor in England were out of character with the new world. A Scandinavian had once inveighed for a long time and with feverish enthusiasm against what she had called the 'Manor House' life and the London slums. She had paused at last for want of breath, and had then been greatly astonished when Millie Pake admitted all of it. 'But it is,' said Millie, 'changing. You should have seen England forty years ago. We're very slow always, but we're kind people really although we've very little imagination.' She envied working-women she knew; they hadn't to keep up appearances. They had a husband and children. She would like to have had children.

But Millie Pake's outstanding quality was her cheerfulness. Now cheerfulness is quite widely condemned in these times. If a man is cheerful he is either stupid and therefore intolerable, or his cheerfulness is a pose, or he is cheerful on principle. Fortunately Millie was so old that she could excuse herself by saying that she was pre-War, became cheerful when she was young and had never been able to get out of the habit. She was not, however, so self-conscious as that. She didn't realize that she was cheerful, and if she irritated anybody by it she never knew it. The truth was that nothing could dismay or frighten her very badly because she was quite certain that when her body died her soul would go to Heaven. This, of course, was, in the light of modern science, so ridiculous that one can only call her a foolish old woman. But, foolish or no, this belief gave her such indifference to danger, and, because she hadn't to worry about herself, enabled her to think so much about other people, that it was undoubtedly a help—an unfair help, many people would say.

It is true that she liked to have cheerful persons about her; that was why she enjoyed the Delaneys so much. They were really cheerful and laughed at quite ridiculous little things just as she did. She did hope, for that reason among others, that they would not be forced to leave the Charles Street house.

She was cheerful partly because she enjoyed on the whole very good health. She really did enjoy it. As far as her body went, she had, when she was very young, wanted to be beautiful. Now she only wanted to be well. She was aware, naturally, of the strange little aches and pains that accompany anybody who is over seventy, but she was, as a rule, too busy to consider them. She had no fear whatever of death, but she *was* afraid, when she thought about it, of a long physical illness which would have prevented her caring for her sister. She was, however, certain that if that trial were allotted to her the Lord would help her to manage. She never spoke to anyone about her religion, but in fact her companionship with the Lord was not like a religion at all. It was like a companionship.

She got a great pleasure out of the tiniest things: the taste of buttered toast at tea, the sound of Big Ben across

the Park, the pictures in the *Daily Sketch* and the leaders
in the *Daily Telegraph* (always so sound and honest: the
Delaneys sent these papers every day up to the Pake
ladies when they themselves had read them), a new novel
lent them by some kind friend, every sort of shop, the
'look' of the sitting-room when the sun shone in through
the window, the 'feel' of her grey silk dress when she
prepared for some little festivity, the singing of the
hymns in St. James's, Piccadilly, demon patience when it
came out (she would clap her hands and cry aloud, saluting its rarity), the flower-stands outside the Christian
Science Church, a drive in a motor-car (kind friends sometimes offered her one), almost anybody's dog (she had
always longed for a dog, but Helen didn't like dogs),
a visit to one of her old friends and a chat about old
times, and, best of all (but this was *very* rare because
she couldn't leave Helen in the evening), a visit to the
cinema. The cinema she regarded as quite miraculous,
and especially were miraculous the lovely faces of the
young women in these pictures.

She was in fact thoroughly urban. She regarded this
little section of London in which she lived as her own
especial village. She still enjoyed a wonderful strength
for walking. Her legs were as sturdy as they had been at
thirty. When someone said to her once that he hated
London because it was so huge, she said: 'Huge! Nonsense! Why, in our village we can cover everything in
about five minutes.'

'Village?' he answered. 'I was talking about London.'

'So was I,' she said. 'I was talking about Curzon Street
village.'

'Oh . . .' he said. 'But I live in Bloomsbury.'

'Well, there's Bloomsbury village and Inns of Court
village and Chelsea village and Camden Town village
and Hampstead village and—heaps more. The best is,
you can go out any evening and do what you like in

another village, and no one in your own village will know where you are or what you are doing.'

Every stone, window-curtain, piece of glass, door-knob in Shepherd Market was known to her, or so she liked to think. She did all the shopping herself. Nearly every man, woman and child in the place knew her, and although she wore funny outdoor hats, tweed skirts, and her nose was often shiny, everyone respected and liked her. Her nickname in Shepherd Market was Aunt Sally, but when she spoke to them you would think, by their deference, that she was Queen of Sheba.

Late in February on an early afternoon she was eating a little cold chicken and potato salad on a tray near the fire (for Helen, who had a little cold, was in bed for the day) when the bell rang and the little maid introduced Dodie Pullet. The girl was a great friend of Millie's, who confided to her all her troubles and told her often frank stories which Millie took with the calm of a veteran life-studier.

To-day Dodie did not pause and smile, as she might have done, at the odd little figure with her skirts pulled up, her feet on the fender, enjoying a chicken-bone in her fingers.

'Come in, dear. It's all right. Queen Victoria did it.' Then quickly as it were from her sharp, intelligent eyes: 'Is anything the matter, dear?'

'It's only——' Dodie was catching her breath as though she had been running. 'Smoke hasn't been here, has he?'

'No. . . . Have some coffee.'

'Thanks.' She drew a chair to the fire. 'Where's Helen?'

'Got a bit of a cold, so I kept her in bed. Why *should* Smoke be here?'

'Oh, no reason. Thanks, dear. It's nice and warm in here. Our room's so cold somehow. Only we had a word or two before he went out and—well, the truth is, when-

ever we've had a word and he goes out I get frightened.
He's so fearfully depressed and it goes on week after
week. And now I'm out of a job too. We shall *have* to
leave here, which Smoke hates, and it's hard luck on Fred
too, because even if he's a month or two without a let
it will tell on him heavily. Besides, we're all so happy
here as we are. We'll never find another place like it; and
then the Delaneys are so cheerful, and you're so sweet,
and even Patrick upstairs . . .' Then Dodie did what Millie Pake had never seen her do before; she burst into tears.
She put her thin arm against her face like a little child.
She was wearing such a beautiful smart frock too, black
with white wings across the breasts, and her make-up
would certainly be ruined. . . .

Millie put down her coffee-cup, took her feet off the
fender, drew her chair to Dodie's and put her arm around
the girl's slender body.

'There, there, my dear! Smoke's all right and you'll
get a job with the greatest of ease.'

Dodie looked up, felt for her case, discovered a minute
pocket-handkerchief, groaned with horror at her face in
the little mirror.

'Oh, damn! I haven't cried for years! Only it *is* getting awful with Smoke. He's jealous, suspicious, sore with
me about anything, with himself about everything. Poor
Smoke! But I tell you, Millie, it's hell having no money.
Hell. He's got it into his head that I will be sleeping with
somebody for cash. Well, I won't. He needn't worry. And
then he's jealous of Patrick Munden. He hates him because he says he's a Bolshie and doesn't wash. But there's
a lot to be said for Bolshevism anyway, and if you're
clever and have got ideas what does it matter whether
you wash or no? But money's the real trouble. We'll *have*
to move, but this address is so useful. . . . Oh, blast!
isn't life bloody? Sorry, Millie, I know you hate my
swearing.'

Millie was holding Dodie's cold hand in her warm one.

'Swear if it helps you, my dear. Have you talked to Meg?'

'No. She'd want to give me some money. They haven't got any too much themselves. Besides, Meg——' She stopped. 'You know how she is. She's the kindest, most generous creature in the world, but she's happy however miserable you are. I don't mean that she doesn't sympa- thize, but I don't think she's ever been unhappy herself. She lives in this world plus another one. I don't mean spiritual. They are *both* material. She's out-size, and one's shy of bringing one's ordinary made-to-pattern size in comparison. You're not out-size, Millie darling.'

'No, I'm not—certainly not.'

Dodie got up.

'I must go and see if Smoke's back. If only he'd sleep——'

'Doesn't he?'

'He's very bad just now. He says he's afraid he'll dream.' She turned, smiling. 'You always do me good. I don't quite know why. But it's a beastly world, isn't it? Hitler, Mussolini, Stalin. So much hatred. Money and food not distributed properly. No one knowing where they're going.'

'I think,' said Millie, 'we all know too much. And hear too much too. It's like Blind Man's Buff—someone al- ways touching you, and you turn round, stretch your hands out, and there's no one there. Also I shouldn't wonder if we aren't being made less stout than we used to be. Pepys went out to see half London burning and then went home and added up his accounts. And I think we all expect happiness as our right. We usen't to.'

'Good-bye. I expect things will be fine soon.'

After she had gone, Millie sat there thinking. Strange how difficult it was to help anybody else! Strange, too, how money was everyone's trouble. After these thousands of years human beings should have discovered a plan whereby everyone had enough, and then they could all put the money problem aside and consider many more important things.

She went into the little bedroom to see how Helen was and found her fast asleep, so she called the maid and told her to keep her eyes and ears open, put on her hat and a strange green mantle for which she had a great affection, took her stout umbrella with which she always walked, and started downstairs.

She had suddenly the idea that she would go and visit 'poor' Claude Willoughby. Herself and Helen always thought of him as 'poor' Claude, not because he *was* poor, but because they felt a kindness for him that had a touch of patronage about it—or perhaps it was only the pitying kindness that all women feel for their bachelor friends. She had never before visited Claude in his rooms and she was surprised at herself for doing so now. Dodie's visit had touched her and made her want to be of some use. As she left the house she felt as though all the inhabitants there were advancing towards some sort of drama. The mild February day that suggested swollen streams, snowdrops and a crocus or two in the country, made Shepherd Market a little shabby and muffled. Everything in the shops looked rather second-rate and there were more slinking cats than usual. It seemed therefore quite in the nature of things that the door in White Horse Street should be opened to her by quite the most unpleasant-looking man she had ever seen in her life. She knew who it was—Claude had often mentioned his landlord. She loathed Brocket on sight, and disliked him all the more that he could rouse such violent feeling in her.

'Is Mr. Claude Willoughby at home, please?'

Although her clothes were old-fashioned there was something in Millie Pake's voice that Brocket instantly recognized. He hadn't been a gentleman's servant all his days without knowing a lady when he saw one, and among his many characteristics was snobbery of a very violent kind.

'Step inside and I'll see,' he said. The hall was dark, stuffy, and smelt of onions and dead geraniums. ''Oo shall I say?' he asked.

'Lady Mildred Pake, if you please.'

'Yes, m'lady.'

He was the eager, obliging, die-for-you-if-you-ask-it English servant. Very like, Millie thought, that butler we once had who had a mania for stealing Helen's clothes.

Brocket seized a trumpet hanging on the wall and shouted, 'Lady Mildred Pake, sir,' then, after a pause, breathing like an eager retriever, he said:

'Mr. Willoughby's in. 'E'll be delighted to see you, m'lady. I'll show you 'is room. Pardon me.' He led the way, and Millie followed the flapping slippers.

'Well, Claude,' she said in her rather hoarse voice.

He was standing, expecting her, and she noticed that he had a little egg on his upper lip and that his scanty hair was ruffled over his thin pate. Brocket had shut the door and vanished.

'What a horrible man!'

'Who? Brocket? . . . Oh yes, he isn't nice at all. Millie, I'm so glad to see you. I was snoozing in that chair and you're my dream . . . really you are!'

She tapped his cheek.

'Come to pay you a little visit. Sit down where you were and let's be cosy. . . . No, I won't take your chair! Here, let me do your fire up a bit.'

Her old knees cracked a little as she bent forward, but she was full of energy as she took the coal off the scuttle, piled it high, broke it up with the poker and made a bright blaze.

Claude watched her in an agony. How could she
know that that coal in the scuttle was all that he had
for the rest of the day and that now he must go shivering
to bed? He was, however, too much of a gentleman to
say anything.

'There!' said Millie, giving the last lump a vigorous
smack. 'That's better! I don't know what you have such
a miserable fire for on a day like this!'

She drew the little cane-bottomed chair forward and
sat there with her broad-toed shoes on the fender in her
favourite attitude.

She looked at Claude. Poor little man, he didn't look
at all well. How she wished she could tell him about the
egg on his lip! But she couldn't, of course she couldn't.
And she would like some tea. It was early—a quarter
past three—nevertheless on an afternoon like this . . .
But she realized that tea would be difficult for Claude
and would involve, probably, the summoning of that
horrible man again. But he would be expecting that she
would demand it, so she said, rubbing her hands together,
her rings flashing their diamonds in the blaze: 'I've only
looked in for a moment. Helen's got a bit of a cold, so
I've kept her in bed, and I said to myself, "I'll go and see
how Claude is!" Most unmaidenly of me' (Millie had
a charming laugh—melodious and rich, with a rather
quizzing humour), 'but we're old enough, Claude, aren't
we, not to need a chaperon? Now you're not to suggest
tea. I've only just had lunch and I shall probably drop
in for a cup with Meg Delaney. The days when Helen is
in bed are visiting days.'

He, on his side, thought what a funny old thing *she*
was with her ugly hat a little askew, her rough old face
so innocent of cosmetics, that queer green cape, her thick
legs, her broad-toed shoes—yet if she walked into the
middle of a hostile African tribe, they would know her
at once for someone important.

The rings on her rather stubby red fingers were old
and magnificent but looked absolutely right on her and
not at all incongruous with her queer clothes. He looked
at the rings rather enviously. After all, she and Helen
could never be really 'up against it' while she had those
rings, and he expected that there were plenty of other
old family treasures as well. But he was delighted to see
her. While she was there, sitting opposite to him, looking
so thoroughly at home, his world was more secure and
he need not fear the enemy.

They chatted for a while very amiably on world
affairs, wondering about the Saar and whether Germany
was to be trusted and what Hitler was like really, and
then something about the *Codex Sinaiticus* and wouldn't
it be better for the money to be spent on the poor, and
so to the 'pictures,' and Millie had seen some photographs
of *Little Women* which she had read over and over again
as a girl, and had Claude read *A Rose in June,* which
of course he'd never heard of, and so to more personal
things—Princess Corleone, Helen's cold, and was Claude
comfortable where he was?

'As I've said, that's a horrid man who brought me
up here.'

'Yes.' Claude dropped his voice and looked about the
room. 'As a matter of fact something very unpleasant
is happening.'

'Tell me about it. Perhaps I can help,' said Millie.

'Well—he's accusing me of stealing things.'

'Accusing *you?* My dear Claude!'

'Yes, really. A little while ago it was some bath salts
belonging to a man called Pierson. You see, we share a
bathroom—a very uncomfortable situation, but there it
is. And one day Brocket came up here and said Pierson
had missed some bath salts. He didn't actually *accuse* me,
of course, but I was the only other person who shared
the bathroom. And then only yesterday he brought up

some coals and said that two library books had been left by Best, another tenant, down in the hall and had vanished.'

'But do you mean to say that he insinuated that you——?'

'Oh, of course he said nothing directly. But you don't know how he looks at me, Millie, and every day he seems to come nearer. I'm afraid of his touching me.'

'Touching you?'

'Oh, not assaulting me or doing anything violent, but just simply touching me. I couldn't bear it. I dream of it at night. If he laid a finger on me I'd be sick.'

'Poor Claude,' she thought, 'he certainly doesn't look well. I don't believe he has enough to eat. He's so very thin.'

'You've been too much alone here, Claude. That's been the trouble. You must come and see Helen and me more. And the Delaneys. I'm sure they'd be delighted to see you.'

'Yes. Young Delaney's been very kind to me already. He took me to a party the other night.'

'That was nice for you.'

'Well, it wasn't really. I didn't know anybody, and towards the end a man spoke who frightened me out of my life.'

'Frightened you?'

'Yes. He said about what the world was going to be very shortly—Communism, you know. Of course I'd heard people talk like that before, but this man was different. He really made you feel that it was true what he said. It was most unpleasant. No personal freedom. No marriages. But it wasn't the details. It was the way he looked. I felt as though I were being stood up against the wall and ordered to be shot there and then.' He smiled. 'Not that it would matter—an old man like me.'

There was something very sweet and touching about

Claude, Millie decided. He had a kind of heroism somewhere although he wasn't very brave. But how could you
be brave when you were over seventy and had no money
and not enough to eat? But she realized that he was, even
in these hard times, one of those who cared more for
others than himself.

'Now, Claude, listen.' She got up and stood looking at
him, menacing him with her finger. 'You've been much too
much alone. Don't you think you haven't got any friends,
because you've got plenty. And don't worry about the
future. Take things day by day. Because the War was
so bad, people think the future must be bad too. It doesn't
follow at all. The Lord does things in His own way and
His own time.'

I wish the Lord had told her not to use all my coal,
he couldn't help thinking; nevertheless he was delighted
with her visit, felt ever so much better for it. He wished
he could ask her to stay a little longer, but he didn't dare.

Millie did then a thing she had never done before. She
went and kissed Claude on the cheek.

He was tremendously affected, and they stood for a
moment together, his hand on her arm.

He didn't speak, and she just nodded and went away.

CHAPTER VIII

The Thunderstorm

THERE may be one or two who remember a very curious thunderstorm on an early March London afternoon in this year 1934.

Why should a thunderstorm that did not last longer than twenty minutes remain in anyone's memory? Well, in part because it sprang out of the bluest, most springlike of afternoon skies. Few people look upwards in London, and perhaps there was no one who saw a cloud, like a blot of ink on a blue tablecloth, spread out of the chimney-pots of Lambeth, throw a cold grey patch over the Thames, turn like a flat crab on to its back and spread out its claws over the Houses of Parliament. The day was March and in that there was a wind, but out of the wind, in Shepherd Market, for instance, or under the eaves of the new Curzon Picture-house it was almost as hot as summer. In the Strand the traffic suddenly piled up to an obstinate halt. The Town just here seemed for a moment to stand quite still, as though all the newspapers in Fleet Street were listening for news. High up in the National Portrait Gallery, all amongst the Elizabethans, an old gentleman in a chair went fast asleep and a beam of sun struck Mary of Scots on the mouth so that she seemed to smile at him. Very pretty. But in the Old Kent Road,

coming up the steps of the lavatory, were two gentlemen
arguing about the Royal Family. 'Bloomin' waste of the
people's money, that's wot it is. Wot good does it do?
That's wot I'm askin' you.'

'It's a symbol,' said the other gentleman, wiping his
mouth with the back of his hand. 'It's a symbol. That's
what it is. Look at the ruddy sun. Warm as summer.'

A novelist can go on with this sort of thing, of course,
for ever and ever. There are the two dogs in Battersea
Park, for instance; and the Princess Corleone coming out
of Claridge's and feeling an ache under her left arm and
wondering about it; and then the soldier on duty outside
St. James's Palace, stamping his feet as he turns and thinking of the new friend he's just made with the posh rooms
in Jermyn Street; and there's the chauffeur of Lord
Pondicherry who's hoping to persuade his master to get
a new Alvis instead of his ancient Daimler, and there'd
be a commission too, wouldn't there? Well, as I mean
to say, there are a great many people in London, and it's
all very easy, as so many writers, nice agreeable men and
women, have found in the last ten years. There's the
stream of consciousness too. *That's* very easy because
one thought *does* lead to another, as Mr. Sterne discovered ever so many years ago. . . . Well, the thing is
to cover a lot of paper—that is, if you want to pay your
income tax. But what do you do if you happen to be
dealing with real people? Real to oneself, that is. The
people are the thing. For instance, Kitty and Alton truly
were there on that afternoon of the thunderstorm. You
can't dislodge them, walking down the slope of the Green
Park in the warm sunshine. That wilderness of walls,
towers and chimneys hems them in.

If you are very modern you will hold them to be no
more than two fish swimming at the bottom of a green
tank. But they are, in my opinion, much more. They
have a passionate wonder, a glittering expectation.

Alton, at least, is happy as he has never been in his life before, because he is telling Kitty about his play. It isn't only a play, of course. It is filled with all the things that his soul has collected during the years of his soul's experience. They are not as yet very original things, except the bit about the young man facing the six old men in the Library and discovering that they are all himself. Kitty thought *that* original although it was probably in Shaw somewhere. He had brought a penny exercise-book and read her some dialogue from it. She wondered that, with the little experience he had had, the dialogue should be so real.

But of course she was absorbed by the young man himself. She was not at all intellectual and always preferred people to literature. And he was quite a new person to her. She had never, for one thing, given anyone such shining, unspoilt pleasure before, and all her life it had been her wish to give people pleasure. She walked along, her tall slim body strong and free, feeling the warm sun on her face and knowing that sense of independent co-ordinated joyousness that is the grandest thing in life. At that moment she bore no one in the world a grudge, had no inhibitions nor regrets.

'The old man blows his nose. The curtain falls,' cried Alton triumphantly.

'Is that the end of the first act?'

'Oh no. The third scene.'

'Is it wise to bring the curtain down in the middle of the act?'

'It's always done now. Cinema technique.'

'I see.'

Strange how very different he was now, consumed by this Art and therefore confident, strong, vibrating with ambition.

'Of course it will only appeal to special people. I mean that I'm interested in it because I'm interested in *you*, but if someone said quite casually "Let's go to the play to-night," and we went to your play, and the first thing we saw was an attic with a girl feeding a mouse just out of its hole—by the way, what would you do about the mouse? Will you have a real one?'

'Oh, the mouse is only symbolic.'

'Yes, but it has to be there. Some mouse has to be.'

What she liked about him was that he was not at all sulky at criticism, as she believed so many artists were. He smiled cheerfully.

'You think the play's rotten?'

'No, no. Of course I don't. Only I told you at the beginning I had no brains—about the Arts, I mean. I hate poems that I can't understand at the very first look, and novels where there's no story and no one you can like, and pictures made of fur and pieces of string. I don't apologize for that. *Very* modern movements always appeal to a small group. If everyone liked them at once there'd be no one for the new artists to fight.'

'What *do* you like in the Arts, then?'

'Let me see. In the theatre I go as far as Tchekov, but I must say I like a good farce or revue better. In novels I like Dickens and the *Old Wives' Tale* and Stella Benson. In poetry Keats and Robert Bridges and Housman. But I like life much better than books. That sounds priggish, doesn't it? but it's true. For instance, what do you feel like when an old woman comes into your shop and wastes half an hour of your time and doesn't buy anything?'

'Oh, that's part of my job.'

'With your love for the country, don't you get mad with impatience and want to rush off and marry a nice girl and live in the country?'

'I've never thought of marriage. I've never been in love.'

'Nor have I. Not for more than a minute. Look at

that cloud! How sudden! There wasn't a sign of it a minute ago.'

Then he asked her a question.

'What do *you* want to do with *your* life? I mean— what do you think it's all *for?*'

'What a terrible question! I don't know. I love being alive, but then I'm healthy and have friends. I think that I expect that something will happen that will change everything—all in a moment!'

'Here *is* something!' he cried. 'It's caught us!'

For there was a flash that flung the grass, the trees, the sheep, into a frenzy of unreal light, then a peal of thunder that seemed to roar at themselves personally as though announcing to them some fearful news; then the rain, shattering down, gates of water descending.

'Oh, run, run! . . . You'll be soaked! This tree——'

'A tree's the worst place! That's where people are killed. . . .'

But they stood there nevertheless although the tree had no leaves. They stood there, both together. The storm took the Park into his hands and worried it as a dog worries a rag.

'It doesn't matter.' She put her hand on his shoulder. 'I was soaked through in the first moment. Home isn't far. I like storms.'

Their faces were stung with the rain.

He turned and kissed her wet cheek.

He began incoherently to speak.

'That settles it. I can never speak to you again. I've done it. I knew I would. Before I came out I saw the danger. I've seen it for weeks. And I'd have managed if it hadn't been for this. . . . The rain, the rain. . . . Good-bye. Good-bye. You'll never forgive me. But I'm not what you think. I'm better—far better. I'll prove myself. . . . You'll see. . . . You'll see. . . .'

And waving his arms like a madman, he started run-

ning across the Park. The rain whirled all about him as
though he were at the heart of a waterspout travelling
with him. He ran. He ran. He was gone.

Millie had often noticed that when her sister Helen
lived very vividly in the past, their room seemed to sink
back with her, throwing off any modernity (it never had
very much) and rising, as a transformation scene does
in a pantomime, with all the feeling, colour and sentiment of King Edward VII. The very chairs and tables
seemed to alter. One old woman's spoken words were
enough. No wonder the Witch of Endor had had so lasting a reputation.

'It's so lovely a day you might almost go out, Helen.'

'You go out, dear. You sit in here with me far too much.
When the sun shines like this I'm walking on the lawns
at Longleat. Do you remember that house-party when
Kitto Baines shot the peacock at two in the morning?
Poor peacock—and you thought I was going to marry
Kitto. You were quite frightened. As though I'd have
dreamt of such a thing. . . . Or did I?'

She got up slowly from her chair and walked, leaning
on her stick, to the window. How handsome she was,
Millie thought, even now! That carriage of the head was
superb and that straight back, a back famous through
England once. Millie remembered how miserably jealous
she had been in the old days. Why could she also not have
had a straight back, and then Kitto Baines . . . ? Following her sister to the window, she shook her head and
then laughed.

'How absurd!' she said aloud.

'What's absurd?' said Helen, not turning her head but
staring at the sun as though she could not have enough
of it.

'I was thinking of Kitto. I was in love with him once,

and dreadfully jealous of you, Helen darling. How silly it seems now! And poor Kitto . . .'

Faintly they heard a peal of thunder.

'Was that thunder?'

'It couldn't be. A fine day like this.'

'It was. There it is again. Nearer now.'

'Come away from the window, Helen. You never know.'

'Never know what?'

'Oh, lightning or something.'

'Nonsense. What a goose you are, Millie! How dark the room is suddenly!'

'I'll turn the lights on.'

'No. No. I like it like this.'

Millie gave a little scream. 'Oh, what a flash! Do come away from the window, Helen.'

'No. I should think not. I love it. Something's happening. Nature shows her scorn of us. That's what I like about a thunderstorm always. Contempt. That's what thunder is. I'd like to die standing at a window in a thunderstorm.'

Millie put her arm through her sister's.

'We'll die together, then.'

'Listen to the rain! Do you remember, Millie, being caught in the rain on the moors near Glencoe? Do you remember sheltering in the hut like King Lear, and Kitto saying "Poor Tom's a-cold"? That was the day I was near to accepting him. If the storm had lasted a minute longer . . . But you were there. You saved me that afternoon. As you've saved me again and again. Oh, what grand rain! What grand, grand rain! It brings me back to my senses, Millie. Sitting there by the fire day after day I don't know where I am half the time. I'm going, going . . . and soon I'll be gone. But standing up to the weather like this I'm all alive again. Listen! It's passing.

That peal was more distant. But how dark the room is!
I can only just see your face.' She turned towards Millie,
leaned down a little, and they stood cheek to cheek. Then
slowly together they moved back to the fire.

'Shall I turn the lights on?'

'No. No.' Helen sank slowly into her chair. 'There.
It will soon be over. Perhaps my last thunderstorm.
"Poor Tom's a-cold." Do you remember how Kitto said
it, looking at me?'

Millie smiled. 'That's better. The room's lighter already. And now we'll have some tea.'

'Help yourself.'

It was clear that Captain Coventry had been already
helping *himself* and now was charming, a little unsteady
on his feet and clearly amused at Bullock's diminutive
stature. Or so Bullock thought. But it didn't matter what
the Captain thought. Lizzie, his daughter, sat in the
shabby armchair by the window. It was a dreary room
and smelt of tobacco and spirits.

The Captain stood there and entertained his guest.
'Very glad to see you, Delaney. Lovely day, isn't it?'

When Bullock had arrived, ten minutes ago, there had
been a most unpleasant woman leaning with one arm on
the mantelpiece. She was handsome in a kind of violent
insolent way. She was heavy under the eyes, over-painted,
running to seed. She had been introduced to Bullock as
Mrs. Agar. And there had been a queer, brown-faced,
black-haired little fellow who, looking like a half-caste,
brought in the drinks. Coventry called him Abel. Bullock
noticed all these things because the child in the window
was his own. That was what he had now the certainty of!
He had met her three times—at the party and twice here.
On the first occasion in this room it had been but for a
moment, for they were just going out, she and her father.
Coventry had apologized but had made no pretence of

staying in. The child had said not a word. So, with these very brief encounters, Bullock was absurdly certain that he had rights over her, that he must care for and protect her, when she had given no sign whatever that she wanted to be protected.

And this was a horrid place. It was here that Coventry held his gambling parties. There were copies of French prints on the walls, an attempt, in the curtains, the fire-place, the sofa, at gay colours; but over everything a film of staleness. Coventry was laughing at him. Well, it didn't matter.

'It's very kind of you, Mr. Delaney, to call on us. Liz appreciates it. Don't you, Liz?'

'Yes,' she said.

Bullock went over to her.

'I wondered whether you'd let me take you out for a drive, Miss Coventry. It's a lovely day.'

'You go, Liz. It will do you good.'

She looked up at Bullock and smiled—a ghost of a smile.

'We have some friends coming . . . haven't we, Father?'

'Oh, they don't matter. Go along now.'

At that instant the light disappeared from the room as though it had been shut off by a dropped curtain.

Coventry went to the window.

'It's going to rain, by Jove! That's sudden. Thunder! Did you hear that, Lizzie?'

Lightning flashed and the room was for a fragment of time really revealed. Bullock would never forget that. The white paste of Coventry's cheek with the red patches, the furniture as though it were of papier mâché. Coventry said:

'I must close the window in the other room. It will rain like hell in a minute.'

Lizzie Coventry had sprung up and, with the strangest

gesture of helplessness, she had flung out her hands. Bullock caught her arm. She trembled.

'Thunder! I hate it! I'm silly, but once in Venice——'

He put his arm round her.

'Look here. Don't be frightened. I don't mean only the thunder. I'll look after you. You're only a kid. You oughtn't to be here. I'm your friend now and always. Don't be angry.'

The thunder crashed as though it were in the very middle of the room. He saw her face, a child's, terrified, her eyes large and distended.

And she had been frightened before. It was as though he had seen her standing like this in some other room. As though he saw it in a crystal or a mirror.

The thunder crashed again and, without knowing what she was doing, she pressed her little body against his. Bullock heard Coventry's voice and found that he was standing close to them.

'Liz is always like that when there's thunder about. It's all right, darling. It will be over in a minute. God, listen to the rain. Who'd have thought it five minutes ago!'

The room was dark. The rain lashed the panes. Lizzie bent down and picked up her book. Without a word she sat down in the chair and began to read.

'I remember once, Mr. Delaney,' Coventry began, and Bullock thought how charming his voice was—'Lizzie and I were in Vienna—know Vienna?—anyway it was a summer's day and we were sitting outside a café, when there was a cloudburst very like this one. It was the time when they had no money—you carried your cash about in a bag. Well, as I was saying . . .'

'Oh, I don't hold with it!' Lady Pender urged the passionate words between her tight lips as though they were weighted with gold. 'No, indeed I don't.'

'She's a terribly stupid woman,' Meg thought, 'and she detests me.' Also the family were behaving very badly, for Meg had made them all promise that they would be there—this the first occasion on which the Penders had come to tea. Bullock had said that he would see a publisher and hurry then straight home. Kitty was meeting a friend. ('Bring them back to tea,' Meg had said. 'Oh no, Mother, I don't think they'd mix with the Penders.' 'How do you know? You haven't seen the Penders.' 'Oh, but I do know.' 'Very well, dear, have it your own way.') Well, but who *would* mix with Lady Pender? *What* a stupid woman! She was called Evelyn. She was dressed too in a kind of black-and-yellow snakeskin, something quite unsuited to her sallow complexion. 'Of course, being out in the East so long you *do* get sallow,' Meg thought.

'They'll be in. They'll be in any minute,' Meg cried joyfully, looking at her beloved Graham. She couldn't help it. He was her beloved now as he had been all those years ago. It was quite possible to love two people at one and the same time.

She would tell Fred all about it. She would say: 'He's so clever, Fred. There's simply *nothing* he doesn't know, *and* he's so sweet. He always had the sweetest nature. He talks in the voice of all the poets, soft, gentle, with every word distinct and full of meaning. Now *you,* Fred, often don't know *what* the words you mispronounce really do mean.'

Graham was thin, brown and exceedingly distinguished, while Fred was burly, florid, and would be too fat if he didn't look out. Not that she was making comparisons between the two men.

She loved them both, that was all, and how splendid to have *two* men to love at her time of life! She knew too that Graham was in love with *her* again. He was saying to himself, 'Why ever did I marry that thin, grumpy . . .?' or wasn't he?

Here Meg pulled herself up, yes, just as she was per-
suading Evelyn Pender to the little paste sandwiches. She
mustn't harm anyone. She mustn't do an unkindness to
anyone. Everyone must be happy. With the sun pouring
in through the window and dear Graham sitting there,
so gently, so comfortably, how could one *not* be happy?

'Oh, I don't hold with it!' Lady Pender had cried. 'Let
the natives once get out of hand and it's good-bye to the
British Empire!' Saying this she tossed her head, clicked
her teeth almost as though they were little castanets, and,
with a wave of her sandwich, commanded all the natives
of India back into their jungle.

'It's too bad,' said Meg, who was always bored with
the British Empire. (The trouble was, she never could
see it! She tried to sometimes, shutting her eyes very
tight, but all she collected were rolling brown rivers, miles
of forest and a missionary.) 'They promised me. Fred is
good about keeping his word too. Isn't the sun lovely?
Graham, do you remember the sun that day on the
Thames? That summer day when Margery Thawe fell
into the river—on purpose, of course, because it was
young Elton rescuing her that made him propose. Dear
me, dear me, what a *long* time ago!'

She wasn't, she reflected, being very tactful to Evelyn,
and at once, knowing that she had done her a wrong, felt
warmth towards her, would have given her anything she
possessed, longed to tell her that that black-and-yellow
snakeskin was the very worst kind of colour. So she laid
her hand for a moment on Lady Pender's shoulder,
saying:

'You'll call me Meg, won't you? Everyone does.'

Lady Pender smiled a tight shoe-pinching smile. 'Yes.
Of course. My real friends call *me* Evie.'

Graham had been very silent. Only now, looking up
at Meg's very simple friendly gaze, seeing her bathed
in sunlight, he remarked:

'I like this room. It's happy somehow.'

'Yes. It is happy,' Meg said. 'It's the house. Fred loves this house as though it were a live thing—Delaneys have lived in it for years and years. We're always afraid we may have to sell it. They want it for flats and are offering a splendid price. As it is we let all the floors and to such nice people. They're all friends of ours. But if one flat were empty we wouldn't be able to manage it. It's a tight squeeze as it is. Try one of those marzipan things, Evie. They're so good. Yes, we hope for the best though. We're an optimistic lot, we Delaneys. Why—where's the sun gone to?'

She moved to the window, and a moment later a flash cut the room as a knife cuts paper.

Lady Pender was quite unmoved. She took another marzipan cake and began to nibble at it, giving it a little careful look between each nibble. Meg went to Graham's side. They stood close together, looking out into the darkness, hearing the peals of thunder, then watching the sheets of determined rain. They did not speak.

Lady Pender finished her cake and looked at them. She stared at the broad back and the thin one. Then, finding her handkerchief, she carefully wiped her lips, looked into a small mirror in her heavy black bag, patted her hair. Then, once again, she stared.

Fred Delaney was a little drunk. He had lunched with three old friends at the Beef Tub, a small hostelry near Apple Tree Yard, and he now saw life gloriously. He was quite steady on his legs, knew just what he was saying, and if life were a trifle intensified, a little more than real, wasn't that a splendid thing? He *knew* that he was a little drunk. That was the *good* thing. The trouble with drinking began when you didn't know. His big body was vibrating with health and strength. With one push of his big arm he could knock this whole shop to pieces, and

wouldn't it look a mess? Pushing his hat straight, smiling
with his fine Irish joviality into the respectable trades-
man's face, he handled the 'shirtings,' pressing them between finger and thumb, finding them, one and all, superb.

Inside his brain one or two notions were running about
and he found it difficult to catch and hold them. Dear
old Meg, for example, had asked him to be back for tea.
Some people were coming. He had promised. Well, he
would keep his promise although he *had* stayed at the
Beef Tub a bit later than he had intended. Then he knew
quite well that he had no right to be ordering shirts in an
expensive shop in Jermyn Street. In the first place he had
enough shirts, and, in the second, he had no right to buy in
a shop like this. He simply hadn't the money. Lastly, the
mirrors in the shop annoyed him. There were so many of
them and, from where he was standing, however he
turned, he saw this big carroty-haired, blue-eyed familiar
laughing at him. The mirrors suggested that there were
many more worlds than one, and that was a suggestion he
didn't care for. One was quite enough for one man to
manage! But was he only one man? Seen side-face, his red
cheek, his rounded chin, the broad shoulder, the stout leg,
here was a complete stranger! He swung about and there
was the familiar old Fred, reassuring him again, but that
stranger was still there. He must be there, hiding in
another mirror. And if there were many Freds, there were
many shops and many Londons. There were *strange*
Londons and behind them *strange* worlds. These mirrors
were doors and one of them might at any moment open.
What would it then disclose? Some brand-new world
where, possibly, men walked about on their heads and all
the windows of the houses were flat to the street! He
laughed at this funny idea and went back to the counter
to finger the beautiful silk 'shirtings' again. He looked
at the decorous assistant very gravely.

'I was thinking,' he said, 'how funny it would be if

windows were flat with the street. If you walked on them
and they splintered. What a noise there'd be!'

'Yes, sir,' said the assistant gravely. 'This blue and
grey is very handsome. It makes up beautifully.'

'Like a film star,' said Fred, laughing heartily at his
little joke. Then, because his legs *were* a trifle unsteady,
he sat down on the hard round chair.

At that moment the door of the shop opened and a big
heavy tub-faced man entered. Fred knew him at once. It
was Mr. Bartlett, Mrs. Van Renn's young friend. Fred
had met him twice at the Van Renns' lately, and a duller
ox of a man you wouldn't find in a day's march through
London. There he sat in the Van Renns' little room, his
legs spread, staring in front of him and saying: 'By Jove,
yes,' or 'You don't mean it!' or 'That's a good one!' He
appeared not to have an idea in his head, and his only
virtue to Mrs. Van Renn must be, Fred supposed, that
he had money and was generous with it. That the lovely
Miss Van Renn was bored with him was probable, although what Miss Van Renn thought about anything was
never very clear.

However, Fred was feeling friendly to all the world,
so from his little chair he said very heartily, 'Hullo,
Bartlett!'

Bartlett's heavy eyes regarded him with somnolent
recognition. 'Hullo, Delaney!' Then he turned at once to
the assistant and said: 'Want some braces. Red and black
stripes.' Then apologetically to Fred: 'Hope I'm not butting in. You go ahead.'

'No, old boy, of course not. Only having some shirts
made up. Grand day, isn't it?'

'Grand day it is.'

Bartlett leaned on the counter, as though he would
smash it to powder.

'You're looking well, old man,' Fred said genially.

'Not so bad,' said Bartlett.

'Seen the Van Renns lately?'

'Yesterday. Was there yesterday.'

'Was it the dark red or the crimson you were wanting?' asked the assistant.

'Hell! I don't know. Let's see them both,' said Bartlett.

Delaney studied genially that enormous back and thought to himself: 'I've got a pretty figure beside this fellow.' He got up, stretched himself and yawned.

'I'll be toddling.'

Bartlett didn't turn from the counter.

'So long, old man.'

'I'll be in again,' Fred said to the assistant and went gaily out, leaving, thank God, all those disturbing mirrors behind him.

He was disturbed nevertheless a trifle about Bartlett. *Did* Alice Van Renn see anything in the oaf? She might. You couldn't tell with her, and Fred was sore to confess that Bartlett had most certainly spent more time with her than he, Fred Delaney, had. For, to be honest, his times with her were extremely brief, always broken into by something. She was for ever going out or coming in when they were alone. Only when others were there did she sit like an image, frozen to her chair.

It seemed to him that he almost sailed along Piccadilly. His hat a trifle on one side, his brown overcoat gaily open, humming a tune, it was as though the world were his ship and he commander.

And then, just as he passed the door of the Berkeley, where the door-attendant, known to him, touched his cap ('A nice fellow,' Delaney thought, 'I never saw anyone help ladies out of taxis better'), there was a rumble as though a lion had growled. He stopped at the crossing and looked up. Why, the sky was black! An instant before and it had been a dancing shining blue. Never mind. He had no umbrella and only a light overcoat, but he would be home in no time. The lights changed, he hurried

across, bought a *Star* from the newspaper man, stood
a moment looking at the racing and seeing that the small-
printed lines danced a little before his eyes, when the
very ground cracked at his feet. He had not noticed the
lightning and so the crash caught him the more with surprise. He really looked at the pillars of the Ritz as
though he expected to see them topple forward. He was
curiously excited, with the sort of realization that one has
sometimes under an anaesthetic. 'By Jove, this *is* the
explanation of the Universe. I've got it at last!'—only
Fred said, and aloud: 'By Jove, the windows *are* all flat,
and I'm trampling on them!'

No one heard him because now, with another peal, the
rain came down in torrents, with a glassy sound, his
slightly intoxicated brain thought, as though those mirrors were crashing about him.

And he ran, a thing that a Londoner hates to do in
public. But he thought, 'I can be home in a minute if I
run.' At the end of Half Moon Street the rain was so
torrential that he stood in the portico of Number 90 for
shelter. 'I'll wait,' he thought. 'It will soon be over.' He
stood there and, very composedly, opened his paper. He
saw a headline: 'LONDON'S DANGER.' It was a leader in
the paper's centre. It began:

There could have been no doubt, we imagine, in the mind of
anyone who heard the speeches made in the House of Commons
last night that the safety of London, in the advent of another war,
is far from secure. It may be that we are witnessing the final
moments of the London that we love. One Air Raid and, so far
as our present Air Protection goes, London will, perhaps, lie in
ruins. London, with her history, her art, her beauty . . .

He had read so far to the sound of thundering waters.
It was as though the sky had opened up and, in a frenzy
of energy, the Minor Gods were playing the game of the
Deluge.

But he saw and felt more than the rain. Removed ever so slightly from actual reality, he saw his beloved City lying, like her windows, flat with the earth. A glittering moon filled his eyes with ironic light, and into the heart of that glitter London rose, her towers white like snow, softly grey like pigeons' wings; the river stood on end spouting a column of water at the cold moon's grin; walls were split and into the air poured the débris of mankind, pictures and coal-scuttles, curtains and fire-arms, 'Tobias and Sarah in Bed' from the Victoria and Albert, Michael Angelo's 'Entombment' from the National Gallery, Mr. Cochran's walking-stick, one of the lions from Trafalgar Square, the air dark with shoes, hats, knives and forks, and the wooden toy horses of a thousand nurseries.

London has fallen! And, after its fall, a great silence. Years of silence—and at last on a moonlight night so still in comparison with the other, a bird's sleepy song, before with a faint whirr of its wings it flies to the trees that envelop Selfridge's bargain basement, where it folds itself to slumber.

London! His London in peril! Of course. Of course. Why had he not seen this before? Its loveliness, its pathos, its roughness and ugliness and tragedy, its gaiety and humanity, its inconsequence, its great multitude of ghosts, the very spirit of its independence, the very helplessness of its appeal to be loved, seemed to come to him as he stood there, and, being a little drunk, he stretched out his arms and enfolded it.

'Come to me, my darling.' (And was it not perhaps wearing the semblance of the lovely delicate body of Alice Van Renn?) 'I will care for you, protect you, hide you from the invader.'

And then, for the rain was less severe, he almost tiptoed the few steps home.

PART II

Charles Street

CHAPTER I

Women Are Motherly

MEG DELANEY, as soon as she recognized that something
had to be done, immediately did it.

People who knew her moderately rather than well
were often surprised at the suddenness with which, out of
what seemed a cloud of absent-mindedness, she became,
all in a moment, practical and efficient. Only her own
family knew that this was so and admired her for it.

She had realized for some time that something must
be done about Rudge, that Caesar, the family Gany-
mede. He was unhappy, poor boy, and that she could
not endure because she was fond of him.

But there was more in it than personal feeling. The
family's ease of mind depended very greatly upon Caesar.
Without that boy everything would be at sixes and sevens,
because he was tireless, methodical, devoted. Because he
was devoted it seemed strange that he should ask so
obstinately for his wages to be raised. But Meg did not
make the mistake so often made by masters and mistresses
about those who work for them. She knew that Caesar
had a life of his own with many things in it that had
nothing at all to do with the Delaney lives. She knew
above all that he was demanding a rise because his old
mother never let him alone on this subject.

She knew too that Fred could not afford to give him

a rise—no rise at least that would satisfy old Mrs. Rudge. And she knew that Caesar was so good and efficient a boy that he could easily find a job elsewhere with better wages.

She knew that the boy loved the Delaneys, that his heart was torn, and that, with a torn heart, you sleep badly, work inefficiently and lose your temper. She did *not* know that, to add to poor Caesar's burdens, he was, for the first time in his life, most desperately in love. Meg was further aware that this problem of Caesar was only one of many problems now beginning to approach the Delaney happiness. It might be the smallest of the problems or it might be the largest. In any case she would at once attack it. She would go to the fountain-head, and the fountain-head was old Mrs. Rudge.

She disliked Mrs. Rudge extremely, and it always upset her to be with someone she disliked. She shared with Millie Pake the belief that if you knew anyone very well you could not really dislike them. Old Mrs. Rudge shook this belief, for the more often that Meg saw her the more she disliked her. Mrs. Rudge was often unwell. She possessed a mysterious Thing that she called her Pain. No one knew quite what it was, for it moved about and no doctor was able to put his finger on it. Meg privately considered that its origins were in eating too much and never taking any exercise. Mrs. Rudge also belonged to that Merry Old England that regarded fresh air as a poison. Now, sitting in the small room over the little shop in Shepherd Market, Meg felt stifled as though she were living inside a camphor ball. She felt also enormous physically, but spiritually inferior to Mrs. Rudge.

Mrs. Rudge was a small woman wrapped in shawls. Her face was covered with wrinkles, and out of the wrinkles there gleamed two little eyes as sharp as pins. But for the eyes you would fancy that she was a poor, weak, crumpled-up little woman whom life, dealing in a series of mean revenges, had reduced to helplessness. It was only her eyes and her voice, which had the sharpness of a drill-instructor's, that showed that there was life in the old girl yet. The room had in it many large sea-shells, the model of a ship, and the dried skin of a baby alligator, for her husband had been a sailor who had found distant seas preferable to matrimony.

She watched her maritime possessions as though any and every visitor had only one purpose in life, namely to rob her of them. But then she watched everything. She resembled a detective in a murder story who may, from the slightest clue, a shoe-lace, a tea-spoon, a cigarette-end, discover the murderer. That the murderer was somewhere about, Mrs. Rudge was always sure.

This suspicion made Meg horribly aware of her own bright colours, her conversation, her spreading proportions. To-day she was wearing quiet clothes, a black dress with silver bands at the neck and wrists, and a black hat. But she had taken off her gloves, and her rings glittered on her fingers. Mrs. Rudge's eyes were fastened on the rings.

'Well, Mrs. Rudge, how are you? Pretty well, I hope.'

'No, mum, I can't say as I feel very well.'

'Oh, I'm sorry. What's the matter?'

'It's my Pain, mum.'

'Oh, I *am* sorry! What kind of a pain?'

'Round my 'eart—then the back of my neck, and then lower, much lower.'

'How horrid for you! It sounds a little like indigestion.'

'Indigestion!' Mrs. Rudge was as scornful as though Meg had suggested that she was a millionairess. 'Ah, well. Them that 'asn't got can't feel. That's what I always say. It's a burden to be borne, and them's lucky that don't 'ave to bear it.'

'Well, I'm very sorry.' Meg knew that the preliminaries were now over and that real conversation must begin. 'I think you're very brave, Mrs. Rudge. Caesar tells me how brave you are. It's about Caesar I looked in for a moment.'

The old lady seemed to stiffen as though she were suddenly all muscle.

'Caesar, mum? 'E's giving satisfaction, I hope?'

'Of course he is—a very good boy.'

'Well, I 'opes he is. That's all. I'll tell you something, Mrs. Belaney.' (It was one of Mrs. Rudge's characteristics that she took a refined pleasure in never knowing anyone's name correctly.) 'If that boy isn't giving satisfaction I don't know any boy in the country 'oo would. That's all I 'ave to say.'

'Of course he is. Perfect satisfaction.' Meg laughed. 'The trouble is that I'm afraid it's we who are not giving *him* satisfaction. He's asking us to raise his wages.'

'Oh, 'e is, is 'e? First I've 'eard of it.'

(Horrible old liar, Meg thought.)

'We think,' Meg went on, 'that he is worth all he can get, of course. He's a very good boy, *very* good boy indeed. The sad thing is that we can't afford to pay him any more. As it is we run the house with no margin, no margin at all.'

Now indeed Mrs. Rudge's little eyes did seem to flash fire. There appeared even an ironical twist to the thin dried lips. *This* woman with her fine black dress and diamond rings saying she couldn't afford it! That was a good one. Oh, a very good one indeed! She, Mrs. Rudge, hadn't once been lodge-keeper at Wintersmoon for nothing.

'You know best, mum, of course. . . .'

'No, of course not. Caesar knows best what's right for his own future. Only I came because I know the influence you have on him, and perhaps you could show him that it would be wise to wait a little and then we'll see what we can do.'

Mrs. Rudge's voice shook. She was in one of her famous tempers.

'Excuse me, mum, but it don't seem right for a lady like you to come 'ere be'ind the poor boy's back and suggest things to 'is mother.'

'I'm not suggesting anything.'

'Oh yes, you are, mum, excuse me. You knows well enough that my poor boy works 'is fingers to skin and bone in your service and 'as done ever since 'e was a little nipper. "Mother," 'e says to me, "Mother, I'm that tired I could just lay me down and die. Don't tell them, Mother," 'e says. "I don't want *them* to know 'ow tired I am. They mean well," 'e says, "but they don't think," 'e says, "they don't think of the long hours and the poor food——" '

'He *doesn't* have poor food!' Meg broke in wildly.

'Ah, not as *you* sees it, mum. *You* mean well, no doubt, but *you* don't see what goes on with that there cook, Mrs. Banter——'

'Ganter!' Meg said. 'Ganter!'

'Ganter or Banter, it's all one as far as my poor boy and 'is food goes. "Mother," 'e says when 'e comes 'ome, "Mother," 'e says, "I may be the son of a sailor, Mother, but that ain't no reason why I should eat what that Mrs. Banter gives me." And then I cooks 'im a nice boiled egg and a 'ot cup of tea——'

This picture was so far removed from the true and cheerfully happy Caesar that Meg could listen no longer.

'I'm sorry, Mrs. Rudge. That really isn't true. Caesar is very happy with us and has *plenty* to eat. He wants to stay with us, we want to keep him, but we *can't* afford to raise his wages, not just now at least——'

But Mrs. Rudge had her head raised as though she were listening to a call from above. Her neck that had before scarcely existed was now a long and skinny one. She beat the air with a dry and withered hand.

'It's my Pain,' she whispered. 'It's my Pain.'

Meg rose. 'Oh dear, I *am* so sorry. Where is it? What can I do for it?'

Mrs. Rudge beat the air quite frantically.

'It's there—in the stummick. And now it's going up. Oh, it's in my chest fearful!'

But Meg had been there before. She put some money on the table.

'Shall I fetch someone?'

'Oh no, mum, thank you. It's a bit better. It's going down again. It's settling in its proper place. I'm very grateful to you, mum, I'm sure.'

'Well, talk it over with Caesar, will you? I daresay he *could* get more somewhere else, but we don't want to lose him and he doesn't want to go. We're very fond of him, you know.'

'Yes, mum, I'm sure . . .'

'Good-bye, Mrs. Rudge.'

'Good-bye, mum.'

Walking slowly homewards, Meg Delaney suffered one of her sharp moments of depression. Mrs. Rudge was *real*, and in all probability the world contained a great number of just such selfish, ruthless tyrants. Mrs. Rudge to Mussolini . . .

At certain intervals Meg had the experience that all optimists and idealists have. A person encountered, a passage read, a word caught and remembered, and the World of Light is suddenly curtained in darkness. It *is* true, then, this that cynics, destroyers, disillusionists, are for ever repeating: human nature is grim, snakes and monkeys we are, no progress has been made. We see ourselves, in those bitter moments, as our detractors see us— weak, complacent, blinded, ever-trusting optimists. We are ashamed. We hang our heads. The bitter moment does not endure. Whether it is our glands, our digestions,

or merely the fact that we were so unhappy as children
that we must needs be happy now, the pendulum swings
back—we cannot deny the love of our friends, the coming
of spring, the succulence of a new potato, the rising of the
theatre-curtain, the glass-green heart of the turning wave,
the tread of the springing mountain turf. A bruised
and mangled world, rich with beauty and terror-veined
promise. . . .

All the same Mrs. Rudge stuck in Meg's nostrils. And
her own sad weaknesses too! For had she not in this
very month taken at least three taxis when omnibuses
would have done? And here they were, Fred and herself,
refusing to raise Caesar's wages, by ten shillings a week!
But raise Caesar ten shillings and Mrs. Ganter too must
be raised. Fifty pound a year more! and the Pullets and
the Pakes threatening to leave! Very shortly another attack on the house would be made, and the raising of the
servants' wages might be the last little feather added to
the already bursting pillow! Fred would yield. He
would sign the house's destruction! And then, as Meg
knew, he would never again forgive himself, his rectitude
would crumble, he would drink and embrace a hundred
Van Renns, Kitty and Bullock would vanish into air.
. . . What of the Joyful Delaneys then?

Seen thus Mrs. Rudge appeared as an old witch riding
her broomstick through the thick night air above Shepherd Market, screaming destruction to the Delaneys.

'I was weak to give her money,' Meg thought. 'How
ridiculous to give the old wretch ten shillings when I
have to hesitate before buying myself a pair of gloves!
It's a kind of blackmail really. I give her money every
time I go there just to stop her going on about her Pain.
And well she knows it. Why am I so silly and so weak?
There's a lot of real pain in the world. Mrs. Rudge is a
sham and I encourage her in her shamming.'

But in the very middle of her self-condemning she was

compelled to stop, just outside her door, and buy some daffodils from a little man with a withered leg.

He coughed and thanked her.

'You are sure they're quite fresh,' she said, knowing they were not.

'They are that, ma'am. Picked this morning.' He looked at her wistfully.

'There isn't any sort of a job——' he began.

'I'm afraid not.'

'You see, my lady, my wife's got the bronchitis and there's the rent due—only five shillings——'

She gave him five shillings.

He looked at her quite angrily.

'I 'ates flowers,' he said, most unexpectedly.

'Oh no, you shouldn't——'

' 'Eartless things. Don't care what you're suffering. Flowers—and your wife with bronchitis and a kid a month old. Sure there ain't any kind of job needed? I'm clever with my 'ands——'

Then something in her face charmed him. He smiled. He spoke to her like a father to his child.

'Never you mind, lady. I'll manage . . .' and went on down the street flourishing his daffodils.

'I must speak to Caesar,' Meg thought. She must see him at once, partly because he would improve the nasty taste of his mother, partly because she could never bear to leave anything suspended. She must come to the crisis. She must finish the thing. And often enough she had spoiled what she was after by her impetuosity.

The room that she loved so much was warm and protected against the outside March rawness. She looked at the William and Mary clock. Three-thirty. That man and his little girl, Bullock's new friends, were coming to tea at four-fifteen.

She took off her hat and gloves and threw them into a chair; in her furs she stood before the fire, warming her-

self, and looking with delighted happiness at the room
just as though she had never seen it before, and especially
at the Rowlandson water-colour she liked best, the one
where they were drinking outside an alehouse and the
coach was arriving and a little boy was flying a kite, the
figures with round rosy faces and stout posteriors, the
colours blue and pink and brown—soft, English, contented.

She had rung the bell and now Caesar appeared, small,
anxious, his large mouth grinning, rubbing his hand on
his black trousers.

'Yes, ma'am.'

'Oh, Caesar, come in. I want to talk to you about
something.'

'Yes, ma'am.'

He came forward and stood close to her, looking at
her, as he always did, with the greatest admiration. To
him she was simply the finest lady in existence. There was
no one worth a gold watch compared with her. Which was
the way he thought because he wanted a gold watch more
than any other thing in the world.

She looked at him and smiled. This lovely friendly
room and Caesar inside it—how happy they made her!

'The fact is, Caesar, I've just been to see your mother.'

'Yes, ma'am.' His eyes withdrew a little, his forehead
wrinkled, his mouth was serious.

'It's this business of raising your wages. It's troubling
Mr. Delaney and myself a good deal. You see, we both
want to do it. We know you are not really getting enough
for all you do and that you could get more elsewhere. We
couldn't bear to lose you. Everything depends on you. The
trouble is, if we give you another ten shillings a week,
then Mrs. Ganter will want it too. That means another
fifty pounds a year, and that would bust us. Mr. Delaney
might have to sell the house. I'm not a very good manager,
I'm afraid, but I'm going to try and economize. The fact

is that the rents of the flats in this house are very small, but if we raise them everyone will go and then we'll be worse off than ever. That's the way it is.'

Caesar looked up at her with so sweet and bewitching a smile that it was all she could do not to put her arms round him and kiss him. There was always something to her especially touching in his small-boyish stature and his grown-up official garments. He was like a boy dressed up for a party. He had rather a hoarse voice.

'What does Mother say?' he asked, watching her with his eyes very anxiously.

She would have liked to say that his nasty old mother had denied all knowledge of the affair, but that would have put him in the uncomfortable position of proving his mother a liar. So she refrained. And *he* would have liked to say that every night now his mother made his life a burden by demanding whether he'd brought it off, whether he'd got the rise, and if not why not, and did he know that he was killing her by his cowardice, and why had she so ungrateful a son who, after all she had done for him, etc. etc. But that would have been unkind to his mother, so *he* refrained.

'Well, ma'am, I hardly know rightly what to say. You've been so good to me, you and Mr. Delaney and Miss Kitty and Mr. Stephen, that I'm sure I'm willing enough to work for nothing, seeing as how I'd rather be working for you and Mr. Delaney and Miss Kitty and Mr. Stephen than the King *and* Queen . . . only . . . only . . . the way it is I sort of feel——' He stopped. He looked at her dumbly. He didn't feel anything of the kind. He was perfectly contented here. It was his mother. This nag, nag, nag, this complaining, these tears—and there *was* something else!

He dropped his eyes, then looked up again full into Meg Delaney's glorious ones.

'You see, ma'am. There *is* something else. There's a girl—I——'

'Oh, Caesar!' Meg was enchanted. 'You're in love with someone?'

'Yes, ma'am. First time. She's working in one of those flats back of the Market. She spoke to me one morning. There's a man spoke to her and she didn't like it. I know him, name of Brocket, owns a house in White Horse Street. Bad lot *he* is, and I told her if she was ever in any sort of trouble she was to come to me, and so we got talking and now—well, now we're going out together. I never was in love with anyone before, but now I am proper. And if Mother hears of it she'll carry on simply awful. That's what she's always been afraid of, me marrying— and so I thought if I had a bit more money, that would keep Mother quiet and so——'

Meg caught Caesar's grubby hand and shook it.

'Now that's splendid. Are you sure she's a nice girl?'

'A *nice* girl! Oh, ma'am!' His rather wistful Cockney face seemed to be lit up with a kind of glory. Glory was also expressed by the tips of his ears and his nose, which were all in an instant rosy. He spoke breathlessly as though he'd been running. 'She's from the country, Mrs. Delaney. Only been in London a month or two. She's beautiful, she is truly. All the men are after her. She's as fresh-looking as the place she come from. And innocent! Why, Mrs. Delaney, she don't know a thing and she's got a voice with an accent in it that's lovely. It *is* truly. But she does want looking after and it was lucky for her she told me about Brocket, because I've got *his* number all right, I have. And if he starts bothering her there'll be murder done in the Market.'

He drew a deep sigh and then said in a sort of holy whisper:

'Her name's Margaret Dundee.'

'Why!' cried Meg. 'It's the same as mine! But isn't the surname Scotch?'

Then Caesar looked at her with so fatherly a gaze that she felt quite young. But his paternal feelings were not for her.

'She's called Dundee,' he said, as though he were confiding a most tremendous secret, 'because she don't know her parents. Never did. She was found on a door-step in the town of Dundee. Brought up in an orphanage.' His eyes opened yet wider. 'It's my belief she's of very high blood. You'd think so yourself, Mrs. Delaney, ma'am, when you see her walking. Like a princess . . .!'

The glory faded. His brow puckered again like a monkey's.

'I can't tell Mother,' he said huskily. 'I just don't dare.'

They were now two conspirators.

'You tell your mother,' said Meg, 'that we're going to do something about the wages. You might tell her, too, that you're looking round for another job, although you won't be, of course. Can your Margaret cook?'

'That was just what I was going to tell you,' Caesar said ecstatically. 'I haven't had more than one of her cakes and some biscuits, but the people she's working for, they've got rid of their cook and made Margaret do it, raising her wages, of course, and she says *they* say they never knew such a cook. Not that she's one for prais-ing herself. You have to drag it out of her.'

'Well, who knows what the future may bring? Any-way, for the present don't you say a word to anybody, Caesar, and keep it dark from your mother. Just come and tell me if anything happens.'

'Oh, I will, ma'am. Thank you very much. You're ever so kind.' Then, backing a little towards the door, he said: 'I'd do anything for you, Mrs. Delaney.'

'More than for Margaret?'

That confused him. Then he grinned.
'That's different,' he said.

She went into her bedroom and changed her black
dress for a rich purple that she dearly loved, brushed
her black hair, put on a pair of long ear-rings of purple
and silver, then returned to sit in front of the fire and
dream for a moment before her guests arrived. 'I'm
motherly, that's true. And yet I'm not motherly at all. I
want to take everyone under my purple wing and do for
them, and yet I don't want to take any of them under my
wing really. I want to be rid of them, to have no cares,
no responsibilities. I love Fred, Kitty, Bullock. How
dearly I love Fred, every inch of him! I love him so that
I must believe in immortality, some kind of continuing
relation with him that nothing can break. And dear Kitty!
How sweet she is and how proud of her I am! And Bullock, what a dear boy, how good and gentle-hearted! Yes,
how I love them! And yet I want to be rid of them all! I
want no ties. I want to go out into the street and do just
as I please, speak to strange men, find out how people
live, take a boat and go to Bangkok, bury myself in China,
ride for ever through Persia. Nevertheless, if I *could* do
these things I would be homesick, worried about Fred,
hoping Kitty was safe and Bullock free from colds! How
tiresome it is! And how exciting too! And how foolish!
Here am I an ageing woman happy as a child because I
love to be alive! I *cannot* learn sense! I *cannot* be quiet
and wise and wear grey clothes and put away my ear-
rings.' . . .

'Captain Coventry and Miss Coventry.'

Meg knew, as soon as she touched his hand, that this
man was dangerous. A bad man, no, for she was wise
enough in her own generation to know that bad men and
women do not exist. Only we are destructive or creative;

in greater or lesser degree there is always that distinction. Creative or destructive of course only, for certain, at the moment of contact; but that which we are frequently we become finally. Nicholas Coventry was destructive. Coarsely handsome now, running to disintegration, his clothes excellent, his eyes hard, inquisitive, active, gay although often apprehensive. She knew at once that he would amuse her, but she was sorry for him, and that she did not want him to be Bullock's friend. She caught the reflection in the round mirror by the window of his tall, straight, thickening body, his too-ruddy cheek, the back of his head (his hair-cut was almost too excellent), and felt an instant addition to the dangers that were accumulating against the Delaneys.

He undoubtedly had not expected so opulent, so brilliantly glowing a lady. He liked opulence and his sensual taste was for middle-age. He held her hand a trifle longer than he would have done had she been younger and slighter.

Then the child caught and absorbed Meg's attention. What a queer creature with that child's body, the beautiful quiet face (for it was beautiful even though a year ago it might not have been), the pallor, the dark hair, the rather shabby grey dress, the quiet watchfulness!

'Won't you sit down? Bullock will be here in a minute. *And* tea.'

The child sat down, on the edge of her chair, very straight-backed, her hands folded. Coventry, entirely at ease, began to produce his charm. 'He's been charming for years,' she thought. 'It's become mechanical. He's thinking of something else.'

She knew immediately that, whereas once he had been able to control his every thought and movement, he was reaching now a decadence when subconscious desires and thoughts begin to have control. Soon his acts also would astonish him by leaping like animals into the arena before

he had given the word. She knew that he was stripping her
in his mind while he talked of Paris and the open-air play
in Verona and robbers at Toledo and a special kind of
pastry to be found only at Avignon.

The child said not a word but with her eyes took in
everything. Indeed, Lizzie Coventry was astonished by
Mrs. Delaney. It was seldom now, poor dear, that she was
astonished at anything, but she had never in all her
troubles and adventures seen a lady like this lady before.
She thought that if you were a woman and middle-aged
and English, you were either a good woman like Aunt
Fanny, or a horribly cheap bad one like Mrs. Agar. But
here was an Englishwoman in brilliant colours, flashing
rings and chains like an actress, and yet a fine English
lady beyond doubt or question. And not only fine but of a
grand size like one of the women in history. Kind, too,
for at the moment of Bullock's entrance Mrs. Delaney
flashed at Lizzie a smile so generous, understanding and
comforting, that the child—who was cold, weary and
almost at the end of her endurance—had all that she
could do to prevent tears from filling her eyes.

Bullock came in with Endless at his heels. That dachshund took an instant and fawning liking to Captain Coventry. This was strange because Coventry kept no dog,
had no scent about his trousers that suggested dogs, food,
or sport, and made no canine effort for politeness' sake.
But it seemed that Endless recognized an old friend, and
even when Caesar brought in the tea, an event that as a
rule commanded instantly the whole of dog, soul and
spirit, he never removed his liquid brown eyes from Coventry's face. As with all dachshunds his intelligence was a
little ironical, a trifle cruel. To surmount the irony of his
ludicrous body he had achieved a humorous criticism of
men and women that made them themselves self-conscious.
He greeted Coventry instantly as a fellow-ironist, which
in fact he was.

Bullock's anxiety caused his mother to love him. Because of it she was more amiable to Coventry than she intended to be, and so they all soon became very gay. What was Captain Coventry doing? Was his work in London?

He looked the serious man of affairs.

'You know what it is—a little business in the City, sometimes not so bad, sometimes damnable. We've been going up and down for years, haven't we, Liz?'

'Yes, Papa.'

'It seems so difficult now,' Meg said, 'to know where the money *is*. You used to be able to say: "There's money. I'll go for it." Now you don't know—no one knows.'

'That suits me,' Coventry said, laughing. 'I'm an adventurer, you know. Always have been. As long as there's bread and butter for myself and my little girl, that's all I worry about. I'm afraid I'm a rolling stone, Mrs. Delaney, and that's a fact.'

'How I'd love to be a rolling stone!' Meg cried. 'Only even nowadays when women can go anywhere and do anything it's difficult. So here I am settled down with a family.'

Coventry gave her a gay buccaneer look as much as to say: 'If you'd like a little jaunt with me I'm sure I could manage it.'

Meg felt she disliked him very much. There was a strain of commonness there which offended her. There was no commonness in the child, however. Meg took her over to a Chinese cabinet that stood in the far corner and opened some of the drawers. In them there were pieces of silk, some fans, a small lacquer tray or two, odds and ends that Meg had picked up at one time or another. Lizzie was fascinated. She had a piece of orange silk marked with little silver figures in her hand and stroked it.

'I love beautiful things.'

'Do you? So do I. In fact my husband is always scold-

ing me for buying things that I shouldn't. What beautiful
things do you like best?'

Lizzie drew a little breath, gave Meg a serious look
as though to see whether she could be trusted, decided
that it was safe, and went on in a low voice that was almost a whisper:

'In Venice once Papa bought me a little painting. It
was very old and there was the Madonna and the Child
sitting under a tree and St. Joseph watching them. Behind them was such a lovely landscape, tiny trees and a
river and a little town all green and blue except there was
a tower that was pink. It was the most beautiful thing
I ever had.'

'Have you still got it?'

'No. We sold it once to pay a hotel bill.'

'Oh, what a shame!'

Lizzie looked, with an odd contraction of her brows,
about forty.

'Oh, we have to do that sometimes, when we haven't
any money, you know.'

'Do you like London?'

'It's as good as another place.'

'Have you plenty of friends?'

'Oh no—not *friends*. We lived with my aunt Fanny
for a time in Westminster. *That* was nice. She had a boy,
Edward, who goes to Westminster School. We were
friends, but I haven't seen him for a long time.'

'What do you like doing best?'

'I like to go walks by myself and see the people in
the streets. And I like reading.'

'What do you read?'

'French books mostly. I like Proust and André Gide.
Paul Morand's good too sometimes. The English don't
write as well as the French.'

Good heavens! Meg didn't know. She vaguely was
aware of the name of Proust as of a Frenchman who

wrote long and difficult books, mostly about homosexuality. What kind of a child *was* this?

'Will you come and see me sometimes?'

'Yes, if you'd like me to.'

'I'd like you to very much. I love walking and riding on omnibuses and seeing the town.' Then she added: 'Would you like that piece of orange silk? I'd love to give it to you.'

Lizzie's hand trembled. 'Oh no, I mustn't . . .'

'Yes, you must. There—slip it into your dress. It's *our* secret.'

The child looked at her, took the piece of silk and looked at it.

'I must tell Father,' she said. Then, after a little pause, added: 'You are very kind, thank you.' She went and showed it to her father.

'Well, really, Mrs. Delaney. That's too good of you. You'll spoil my little girl.'

Five minutes later they departed. All that Meg said to Bullock was:

'I don't trust that man, Bullock.'

'No—nor do I.'

'But the child's a darling.'

'Yes, she is.'

'What are you going to do about her?'

'See that she's safe.'

'Yes,' said Meg, kissing him on the forehead. 'You're right. She's worth saving.'

CHAPTER II

The House

FRED DELANEY stood in the hall of the Charles Street
house hiding an annoyance with his brother Larry which
was by no means new to him. He had experienced it first
when, at the age of two or so, Larry, crawling under the
table beside him, had pinched his leg to draw his attention
from dreaming to something practical. Larry had been
doing the same thing ever since. He stood now, very
smart in his deep-blue overcoat, his faintly yellow gloves,
his soft dark-blue hat, advising him about the house.

'Sell it, old boy! Don't be such a bloody fool. The
strain's simply killing you. You're getting to look like old
Ma Plunket who can't make up her mind whether to sell
her shell-backed chairs to Corleone or not. One day she
thinks she will, another day she won't, and that's after my
getting Corleone to lunch in her house, which is a thing
she's longed for all her life, and I had to work like the
devil to bring it about, I can tell you. Old Plunket's been
in her bed for a week with a sort of nervous breakdown,
and you'll be the same if you don't look out.'

Larry's voice, which had all the decisive pressure belonging to a man who was ever selling things to people
who didn't want to buy, went echoing up the stairs, and the
whole house shivered with disgust.

163

It was unfortunate, but Larry was just the kind of man the house couldn't endure. It was for the house Fred Delaney was annoyed; he never minded Larry half so much in the street. But, as often before, it was Larry's implication that he, Fred, was a dreaming ass that irritated him so especially. A dreaming ass when he had kept the house together all these years, when he had managed all these difficult people with tact and adroitness—a thing that Larry could never have done, for he had tact with people only when he was intent on making a bargain.

He had certainly no tact now. He struck Fred on the shoulder with a horrible brotherly patronizing geniality.

'You're sentimental, that's what you are, old lad. You and Meg are two of the most sentimental people I know.'

To be sentimental, to have no humour, to believe in God, to dislike cruel sports, to have trust in whatever Government may be in at the moment, these are the charges that any decent person in these days must rightly resent.

'Sentimental, am I?' cried Fred. 'Just because I want to keep the house we were born in and our fathers lived in before us. Pity more people haven't sentiment if that's what sentiment is. Now you get out, Larry, before I kick you out.'

'All right,' said Larry. 'Don't lose your temper, old boy. What I say is true though. You can't keep the house unless you raise the rent, and if you raise the rent you won't get the tenants. There you are—in a nutshell.'

'Why shouldn't people pay higher rents? Look what they are asking for flats all round here. Twice as much as *we're* asking.'

'Exactly. That's just it. Flats, yes. Poky rotten flats, many of them, but they're modern with modern gadgets. 1934. That's what *they* are. People are afraid of old houses these days. Think they're full of rats and ancient privies. *I* know. I go about and hear things.' He caught his brother's arm. 'By the way, you don't want to sell that old clock of yours? If you're hard up, I mean. I'm sure I could get a pretty penny for it. I know just the party. Old Lord Ragadoon. He's mad as a hatter, but he's got lovely things. I know I could persuade him.'

That was the last insult.

'Go on, Larry, get out. You don't understand me and you never have. I wouldn't be you for all the gold in America.'

'All right, old boy. I'm going. See you soon.'

And Larry went.

After the door was closed Fred stood there in the dim morning sunlight, looking up the stairs as though he were asking a question. In actual fact he didn't know what he was doing except cursing Larry. He always felt a small boy when Larry had been at him, and he felt that now.

But in some respects he was one—the kind of twopence-coloured strain that hinders maturity was in him as it had been in Robert Louis Stevenson, Scott, Tom Moore, Goldsmith, in almost every Irishman and Scotsman perhaps. Not that maturity isn't there, but through it there runs the silver skein of playing at life as Stevenson played at his toy theatre. This Fred Delaney had, a strain neither in his wife nor children. For Meg did not *play* at life— she embraced it with both arms—and Kitty and Bullock were, like all their generation, in many ways, mature before their time. Fred Delaney was the only child in the family and the only poet.

His visions of Ireland, London, this house, his wife, women, were all poetical: that is, filled with music, colour, fantasy, twice as deep as they looked and gone before they were grasped, but leaving in their wake some lasting tune, some permanent colour.

But his trouble was that he could not communicate any of this. He might burst out, as he had done on that New Year's morning to Munden concerning London, but those outbursts were rare. He had a true positive belief in things: stone and mortar and brick and clay and oil and steel and silk and cotton—these materials and the shapes man made of them—as being sentient, responsive, depending for their life a little on the human souls with whom they were. And he reconciled this new machine age in which he was placed absolutely with the world of truth and beauty. Man would subdue it and transform it as, so often before, man had subdued and transformed its ancestors. His beloved London in which now so many lovely buildings were tumbling down had, he believed, an inner spirit that would conquer all that it absorbed. But destruction—real total destruction—that he had not counted on!

Ever since, on the afternoon of the thunderstorm, he had read in the evening paper that casual article about raids, fire bombs, poison gases, a fresh and most poignant anxiety had grown round his heart. This could not harm his fundamental happiness, but it made him something of a man-at-arms guarding with his life the treasure-house of the King. It had increased the poignancy and tenderness of his love of London. She might, like any and every human soul, have evil in her—wicked ways and filthy slums and crooked politics, noise and stench and confusion, but these things were only because she was alive and composite and real. And as with London so, in the heart of her, was this house. She also was threatened with destruction. With something more imminent and perilous.

As now he looked up at that old staircase, dimly laced with sunlight, his heart ached with love for her. That might, as Larry had said, be sentimental, but everyone was sentimental about something!

He ran up the stairs and, as he had so often done before, hastened to the very top of the house. Here, up some little wooden stairs above Patrick Munden's flat, was a

grimy little attic room with one small window looking
right over the town. He flung it open and leaned out.
Spring was in the air, the sun bathed benignantly the roofs
and chimneys that lay now in a sea of glitter from which
rocks and monolithic creatures and helmeted warriors and
extended blackened arms uprose to the blue sky. Higher,
higher, in flying ship he might go and from that clear sky
look down on this black glittering sea and discern perhaps
in some pale line on those waters minute bodies moving as
germs move in a doctor's chart. Detach one of those
germs, and from its miniature life proceed the Mozart
Violin Concerto, the 'Hailstone Chorus,' the dark self-
portrait of Rembrandt, King Lear's heath, and the revela-
tions of Einstein. Miraculous miracle! Wonder of the
stars! . . . The murmur of all life came to his ears. He
dropped, he dropped, and there was once again the faint
pain in his left temple, the slight occasional stiffness of
his right leg, the steady friendly beating of his heart. He
closed the window and thought of Mrs. Elizabeth
Montagu. Why that Queen of Blue Stockings? For no
reason except, of course, that she had been in that house,
and the Mrs. Pasket Delaney of that time whose journal
in a salmon-coloured cotton-cover manuscript book Delaney possessed (it was dry and dull; otherwise he would
have published it) recorded numbers of times: 'Mrs.
Montagu came. . . . Mrs. Montagu present. . . .
Mrs. Montagu held forth to my thinking far too frequent.'
That was after her marriage, when she moved to the
house in Hill Street, where, as Hannah More said, 'She
lives in the highest state of magnificence,' which meant
Chinese taste and a whole room painted by the brothers
Adam. Mrs. Delany too—no ancestress; only one E—she
was in the house, and that always brought Swift into it,
the Duchess of Portland and Lord Chesterfield. However, now his back was aching, for the attic roof forced
him to stoop and the sun was hot on his forehead.

But he was cheerful again now. London, Mrs. Montagu, the brothers Adam—how insignificant and unimportant Larry was beside these! Once again, as so often before, the house itself had taken him and consoled him and whispered that Time was not and Beauty could not die.

He stepped down the little wooden stairs, humming a tune, and knocked on Patrick Munden's door. This was the humblest and cheapest of the flats, and indeed was not a flat at all but just two rooms, and Munden, being a careless young Communist to whom all things were in common, never locked his door. Fred knocked again, then, getting no answer, poked his head in. The room was in fairly decent order although books were piled on a chair and one boot, lonely and gaping for company, stood in the middle of the floor. Fred wandered about, calling 'Patrick! Patrick!' for who knew but Patrick might yet be asleep after a night's Communistic celebrations? No answer, and Fred was about to go when a single sheet of paper stirred, by his movement, from the table, tumbled to the floor. Delaney, thinking it might be one of Patrick's poems, stooped, picked it up, realized that it was Dodie Pullet's handwriting and unavoidably read the first line: 'Patrick, my sweet, I can't manage five o'clock because Smoke . . .'

He read no more and was ashamed that he had read any. He was ashamed for himself, for Dodie Pullet, for Smoke, for Munden. . . . There was, of course, nothing in it at all: girls wrote like that in these days to the merest acquaintance, but it fitted, fitted too damnably with his own uneasiness. Munden was the sort of young intellectual with whom girls like Dodie—nice girls, clever girls, unsatisfied girls—did fancy for a moment that they were in love. Munden, like any other young man, let his brains be what they may, was attracted by physical beauty. Smoke could be no pleasant, easy companion just now.

Figures in the Rain! Figures in the Rain! Delaney, from
the superior vantage of his added years, felt a great kindness, sympathy, tenderness for all of them! The stinging,
unsatisfied, melancholy loneliness of the lust of the flesh!
Did he not, like every other vigorous man, only too
desperately know it!

But behind the sentimental kindliness there were stern
facts. If Smoke, in his present state, knew of this, to what
tragedy might it not urge him! It seemed to Fred, listening there in that empty room and staring at that empty
boot, that the house, his friend and companion, was pressing upon him, urging him to take some step, to move forward and halt some danger. But could he? He was the
friend of all of them and yet he had never before, perhaps, realized with such vivid acuteness the remoteness
of one human being from another.

He felt as though his love for this house in which they
were all living together should give them some sort of
common bond. And yet it did not. If he went to Munden
and said, 'Look here, old man, because we are living
under the same roof don't make Smoke Pullet unhappy!'
he would be committing some interfering impertinence.
To Smoke, of course, he could say nothing. And to Dodie?
A word, perhaps—a very, very careful word. Useless.
And yet the house was on every side of him, urging, pressing upon him, pleading.

He shook off the fantasy, went out, closing the door
softly behind him. He wasn't much use, he concluded;
sentimental, Larry had said, weak as he well knew, happy
with only selfish reasons for happiness. God help us poor
men all!—In spite of the Mozart Concerto we're a feeble
lot!

Outside the Pake door he paused again. Should he go
in and give them the glory of the morning? He often
visited them and he knew that they liked to see him. Something now prevented him. For one thing, he did not want,

now when he was already distressed about the Pullets, to hear Millie say to him that she was afraid—that she was so very much afraid—that they would not be able to afford . . .

He had a sharp sense that, behind that closed door, drama was developing. The drama of old age. Twenty years ago those two old ladies would have seemed infinitely removed from him, he was so young and lusty, they already fifty or more, their lives, their *real* lives, already behind them! But now he was himself through two-thirds of his life, and already for him past, present and future were so confusedly mixed that he was one with these old ladies, at the verge of death, as he was with that infant realizing for the first time that smother of apple-blossom in his uncle's garden in Wiltshire.

With Time or without it the old Pake ladies had brought their own lives, every fragment of their experience, to enrich the house. They had added their gifts to the decoration of that edifice of beauty. He remembered one afternoon when, going in unexpectedly, finding Lady Helen alone except for the little maid, he had found her lost in the past as though she had been under a spell.

She had not been bemused or bewildered. She had said to him at once: 'Sit down there, Fred, and keep me company.' Keep her company he had and passed with her into a world where it was always afternoon—the carriage, the horses straining, had risen to the top of the hill, and there, sunlit in the evening hush, the whole map of the country, coloured orange and dark umber, silver-grey and purple, lay in tranquillity beneath them. There had been no sound until someone had said: 'Time to go back. The Laceys are coming for dinner.' (The Laceys or whoever.) So down the hill they had gone, rolled under the old grey arches, blinked a little in the fire-lit dusk of the stone hall, gone slowly up the wide staircase to see the clothes laid out on the bed, to hear the clock ticking and the fire murmuring and the last twitter of the evening bird beyond the window.

Now there was poverty and pain and a foreign world. But there was no sadness. Beauty once caught could not be lost! Helen was brave and would take what came with no whining grumble. So also he. Experience of life was enough, even at its bitterest, for any bold adventurer.

So down the stairs he went, softly, humming his little tune. And then once again he paused. For now he was outside the Pullet door. Should he knock and enter? It was nearing lunch-time and, more than likely, they would both be out. But Smoke might be there. He might say to him a cheery word or, on the other hand, he might stir that unhappiness to some violent suspicion. Should he venture? Should he leave it alone? Something told him, as though the house were answering his question, to let it go. He felt deeply sympathetic with Smoke. Here the feminine strain that is in all sensitive men made him long to comfort and reassure. But, at the moment, it was wiser to be silent.

He would find Meg waiting for him in the room below, for the children were out and they were to have luncheon alone. Meg! Meg! How she assured and consoled and strengthened! How deeply, how deeply he loved her!

He ran down the last steps of the old staircase and, as he opened the door, called out joyfully:

'Meg! Meg! Are you there?'

CHAPTER III

April in the Painted Room

KITTY DELANEY, on an early day in April, went to luncheon with Sarah Grafton. It was a very intellectual luncheon in Sarah's lovely little house in Chelsea. There were present among others Lady Marble, Mr. Luke Armstrong, the brilliant essayist, Amelia Gracie, the yet more brilliant novelist, a stout, smiling foreign gentleman called, Kitty thought, Gramophone, or something very like it, but everyone addressed him as Voltaire (she didn't, of course, know the point of this), Mr. Pankhurst the famous critic, and Garfield the painter.

Kitty was altogether unsuited to this company and was present only because she liked Sarah Grafton so very much. Last year at a picture show whither an artistic friend had borne her, she had seen a little painting of a lady looking at a mirror. She had cried aloud in the regular Delaney fashion, 'Oh, I do like that!' and a tall, beautifully dressed woman with grey hair standing beside her had said: 'I'm glad. I painted it.' They had talked and in five minutes were friends. Kitty liked Sarah Grafton for every possible good reason. Sarah was an excellent painter, influenced by Sickert, Matisse, but not too much. She was a wealthy American who had lived in London for many years. She entertained the very clever people but was not herself supercilious or intolerant of those who, like Kitty, knew nothing about Art. She was kind and generous and gay, over fifty but interested in everything. When Kitty went to her luncheons she didn't mind that she had no artistic gifts or interests because Sarah did not mind and she liked to listen.

These very clever people always seemed to her peculiar because they were so kind and so cruel all at the same time. They were kind with their hearts and cruel with their brains. For instance just now, while the sole in an extraordinary brown sauce was proving so lovely, they were admiring a novel which, although Kitty hadn't read it, she nevertheless knew all about. It was one of those novels that for all she could see in them seemed to her to have returned to the elemental style of 'The Cat was on the Mat. This is the Pen of my Aunt.' She could herself, she thought, quote sentences from it although she had not read it.

'The wind ruffled the hair of old gentlemen going to their Clubs. As Myra poured the tea out of the silver tea-pot, asking the Colonel from India whether he liked one lump or two, Mrs. Monks grubbing in the dust-bin found a cigarette and a broken comb. The Queen was passing down Bond Street, and in spite of the wind the gentlemen took off their hats.'

'I know as much about it as they do,' Kitty thought, feeling very clever, but Luke Armstrong in his high piping tones was saying: 'You can only take the subconscious so far. What we want in the novel is to return to Giotto.' Wasn't Giotto a painter? But never mind. What Kitty really wondered was why Mr. Armstrong must be so dirty? She had wondered that often about Patrick Munden, but after all, Patrick was a young poet with very little money and Communist beliefs. Not, of course, that all poets and Communists were dirty—far from it—but Patrick had his excuses. She couldn't see what excuses Mr. Armstrong had, coming to luncheon in Sarah's beautiful house, all gold and rose and the staircase lined with such exquisite drawings. She wondered, as she decided that she would never taste sole as lovely as this again, how Mr. Armstrong could succeed in always being *half* shaved, for she had met him in Sarah's house before and that was always his condition. And why he must wear that soft collar of a dirty grey, and did he ever wash his hands? They all smiled and were ready to be generous to everyone until someone mentioned poor Mr. Hacking, who was, it seemed, in the Foreign Office and couldn't keep a wife. He had apparently had two and lost both. They fell upon Mr. Hacking, rent him to pieces and threw bleeding fragments of his body in the air. He was, it appeared, mean, tactless, vain, ignorant and time-serving. Yet he was also, she gathered, a friend of all of them. Then Amelia Gracie mentioned her little boy who had just gone away to school for the first time, and, in spite of herself, tears filled her eyes and she told them of his first letter home and his homesickness and how she couldn't endure to be without him. She spoke as the very simplest of mothers, brilliant and devastating novelist though she was, and they all took her as that, giving her advice and consolation, surrounding her with comfort and kindliness. Voltaire was almost in tears and said: 'Ze poor little fellow. Your English public schools they make me very seeck!' Only Mr. Armstrong became a little restless under this domesticity and murmured, 'All the same, Braque is beginning to be as old-fashioned as a Christmas card,' which, although it had nothing to do with Amelia's child, roused fury in the heart of Voltaire, who had evidently known Braque well in Paris and had even sat as a violin for the central motif in one of his most famous pictures.

At the word Braque Kitty pricked up her ears. That was the name on the painting in Hanover Square, and

at once the world was illuminated for her, a wonderful
harmony seemed to reconcile her with everyone in the
room and, to her own surprise, she heard herself saying:
'Braque's a beautiful painter. I don't think he'll ever be
old-fashioned.'

Voltaire, who was sitting next to her, and had obviously, until then, thought her a pretty but uninteresting
girl, turned now a kindly gaze upon her and said confidentially:

'You must come and see my little collection—yes? I
have a Picasso of the blue period. *Exquis.* Also a Miró
and a Dali.'

This stirred Mr. Garfield, who, in his mildness and
look of rather simple blind inattention, resembled a
penguin, to burst into a frenzy very unlike his innocent
face. He flapped his arms and cried: 'Miró! Dali! . . .
Dali, Miró! What are you talking about? Those impos-
tors! Don't you realize that you must paint what you
see? Didn't Cézanne do it? Everyone from the Spanish
cavemen to Cézanne——'

'Miró paints what he sees,' Luke Armstrong said in
a voice which was like that of a mosquito singing in space.

'Then Miró should be in a madhouse, and Dali—the
whole damned lot.'

'But,' pursued Armstrong in a maddening manner and
examining a finger-nail that was blacker than it ought
to be, 'Dali is expressing *what* he sees and then more than
he sees. What he sees is a trifle compared with what he
doesn't see. . . .'

'Oh, how boring! How boring!' most unexpectedly
cried old Lady Marble. 'You're talking like the people
in clever young men's novels. Why can't you all be real
for once? I have a garden, a lovely garden, and there isn't
a rose in it that wouldn't put you all to shame. Dear Sir
Edward Burne-Jones, he was a delightful man and no one
has been able to draw like him since he died. Then there

was Mr. Browning and Robertson of Brighton. You should have heard him preach. And dear Sir Henry Irving. He enjoyed his supper more than anyone I've ever known. And a beautiful luncheon you've given us, Sarah dear.'

This was the signal for the ladies to go upstairs and to admire, as they always did, the drawings on the staircase.

'Yes, it *is* a beauty, isn't it? Cotman. And that's a Turner. Very fine, isn't it? No, dear. I'm afraid Monday I am *not* free—almost any other night.'

Safe in the beautiful drawing-room, Kitty had a word or two with Sarah.

'I think I'm in love, Sarah, at last!'

'Oh no, dear, are you? I *am* so glad!'

'I'm not sure. I may not be. It may be only that I want to help him so very much.'

'Help him?'

'Yes, he's a young man in a shop, with a dreadful father. He's very clever and he's writing a brilliant play.'

'Oh, darling, do be careful!'

Sarah laid her hand on Kitty's.

'I know that kind so well. Nowadays when classes seem to be vanishing it's so easy to make a mistake. A man isn't better or finer just because he's in another class. So many women think so.'

'Sarah—if I'm in a difficulty—if I want help and advice —may I come to you?'

'Of course, darling, you may.' Sarah's hand tightened on Kitty's. 'I'm such years older than you, but we're alike in that, that we both want to help people. Only helping people isn't easy especially if your own feelings are roused. It's so hard sometimes not to make them dependent on you, and then perhaps you suddenly find you've come to the end of it. It isn't your fault that you have, but it *is* your fault that you've made them taste a kind of life that, without you, they'd be lost in. You've spoilt them for their own and given them no other. I'm preaching but—*moi qui parle,* I've been through all of it. . . . Is he in love with you?'

'Yes, he is—or thinks he is.'

'Is he very young?'

'Yes—very.'

'Well—be careful.'

'Yes. I know. But I rush on. I see something ahead of me so clearly——'

The men came in. Kitty said good-bye. Sarah looked after her anxiously as she went out.

The Braque was not in the window and Kitty felt a pang of disappointment. It had been there for weeks and weeks. Now the colour seemed to have died out of the Square, which to-day was trailing little webs of mist, and overhead there was a sky sulkily on fire. Kitty entered Zanti's to find Mr. Zimmerman *and* Alton Foster. She had been twice to the shop lately and once Mr. Zimmerman had been there. He was a stout little man, with a grey moustache and eyes slightly bloodshot. He was immaculately clean and his high collar creaked as he moved his neck about. Kitty felt extremely foolish because now he was seeing her for the second time and most certainly would expect her to buy something. Alton had given her one glance and then buried himself behind the little desk in the back of the shop. Kitty was very unhappy. She realized the truth of all that Sarah had said to her, and yet the sight of Alton, a slave to the stout, bloodshot Mr. Zimmerman, made her only the more determined. Never mind whether Alton loved her or she Alton—he must be rescued from this. Her heart was beating quickly. She felt with every meeting with Alton a nearer approach of some possibly fatal climax. What she really wanted was to put her arms around him, comfort him and tell him

that a millionaire would produce his play Tuesday fortnight. Meanwhile Mr. Zimmerman was showing her
things. He was opening drawers and bringing out trays.
'I can see that you care for beautiful things. There is
no necessity to buy. Mr. Zanti who founded this business,
he always said: "Show things! Show things! Let the sun
shine on them and the air blow on them! Don't keep them
buried." I have not his eye—his taste, his sensibility. No
one will ever have again. He was a magician. But see,
madame. Here are some beautiful things—is it not so?
This is, of course, Chinese. The head-dress of a bride.
Silver gilt filigree openwork, with applied ornament in the
form of a temple, dragons and ho-hos. Yes, that is a king-
fisher feather. It is decorated, as you see, with pearls.
This is very handsome. A sixteenth-century cameo portrait cut in a dark onyx—look at the enamelled setting,
madame. We know that as the "Peapod" style. The
enamel, as you see, is green with little white "peas" and
has small diamonds set on each pod. And here is a beautiful thing—a brooch—ovate mounted in gold, the central
ornament, you will notice, is carried out in fine gold mixed
with tiny pearls, mounted on a ground of purple foil, the
whole surrounded with a ring of brilliants. Eighteenth-
century. And this—this is the most beautiful thing we
have. Cellini, madame. Oh, undoubtedly. A museum piece.
See how perfectly the gold-work is modelled. A mixture
of *repoussé* and chasing. See how the stone was chosen
for its beauty of colour, never mind the form, and then
cut *en cabochon*—the diamond is backed with black, and
the beauty of the stone depends very largely on the shade
of the black. Ah! he was an artist, Cellini was—and what
happiness and joy a true artist can give to the world so
many hundreds of years after he himself is gone!'
     Kitty saw that Mr. Zimmerman was quite transformed
while he was handling his treasures. A kind of beauty
shone from his little fat stiffly-clothed body. The whole

shop had a kind of glow, the same glow and colour that
the Braque had given to the Square. And this beauty too
involved the bent, humble form of Alton Foster. She
looked for an instant across the shop to him and she
seemed to see a genius there, a greater genius than
Tchekov or Shaw. It had been given to her, it was her
mission to rescue him from the Dragon!

Mr. Zimmerman was saying: 'If you will afford me,
madame, one moment. I hear the telephone ringing from
the other room. It is a message I am expecting. Forgive
me. The young man will attend to you.'

The stout little body scurried across the floor and disappeared. The young man came quickly over to her. He
looked at her beseechingly.

'We have only a moment. Tell me. You are not angry
with me?'

'Angry—of course not.'

The light of his genius still suffusing him, she thought
he was adorable.

'But I haven't see you—I haven't heard from you—
I'm going mad.'

She was happily maternal.

'Now, Alton, you mustn't be like this. We are friends.
Nothing can change it.'

'No. Nothing can change it,' he repeated, staring into
her eyes.

'Then you mustn't worry. You mustn't be upset. I'm
going to do something to get you out of this. Have you
wrtiten any more of the play?'

'Yes. Another five scenes.'

'Good heavens! It must be getting frightfully long.'

'No—one scene is only one line. It is the most important
scene in the play.'

'You must let me see it. How is your father?'

'Just the same.'

'Yes, he always will be. I'm sure of that.'

He began to be greatly agitated.

'The worst of it is, you are making me see everything differently. Neither my father nor sister are the same to me as they were. And they realize it. But I don't care. If you'll only let me see you sometimes, nothing else matters. You are inspiring me. My old life, before I met you, is dead.'

Kitty felt a chill reminder of Sarah Grafton's warning. Nevertheless, now she had begun she must go on.

'Please—tell me—how soon will I see you?' he said.

'I'll write. Very soon. Very soon—I must go. Now, Alton, don't be unhappy. We are friends always—remember.'

She gave him her hand, and then before he realized it she was gone, just as Mr. Zimmerman came hurrying back into the room.

In the Square again she was appalled by her weighty sense of responsibility. It should not be as Sarah had said. Was she in love with this man? She did not know, but she felt an imperative, protective necessity to do anything, everything for him.

And suddenly she knew. She would go now, at once, this very minute and see his father. She would tell Mr. Foster that Alton had genius, was wasted where he was, must be given help, freedom. . . .

Almost before she knew she was doing it she had summoned a taxi.

She looked at once towards the painted walls. It was impossible not to do so, for now they seemed more intimate to her, a little closer, and their tender soft colours more appealing. She felt this time an impulse of almost furious irritation at the vulgar daubs that here and there concealed them. There was one place in especial where a horseman in silver armour riding along a path under dim peach-blossom vanished into a violet crimson sunset with blue waves like rolls of cloth tumbling on to papier-mâché rocks. . . .

Miss Foster had admitted her and was talking. Mr. Foster had been painting when she entered and had laid his canvas down on the floor. He looked as spruce as ever and there was a flower in his buttonhole. She knew that they were surprised and excited to see her. What had she come for? What was her game?

'Tea—tea,' said Mr. Foster. 'Lucy—crumpets. Miss Delaney must test our crumpets!'

'Oh no!' she cried out almost in horror. The thought of another vast tea was simply appalling to her. 'On no account. Last time—you remember?—I said I never had tea.' She laughed, and Lucy Foster choked when Kitty had expected her to giggle. She choked as though she would die. Mr. Foster paid no attention whatever, but regarding Kitty with the utmost blandness said:

'You wouldn't insult our hospitality, Miss Delaney. I am sure you are far too kind and generous for that. Only—you have taken us by surprise. Had we had warning—— But, as it is, the little baker's shop down the road—only a door or two. Lucy won't be a moment. Not a moment.'

Kitty noticed that when he mentioned crumpets there was a certain unctuousness and realized that her visit had given him an opportunity for food that he could not without her have had. He was determined on his tea. Lucy should go for the crumpets. She did, hurrying away with little chatting noises and wearing a hat like a small coal-scuttle.

They were alone and Kitty did not care about it. It was not that she was frightened, for what could an invalid do? Even though he were but partially paralysed she could deal with him, and Lucy, in any case, would be but a few moments. She was wondering whither her Delaney impetuosity was leading her. She had no right to busy herself about Alton. He himself was so *naïf* that in all probability both his father and his sister knew that he was in love with her. They must, of course, suppose that *she* had some interest in *him*. It was, however, the gaze that Mr. Foster now fixed on her that made her uncomfortable. It was kindly, beneficent, and quite frankly aware of her pleasant appearance. She was wearing her luncheon-party frock, her colour was high, her head erect. She knew that he was admiring her. But he was also ironical, even, could it be a little patronizing? Oh! what a foolish thing she had done, in coming thus impetuously! And how truly paralysed was he? Could he, for instance, raise to its full extent one of his strong stout arms? The fact that his face and neck and thick brown hands alone were visible, and that these seemed to pulsate with superb health, made the rest of him dangerous! A double danger in its invisibility. Her chair was decidedly close to his couch. She got up, examined the paintings on the walls, then, turning to him with a charming smile, said:

'I came on an impulse, Mr. Foster. I wanted to speak to you about your son.'

'Yes. Of course.'

His whole body, under the rug, made a movement. She wondered whether she ought to offer to assist him. But of course not. That would be most dangerous. There was an implication of helplessness in his effort which touched her. However slight the paralysis, it must be terrible for so strongly built and otherwise healthy a man to lie there, day after day, at the mercy of that imbecile, his daughter. Why should she fear him? She had never been afraid of anyone her life long. She came and sat down in the chair again.

'I think Alton has great talent. I have read part of the play that he's writing and I think he's being wasted where he is.' Before he could speak she went on. 'I'm afraid I must seem dreadfully interfering to you, Mr. Foster.

I'm afraid, too, that I've made Alton restless by being interested. That means that I feel responsible a little. I want to help.'

His reply was utterly surprising. He leaned his whole body over, moving it, as it seemed to her, in one rigid piece, and his hand, touching the floor, raised the canvas. Moving his hand very stiffly he turned the picture towards her. He said:

'What do you think of this?'

She was honest and fearless, so she said:

'I don't like it.'

'You think I'm a bad painter?'

'I know nothing about painting. I'm quite inartistic. You mustn't pay any attention to my opinion.' He was staring at her and breathing heavily.

'You're the first person—the first from the outside world, Miss Delaney. I can move my hands very little. I cannot sit up properly. It's a miracle I can paint at all. God's miracle. What do you say to that?'

'If it makes you happy——'

'It doesn't make me happy. I know this seems bad to you because you're used to old-fashioned painting. You like that milk-and-sugary stuff on the walls. You do, don't you?'

'Yes, I do.'

'I thought so.' He sank right back flat on his back, his mouth scornfully grinning. 'It doesn't matter what you say—what anyone says. . . .' Then his voice changed. It was soft and friendly. 'So there we are, Miss Delaney. You think I'm no painter and I know I have genius. You think Alton has genius and I know the boy's a damned fool.'

'He isn't a fool,' she broke in hotly.

'Oh yes, he is. Do you think his own father doesn't know? He's a weak, silly, sentimental fool and I don't want a beautiful woman like you to waste your time over him.' His body moved again. 'Listen, Miss Delaney. I'll tell you something. I'm getting better. There's improvement every day. I'm getting stronger. Soon I'll be on my feet. Soon my arms will be strong and then I'll show them the painter I am!' He grinned all over his face like an excited schoolboy.

'Don't you think I speak well for my station in life? Do you know what my father was? A farmhand down in Glebeshire. There were ten of us and we lived in a pigsty. But I was the handsome one *and* the clever one and there was a lady in the village, a charming lady, *she* taught me——'

'How long is it since——?'

'My accident? Twenty cursed years. I'm forty-five. My white hair makes me look older, doesn't it?—and I've got stout lying here. My dear wife, under God's governance, died five years ago.'

Kitty said: 'It must have been terribly hard for you.'

He grinned again like a naughty boy.

'God's been looking after me. God gave me the accident so that I should have a chance to show what a strong man can do. Do you believe that God looks after each one of us?'

'I don't know.' She had no idea as to whether he was sincere about God or was scornfully mocking. She could not tell at all. Also, being of her generation, she was sceptical about God.

'A bit roundabout way of doing it, though, don't you think? I was the strongest lad in Glebeshire. When they heard I was bathing all the girls would come closer to have a peep. Bit vulgar, aren't I? I'm everything, Miss Delaney—vulgar and refined, religious and pagan, clever and stupid, artist and Philistine, weak and strong. . . . But you want to be talking about Alton, not me. Are you in love with Alton?'

She looked him straight in the eyes.

'I don't know. What do you mean by being in love, Mr. Foster?'

'Why, wanting to sleep with someone, of course. There, I'm vulgar. One thing with one person, another with another. And that's why I've changed with you, Miss Delaney. It's a compliment really. I was all manners the other day, wasn't I? But as soon as I saw you were a real person I had to be real too. It's because you're real that it's silly of you to fall in love with Alton. Go to bed with *him* and you'd find he wasn't real at all. Now if *I'd* been fit and strong——'

Kitty got up. He said:

'Now don't you be shocked.'

'I'm not going,' she said, 'because I'm shocked, but because I see we can never agree about Alton. You don't understand him in the least.'

Mr. Foster laughed joyfully and she saw his whole big body quiver under the rug. Then to her own surprise, and even horror, Kitty found that she was laughing too. It was one of the troubles of the Delaneys that they found themselves laughing at the very moment when they least wished to. Meg and Bullock were especially victims of this unfortunate habit.

'Don't understand my own son—that's a good one! I understand both my son and daughter, and how it came to be *my* seed created them I'm at a loss to understand. I am indeed. Lucy's a fool and Alton's a weakling.'

'He's only a weakling because he's given up his life to keep *you* in comfort.'

'Don't I know it? Would anyone but a weakling stay at home looking after a crippled father? Sloppy sentimentality—and the more that he hates the sight of me!'

'And what would you have done if he *had* gone away?' Kitty cried.

'Oh, I'd have cursed him and told the world what an ungrateful child I had. But I'd have managed and admired

him the more. Here now—sit down again. Stay a while
yet. It does me good to look at you.'

Kitty sat down.

'Your daughter's a long time with the crumpets.'

'She'll be back soon.'

'I believe you told her to stay away.'

'I did say to her that when you came again she was to
see and stay away so that we could have a talk together.'

'*When* I came again! How did you know that I would?'

'Oh, I knew you would—to see me just as much as to
see Alton.'

He smiled a really charming smile.

'Draw your chair closer. You needn't be frightened of
me. I haven't the strength of a child. There! You're putting the chair on the painting! Not that it matters! Take
my hand for a moment! Do you feel how strong it is!
Now put your hand on my arm! Weak as a baby's. I'm
in your power entirely, dear Miss Delaney.'

The flesh of his hand was firm and strong, but there
was no resistance in the bones of it. She touched his arm,
then she took her gloves, her furs from the table and
moved to the door.

'Now I'm really going.'

'And when will you come again?'

'I'll come again if you'll promise to do something about
Alton.'

'Do? What do you expect me to do?'

'Let him have his chance with his play.'

'Of course he can have his chance with his play. What's
to stop him?'

'Not while he has to work in that shop.'

'Do you want him to give up a safe job, then?'

'I'll find something.'

'You can do what you like if you'll only come and see
me again. I'll paint something like the pictures on the wall.
Just to please you.'

He looked at her, as she stood by the door, every inch of her, from head to foot. Then, with that same strange resolute urging of his whole body, he turned himself and lay with his face away from her.

She thought for a moment that she would pick up his painting for him. Then, deciding against it, she went without another word.

Meg was out. Bullock was out. Fred Delaney was fast asleep in front of the fire. She bent over and kissed him, once, twice, thrice. At the third kiss he awoke. He grinned.

She stood in front of the fire, for the April afternoon was cold.

'What were you dreaming? You were giving little moans.'

'Yes—of pleasure, darling. For I was flying through the air, an angel in each arm. At least I think they were angels. And I kissed first one, then the other, slowly, melodiously. They were wearing only the thinnest of draperies. What have you been doing? . . . Oh, Lord, see how late it is! I must go and dress.'

She took a round fat-cushioned stool and sat at her father's feet. She leant her head against his thigh. He rested his hand against her cheek. They were blissfully happy. He bent forward and kissed her cheek.

'Darling . . . I've told you I must go.'

'No. Wait a minute. It isn't six yet. Yes. I think I'll tell you.'

'Tell me what?'

'I've been engaged in an adventure for several weeks —even months.'

'I know you have.'

'It's very simple. I went into an art-shop in Hanover Square. There was a young man behind the counter. I liked him somehow. I paid a call on his family. He has a sister, a father, no mother. The father is very peculiar.'

'How, peculiar?'

'He's a big stout man of forty-five, with white hair and a buttonhole. He is paralysed—or partly—and paints dreadfully bad pictures. The young man has talent and is writing a very clever play.'

Fred spoke lightly, but he strengthened his hold round his daughter's neck.

'It all sounds most unreal.'

'It is—and it isn't.'

'Are you in love with the young man?'

'No—I don't know. But it's an adventure. I want to help him—in fact I *must* help him. His father says he's no good.'

'Then he probably isn't.'

Kitty went on, looking into the fire.

'You know I've never known anything about pictures. Well, this adventure is surrounded by beautiful things. First there was a picture in a shop in Hanover Square, then in the shop where Alton works his master showed me the loveliest jewels, then in the room where they live, these people, the walls are painted all over—by two young men who had the place once. That's why this adventure is new to me. I seem to be moving into a new world.'

Delaney watched her with loving tenderness, and anyone seeing him now for the first time would have thought him a good wise man.

'Darling, I've been moving into new worlds once a week all my life. At least I always *think* they're new. But no—same old game, same old faces, same old result.'

Kitty caught his hand and kissed it.

'I think this *is* perhaps new for me. I don't think I'm in love exactly, but I want to help as I've never wanted to help anyone before. But it seems so difficult to help without doing harm.'

'You're right. It is.'

She twisted round and looked in his face.

'My generation—because we have no rules, because we can go anywhere and do anything—it's hard for us to know where we're going. Now you and Mother and Alton's father and Sarah Grafton and Millie Pake— you all seem quite definite. You may do the wrong thing, but you see where you are. We have nothing to guide us. . . . I don't know. I wouldn't *be* your generation for anything, but sometimes—your advice isn't so bad.'

Fred Delaney shook his head.

'I'm no good at advising. I'm always getting into a mess. But I love my wife, my children, this house, London, beautiful women. I try not to hurt other people——' Then he caught her close to him.

'But don't *you* get into a mess, darling. I'm so fond of you. So's Meg. We're all of us so happy together. Don't lose your heart to someone who isn't worth it. Be proud. Not *conceited* but proud. I've had no education. I'm as ignorant as I can be, but I believe in other people being swells—fine characters, I mean. They tell you in these days that nothing matters, it's a sort of wolfish world. But it isn't. Cervantes and Raleigh and Sidney and Sam Johnson didn't think so. I can see what fine conduct is, even if I miss it myself——'

She kissed him on the eyes gently. Then she got up.

'I don't think you need worry. Only it's *interesting.* People are *interesting.* I've shut myself up, watching, never sharing in anyone's life, except ours at home. Does it matter, do you think, if one *is* damaged a bit? I'm not a lily in a vase, you know.'

He looked at her for a long time. She returned his gaze.

'You mustn't ask me that. I love you too much. I don't think you *can* be damaged. I've often wondered when the time would come for something to happen to you. Of course, you've got to take risks. Only—looking back— I'd give a lot now not to have done some of the shabby

things I have done. You'll never be shabby, Kate Delaney
—never.'

They went together to the door, his arm around her
neck.

'I've got to have the bath first,' he said. 'I'm in a
greater hurry than you are.'

'Where are you going, sweetheart?'

He hummed a little tune. Then burst out laughing.
'Wouldn't you like to know?'

Then, as he turned into his tiny dressing-room, taking
off his coat as he went, he threw back over his shoulder:
'Yes—shabby. That's what I am!'

CHAPTER IV

Closing In

AND what had been happening to Claude Willoughby
during these last weeks?

To the episodes of the bath salts and the library book
one more had been added—Colonel Badget's gold-topped
walking-stick. *This* no one had accused Claude of stealing.
Brocket, standing in the doorway, had simply said:

'Colonel Badget has lost his walking-stick. Funny what
goes on in this house.'

He had cast a sombre eye on Claude, who had snapped:

'Yes, it is. Why don't you look after things better,
Brocket?'

This spirit on his part surprised Brocket, who answered:

'There's more in this than meets the eye, Mr. Willoughby.'

'Badget probably left it somewhere.'

'He says not.'

Then Claude took a resolution. He went downstairs
and called on Badget. He did this to clear the air. Everything now was so mysterious in this house. It seemed to
Claude, who was sleeping very badly and not eating
enough, that there was always someone hiding round
the corner. He would wake up in the middle of the night
and feel certain that there was someone in the room.

He did not switch on the light, because he would lie there
in order to hear that someone moving. And it seemed to
him that he did—someone moving very carefully so as
not to knock into the chair or the table.

Claude lay there in the dark, the sweat gathering on
his forehead and his heart thumping. At last he turned
on the light and there was nobody there. There was never
anybody there.

He fancied that everyone in the house now regarded
him as a thief. He almost overheard, it seemed to him,
the conversations of Badget, Best and Pierson. He fancied that, on his daily morning encounters with Pierson,
there was a hinting, a suggestion, a curious suspicious
glance from those bottled eyes under the toupee. It did
not seem to him impossible that one fine morning he would
wake to find a police-officer standing inside his room. For
a gentleman of high family and absolute rectitude these
imaginings were torture.

So one morning he went, on a sudden impulse, down to
visit Badget. Badget was the king of this castle. He was
the man with the money, the only tenant to whom Brocket
paid deference. Claude had the fear of him that anyone
who is penniless and helpless has of anyone who needs
not to consider money. It is a peculiar fear that shames
the possessor of it.

Claude knocked on Badget's door and heard the shrill,
rather whistling voice from within cry:

'Come in! Come in!'

He went in and found Badget, his long thin legs
stretched out in front of him, comfortable in his armchair, reading the newspaper.

Colonel Badget was long and thin, with the high bony
face of a complacent giraffe. He was not at all a bad
man. He was even a good one, for he supported a ne'er-
do-well brother-in-law, the unhappy wife of the same,
their children, his own fearfully ancient mother, in the

most noble fashion with never a murmur. He did no one in the world any harm. He was, in his own way, religious and extremely proud of his country. So he may be called a good man. He was, however, encased and enveloped by an overwhelming unquestioning self-satisfaction. He not only thought himself a good man, but a man quite perfect in every way. It would not be true to say that he despised other people. He did not. Scorn implies some sort of comparison. He was religious because it was agreeable for God to have such a man as himself to believe in Him. Here his really kindly nature was involved. He was patriotic, because, having been born English, it was natural for him to believe in the country that had given him birth. He had never married because, unlike Sir Willoughby Patterne, he needed no admirers. He was himself sufficient for that pleasure. And in any case sexual emotion was outside his dignity because it implied a certain levelling.

It would be wrong to call him arrogant. With his staring, slightly surprised eyes, protruding chin, long neck that contained a fine Adam's-apple, shrill tones of voice, immaculate but inhuman clothing, he was incapable of patronage because that involved a considered relationship.

You might have thought that he would be lonely, but he was not so, because, having for consideration and constant observance an absolutely perfect person, the minutest happenings to that person were of importance and interest. Physical ailments were for him a constant preoccupation. It was, for example, a piece of high and curious impertinence for the common or garden cold to make itself felt in so immaculate a nose or throat. He felt a humorous, almost friendly indulgence towards such a cold, rather as Napoleon would have considered an urchin who took his handkerchief. Further intrusion than this upon his person, however, was, on the part of an ailment, indecency. He had of late been conscious of certain rheumatic pains in the right groin. At first he addressed the rheumatism with such disdain as to be practically inaudible. The rheumatism remained. His disdain changed to anger. Still the rheumatism lingered. He paid a visit to his doctor, Sir Hector Firebrace, who was almost as arrogant as himself. Together they addressed the rheumatism in such terms that it should have shrunk trembling away. Instead of that it awoke him in the middle of the night and bit his left elbow.

He was quite aghast with astonishment—the same surprise with which he contemplated, from a vast distance, the London County Council, shop assistants, crooners on the radio, Communists, and indeed all foreigners, including the Scotch, the Irish and the Welsh.

It must be emphasized again, however, that he was not an unfriendly man any more than Alexander the Great was unfriendly. He greeted Claude Willoughby now with a kindly welcome. He did not get up from his chair, but he did lay his newspaper on his bony knees. He had seen Claude before on several occasions but had never enjoyed a real conversation with him. Not that he ever enjoyed a real conversation with anybody, because he considered his words precious and was sparing in his use of them.

To Claude the room seemed very rich indeed but rather over-burdened with large heavily carved pieces of furniture. There was a vast sideboard, a massive table, a towering chimney-piece, and great beetling bookcases filled with heavy gilt volumes that all looked like Burke's *Peerage*.

Badget, when he was reading, wore spectacles (he considered his eyesight distinctly impertinent in its more recent behaviour). These spectacles now slid to the end of his long nose, waiting deferentially until they should be in demand again.

'Ah, Willoughby, come in. How are you?' And then, as he extended his long, cold, bony hand, 'What can I do for you?'

Claude hesitated. He felt oddly like the small boy he had once been at Harrow when, summoned by his house-master, his small hands pressed with nervous anticipation his thighs. He had acted on impulse in coming. He had not realized that the room (which was papered with a stiff, dark, bronze-coloured wallpaper), the furniture and, of course, Badget himself, would appear so altogether overwhelming. However, he had come about the walking-stick, so he would begin about that.

'I was very sorry to hear from Brocket yesterday about your walking-stick.'

'My walking-stick?'

'Yes—that it had been stolen.'

'Ah, certainly—I had forgotten.'

(This had the double effect of making it appear that Badget had dozens of gold-headed walking-sticks, and that Claude was a fool to have come on such a business.)

Claude thought—have I the courage to sit down? Certainly he should ask me to do so, but of that there seems no sign. Have I the courage? Yes, I have. He sat down on one of those dining-room chairs that are so ugly and uncomfortable that only excellent food and drink can help one to forget them.

'Well,' he said with nervous cheerfulness, 'I'm delighted—I mean it's agreeable that it's a loss of no importance. I understood from Brocket that it was rather an important stick——'

'Not at all. Not at all.'

'Of course, we can't tell for certain that it was stolen, can we?'

'Stolen? Stolen?'

'Yes—I understood from Brocket that you thought it had been stolen.'

'Who said that?'

'Brocket.'

'He did, did he?'

'Yes, he did.'

'Damned impertinence.' Badget sat up in his chair, felt his shoulder tweak, and gave a little cry, rather like that of a chicken just emerged from the egg.

'Brocket said that?' He pushed his spectacles back on to his eyes and stared as though he were seeing Claude for the first time and were wondering why, in heaven's name, he was sitting on that chair without having been first asked to do so. However, Claude stood, or rather sat, his ground.

'Yes, he did. Distinctly. "Colonel Badget thinks his walking-stick's been stolen." That's what he said.'

'Damned cheek! Mentioning it.'

'That's why I came in to see you,' Claude said. 'It isn't the only thing that's been lost in this house. There's been quite an epidemic.'

'Epidemic!' Badget cried, startled.

'What I mean is a number of things have been missed —Pierson's bath salts, some library books, and now your walking-stick.'

Badget began to feel a sort of disgusted annoyance creeping up his spine. What was this miserable-looking, shrivelled-up nonentity doing in his room at all, and further than that, how did the miserable little nonentity have the cheek to sit on *his* chairs and talk about *his* walking-stick?

Further than that again, how dared the miserable little nonentity have the insufferable impertinence to compare Pierson's bath salts with *his* walking-stick?

All this made his neck rise and his Adam's-apple agitate. On the other hand he was a kind man and realized that Claude was a poor little pitiful, a sort of beggar at the gates—so he bent his long neck over the side of the chair, blinked behind his glasses and said benignantly, 'It's nothing—kind of you, Willoughby, to enquire.'

He might have been referring to his rheumatism, of which, at the moment, he was actually thinking, but Claude burst out:

'The point is, Badget, we must discover the thief. The point is that until the thief is discovered, everyone in this house is under suspicion. Now where did you see your walking-stick last?'

This direct attack was very disconcerting to Badget, who was not accustomed to this kind of Scotland Yard question, so, quite feebly and mildly, he answered:

'I don't know. I may have given it away.'

'Given it away!' Claude was staggered by Badget's reply.

'Little things, you know.' Badget waved his hand. 'Little personal things. One gives them without thinking. I knew a man once who made a list, and after his death, his small odds and ends, trifles, his friends had them, cherished them——'

'But,' said Claude, 'if you gave a walking-stick away wouldn't you remember it?'

'Might not,' said Badget.

Claude fancied then that Badget was looking at him with a stare of cold suspicion. He couldn't tell, of course, that Badget was at the moment not thinking of him at all but was holding a little earnest, one-sided conversation with his rheumatism, as thus:

'How dare you bite my shoulder? . . . If you don't go soon I shall have to take serious steps. . . . Do you *realize* what you're doing and where you are?'

But Claude, seeing that haughty, cold stare behind the spectacles, and the thin, arrogant lips and the pointed, hat-hanging chin, thought to himself: 'He is sure that *I* took his walking-stick just as Pierson is sure that I took his bath salts. This is awful. They are closing in on me——' His agitation drove him to his feet. He began, stammering:

'It's all very well. You may take it calmly yourself, Badget. But it's very unpleasant for me. Very unpleasant indeed—unpleasant for all of us. It must be cleared up.'

'*What* must be cleared up?' Badget, leaving reluctantly his rheumatism, enquired.

But before the question could be answered there was a knock on his door, the door was opened, and rosy-faced little Mr. Best stood there.

Mr. Best was short, square-shouldered, stumpy-legged, rubicund, with bright-blue excited eyes, and he wore gay colours; a Club tie and sometimes a canary-coloured waistcoat. He was cheerful, insensitive, ceaselessly talkative, one of the supreme bores of London Clubland. He belonged to four Clubs and was in one or other of them all day and half the night. Members melted before his approach like the snow before the sun. He always gave them warning, because he began to speak, at a distant sight of a member, in a loud, echoing voice. He was happy, insensitive, good-natured, always in excellent health. He liked to tell a bawdy story and so Pierson simply detested him. He came often to visit Badget because Badget never ran away. This, Best thought, was because Badget was interested. It was, in reality, because Badget was thinking of himself and heard scarcely a word that Best said.

He began the moment he was in the room.

'Hullo, Badget, old boy! How's yourself? Top of the morning to you. Slept like a top, I did, and wasn't in till three. Jolly evening at the Club with Bicester and one or two more. You know Bicester? Chap shot all that game in Africa. Masses of buffalo, herds of rhinoceros——' Then he saw Claude and was buoyantly surprised to find him in Badget's room. 'Hullo, Willoughby! How's yourself? Hope I'm not interrupting. Tell me if I'm in the way.'

Badget nodded his head, which Best could take for acceptance or dismissal just as he pleased. Best took it happily for an invitation, strode to the window, whistling, looked out with his hands in his pockets, then turned and regarded Claude Willoughby. Poor old devil! What a thin scrap of a miserable old boy it was, with his anxious expression, his wisps of grey hair, his worn and faded suit!

Claude felt that he must explain his presence.

'Good morning, Best,' he said with dignity. 'The fact is I came in to see Badget because of the things that have been stolen here lately.'

'Stolen!' Best cried. 'Stolen! By God, you don't mean it? What's been stolen?'

'Well,' said Claude, hesitating before Best's energy as he always did, 'we don't actually know that they've been stolen. That's perhaps going too far. Anyway, they're missing. Some bath salts of Pierson's, your library books, and now Badget's walking-stick.'

'I say, Badget, your walking-stick been stolen? I'm most awfully sorry. Rotten luck. Rotten luck. Hope it wasn't valuable. I had a walking-stick once, ivory, you know, and all that, thought no end of it, given me by an old uncle of mine, had it in the family for hundreds of years. I valued that stick, I can tell you, and one day——'

'I don't know,' said Badget, with a wrinkling of his nose, a favourite gesture of his, expressing a kind of bored remoteness, 'that it has been stolen. May have given it to somebody.'

'Oh, that's all right then. I thought Willoughby said——'

Claude felt that both men were regarding him with dislike. He began to stammer.

'I only said . . . I thought that as Pierson's bath
salts——'

'But, by God,' Best broke in, 'it may be right—there
may be a thief in the house. I shouldn't wonder. Now I
come to think of it, there's a tin of Bath Olivers I was
looking for the other night, couldn't find it anywhere.
I rang for Brocket and said, "Brocket, there was a tin
of Bath Olivers," and Brocket looked a bit green about
the gills. I remember thinking so at the time, now you
remind me, and Brocket——'

'Brocket,' Badget interrupted judiciously, 'is quite
above suspicion. It's to his own interests to see that nothing in the place goes wrong. I can't say that Brocket is
ideal in every respect, but he's honest. I have always
found him so.'

'Oh, quite, quite,' said Best. 'But if it wasn't Brocket,
who——?' He broke off and stared with his bright blue
eyes at Willoughby. 'Whom do *you* suspect, Willoughby?'

'Oh, I shouldn't like to say that I suspect anybody,'
Claude said hurriedly. 'I only thought that it's unpleasant,
these things happening, and that perhaps we ought to
do something about it. But if Badget thinks that he gave
away his walking-stick——'

Badget slowly rose, his long legs following his long
body in a kind of dignified procession.

'Ever had rheumatism, Best?' he asked.

'No. Can't say that I have. Wonderfully fit for my
age. Fifty-eight last birthday, and see me stripped you
wouldn't think a thing wrong with me. As a matter of
fact there isn't. Not a thing. I put it down to my morning
exercises and two rounds of golf every Saturday. Morning exercises in front of an open window, stripped to
the buff. You try it, Badget.'

A faint look of disgust spread over Badget's features.

'Well,' said Claude, 'I'm glad everything's all right.
I really am. Yes—well—thank you very much. I must be

going.' And out of the door he slipped without a word
from anybody.

Safe in his room again he thought: *What* a fool you've
been! What did you think you were gaining by going down
to Badget like that? Didn't you know Badget well enough
anyway to realize that you'd get nothing at all by making
any sort of appeal to him? . . . and then that fool Best.
. . . Claude stood there and his thin cheeks slowly flushed.
How they'd *looked!* And Best, when he had talked about
his ridiculous Bath Oliver biscuits, hadn't he suddenly
turned to Claude and fixed his unpleasant blue eyes on
to him? Oh, they suspected something! No doubt of it.
And soon Pierson with his ridiculous toupee and bombast
would join them and they would put their three silly
heads together. Afterwards Brocket would be called in
and of course *he'd* have nothing good to say about Claude.
They would perhaps search his room while he was out.
They had perhaps already done so. And they would be
spying on his every movement. Oh, he must go, he must
go! He must pack up and leave at once! But whither?
And he could not go until he had paid this present quarter's rent which Brocket had most surprisingly allowed
him to suspend. He had even, it seemed, been glad to do
so. Was it, Claude thought, because now he, Brocket,
would have a hold over him? He hadn't thought of that.
He was held, a prisoner, unless he could pay that rent,
a prisoner in this house where everyone thought him a
thief.

Distracted, he began to walk up and down his small
room with nervous, agitated steps. What was he to do?
Oh, *what* was he to do? He thought of Millie and Helen
and those kind jolly people the Delaneys, but his natural
pride and dignity prevented him from applying to anyone
for money. It *hadn't* prevented him from saying to
Brocket, when that stout unpleasantness had remarked,
'Well, Mr. Willoughby, I don't mind for this once. Leave

it over to next month, if it's easier for you.' 'Thanks very much indeed'—a horrible memory, and the more horrible now when he realized the true reason of Brocket's complacency. But he couldn't speak to the Delaneys about it, not that lovely young girl with whom he had shaken hands, nor that kind young boy who had taken him to the party.

He went yet once again and looked at his beloved things in their cupboard. No, he would *not* sell them—not the gold snuff-boxes nor the silver christening mug, nor the miniature of his mother, nor the gold brooch with pearls, nor the Marie Antoinette cup and saucer.

There were other less important things there too, but they—although precious to himself—were quite valueless to anyone else. Then, like a flash, thinking of these things and having also Best and Badget in his mind, there illuminated his brain and being something that Badget had said to him about a friend of his who had left all his odds and ends to be selected by his friends after his death. Now, thinking about it, Claude did not find it foolish at all. He would leave these precious possessions one by one to his individual friends. He hadn't very many —Millie and Helen Pake, the nice Delaney boy—oh yes, and old Hare down in Winchester whom he hadn't seen for years but cherished the memory of, and Cluttock who went flower-hunting in the Andes, and—

He began to grow greatly excited, waving his hands about, talking to himself. Oh really, what a *beautiful* idea! He had something to live for, or rather to die for. And these things that he loved so. They would not, after he was gone, be neglected or despised—years later someone would be saying: 'Yes, that's the very cup and saucer Marie Antoinette drank her coffee out of. An old friend of my father's, Claude Willoughby——'

He heard a sound, looked up, and saw Brocket standing there.

He placed on the table one of those unappetizing envelopes that consist of a window of celluloid apparently surrounded by a wall of dirty whitewash. Why does the clothing of a bill always have the appearance of a pawn-shop furtiveness?

'Post,' Brocket said laconically, then, turning to the door:

'Have a nice talk with Colonel Badget?'

'That'll do, Brocket, thank you.'

'All right then. I'm not interfering.' Then his body stiffened. 'Only you look here, Mr. Willoughby. It's *my* house and I'm not going to have one of my tenants sneaking round complaining to the other tenants and hinting that if someone's been taking things in this house it's someone's proper place to find out 'oo's done it.'

The dirty apron above the unwieldy stomach quivered with agitation. 'It may be my place or it may not—but when a gentleman's behind with the rent it's not for *him* to complain——"

He had advanced again into the middle of the room and now was staring at the little collection of things in the cupboard. The glass door was open.

'Pretty lot of things you've got there, Mr. Willoughby, I must say.' He began to scratch one of his arms. 'Old, some of them, I shouldn't wonder.' He moved forward.

Claude stepped in between Brocket and the cupboard.

'You'd better leave those things alone, Brocket,' he said. 'If you touch one of them with your dirty hands I'll—I'll murder you.'

The two bodies were almost touching, the one so fragile that a twist from Brocket's grey arm would surely snap it, the other stout, heavy with the imponderability of a feather bolster. Claude caught very strongly the aroma of Brocket's breath—beer, bad tobacco, ill-conditioned stomach.

The room tilted and rocked. For an absurdly conscious

moment he thought that he would faint and nothing could be more humiliating than to subside into the arms of Brocket! The blood of the Willoughbys came to his rescue. He closed, with trembling hand, the cupboard. He moved away and took a deep breath of fresher air.

'While I'm tenant here,' he said, 'this is my room and I'll trouble you not to come in here another time without knocking. You shall have the rent in a day or two, and after that'—he drew a deep breath—'you can find another lodger.'

Brocket had been really, for a moment, frightened. He was not, as life went, a very courageous man, and there had been something about old Willoughby's face, something. 'Why, you'd have thought,' he said afterwards downstairs, 'he'd have stuck a knife into me if he'd had one, the old bastard.'

But now he had recovered and, arms akimbo, he said:

'Easy enough to find another tenant, Mr. Willoughby. But I don't know as I want to. And somehow—I'm thinking—I don't know as how I'd be leaving too quick —not until this funny stealing business has been cleared up.'

He was gone, but the room seemed still to contain his presence. How hard is it in this world of so many dimensions to be rid of a haunting presence—for we live in imagination quite as truly as in physical fact. The murdered are not quiet in their graves, for as you close down the soil on one, like a worm, the twister is coiling above-sod there by the graveyard wall! Claude had never murdered anyone, but the very thoughts that he had had about Brocket gave that fellow a worm-like quality.

And there was a stench in the room. Claude went out.

Quite late in that same day he was in Charles Street. He had heard the echo of Big Ben strike across the Park ten o'clock. He had come out because of a crazy mad notion that he would pay a call on the Delaneys. Now, at this hour! But just as he was beginning to fear the Shepherd Market house, beginning to feel that it was closing in on him and threatening him with some horrible disaster, a disaster now linked in his mind with the cold atheistic prophecies of that man at the party, so the house in Charles Street was standing to him as a symbol more and more of warmth, friendship and understanding. And old man's fears are grim, because he is half a ghost already. He sniffs the windy spaces of the immortal world into which he is stepping.

Now he looked at the Charles Street door and did not dare to push the bell. He walked about. There was a thin early April air blowing and not a soul in the street. All the doors were dead, the steps cold. The street was as chill as though with the blasé indifference of brick-and-mortar history it was callous about all the blood and bones that had passed its way. Little cries of laughter, a jest or two, a love spasm, a prayer for help, the clink of a coin . . .

Claude passed, hesitated, passed again, a thin old man in a cold bare street.

CHAPTER V

Tower Idyll

'LET's all go to the Tower!' Meg cried. So very deceitful did she feel that she wondered that they could not all see her blackened and corrupted heart. She said 'The Tower!' because only the day before, looking at a Picasso drawing in Tooth's window in Bond Street, Graham Pender had said to her: 'You'll laugh at me, but Wednesday afternoon I'm going to visit the Tower all by myself. Haven't been there since I was a kid. I've been meaning to go for years.' Then, looking at the Picasso, which was of an enormous bearded Hercules carrying a struggling pink-bosomed lady in his arms; 'Funny that should give one pleasure. It's very ugly really.'

Temptation is for ever coming our way. It isn't as though we asked for it. Meg had had not the slightest intention of finding her path to the Tower on that Wednesday afternoon. The Tower! What a place! Most certainly not. And then on the Tuesday evening Fred Delaney had cried out to them all: 'We're free to-morrow afternoon. I know we are. Anyway we've got to be. It's time for a Family Expedition. Where to is the question.'

All self-respecting families in these days do all they can to stay apart. And perfectly right. Because you have sprung from the same loins and sinews is no reason for liking. Two dusty old people who have paid your school

206

bills and hindered your enjoyments have obviously no
real claim on you. The Delaneys, however, loved one
another and, better than anything else, enjoyed being
alone together. This was difficult to achieve in these
modern restless days. Someone was for ever breaking in!

So, at certain times, they almost guiltily arranged
together that they would creep off somewhere and have
an afternoon to themselves. When they were in the country it was easy enough, but in Town not so. They had
generally found that museums and collections of things
saved them from their friends. They knew the London
Museum, the Victoria and Albert, the Wallace, the gallery at Dulwich, the Science Museum very intimately.
They had even been up to the top of the Monument
together and stayed there for quite an hour or so. They
always pretended on these excursions that they were
visiting London for the first time, and were very friendly
and inquisitive with the guides and attendants, whom
Fred always surprised at the end with the largeness of
his tip. They always dressed on such occasions very
quietly and told one another how greatly astonished the
Vicar would be at all they had to tell him. They always
bought a lot of postcards.

On this Tuesday evening they had been discussing this,
that and the other. Kitty was reading a new novel called
Matador and was wondering aloud whether horses had
the same sense of fun when they were torn apart by the
bull as foxes were confidently supposed to have when torn
apart by the hounds. Fred had been looking at a picture
of Miss Paget's Golden Miller winning the National,
and Bullock had been reading about Mussolini's scorn
of the League of Nations.

When Fred suggested a family expedition they all at
once agreed. Behind their current topics had been lurking
their especial personal problems, and, as always when
the hard world was driving from without upon them too

severely, their impulse was to move inwards towards one
another. One afternoon alone and they would go forward
with renewed confidence.

That was why Meg Delaney had an awful sense of
treachery when she cried out, 'The Tower!' She knew,
better than any of them, what these family expeditions
really meant, and for the first time in her married life
she was planning to betray them. And yet—what nonsense! In all probability Graham would not be there; in
further probability they would not see him if he *were*
there! The Tower was a very large place and there were
many, many suits of armour. And if she did see Graham,
what of it? She felt no real treachery to Fred in her heart.
She loved Fred more than twenty Grahams. It was only
—it was only—Graham was different from anyone else
with his shyness, his romantic sensibility, his modesty, his
vast knowledge. He had once been in love with her. He
was in love with her still. Was there any harm in that?
The point about being in love was that you should not
hurt anyone else. It would not hurt Fred if Meg were
to tell him this very night: 'Graham Pender, who has
white hair and has been married for years, to whom I was
once engaged, is in love with me. You don't mind my
seeing him sometimes, do you?' Fred, laughing, would
certainly reply: 'See him! See him! As often as ever you
like!'

It was all this everlasting search for something. Everyone for ever searching! Here was Meg, middle-aged,
deeply in love with her husband, perhaps the happiest
woman in England. . . . Yes, and what then? Only the
glamour, the colour, the light that never was on sea or
land. Fred did not possess it for her—how could he when
he was now part of herself? Moments in life provided
it—the distant swirl of music, first crocuses on a garden
lawn, the sea on a fine afternoon just before dusk. Oh,
a thousand things in life and nature, but there shifting,

intangible. It stayed with you only in a piece of work or a human being. And there too it stayed only so long as you did not realize it. The piece of work ends and the light dies, the beloved is secured and the spell is over! She knew that well enough. Married to Graham it would never do. Fred, dear, dear Fred was the permanent joy of her life. But Graham—just now, for this moving vanishing summer—had the glamour!

And yet there *was* something wrong, something traitorous at the heart of it. No one cared any longer for stuffy laws or conventions. Yet doing away with them had not really made any human relations easier! How odd that was! There was, as Fred always said, a world *below* the world, a world whose laws did *not* change; human beings, by their habits, fashions, half-discoveries, conceits, patronages, fears, try as they might, could not affect it.

Meg looked at them—Fred, Kitty, Bullock—sitting around, close together, and loved them with an almost tigerish love. Nothing must imperil them, nothing must hurt them—they must be happy for ever and ever! She got up and went round kissing each one of them solemnly on the forehead.

'What's up?' Bullock asked. 'Feeling sentimental?'

'I suppose I am. I'm a woman of sentiment.' She looked Fred straight in the eyes. 'No. Don't let's go to the Tower. It's a stupid place. I don't know *what* made me suggest it.'

'On the contrary,' Fred said. 'An excellent suggestion. I haven't been there since I was six, when I hid behind a Beefeater and made my governess cry with anxiety. The very place. We shan't see a soul we know there.'

'Oh, but we may!' Meg said wildly. 'You never know. Everyone may suddenly decide to go to the Tower.'

'What nonsense!' Fred cried. 'Look here, Meg—I'll make you a bet. I'll give you five pounds for a new hat if we see a single soul there we know.'

'*You* know or *I* know?' asked Meg, who adored a bet.

'Whom we *both* know. And who do you know anyway I don't know?'

'Lots of people.'

'Well, you oughtn't to.' He stretched his legs and yawned. 'Boys and girls, I am going to bed. To-morrow you're all for the Tower.'

The three of them sat cosily in front of the fire after Fred was gone. Kitty was reading her novel, Meg staring in front of her smiling at the fire. She was thinking to herself: 'I shall soon be old and I don't mind that in the least, but let's have all the harmless fun we can.' And then a thought struck her like a coal leaping out of the fire and burning her cheek. 'What about Lady Pender? Does she like you, do you think? . . . No, she doesn't. There's no doubt. She doesn't like me at all.'

Bullock, his tongue protruding between his teeth, was writing in a little notebook. He wrote, then looked up and beamed at the fire.

'Is it good, darling?' she asked. 'As good as Mr. Wodehouse?'

But he wouldn't tell her. He grinned at her with love and confidence, but he kept his secret. For he was, for the first time in his life, planning a novel. This Lizzie Coventry had done to him. She had said: 'Why don't you write a novel? I'm sure you could?'

'Why do you think I could?' he had asked her.

She had given him a comprehensive answer.

'Because you are interested in people. Because you see things in a funny way. Because you can tell stories.' She had explained her views on the English novel. 'English writers don't know how to be serious and funny at the same time. That's why I like French writers better.'

There was perhaps no one in the whole world *less* French than Bullock, but he read Lizzie a description of two ladies lunching at the Ritz and she had laughed.

She laughed very seldom, but when she did she was suddenly so care-free and happy that his heart ached. He had presented to him then, out of the air, the subject for a novel, a serious, almost tragic subject. He was quite overwhelmed as he contemplated it, but all the tenderness and brotherly care he felt for Lizzie Coventry was at the heart of it.

'Only you will have to take much trouble not to be sentimental,' Lizzie had said. 'The English are so very sentimental.'

'I suppose they are,' Bullock said. 'But our novels now are very brutal. Everyone in them is very savage to everyone else.'

'That's another kind of sentimentality,' Lizzie had said.

He loved her, but he ought not to tell her that for another two years at least, so he thought that he would sublimate this emotion by putting it into a novel and he would disguise his emotion with his sense of humour. Characters were already crowding in upon him. He felt all the exuberant happiness and confidence of the creator before he has begun his creation.

Meg, staring into the dying fire, said: 'If I were granted a wish now I know what I'd have—a long and painless old age. I'd like to live on and on, seeing what is going to happen——'

'You'd be lonely without us,' Kitty said.

'Oh, you'd all have to live on too.'

'And all have painless old ages?'

'Of course.'

'Then that would be at least six wishes. And suppose we had no money, as would be more than likely?'

'We'd *have* to have money.'

'And suppose there was a World War, an awful one as it would be?'

'That would be all right if we knew *we* were going
to have painless old ages!'

'Mother—how selfish!' Bullock said, closing his little
book.

Meg sighed. 'Yes, I suppose it is.' She jumped up. 'I'll
have six wishes! One—no more war. Two—the Delaney
family *all* to have long painless old ages. Three—the
Delaney family all to be rich. Four—everyone in the
world to have enough to live on. Five—a cottage in the
country. Six—universal tolerance and understanding.
There! I think I've accounted for everything!'

Kitty laughed. 'How dull it would be!'

'What do *you* want, then?' Meg asked.

'I want—I want—I don't know. Love. Discomfort.
Unexpected rewards. Understanding. More understanding.' She stood up and put her arm round her mother's
broad waist. 'I want to grow, and I expect one does that
best in difficulty. Am I priggish?'

Meg kissed her.

'No, dear. I don't think so. It's so hard to say what
one is. At this moment I'm happy and wicked and greedy.
I'm off to bed with your father.'

They went down to the Tower in the family car, which
they placed under the watery eye of a little purple-faced
man with a game leg and a stiff arm, in company with
other family cars.

All the cars rested there together under the brow of
the Tower and seemed not very comfortable about it.
The combined grey-piled authority of Tower, sky and
river was too strong for them. In fact, under the beetling
frown of unperturbed history they ceased to exist.

The Delaney family, dressed, they hoped, as though
they were just up for the day from the country, moved
towards the entrance. The effect of that mass of frown-
ing menace upon them was strengthened by the fact that

excavations were going on in the moat. On the other side
of the parapet there were numbers of young men with
cameras, little boys, a brooding Alsatian, and men digging
in slimy mud. Curious how sinister this appeared to the
Delaneys! At any moment skulls might be discovered!

At the entrance a Beefeater, a little the worse for wear,
showed them that they must purchase tickets on the other
side of the road. The entrance to the ticket-office was
filled with a stout lady and two fat little girls. One little
girl was sobbing bitterly. It seemed that she did not wish
to go to the Tower. Quite suddenly she broke into a
tempest of rage and beat upon the stout lady with her
fists, screaming: 'I hate you, Miss Franks! I hate you,
Miss Franks!'

Miss Franks was imperturbable.

'I want tickets for everything,' she said to the ticket-
vendor.

'The Armouries?'

'The Armouries.'

'The Regalia?'

'The Regalia.'

Only then, with the grey and red slips in her hand, she
turned to the screaming child and said: 'Hilda, remember
the snails and oysters.'

The Delaneys were fascinated by this mysterious reply.
The incident had this importance, that for many a day
thereafter any rebellion on the part of a Delaney would
be checked by the threat: 'Remember the snails and
oysters!'

'Do you want to see everything?' the pale, anxious-
eyed lady behind the counter asked.

'Everything!' Fred Delaney said firmly. 'You see, we're
up on an excursion—only three-and-six return, but bringing the children *is* expensive and we don't know when
we'll be up again, so we do want to see everything, including the Little Princes *and* the Block. . . .'

But, through the entrance and walking towards the Traitors' Gate, all his gaiety left him, for standing to the left with Byward Tower behind her was the beautiful Miss Alice Van Renn. He concluded that his Irish blood was mastering him. She was a lovely spook; he had but time to realize that she was wearing a cherry-coloured dress and that a jewel of some sort sparkled in her little hat, before she was gone.

Many people were hurrying about; the sun for the first time pierced the grey and threw a faint primrose glow over walls and towers. He stared. He shrugged his shoulders. He caught his daughter by the arm.

'Kitty, don't leave me. I'm frightened.' He grinned at her. 'It may be that once we are inside this place we shall never get out again.'

'It will be all right if we are together.'

'*You're* all right, aren't you? You don't see anything?'

'See anything?' Kitty stared about her.

'Yes. Not Lady Jane Grey nor Anne Boleyn nor Henry the Eighth nor Colonel Blood.'

She had forgotten him. She was staring at the Traitors' Gate.

He stared also. 'We ought not to have come,' he thought. 'Everything I have done this year is leading inevitably to some catastrophe. And this is the centre of the world—the evil, spell-binding centre. This place stinks of death, torture and the savagery of man. This is the den of the London monster and I am betraying my innocent family. . . . Good God, *was* that Alice Van Renn? Is she beginning to obsess me so that I see her everywhere? Has it become so evil with me that I can only rid myself of this wretched obsession by sleeping with her?'

But there they were, all four of them together, his arm through Kitty's, and he was happy for the most ridiculous reasons, that the primrose sun was shining, that Bullock's round face was so charming, and that his own heart, not

yet impeded by any foretaste of destruction, was beating
with such strong regularity in his breast. *Had* that been
Alice Van Renn? But Meg was talking to the kindly Beefeater.

'And *this* is the Traitors' Gate?'

'Yes, ma'am. Here passed on their way to prison or
execution Edward Duke of Buckingham, Sir Thomas
More, Queen Anne Boleyn, Thomas Cromwell, the Earl
of Essex, Queen Katherine Howard, Jane Seymour . . .'

He was reeling off his piece like a child at school, his
round chubby face and white walrus moustache giving him
so innocent an expression that Meg interrupted: 'That's
enough. I hate to think of it. And were you a soldier once?
What made you become a Beefeater?'

'Well, you see, ma'am, it's a permanent job, and being
a bachelor——'

'What! Do you mean to say you're not married?'

He clicked his uncertain teeth together with great satisfaction. 'No, and I reckon I'm safe now, being sixty-seven
next birthday.'

'Don't you approve of marriage, then?' she asked,
greatly interested.

'No man in his senses would ever marry, ma'am, but
he isn't *in* his senses half the time, and it's just those unfortunate lapses——'

She was interrupted by Fred, who wanted to move forward, but she hated to leave the dear old man, with whom
she would willingly have talked all the afternoon.

'So extraordinary,' she said, putting her arm through
Bullock's as they moved forward. 'He talked like a Professor. He's *so* right. I can't think what men ever marry
for.'

'I can,' said Bullock. 'If you love someone . . .'

He sighed and she pressed his arm close to her side.
She was aware with a moment of acute surprising jealousy
that in a little *he* would be married and Kitty would be

married and she would be old. . . . Life moved so swiftly that, with the flick of action, just as the sun now moved behind a cloud, all would be over. This Tower would remain. Long, long after she, so alive, so vigorous, was forgotten, these walls would stand and another Beefeater would be repeating, 'Here passed on their way to prison or execution . . .'

But now they were looking at the line of the old Roman wall, and now climbing steps into the White Tower, and here is the Axe, the Execution Block, the horrible little waxen figure upon the rack, the thumbscrew. . . . Here too were children, mothers, fathers, loving couples, raucous young men, Miss Franks and her charges, two old ladies with large umbrellas, a bearded guide with a group that clung to him like ducklings to their mother, and a long thin Beefeater looking at them all with so grave a distaste that Meg's heart ached for him. Over all was a pale shadowed light and the air was chill. The Execution Block! The Delaneys were fascinated by it. Deep in its greasy shining oak were grooves wherein the axe had dug. It seemed, as they stared at it, to move. It had an unctuous satisfaction as though it said to them: 'I at least have performed efficiently my duty in a world where everything is always mismanaged.'

'You know,' Fred said, turning from the model of the rack to the block and back again, 'at the very first threat I would have confessed anything, given *anyone* away. Yes, all and every one of you. At the first stretch I would have condemned you all to the flames. That's the kind of man I am.'

Meg nodded. 'We wouldn't have blamed you. We would have understood, I'm sure.' Then she saw that the fat child who had turned crying on Miss Franks was close beside her and staring at the Block with wide-eyed, white-faced terror. Its lips were moving.

She touched the child's arm. 'Don't trouble, dear,' she

said. 'They don't do things like that any more and never will again.' (Don't they? Won't they? Are we any better?)

'They cut off your hair first,' the child said, staring up at her. 'And sometimes the axe missed the first time. It was like that with the Duke of Monmouth. He asked the executioner to take care to do it the first time. But he missed. He did it four times. I know because I've read it.'

She broke off. She was still staring into Meg's handsome kindly eyes. Meg saw that she was trembling. Meg kissed her.

'No one's ever going to do that to you, darling. Nor to anyone. We're so much kinder . . .'

Miss Franks had hurried up.

'Well, I'm sure. Hilda, what did I tell you? I beg your pardon. She's been told a thousand times not to talk to strangers.'

'Take her up and show her the armour,' Meg said cheerfully. 'I can see she's an imaginative child.' She stopped, for there, starting up the staircase to the next floor, was Graham Pender.

Then he *had* come, and he was alone. Her heart began frantically to beat and she was reminded most absurdly of a day long ago when, as a child of fourteen or so, she had been lost in Monte Carlo and had wandered through some gardens with a yellow-faced, shining-haired young man who had said he loved her and would feed her with fried snails in a little place he knew. Snails! Snails and oysters! But now they were climbing the little staircase and, most unexpectedly, were gazing at a gigantic model of the Battle of Waterloo. A guide with spectacles and black bushy eyebrows became one of their family in a second of time. Eagerly he said to Kitty: 'You look through this glass, Miss. There! Now don't it come out clear? Yes, sir—move along this way. That's Wellington—next to him riding on the silver horse!'

'Well, this *will* be something to tell the Vicar,' Fred said. 'He's so especially interested in Napoleon—our Vicar at Little Frampton,' he explained to the guide. 'We've come up on an excursion and the last thing the Vicar said at tea yesterday was—"I don't suppose there'll be anything about Napoleon in the Tower. I hardly see how there can be." Little he knew! Look, Hilda,' he cried to Kitty, 'at all the soldiers—thousands of them. Why, Waterloo must have covered the whole of Belgium practically.'

So Meg had slipped away on the other side of the gigantic model and found Graham in an alcove studying some helmets. They were miraculously hidden from view.

'Well, Graham,' she said.

He was vastly astonished.

'Meg! You——'

'You told me. You said you were coming to-day, so when the family decided on an expedition I suggested the Tower. They're all over there looking at Waterloo.'

His thin distinguished face (so very much more distinguished than any face that she had seen since Forbes-Robertson's) flushed. He said:

'Then this is the place and this is the moment to tell you that I love you, Meg. That I have always loved you and will always love you. What am I to do about it?'

'And I love you too, Graham. But I also love my husband better than anyone else on earth. I'm happily married and I adore my children. So there is nothing to be done about it.'

The bearded guide, his flock close about him, arrived at that moment, and began: 'Nothing here is worthy of especial attention, but we shall see in a moment two curious figures, "Gin" and "Beer," brought from the buttery of the Royal Palace of Greenwich at the end of the seventeenth century, also the cloak on which General Wolfe died at Quebec. . . .'

Graham looked into her face like a child asking for comfort. 'No, Meg, I suppose nothing. But if I could have you in my arms only once. Just one night. After that I wouldn't mind, I think. After all it ought to be my right, I think. It was *meant* to be——'

Meg shook her head.

'But not now. You see, Graham, we're old. We would hurt people even though they didn't know of it.'

'Isn't that rather conventional? What harm can it do to anybody? You won't love anyone less because you love me a little. You'll be enriched and so will I. You're right. We'll soon be old and this is the last chance of our lives. Listen, Meg. Come away for a night. I have to lecture in Oxford in June. We could stay near there. Somewhere like Evesham. Some little place where no one would see us.'

She put her hand on his arm.

'You'd be disappointed. It wouldn't be what you think.'

'It would be better than I think—far, far better. I'd have something to remember and cherish. You too. It would give us a bond.'

'We have a bond. Nothing can break it. Being together for a night wouldn't strengthen it.'

She heard Fred's voice. 'That's *most* interesting. Now for the armour. Where's Meg got to?'

She slipped away. She caught Fred's arm. 'All the armour's upstairs, I think.'

'Weren't you interested in Waterloo?'

'I hate battles.' As they all moved to the staircase she caught a swift glimpse of Graham's passionate beseeching gaze.

In the Horse Armoury they collected, for use in Little Frampton, some really splendid things. There was, for instance, the case with the richly ornamented helmets of the sixteenth century.

'I think,' said Fred, 'we'll have *that* one for the centre of the dining-room mantelpiece. My idea is that we line it with glass and then grow ferns in it. And *that* one shall have Meg's odds and ends, the things she leaves all over the room. And *that* one will do splendidly for snails and oysters.' He asked the mild learned custodian: 'Do you think you could steal a helmet for me?'

The custodian solemnly giggled.

'A heap of people make that joke, sir,' he said.

'Oh, but I'm quite serious,' Fred answered, and looked it. He spoke in low confidential tones. 'I'll pay you an excellent price. If you're caught I'll buy your ticket to Australia.'

The custodian shook his head sadly.

'You'd be disappointed, sir. Even if you got away with it safely, what would you do with it?'

'Plant ferns in it,' Fred said. 'In Little Frampton we have about forty varieties of ferns. They say that people come from all over the world fern-hunting at Little Frampton.'

Kitty expected the custodian suddenly to turn upon her father that hullo-here's-a-lunatic look that she had seen before in the eyes of guides and custodians. But not so. There were so many queer visitors every day that he thought nothing of this one.

'I expect you're right, sir,' he observed mildly. 'I collect cigarette-cards myself—for my little boy.'

They had seen, however, at the end of the room the gilt armour of Charles I on his horse, and he surrounded by figures of cuirassiers and pikemen. The bearded guide was proclaiming: 'Face of king and horse carved by Grinling Gibbons, and at the base you will observe nine small cannon made for Charles II when a boy.'

But what Fred Delaney observed, half hidden behind the large case of armour to the left, was the lovely cheek and nose surmounted by the little hat with the sparkling jewel of Miss Alice Van Renn. He threw a quick look about him. Meg, her arm through Bullock's, had wandered off to see the armour of James II. Kitty was talking to the custodian.

'I thought you were a spook,' he said to Miss Van Renn.

She was dove-grey and silver and moth's wing and moonlight on water. Chastity whose purity was lit with fire. As naked to him as though she had risen from the waters of the armoured and brutal past, the Venus of all cruelty and indifference. Fragile, created out of foam, flower petals, silver web. And a lot more nonsense. A bitch. He longed for her with such sexual desire that the top of his head stuck to his hat, or it felt like it. He knew why men strangled ladies who resisted them. He knew why men spent thousands of pounds which they hadn't got in a jeweller's shop. He knew why Troy fell. He knew what sailors felt on reaching port after being at sea for three months. He knew why Antony threw empires away. He understood thoroughly Don Juan, Christina of Sweden, the Walrus and the Carpenter, and Rasputin. And, his imagination running ahead of the event, he was aware of the chill disappointment of all the gentlemen through history who have escaped out of the window at three in the morning in their shirts. All this he saw while the armour of the kings of England swam, reeled, swung into curtains of swaying gold and silver and resolved finally into the nine little cannons of the small boy, Charles II.

'I'm not a spook,' Miss Van Renn said. 'How are you, Fred?'

'You're a spook to me,' Fred said, putting his hand inside his collar to push it forward a little. 'Always. I never get more than a minute with you anywhere.'

'Oh, I don't know,' she said, appraising him quietly with her most lovely eyes (and he felt his stoutness rising within him, a shame and a derision). 'We see one another fairly often, I think. Tea, luncheon, a walk or two——'

'Yes, and I don't know why it is, but there's always

someone interrupting. It's a sort of fate. I've got my family with me now.'

'Yes, and I've got Mr. Bartlett. He's examining the helmets.'

'Oh, damn Bartlett! I can't see what you find in him. He's the most crushing bore——' He pulled himself up and said quite piteously: 'Can't you see, Alice? Can't you understand? I want to be alone with you. I want to take you out one evening—somewhere quiet—I want—I want——' He came beside her, pressing his stomach against the glass case, catching her hand. 'You know what I want——'

'Yes,' she said, letting him hold her hand. 'I do.'

'Well, then——'

'Well—what?'

'Let me see you——'

'You can see me—whenever you want.'

'No—but alone.'

'And then—what?'

'I want to tell you.' He was choking. It was as though all the armour in the room were closing in upon him. 'I love you. I *have* loved you——'

'Here *is* Mr. Bartlett,' she said.

That irritating, stout bovine figure advanced happily towards them.

'Hullo, Delaney!'

'Hullo, Bartlett!'

'Fancy finding *you* here!'

'Yes. Never thought I'd see anyone I know.'

'No. Nor did we. Did we, Alice?'

'Didn't we? I never thought about it.'

Fred moved away. 'So long, Alice. See you soon.'

'Why, of course.'

'So long, Bartlett.'

'Oh, darling,' Meg greeted him. 'We must hurry. They close at five. It's the dungeons next.'

It was first the dungeons in which, as the bearded guide explained to his devoted flock, 'No prisoners have *ever* been drowned at high tide. Romantic idea I *will* acknowledge and popular because, ladies and gentlemen, we are all partial to horrors, and rightly so, but facts are facts and these dungeons in which you are now standing are more than ten feet above high-water mark.'

'The guide-book calls them the basement,' Fred said disconsolately. 'There's romance for you!'

Followed the Beauchamp Tower where pathetically 'Jane' is cut into the wall, followed the Regalia where jewels, looking more like paste than any paste, blazed to the memory of Colonel Blood, and so—there they all were—on Tower Green.

It had become, while they were tumbling through history, a lovely serene and mellowed April day. The Green, with its small square plot, paved with granite, gazed mutely into a sky of shriven blue, mild, temperate with the shadows of a primrose dusk stealing in veiled light behind the Tower. Here, on this spot, suffered

> Lord Hastings
> Queen Anne Boleyn
> Margaret Countess of Salisbury
> Queen Katherine Howard
> Jane Viscountess Rochford
> Lady Jane Grey
> Robert Devereux Earl of Essex

Fred took off his hat.

'Let us pray for the souls of all departed,' he said.

There were two gigantic ravens, their wings clipped, hopping on the grass. One of them, a really enormous bird, fixed Delaney with a cocked, inquisitive eye. Fred bowed.

'Henry, Eighth of that name, receive my condolences. You were evilly entreated by women—more sinned against than sinning.'

Henry VIII winked at him in agreement, then pecked at a feather. The scene was now of the deepest tranquillity. Miss Franks and her charges, the bearded guide and his flock, all had vanished. The little houses, like the discreet and decorous homes of a Cathedral precincts, sat in a row of daffodils and primroses against their walls. A white-wing-flamed seagull swooped against the Tower's grey. The sky grew ever more primrose. The granite slab was warmed in the gathering light. The four moved down the hill, up the steps to the parapet outside the Beauchamp Tower looking to the river. So tranquilly flowed the Thames, a barge slowly slipping by; a faint ruffle of wind threw multitudes of tiny grey feathers on to the waters. There was a scent of flowers. Also of tar.

They leaned on the parapet, their bodies close together.

'You know,' Fred said, 'it is charming when we're alone together. Better than *anything* else.'

'Much better,' said Meg.

'However delightful other people may be.'

'However delightful.'

'You know,' Kitty said, 'when we're by ourselves like this every problem seems to be solved.'

'The cruelty of the past doesn't matter.'

'Nor the blindness of the present.'

'Nor the hazards of the future.' Fred Delaney's hand was on Meg's shoulder. Very lightly he kissed the lobe of her ear. 'Darling Meg.'

As they moved away Fred said:

'Well, I won my bet. There wasn't a soul we knew. I said there wouldn't be.'

'Not a soul,' said Meg.

'Only Henry the Eighth,' said Kitty.

CHAPTER VI

Time Piece: Young Man on Paper

Fragments from a Journal

. . . UNTIL now, it is sad to reflect, I have written nothing in this Journal worth a tinker's curse. That is perhaps not very surprising when one considers what punk most Journals are, and that Pepys is the only amusing one and Barbellion's is interesting mostly because we know he's going to die very shortly. Evelyn's is good in places, there are one or two French ones, and I read all of Arnold Bennett's, and he must have been a jolly good fellow, I think, although he cared more for hotels than they are generally worth. Then there are the egotistical ones like Marie Bashkirtseff's, but undoubtedly it's the hardest thing in the world to write a good Journal without being self-conscious and yet be interesting to other people. But one oughtn't to write with other people in mind and I'm certain I shall never show this to anyone else except perhaps Lizzie. It's Lizzie who now makes the whole difference. I see I began this about five years ago, and there are now about five exercise-books full, but it's all the most awful rot—Aug. 5, 1932. Boulogne. Bathed. Saw dark girl with beautiful legs. Lost twenty francs Casino. . . . That sort of stuff.

But this is different. I want to be absolutely as honest as I can so that I may know myself better for Lizzie's sake. Also it will help my novel. Because I've never really tried to write before, I can see that quite clearly now. Trying to make jokes for *Punch* isn't really writing, although *Punch* is awfully good if you like that sort of thing. Of course people like Munden simply hate it. Then there was a time when I thought I'd write like Wodehouse, but I see now it's no use trying to write *like* anyone. What you've got to be is yourself, but then is there any real self for me to be? Lizzie says there is, and that's why I'm going to try and write a novel that, however bad, is mine and mine only.

But first I'm going to be utterly honest to myself on paper to see where I am.

I'm not in any way remarkable, of course. That's the first thing. I'm just like thousands and thousands of other men of my own age. But I'm going to put one thing down right away. I'm awfully happy. That would sicken almost anybody if they were to read it, because undoubtedly it's wrong for anyone to be happy to-day with the awful state the world's in, so many unemployed and probably a World War in a month or two. All the same I said I was going to be honest and so I must be. I'm happy, I suppose, for three reasons. The first is that I've got in Father, Mother and Kitty the three grandest relations in the world. Secondly, I'm in love with Lizzie, who is only a child at present but simply beautiful in every way; and thirdly, I'm in excellent health—there's nothing the matter with me physically in any way whatever. I'm making a bit of money too—I made £136 : 4 : 3 last year, and this year so far I've made £83—£35 from *Punch*, £15 from a short story, and the rest odds and ends.

Do I feel it wrong to be happy? I honestly don't. Of course I have my worries like anyone else. We may have

to sell the house, which would be frightful after its being
in the family so long, and I hate the world to be in the
mess it is. Ought I to do something about it? People like
Munden feel that I ought. He's working away all the
time. The trouble is I don't know what I'd work for if
I *did* begin. I don't like Stalin any better than Mussolini
or Hitler, and I feel we've got the best sort of government
here in England. It isn't perfect, of course, but at any
rate we're free in England to say and think what we like,
and that's worth everything else.

The next thing is that perhaps father, mother, Kitty
and I are much too satisfied with ourselves. But then
father and mother are really remarkable. I don't see how
you can think them anything else if you really know them.
They are entirely free of all the worst faults—meanness
and jealousy and cruelty and spitefulness. And when you
live with people like that all the year round it's a great
piece of luck undoubtedly.

But I must say I believe in families like anything. I
know most people think them rot these days, and in my
generation lots of people laugh at their parents because
they seem to them slow and sticky. But this must be the
parents' fault partly. And another thing is that my generation will be parents soon themselves and then *they'll* be
laughed at. But with us it's never been like parents and
children. Almost the first thing I can remember is bathing
at Eastbourne or somewhere and my being carried into
the water by my father and my not being frightened because he was laughing, and I knew he wouldn't be laughing if it was dangerous. It seems to me he's always told me
everything from the very first, about money troubles
which we've always been in, about the women he's in love
with, and he explained to me all about sex in the simplest
way before I went to my Private. I remember he told me
I'd find I got in a mess sometimes because beautiful

women were beautiful women and there was no use pretending they weren't. But then he's always been more
passionate than I shall ever be. He's a bit of a poet, I
think, which I'm certainly not, and the Irish is stronger
in him than it is in me. Then I'm afraid women will laugh
at me because I'm so small. I've fancied myself in love
heaps of times, but I've only had a woman once and that
was beastly. And I never was *really* in love until I saw
Lizzie. All I want now is for her to grow a bit and then
we'll marry and then we'll have children, which is the
grandest thing I can imagine.

Then I must say a word about my mother because I
simply don't know what my life would have been if she
hadn't been there. She's most unusual. There's no doubt
about that. You'd think from the way she talks and be-
haves that she's all over the place, but as a matter of fact
she isn't. She seems careless and to say the first thing that
comes in her head, and always to be rushing about.

The truth is that more than most people she knows
just what she's doing. She's always throwing herself into
other people's lives and helping them, not because she
wants to do good but because she's made that way. Then,
although she never says anything about it, she's really
religious. She thinks there's a God and that Jesus Christ
is alive and is with her wherever she is. I don't believe
that myself, but it makes her happy, and she's so happy
that perhaps she's right after all. What I say about religion is that each man must go by his own experience and
it's silly rot to laugh at someone because he doesn't think
as you do. And anyway I know I'm not just chemicals as
Munden thinks, or I couldn't love Lizzie as I do.

Well, now about Lizzie. You couldn't call her beautiful, I suppose, although she's beautiful to me, and she can
look beautiful sometimes when she's thinking of something she can't see. She's just my height, which is very

pleasant for me. Although she's only sixteen she's very
old for her age because she's travelled all over the world
with her father and seen everything—many things it's
terrible for a child to have seen. And because she's seen
everything and knows exactly how cruel and wicked people can be, she's reached a kind of calm although she's
often very unhappy. Her father's the worst man I've ever
known in my life, and yet he can be very charming and
amusing. He's bad because he's got no sense of right and
wrong at all and doesn't mind how much he hurts anybody
if he can get what he wants. The funny thing is, I think
he loves Lizzie in a sort of a way. She's the only human
being he does care for at all. He's going downhill all the
time, and I expect that once he was most charming and
very handsome and really did want to be a decent sort.
But now he's past caring and hasn't any strength of will
at all, and soon, I'm sure, there'll be some dreadful crash.
When that comes I must be there to keep Lizzie safe and
see she comes to no harm. Can I honestly say that Lizzie
loves me as I love her? No, of course I can't. She doesn't
trust anyone in the world except her aunt with whom she
lived for a while in Westminster. She's seen so much to do
with sex that's horrible that she hates it all and tries to
keep herself from contact with anybody. But I think she
is *beginning* to trust me, and she liked mother very much
when she went to our place to tea.

An illustration of the unexpected, unusual person Lizzie is I will give here because it is still very much in my
mind. On an afternoon last week we were in the National
Gallery. We go there quite often because we are sure we
won't see anyone there we know. Also, in the first place,
because Lizzie really loves pictures and knows a great
deal about them, and now I'm beginning to know something too because of what she's told me. We had sat down
in the long Italian room and I had just asked her if she

would write down for me the six pictures she liked best in the Gallery. I have the bit of paper in front of me now.

She wrote:

For young Mr. Delaney—

I, Lizzie Coventry, solemnly declare that, in all the National Gallery in London, England, the six pictures I like best are:

Christ and the Magdalene	.	Titian
The Entombment	. .	Michael Angelo
The Painter's Daughters	.	Gainsborough
Death of Procris	. .	Piero di Cosimo
Windmill on Mousehold Heath		Crome
Baptism of Christ	. .	Piero della Francesca
The Graham Children	. .	Hogarth

I know this is seven but I couldn't leave the Graham Children out.

N.B.—I don't say these are the *best* pictures. They're the ones I'd like if I had a house.

I'd just told her where I agreed and didn't agree when we saw the oddest figure coming towards us. This was an old man with an untidy grey beard, an old grey felt hat shoved down on his head, a plaid shawl over his shoulders, and brown velveteen trousers. He carried a heavy knobbly stick and was shuffling along as though he couldn't lift a foot from the ground. He was muttering to himself as he went, and yet I must say he didn't give one any notion of senility. When he came nearer I saw that he had the sharpest, brightest blue eyes I'd ever seen.

Well, when he was just opposite us his stick slipped on the surface of the floor and I thought he was going to fall, so I jumped up and caught him by the arm.

He turned on me quite savagely and snapped: 'I'm all right, young man. Think I can't look after myself?' I'll confess I was pretty aggravated and was for telling the old fool he could drown for all I cared, but it was Lizzie who said with the utmost sweetness:

'The floor is slippery, isn't it?'

He said: 'Yes. That's why I'm allowed to keep this stick.'

Lizzie, when she lets her real self come out, is like no one else I have ever known. She is so compassionate that, although she is herself only a child, she is like a mother to anyone in distress. People might often think her hard if they hadn't seen her on one of these occasions. She seems so cold and indifferent to so many people. But this old man roused her tenderness. She looked at him so sweetly that he was conquered at once and came and sat down on the seat beside us. He talked then like anything. He never stopped. He said his name was Lord Ragadoon and I knew then at once who he was, an eccentric old man, very rich, a collector of fine pictures and furniture, many of which he stored away in an old castle in Ireland while he himself lived all alone in some messy untidy rooms in London. People of course said he was mad; but he wasn't at all mad, it seemed, in the auction room. Well, he sat there talking to us about one thing after another—pictures, with stories about Velasquez and El Greco (he said he was the greatest painter who had ever lived), and the best A.B.C. shops for toasted buns, and the iniquity and ignorance of doctors, and a cure for rheumatics, and two cats he had called Hore and Belisha. And he laughed a great deal, or rather shook and rumbled in his beard. He had taken, it was clear, a great liking to Lizzie, and he took her hand in his gnarled hairy one and patted it. She talked away and laughed and was simply adorable. He made us both give him our names and addresses, and when he found I was partly Irish he was delighted.

As I sat there, next to the funny old man with the grand pictures around us, I can't explain why it all seemed so Londony. It was somehow like Dickens with a smell of smoke and tobacco (which came from old Ragadoon's clothes) and it had the *stillness* of London. You felt as

though this grand Gallery was planted there in the very
centre of crooked chimneys and narrow twisted streets
and fish-shops, and the river with its mud and old ships
and the Houses of Parliament dusky on a winter afternoon although the lights were on. I seemed to hear Big
Ben striking right along the Gallery floor. I have put this
down just as I felt it. It was so quiet and homely, and I
loved Lizzie twice as much as ever before. At last he got
up and, nodding and smiling back at us, went shuffling
away.

Then, strangely enough, this little incident led to another—a rather bold one on my part. Lizzie told her
faher about Ragadoon and at once that rascally parent
began to lick his lips over the prospect of getting some
of that old eccentric's money. He tried to persuade Lizzie
to bring the old boy to their place, and of course this
Lizzie refused to do. Then he had a violent scene with
her. What exactly happened I don't know, for she refused
to tell me, but there was a slight bruise above her left eye.
She seemed to be indifferent, almost contemptuous. I know
her well enough now to realize that that was her pride.

She lived alone, all to herself. She had seen that life
was so dangerous and that it could be so humiliating if
you allowed it that she had created a self-defence, self-
remoteness that no one was going to penetrate. I could
discover two persons only in the whole world for whom,
in her secret heart, she longed, her aunt Fanny, Mrs.
Carlisle, and Mrs. Carlisle's son Edward. If she spoke
of them her voice shook a little; there was longing in
her eyes, poor darling Lizzie . . . darling, darling Lizzie. . . .

Anyway I was sure in my own mind that a crisis in
Coventry's affairs wasn't far away. He was for ever
drinking and day after day having the most horrible rows
with that beastly woman, Mrs. Agar, who was calm
enough herself and used to let him storm, but I never

knew a nastier woman. When you are going downhill and are becoming seriously frightened of consequences your eyes get a funny half-open look as though you were half-closing them so that you might see some object in the distance more clearly. Coventry had that look now, and sometimes he would draw his breath sharply as though he were out of breath from running. I saw too that Lizzie was herself beginning to be apprehensive as she had not been before. In fact, half an hour before I wrote these words I was with her and I realized fully that she is expecting something dreadful to happen. May it not be long before I can protect her and watch over her and see that she is happy and safe!

But now I must write something down about Fanny Carlisle, because she is, I think, going to be important both in Lizzie's life and mine. I decided that I must go and see her, so without giving myself time to think of the cheek of what I was doing, one fine afternoon about four down to Westminster I went, rang the bell of the Carlisle house, and, to a stiff-faced old-family-servant kind of woman, said I wanted to see Mrs. Carlisle. She of course asked me my reasons, so I gave her my card and said she was to tell Mrs. Carlisle that I was a friend of Miss Lizzie Coventry's. The old family servant's brow darkened at that and she gave me the stiffest kind of look, but she disappeared with the card and a minute or two later said Mrs. Carlisle would see me. She showed me upstairs to a jolly drawing-room rather full with things, but then I don't like a room to be quite empty except for an unintelligible picture and a vase with flowers made of white linen. There was a grand Japanese screen and some good pictures, and everything as bright as the sun. These details, I suppose, have nothing to do with it except that the brightness and freshness were all part of my idea of Fanny Carlisle. I'll acknowledge quite frankly that she and I took to one another at once. She is a lady getting on for fifty, I should think, and reminded me a little of a smaller edition of mother. She wasn't modern in dress or hair or anything; just a rather stout, middle-aged, cheerful English lady who probably was forbidden to read Rhoda Broughton's novels when she was a girl. But I've never seen anyone look more honest or kind, and she had a sort of gentleness that comes from understanding people and being tolerant. I know she was awfully surprised to see anyone as small and boyish-looking as I am. I'm accustomed by now to people having that impression when they first see me, so I always try to be quiet and sensible. It is much more dangerous for someone of my appearance to say anything without thinking first than it is for someone like Patrick Munden. I always have to remember that and try to see myself as others see me.

I sat down, and Mrs. Carlisle asked me what I had come about; I told her at once that I loved Lizzie and hoped in two years' time to marry her. I said that I thought that she trusted and liked me but didn't love me. I said that she cared more for her father, Mrs. Carlisle, and her cousin Edward than for anyone else. Mrs. Carlisle was very much moved by this and seemed at once to trust me, because she told me something of what had happened when Captain Coventry, her brother, and Lizzie had stayed in their house. She said that he had behaved badly, they had had a quarrel and he had left, taking Lizzie with him; that since then they had never seen him or Lizzie and that they had always loved Lizzie very much. I said then that I was sure that Captain Coventry would soon be in some very bad trouble, and if that happened would they help Lizzie? Mrs. Carlisle said at once that of course they would love to. I told her something about my family so as to reassure her, and said that I thought that she and my mother would get on like anything. Afterwards she said, smiling, she hoped I wouldn't mind but I *did* look very young, upon which I said I wasn't as young as I looked and practically earned my living by writing. I said 'practically' so as to be quite truthful. She asked me what I wrote, and I said I wrote for *Punch* and when she saw anything with the initials 'S.D.' that was me; and she said that they took *Punch* every week and she'd look out for those initials. That was practically all, I think, and I must say I liked her very much.

Afterwards I told Lizzie that I had been and I thought she might be angry. But she wasn't at all. Only she was more moved than I'd ever seen her. She asked ever so many questions, saying the servant at the door was Janet and I hadn't seen Edward, had I, and about things in the room. She remembered every detail. Then she looked at me very gravely and said: 'Why do you do these things for me?'

'Because I love you,' I said. 'And whether you love me or not I am always going to look after you unless you ask me not to.'

She said then for the first time that she would be very fond of me, but she was afraid to because life was very cruel, and as soon as you liked someone or something it was taken away. She said, too, as though she were a hundred years old, that it wasn't worth while for anyone to be fond of her because she had been damaged, spoilt. Everything, she said, had come to her much too early and she had lost all her trust and belief in things too soon. Everyone lost it in the end, she said, but there were generally some happy years first. So I laughed at her and said that wasn't true, that my father and mother were well on in life and hadn't lost their trust in anyone or anything. Lizzie said that that was because they didn't see life as it was. It was like romantic novels which tried to end everything up happily.

I said there were lots of happy people, people who loved one another all their lives, and that I should love her always, whatever happened. She looked at me and suddenly laughed. 'I think we're both very silly,' she said, and for the rest of that time she was happier than I'd ever seen her before, and I kissed her before I went home. I think the knowledge that I had been to the Carlisles and the knowledge that her aunt Fanny still loved her meant a tremendous lot to her—so I really had done a good deed for once.

Meanwhile Coventry lately has really seemed to accept me as one of the family. His behaviour would seem to me very extraordinary if it were not that I believe that he is becoming drawn into his own troubles and difficulties so far that he has ceased to bother about anything outside them. He allows me to take Lizzie out where and when I please. Sometimes when I bring her back in the evening, after we have been to the theatre or the pictures, I find play in his rooms at its height. Their sitting-room is not large, but it is wonderful how many people Coventry manages to squeeze into it. The place is thick with smoke and everyone is so intent on what is happening that no one pays any attention to us. Once the brown-faced half-caste at the door has admitted us, that is enough. Lizzie slips at once away to her own little room and there she stays. What fears and terrors she must have then, although she tells me nothing—only that there is quarrelling sometimes and a scuffle, some drunkard thrown out or some argument about the cards. Well, this can't last for long! That's one good thing.

Meanwhile this has become the centre, the object of my life. When I return to my room in Charles Street I feel as though here in this quiet street is the heart of the real world. I'm neither very clever nor very wise—in no way exceptional at all—but I do know that the kind of love we have for one another here and the love that I feel for Lizzie, this love is the one certain fact that I know about life. No one can explain it away or give it the easy explanation of sensuality or self-interest. Every kind of trouble and cruelty and uncomfortable change can bluster and blow on every side of it, but in itself it is sufficient reason and explanation of life and, I am sure, is a promise of much greater, finer and wiser things to come. Thousands upon thousands of people alive to-day love one another as we love one another. Life must be a battle, I suppose, otherwise where would growth come from? I don't put these things very well, or in any new way, but when I think of Lizzie in her little room and all that robbery, greed, cruelty going on in the room next to her, I seem to understand why there are these opposites, two worlds at war. If there were nothing to fight for, what would happen to one's muscles?

I'm much too shy about these things to say them aloud to anyone. When I am older I shall understand more— or perhaps less? At any rate this is what I understand now. Here in Charles Street where, as I write, late, everyone else in bed except Kitty, who is at a party, there is not a sound, only the clock ticking and saying, 'Yes—yes— certainly—yes.'

CHAPTER VII

Time Piece: Death of Anybody

WINDSOR LAD had won the Derby, and Mrs. Bathorne, who had put her money on Colombo, gave a light-hearted laugh and told Meg that it didn't matter in the least. 'My little all,' she said. 'Gone. I start, once again, from the gutter.' Old Mrs. Van Renn said, 'Nonsense, Violet. You've always your diamonds.' Mrs. Bathorne smiled complacently at the large glittering ring on her finger and answered, 'Stuff, darling. They're all pawned. This is paste.'

It was a hot afternoon in June, and Meg, who was in some queer way apprehensive, wished that the Three Witches would get up and go.

They sat about the room, rather close together as though summoned from the vasty deeps by Shakespeare himself—Mrs. Van Renn, Mrs. Bathorne and Lady Perivale-Hawder. Meg had not invited them. Mrs. Van Renn had called (WHY? Meg asked herself), and Violet Bathorne and Muriel Hawder had come together. They were the type of old ladies common enough in our perverse generation. In Millie Pake's youth they would have been *real* old ladies, secure in lace cap, footstool, and wise sayings. They would go to bed at ten and have a long sleep. They would be wise about life, knowing everything, severe on folly, tickled by scandal, generous and helpful in trouble that approached them personally, fond of their food, strong, equable, living to ninety.

But Mrs. Bathorne and Muriel Hawder, seen from the rear, walking along almost any street, appeared like girls of twenty. Front view, their eyelids lifted in cold and perpetual surprise, their hard red mouths, the powder lingering in the crevices of their salmon-pink cheeks, their smart hats, stockings and shoes, they looked older and deader than Time. Naked their bodies were a litter of bones. Clad so smartly they had slim figures. Every inch of their persons demanded an unwavering vigilance. Very costly too. Mrs. Van Renn was poor, but the other two won at bridge, struggled for inside tips on the Stock Exchange, had a man or two to wheedle, sold their possessions, ate nothing, lived on a cocktail a day. What *was* miraculous about them was their energy, for Mrs. Van Renn was all but seventy, Mrs. Bathorne sixty-five or -six, and Muriel Hawder a trifle more.

Practically they never slept. They pushed, urged, fought their way into parties, and could be seen at two in the morning at the Ruritanian Ministry listening, with half-closed eyes, to M. Dimanchenko working his way through all the Hungarian Rhapsodies. By eight-thirty of the morning they were telephoning vigorously, and by ten o'clock they were in Miss Sheepshanks' Beauty Parlour.

This lack of repose led to a half-crazy, half-brooding glint in the eye under the perpetually astonished eyebrow. A look of apprehension too. And then quite suddenly they vanished. Someone said at breakfast, 'Oh, Muriel Hawder's dead'—and that was that.

But Meg, now, surveying them, wished—oh, how she wished!—that they would get up and go. The afternoon was close, but that would not altogether account for the apprehensive brooding of this room and house. She felt as though something terrible were happening or about to happen. It might be, of course, in part, her own sense of guilt. Since that meeting in the Tower she had had half a dozen encounters with Graham Pender, and at the last, in this room, they had embraced with a passion that had in it nothing either spiritual or philosophical. Fred, had he been present, would have knocked Graham down. There would have been no complacency or tolerance. She could not cheat herself any longer. She had detachment enough also to realize several other things: that there was nothing aesthetically beautiful in the physical eagerness of a stout woman of middle age, that such embraces led inevitably to one issue only, that modern scorn for religion and marriage made adultery no prettier than it had ever been, and that she in fact scorned neither religion *nor* marriage, that she was grievously unfair to Evie Pender, who might be a fool but nevertheless loved Graham, that she herself, Meg Delaney, loved her husband Fred Delaney more than ever before, that the possibility that Fred Delaney had already spent the night with Alice Van Renn (and old Mrs. Van Renn was paying a call, perhaps, *because* it had been so) excused nothing— her realization of all these things did not prevent her extreme boredom with these old ladies, nor her conviction both of sin and of the exciting drama that life, even when you were over forty, provided.

She was forced now to attend to Violet Bathorne, who was insisting that she should share in her grievances:

'I know, darling, you *look* contented enough. I always think both you and Fred are *maddening* as far as looks go—but you must realize what I feel—to be pushed out of the door, practically *pushed* out, and only because Clara has had this money left her. No other reason whatever. And now she's taking up all these Bolshevik young men and going to suppers in coal-cellars, and she's writ-

ten a letter to Hitler saying that she is of the purest
Aryan blood, but she wants him to understand all
the same that she sympathizes with the Jews and hates
anyone so narrow-minded . . . and *only* because she
had this money left her, and *why* that old man *did*
leave her the money no one can understand. Everyone
thinks it *very* fishy, and I'm really one of her best friends,
if she only knew it, always defending her, and so I told
her this morning, and yet she simply *pushed* me through
the door. . . .'

Meg had to pull her mind back as one pulls one's dog
when it has seen another dog. Clara? Who was Clara?
Oh, of course, Clara Merlin who had been left all that
money by old Colonel Woodhouse. . . .

But when at last she answered, 'I haven't seen Clara
since . . .' she found she was confronted with Muriel
Hawder.

'But tell me, dear. I'm sure you went to the first night.
Didn't you think it *stupid?* All about people at a holiday
resort—as though one cared. I certainly thought the
Hyson girl pretty sitting on that rock, but Freddie Carl-
yon was so stupid. I was *determined* to go on to the "Al
Fresco" afterwards, but he said he had to be in bed early
because of polo or something the next day. . . . Yes,
Touch Wood, that's the play. Who *wants* to know how
people like that live, although I suppose they do run the
country now and we've *got* to get used to it. . . .'

Meg was used to Muriel Hawder's gabble. Muriel
modelled herself on the Corleone and had acquired a
pitch of voice as ugly and rasping as a creaking weather-
vane. She spent her days in arranging to be taken to the
theatre and opera by reluctant males. She would telephone like the wind through the wallpaper and say: 'Any
time in the next fortnight. I hear it's *such* a good play.
You get seats and we might have supper at the Cosmo-
politan after.'

But Meg knew that Mrs. Van Renn was her immediate
business. And she was. She said:

'I was so glad to see Fred yesterday afternoon. He
came in for a cup of tea. He was looking superb.'

Meg realized several things: that Fred had lied to her
because, last evening, he had said he had been all day at
Epsom, where he had had a tiresome piece of business.
'Came straight back,' he had said, kissing her. She realized also that old Mrs. Van Renn admired Fred greatly
and, had she been a little younger, would have entered
into competition with her own dear Alice. The battle that,
months ago, on that New Year's Day, had first been
joined, was now all about her ears. *Not* a battle between
herself and Fred—she was sure that nothing could injure
their relationship. But a battle for her own integrity and
purity of soul, for Fred's, for the possession of this house,
for the safety and well-being of the house, London, England, all that was right and good in the world. She was
not at all dismayed by her sense of peril and apprehension. She rose to it gladly. But, all the same, her alarm
was real, and the first thing she would do would be to
rid herself of the Three Witches. So she rose and pushed
the bell. 'Only,' she said, smiling, 'I've forgotten. I *have*
to send Caesar with a message.' It was enough for them.

They all departed. Muriel Hawder began to Mrs. Van
Renn, as she went out, 'It's a Cochran first night. The
twenty-fourth, I think. I'm going to see if . . .' She was
already deep in her next campaign.

Caesar didn't come, which was as well, for Meg had
nothing to tell him. He could clear the tea away. He had
been depressed lately. She must go and see his horrible
old mother again. She sighed. The house weighed on her
head like a ton of coal. She could scarcely breathe. Something was the matter. And in this house. It gave her no

surprise at all when the door opened and Millie Pake stood there.

Meg cried out: 'What's the matter? What is it, Millie?'

'Yes. Something terrible has happened,' Millie Pake answered.

Millie Pake, earlier on that afternoon, had been turning some clothes over. Helen had stayed in bed that day because—well, because she had not wanted to get up. More and more now she stayed in bed, and it was as well, for more and more she lived in the past (or was it in truth the present if she thought it was?). Living thus in one room or another, bed or chair—what did it matter? In bed she was warm, for, although now it was June, Helen shivered in the sitting-room.

She was about to die, as Millie well knew. A few months more and she would be gone and Millie would be alone. Millie had always been one to face facts, and the one that she faced now was that she was in excellent bodily health, that she would have two pounds a week to live on, that she would *never* live with her brother, that no one would want her, and that she would miss Helen every minute of her waking day, that she would probably, thus poor, hungry and unwanted, live for years.

She was neither sentimental nor despondent at this prospect, but she *was* a little frightened. Try as she might she could not altogether calm her fears. Suppose the little dividends that still trickled into her lap ceased altogether? Suppose her health did suddenly fail? After Helen was gone she could not, she knew, afford to go on living in this flat, although she would like to, because Helen would be nearer to her here than anywhere else. Where would she go? Nothing in the world is such a bore to even the kindliest people as a very poor, single old lady! She knew that there were societies for aiding old gentlepeople, and very good things they were; but she thought, with an ironic shudder, of herself receiving some coals or a nice warm blanket at Christmas.

Well, what of it? She had had really a lovely life, and Jesus Christ would remain in company with her however poor and tiresome she was. She had no patience with the old people in novels who whined and lamented. Jesus Christ was often so close to her that she heard His voice, and it had, often enough, a touch of irony about it. He had never had, she fancied, a great deal of use for lame dogs, nor had she herself. He would dislike it very much if she showed any sign of becoming a lame dog, and certainly that was not what she was going to be. She had had an Aunt Sybella once who, in spite of arthritis, a weak heart, and losing all the hair off her head in a fire, had been, to her ninetieth year, full of spirit, wit, and scorn for her fellows. Millie did not scorn her fellows, but where Aunt Sybella had gone she could follow.

Sitting there now, turning over her dresses, listening for a second lest Helen should wake and want her, she did wish that she could buy some new clothes. She was old and no beauty, but a dark wine-coloured evening frock she had seen in a Hanover Square window had filled her with longing and desire. She had turned these old dresses again and again, and the grey silk was so familiar that it was ashamed to look her in the eye. She stroked it affectionately. Poor old dress! Surely one gave the clothes, the furniture of which one had been for a long time fond, some kind of living, sentient personality? No. That was nonsensical sentiment. She was sick of the old dress, and that was the truth.

The mad notion came to her of stealing the wine-coloured dress. No good. She didn't know how to set about it. How *did* you steal things? That was the worst of an honourable upbringing, the sort that she and Helen had received.

Her mouth full of pins, she grinned. Then she stole to the bedroom door and saw that Helen was quietly sleeping. Then she heard a sound.

She had been sitting with the door into the passage, and the door beyond that, open because the afternoon was close. Now she fancied that from the flat below, from the Pullets' flat, there came a noise.

She went into the passage and stood at the hall-door listening. Imagination. On an oppressive afternoon like this you fancied things. There was no further sound. All the same she was uneasy. She could hear the beating of her heart. The house, in the silence of the oppressive June afternoon, seemed nevertheless to be full of noises. Around and about her beating heart and mingling with it were rustles and whispers as though boards were creaking, plants rustling, clocks ticking. But when she forced herself to hear *beyond* her heart there was no sound at all.

Nothing had happened. And yet, as though she had been commanded by someone stronger than herself, she moved down the stairs.

On the next landing she saw that the flat-door of the Pullets was ajar. This was so unusual that her earlier fears were now confirmed and came running back to her, whispering as they came 'I told you so.' Well, it was no affair of hers. No doubt one or other of them had but just come in and forgotten to close the door. At a moment Smoke or Dodie would be there. (She could hear Dodie's pleasant warm voice crying, 'Smoke, you idiot, you forgot to close the door.') He, or she, would look out into the hall before closing the door, and then how foolish she, Millie Pake, would seem, standing there without any reason.

She went back to the stairs, but then no one came. She waited and now heard quite clearly, from within the flat, the sharp meticulous ticking of a clock. It was, at least, careless of them to leave the door open. She went back and knocked on it timidly. There was no answer and she knocked again. Then she rang the bell. She heard the bell ring, the clock tick. For the rest the silence was intense. She pushed the door wider. Suddenly into the outer hall came the pale Siamese cat that Dodie Pullet had possessed for some two years—possessed, as she often said laughing, in pretence only. There was never a cat more unpossessable. Aloof, unperturbed, this creature moved like an ironical spirit to the head of the stairs. Then it turned and looked at Millie with eyes of cold ironical disdain. But Millie was not looking at the cat. On the surface of the carpet over which the cat had stepped were tiny paw-marks of blood.

Millie did not, if life gave her a crisis to deal with, fear or hesitate, but for a moment the lower staircase swung up at her, suspending the cat as though it would hurl it into space. A second later all was solid and material. She walked into the sitting-room. The bedroom door was wide open. First she saw the reflection in the long deep mirror that stood opposite the bed. In the mirror was the bed's width, the fresh piled pillows, and Smoke in his pyjamas, sloping over the bed, the upper part of his body hanging towards the floor. From his chest blood was dripping, and she saw quite clearly in the mirror the tiny cat-marks proceeding from the blood-pool on the carpet to the door.

She turned to the reality, saw the revolver on the floor, the crimson bedroom slippers on his feet, and the signet ring on his finger shining in the sunlight that poured in from the bedroom window.

'Oh, poor, poor Smoke!' she said aloud, facing her own reflection in the mirror. Instinctively she made no movement. She knew that he was dead. She knew at once that she must disturb nothing because of the police. She saw that there was a letter on the table beside the bed.

Where was Dodie and what must she, Millie, immediately do? It might be hours before Dodie returned; she must find out at once where Dodie was so that she might telephone to her. She went back into the sitting-room and discovered then that her legs were weak beneath her. She sat down on the sofa and looked about her at the metallic furniture, the black and white decoration, and a large cluster of silver-tinsel branches and leaves in a high white vase.

'Oh, poor, poor Smoke!' she thought again and found that she was crying, tears rolling down her dry cheeks. She did not attempt to stay them but only sat there, clasping and unclasping her hands. Where was Dodie? She *must* be found. She got up then and moved about, looking if she might find some engagement-book or pad. But the room was icily bare. Not a thing about, only in a corner near the window a very modern basket made of twisted white wood, cushioned in black—the home of the Siamese cat. Then, like a knife cutting paper, there were voices. A moment later Dodie and Patrick Munden stood in the room.

'Why, Millie——' Dodie stopped. 'But where's——'

Millie said, 'Wait.' She rubbed her wet cheek with the knuckles of her hand.

'But where's——' Dodie said, and moved towards the open bedroom door.

Millie put her hand on her sleeve.

'No, don't. . . . Smoke's hurt. Don't go in for a moment.'

But Munden strode past them both. For a moment he disappeared. Then he returned, closed the bedroom door and stood with his back to it. He looked Dodie straight in the face.

'Smoke has shot himself. He's dead.'

Dodie moved towards the door.

'No, you're not to go in. Not yet.'

She was furious. 'Of course I am! Do you think I'm
a child?' Then she said what Millie had said: 'Oh, poor,
poor Smoke!'

But Munden didn't move.

'No. . . . Wait . . . until the doctor's been.'

'Oh, the doctor!' Millie cried. 'Doctor Roach. . . .'
She went across to the telephone.

Dodie spoke like a man. 'Get out of it,' she said to
Munden. 'This isn't *your* affair.'

Munden let her pass. He stood looking in front of him
while Millie telephoned.

'Yes, Doctor Roach, please. . . . This is Lady Mildred Pake. . . . Oh, is that you, Doctor Roach? Could
you come at once to . . .' She moved away from the
telephone, saying to no one in particular: 'He will be here
almost at once.'

Dodie was in the room again and said: 'No one is to
touch anything. The police will have to come.' Then looking at Munden she said (she was holding in her hand a
sheet of notepaper) : 'This is what he says:

'DARLING—For a long time I've thought I would be better out
of your way. I know you're fond of me and I thank God for it.
I know you're in love with someone else too. And I know I'm
useless and an encumbrance. I'm perfectly sane as I write this and
quite happy—sane enough to fancy I may be given a chance somewhere else. If I'd had some brains I might have got somewhere,
but in this new world you're quite useless without brains. Perhaps
where I'm going they'll give me some brains. Remember, darling,
I'm quite sane and quite happy.

'Your devoted
'SMOKE.'

'They'd like to read this at the Coroner's inquest,'
Dodie said. 'But they won't. And no one's to tell them.
Do you understand?' she said, looking at Munden. She
tore the paper into tiny pieces.

'I shan't tell them,' Munden said.

She bent down and picked up the fragments of paper. She went back into the bedroom, closing the door behind her.

'We're in love, but we're not lovers,' Munden said in a dull, almost sullen voice to Millie.

Millie said: 'I ought to go in there to her.'

'No. Leave her alone. Poor Smoke! What a hell of a life!'

'It's not my business,' Millie said. 'Why didn't you —— '

'Why didn't I leave her alone? Because life's a mess, a silly blasted mess. My love for her is the only decent thing I've got. And it wouldn't have made any difference. Smoke's better dead, and so would millions alive to-day be.'

Millie shook her head. 'Of course I don't think so. But I *do* think Smoke will be happier where he is.'

Munden glared at her. 'That rot!' Then he lowered his head almost as though he were praying. He raised it again. 'Please forgive me. I don't mean to be rude. All that seems nonsense to me. . . .'

Millie said: 'I think you don't see far enough. You must see a very long way. I don't think death's very important, and perhaps you'll find that out now you're in love. . . .' She gave a little anxious movement. 'I don't like her being alone in there.'

He answered: 'She's wise. She's sane. She'll let no one help her either now or ever. Smoke was the weak one. Men *are* these days compared with women.'

Millie turned her head away. In spite of herself she was crying again and she didn't want this fierce young man to see her weakness. To her great surprise he put his arm around her and led her back to the sofa.

'Sit down. It must have been an awful shock to you. I was fond of Smoke too, you know, and yet I can't help loving Dodie.' He patted her shoulder as though he were her mother.

Doctor Roach came in. They told him what had happened and he went into the bedroom.

Millie thought, 'I must tell Meg.'

CHAPTER VIII

Time Piece: Duchess of Wrexe's Ball

LITTLE Brun was one of those who dined with the Corleone before the Duchess of Wrexe's ball. 'Little' was indeed the word for him now, poor man. The neat, dapper, inquisitive recorder of 1900 was now in 1934, shrivelled, meagre and wan. Only his sharp little eyes and the Legion of Honour in his buttonhole had colour. What was his age now? Anything from seventy to ninety. No one cared. His own world was gone, shrivelled like himself to nothing. He detested and despised this present one. His odd weaknesses, that he loved good food, good wine, malicious gossip, were in evidence to-day as forty years ago, for he disliked and despised his hostess and should not therefore be accepting her hospitality. But he was present once more to assure himself of the end of all things and especially of England. *Not* of English Society —*that* had gone long ago—but of England herself as a power and a glory. This might once have saddened him, for he had always loved England, but he was now altogether beyond any emotion save a rather greedy bitterness. His stomach was still in good order and so he could enjoy Corleone's excellent food. But the conversation! As he sat there he thought of the great ladies of the London pre-War world—Lady Ripon, Mrs. Keppel, Lady St. Helier, Mrs. Willie James—and he blushed for this yellow-haired chattering monkey, and the world that tolerated her. Corleone, the widow of an Italian nobleman, talked much of her adopted country. She had still a palace in Venice with a Veronese, a Tintoretto, and a handsome gondolier. She screamed, she laughed, and once and again her small pale eyes had a look of frightened appeal. Some young friend of hers had written a wonderful novel about the miners in Wales.

Brun interrupted. 'You should read *Germinal*. Oh, I know no one ever *thinks* of Zola now. All the same it's a great work, terrible, dark, underground. A marvellous prophecy, too. These young men, what do they know about miners?'

But no one paid him any kind of attention. The ladies on either side of him talked across him. They were laughing at the young Duchess, whose Ball they were attending. The girl's old mother, they said, was a terror. Brun thought of *his* old Duchess all those years ago! Had she entered the room at this moment! Oh, but didn't he wish she could!

At one remove from him was sitting Larry Delaney, an amusing fellow whom he had known idly for years in London. Delaney seemed to Brun prophetic of a coming return to absolute barter—'Give me shoes; I give you shaving-cream.' Only, while the world still had a real possession or two, Delaney dealt in Louis XIV beds and Tang horses and Venetian shell-back chairs. Delaney was a common coarse fellow, but Brun liked him for his irony and good spirits. He was vulgar, greedy, selfish, but he was perceptive. His voice was raised a little now and he was talking about his brother:

'Fred? . . . Why, yes, Princess, you can see him to-night if you wish to. He'll be there *with* all the family.'

'You always speak contemptuously of your brother,'

Corleone said. '*I* think he's charming. He doesn't rob us as you do. I wish I saw him more often!'

'Rob you! No!' Larry said, laughing. He regarded his hostess with bold impudent eyes. He had no respect for her. He knew her greediness too well. 'Fred would rob nobody. He is altogether honest. Perhaps that's why we patronize him, for we all do. That and his happiness. His whole family are happy always.'

'Impossible,' said Captain Merivale Basting, a pink-faced, good-natured imbecile whom Larry despised because he insisted on his War courtesy-title. 'No one is happy always.'

'Ah,' said Corleone. 'That is his wife—the big fat blowzy woman—forgive me, Delaney—your sister-in-law —but of *course* she is happy. She is religious and does not think about diet. She talked to me at some cocktails somewhere once about Jesus Christ—as though He were in the room, I mean.'

Delaney was irritated. After all Meg *was* his sister-in-law and a damned fine woman. But he grinned friendlily, for always, one must remember, there were things to buy and sell. He had drunk good wine, however, and was impatient with the stupid women on either side of him (also he detested the rosy cheeks of the 'Captain'), so he lost some of his caution. He leaned forward, turning his smiling buccaneer face upon all of them. 'But they *are* happy, my brother's family,' he said. 'And it isn't only Freudian or a kind of clever hypocrisy either. It's quite real and comes from real causes. I'd say it's because they all four of them take long views and are devoted to one another—really love one another, you know. What I mean is that they aren't frightened by every little thing that turns up, as most people are these days. They take a long view. After all, if they do lose their money or get cancer or a war comes—well, history's a long time making!'

'It's all very well if you've plenty of money,' Miss Nancy Mohun, a girl as beautiful as she was sincere, as sincere as she was stupid, remarked.

'But they haven't,' Delaney went on. 'They have very little indeed. They take in lodgers.'

'Family love,' Corleone said. 'How appalling!'

'Yes, I know,' Delaney answered good-humouredly. 'That's why we all patronize them. I myself think them very tiresome often enough. All the same, they're the best people I know anywhere.' And so much for you, you old bitch, he thought, enjoying the *bombe surprise* and wondering whether Miss Mohun were really a virgin, as gossip sarcastically reported.

'All very old and stale,' Brun thought. 'Stale and old. Old and stale.'

The dining-room was, in the fashion of that year, entirely white: white curtains, white table and chairs, flowers made of white silk in the white vases. The women moved and their sheathed bodies, crimson, gold, silver, white, black, were like echoes from the movements of a dance that had once been fresh and exciting.

'It's all lost its spring,' Brun said, as though to himself.

Delaney answered. 'There's still a lot of fun going.'

'I suppose so. I'm very, very old. Never felt older than to-night.'

'Wait till we move on.'

'Ah, move on! I've seen some balls in my time. This one——'

'Different, of course,' Delaney said. 'Not so grand. Possibly more lively. Grand in its own way too. As I see it, this is a more real world, this new one.'

'There *is* a new one, then—not only the pale corpse of the old?'

'Why, of course.' Delaney laughed. 'Only it's rough, hazardous, cynical like all new worlds.'

'I thought new worlds were young, idealistic, full of hope.'

Delaney grinned. 'Don't you believe it. New Athens, the Renaissance in Florence, Elizabethan England, America in 1790. Fierce, vulgar, scornful.'

'I'm tired,' was all Brun said. 'I've seen so many new worlds in the last twenty years.'

They all moved on, crowding into the motors, slipping away through a flare of light, cries and voices, pools of darkness, and at last into the wide, rather pathetic emptiness of Portland Place.

There was a broad red carpet and a crowd of feminine faces, hoping that from one car at least some film star would emerge. No, but to-night there would be Royalty, so the crowd grew and grew. A sleek black cat ran, furtively, before the policeman could prevent it, across the strip of red carpet.

Brun moved up the steps into the hall. He waited for their party to assemble and, looking back through the open door, saw the London night sky pale blue and tender like a beneficence. He was very soon to die and, once again as so often before, asked himself why these moments of such perfect beauty should occur, or rather why he, nothing, the child of nothing, destined for nothing, as he so firmly believed, should have so deep a perception of beauty. There had been perhaps no period in the world's history so altogether pagan as this present one—and yet religion would undoubtedly return in one form or another. Man could not live without it—childish, brave, pathetic man. One intensely brilliant star glittered above where Broadcasting House so confidently had planted itself, and the London hush, ancient gentleness, ran like a sleepy flood about men's feet.

'There they are,' Larry Delaney's voice said at his side. 'My family, I mean'—and little Brun, for some no-reason, remembered how, in this same house, all those years ago, he had greeted Rachel Beaminster and wondered what her life would be.

Meg Delaney, radiant, excited as a child at a circus, came sailing up the steps, followed by Fred, Kitty, Bullock and little Lizzie Coventry. Through Connie Beaminster she had obtained invitations for Lizzie and the Graham Penders. The great question had been—could Lizzie be made to look old enough? But Lizzie had reassured them. Her hair had been pulled back and fell to a little roll of curls that crowned her pale thin neck and shoulders. She wore a white dress with a rather long skirt, and over her bosom a thin gold chain of coins curiously cut. This, she said, had been given her father by a lady in Dubrovnik for some service he had rendered.

She looked young, certainly, but not a child. Her face was as serious, Bullock told her, as though she were going to be married.

Larry introduced them all to Brun. Brun looked at Meg with curiosity. So this was the happy blowzy lady who was so frankly a Christian! She was certainly not blowzy to-night. She carried herself magnificently. In her black hair was a small tiara of diamonds. Her dress, he thought, was of a rich deep purple with a short train. She reminded him, yes, more than anyone he had seen for a long time, of the ladies of his youth. Not that she was old-fashioned; her gaze was clear, unhypocritical, courageous. Her large dark eyes sparkled with the anticipation of pleasure.

'I came as a child here once,' she told him, 'with my father to tea with the old Duchess—and wasn't I frightened! I'll never forget that old woman sitting by the fire at the end of the long drawing-room, and we had to walk all that long way. I thought my drawers were coming down. There was a big grey Persian cat, I remember, and little marzipan cakes.'

Little Brun asked her about her father. He had known him well. 'This is the child of that old scoundrel,' he thought.

'And poor Rachel Breton. Of course she was years older than me. But how I used to admire her! It was her Russian blood, I suppose, made her seem so romantic. Ah, dear me—I was dreadfully sentimental then—am still for that matter!'

As usual Meg had been standing there talking in people's way when they should have been moving like sheep and goats, men one way, women another. Kitty felt one of those momentary impulses of wishing her mother were different, *more* conscious of what other people were doing.

'Come along, Mother. We're holding everything up.'

'Are we, dear? . . . Well, Mr. Brun, we'll be having a talk later, won't we? Where are we all? Lizzie, come with me, dear.'

Two minutes later they all met again and began, with so many others, to climb the great stairs.

The young Duchess knew well enough what everyone was thinking. She had not been married long enough to make many friends. In her own country town there had always been a plentiful supply of cats and monkeys. After all London was only a larger town. In any case she could not be unhappy nor alarmed because her husband, who loved her so much, was standing beside her and seeing her through everything. Looking down the staircase at the figures pressing up towards her, the men magnificent with their orders, the women as beautiful as once, in Cherry Minton, her small town, she had imagined that in fairyland they would be, it had the quality of dream, of nowhereness, of perception and touch and hearing being all at the mercy of the stroke from a clock as Cinderella once found it. . . . She was shaking hands with the Prime

Minister, who was exactly like the Cherry Minton doctor, and, in spite of the decorations and evening clothes he was wearing, there was surely a pipe in his mouth and the clothes covering his sturdy body were of the rather faded pepper-and-salt that old Doctor Warnsley never varied for twenty years. Looking into one of the kindest, most trustworthy faces in the world, she grinned, just as once she had done when Doctor Warnsley asked her to put out her tongue.

'Balls in general,' Mr. Baldwin said to her, 'are a weariness of the flesh to me. But not this one. . . . How are you, Wrexe?'

Mrs. Baldwin gave her a very motherly look, taking everything in and deciding immediately what to do about it.

People are saying, the Duchess thought to herself: 'She's not bad-looking. Holds herself quite well. Must seem funny to her after the life she's led.'

She remembered how her husband, kissing her in his dressing-room that evening, had said to her: 'One day we'll go to Cettinje. That Dalmatian coast's lovely. In Cettinje there's the old Montenegrin palace, shown to tourists, ten dinars a time. Most melancholy place you ever saw—hideous furniture, and hundreds and hundreds of family photos, Victoria's family—all of them, German, Italian, Greek, Russian, Montenegrin. Lots of the too poor Russians. All so grand, in groups, in every kind of uniform, the ladies in immense hats—all so grand, so commanding, so powerful. Now all dead—many of them murdered. None of them mattering a damn. There are some nice people in London you'll make friends with. We'll laugh at the others—together.'

But she didn't feel inclined to laugh as she saw them coming up the staircase. She felt a great tenderness—but then she was very young and, as yet, not at all cynical.

Meg, with her husband, sailed into the grand ballroom like the queen of some gipsy kingdom that despised its neighbour, Ruritania, for insipidity. She would indeed have made the late lamented Flavia look like one of those white silk flowers in Corleone's dining-room. Meg sometimes read books by very clever men who poured contempt upon parties. This she always thought *must* be a pose. For who could but adore parties? And a ball like this one? She was ageing. Her vitality would go, her zest, her sense of fun. This might be her last great ball. So—she would savour every slightest tang of it! But, more than this, she was in her own absolute world. Were Fred, poor dear, a millionaire, instead of penniless, she—Meg—could give a ball that would astonish London. And yet there was something here that the house itself, so triumphantly aware of its own past history, gave, something that no one could imitate. It was not the portraits of dead Beaminsters—Lely and Van Dyck and Reynolds and Gainsborough—gazing perhaps rather apprehensively from the walls—apprehensive because ancestors to-day were worth nothing except for the prices they might fetch at Christie's—nor the superb crystal chandeliers, nor the splendid Adam fireplace—possessions, however beautiful, do not give England and London their quality—but rather the certainty, arrogance, defiance of time, that the building and the human beings moving with it asserted.

All sailed along together. The quality that made Englishmen so rightly hated, but that should also have made them trusted—the simple, childlike certainty of permanent survival and unchallenged superiority. Was that great quality to end now? Was England's contribution to the little adventures of this pigmy star concluded? Meg at least did not think so, for to her it was like coming home to a family gathering after a long exile. Whatever form the future world might take, there would still surely somewhere be this English calm, this English arrogance of common sense. She and Fred and Kitty knew everyone, and danced, laughed, chattered almost, as Larry ironically observed, as though it were a Delaney party. Bullock never left Lizzie's side. But there was one thing that didn't occur to Larry, something that, behind the scene, never left the Delaney consciousness for a moment—Smoke Pullet's suicide.

We are all aware of those events that bring us quite suddenly into a new reality, a world of experience that makes our everyday world as thin as a Japanese wall. Before the new experience we alter our scale of values and climb into a fresh comprehension of existence. For the moment only. The force of the event slackens. It is not, unless there is a world catastrophe, repeated. It thins to the shadow of a skeleton on the ceiling. But we are changed.

Smoke's death had so affected the Delaneys. For Meg at least it was something towards which she had for a long time been moving. There had always been something 'fatal' about Smoke, and with that ill-omen of his personality the house too had been stained. She believed, being simple and old-fashioned, very definitely in the powers of evil, and in fact welcomed the conviction that life was a battle. She had been sure, ever since that New Year's Day when her brother-in-law and Alice Van Renn had appeared in the doorway, that this year 1934 would be 'the very devil of a battle'—for herself, for Fred, for the house. Through the spring she had been preparing to meet it; now, with Smoke's pistol-shot, the fight was really engaged. She was sensible. She did not feel it a great tragedy either for Smoke or Dodie. But she had liked him, been deeply sorry for him. His death had thrown an atmosphere of ill-omen over the house, the flat was empty, she fancied that people looked at herself and Fred as though they might have prevented it—and there was, she was certain, worse to come.

So that, perversely, she intended to enjoy this ball with all her might. Who knew but that, within a month or two, she and Fred might be out on the street? 'Who knows but the world may end to-night?'

She was sorry for poor Smoke, for Dodie, for Patrick Munden, for all and everybody, but life was larger and longer than personal misfortune, and God meant you to enjoy the delightful things as they turned up. This was one of the delightful things.

She had a word with Royalty and talked and danced with all sorts. In spite of her weight and size she danced beautifully and with so great a spirit of enjoyment that it was a delight to watch her. Young Rawdon Temple languidly commended her: 'You know, Mrs. Delaney, you look as though you hadn't a trouble in the world.'

'Do I? That's odd—because I have a number.'

Temple was a tall, very thin young man, in the best society because he had married a scion of the house of Wintersmoon, but famous in certain circles too because he wrote the longest possible poems on the tiniest possible objects. There was his epic, 'The Snail's Journey,' and a vast unfinished poem, 'The Flea's Chronicle.' He took himself as Munden took himself, very seriously, but they represented two opposed worlds. Meanwhile, perhaps because he wrote so much, he spoke as little as possible, and when he did speak it was with the air of despatching from Heaven a few grains of manna upon the starving Israelites. Meg found him exquisitely absurd.

'How's your poem about the frog getting on, Mr. Temple?' she asked him. He looked at her, but there was no mockery in her innocent gaze. So she was just a fool.

'Very well,' he answered her kindly.

Her next partner gave her one of the real shocks of her life. This was Colonel Robert Beaminster, first cousin of the present Duke, a handsome kindly man, some forty years of age, more than a distinguished soldier because he was interested in the arts and had a little house, filled with beautiful things, in Wiltshire near Wintersmoon. When they had danced a little while he said: 'Mrs. Delaney, do you think Fred and yourself would object if I asked Kitty to marry me?'

'Kitty!' Meg stopped where she was. He gently urged her on again.

'Yes—why not?'

'But you scarcely know her!'

'Oh, but I do. I've met her numbers of times, especially lately. Of course I'm old. I know that. Nearly twenty years too old. I've been in love before, of course, but never like this. I fancy myself young for my years. I——'

'But has *she* any idea?'

'Not the slightest. We're friends though, I think. I've money enough and, so far as I know, no ruinous habits. I'm not terribly set in my ways although I've been a bachelor so long. I'm old enough to be sure. I love her body and soul, as they used to say in the old romances.'

Meg smiled, a divine, maternal infantile smile. Oh! if Kitty could or would! It would be the loveliest, most perfect thing! Of course he *was* older, but Kitty was mature, not one of these chicken-headed, idiotic girl-babies.

'Object? No, of course not. But it's absolutely for Kitty to say.'

'Yes, of course.'

Meg stopped.

'Wait a minute. I can't dance any more. Let's sit here.' They sat down.

'Since when have you thought of this?'

'Oh, for some time. I loved her at sight, I think—about a year ago. Do you . . . does she like me, do you think?'

'I can't tell, of course. To be quite honest, she's never mentioned you to me.'

'No—she'll have to get used to the idea. I don't mind how long I wait.' He jumped up. 'As a matter of fact, since you say it's all right I'm going to ask her now. She said that the next dance should be mine.'

Kitty was approaching them. Beaminster said to her: 'Do you mind if we don't dance this, Kitty?'

'No, of course not. I've been dancing a lot. Are you all right, Mother?'

'Perfectly all right, darling.'

Beaminster led her off. He took her out of the ball-room, up some stairs, into a little quiet room that contained only one picture. Beaminster closed the door and they sat down. The music came to them faintly like the refrain of a river.

'Look at that,' Beaminster said. 'It's my favourite picture in the house. It's by Tintoretto and is a study for the big Manna picture in Venice.'

'Yes. It's beautiful,' said Kitty.

'I should think it is. Look at those blues and silvers and the deep red of that woman's dress. And see how active everyone is. In Tintoretto's pictures everyone is doing something urgently. That woman bending down to pick up the manna, holding the baby by one hand. . . . The interesting thing is that El Greco came to Italy as a very young man and was greatly influenced by Tintoretto. You can see it—the long extended bodies, the opulence of some of the figures, a sense of light and thunder, the dramatic intensity . . .'

He suddenly took her hand.

'Kitty, I want you to marry me.'

She sat there staring in front of her. Then she turned and looked at him incredulously.

His hand trembled on hers.

'Yes. Don't be surprised. Although of course you must be. Think it over. Get used to it.' Then, holding her hand more tightly, he went on urgently. 'It's a new idea to you, but I think I fell in love with you a year ago. The very first meeting. There was a kind of quiet happiness about you. . . . I've been in love before, but never like this. I was engaged once, but we both found it wouldn't do, and so this time I've waited a year. Of course I'm forty. You may think that makes it impossible. But it doesn't. I'm very strong, perfectly healthy. Our children would be thirty or more before I'd be anything like an old man.' His voice trembled.

She was incredibly touched when she saw that his eyes were full of tears. She looked at him gravely as though she wanted him to realize how greatly she felt honoured. But she shook her head.

'How kind you are and good! I like you so much. But it's impossible, I'm afraid—and must always be.'

'I expected you to say that. I knew you must. You must think it over. See me a little. Get to know me. I don't mind how long I wait.'

It had never remotely approached her—the idea that he loved her. He had been only one of a number of nice men she knew in London. Thrice before men had asked her to marry them, but on each occasion she had known that the proposal was coming.

But the queerest thing of all, she thought, as she stared at the woman in the red dress bending down to pick up the manna, is that, six months ago, I might have accepted him. He is charming. I might have grown to love him. Mother and father would be delighted. Everything is right about it except possibly his age, but I had always, until lately, liked men older than he is. And now what prevents me? It could not be a young man in a curiosity shop, nor that shop itself (the strange name Zanti going on through the years—Spain, Cornwall, London, although of course she knew nothing of this) nor a picture in a shop window, nor a wall beautifully decorated, nor the crude paintings of a man laughing up at her from his

couch—none of these things, all of these things . . .
simply a new world of which she was now citizen, a
world to which Robert Beaminster could never, never
belong.

He went on: 'I don't want to pay compliments, but
you are different from anyone I've ever known. Life is
such a mix-up, isn't it? The kind of confusion that Shakespeare and Keats felt. So much nastiness—our bodies,
our thoughts, our mean shabby acts. I don't understand
any of it. Who does? The moment I saw you I felt that
there was *no* confusion—you were someone to live by.
You moved so quietly and honestly——'

She broke in: 'Please! You're altogether wrong about
me. I'm terribly ordinary—not even *half* educated. I'm
nothing yet at all—I've got everything to do, to learn.'

'We'd learn together.'

She shook her head again.

'No. I want you to realize *why* it's impossible. Six
months ago I had no idea of anything. I had my home
and my friends. I went about like any other un-ideaed girl.
I'd read nothing, seen nothing, thought nothing. Then little things happened, apparently unconnected. I met someone, I saw a picture somewhere . . .' She smiled at the question in his eyes. 'No. I'm not in love. Or I think not. But
I do realize now, as I didn't a little time ago, that there's
a world of experience waiting for me that I must accept.
If I don't I miss everything. I suppose that's true of everyone—only perhaps I shall never see it so clearly again.
Things cloud over, I expect, as one gets older.'

'And I'm not in that world of experience? I could
never be?'

'So it seems to me now.'

He took his hand from hers and got up. He stood,
looking down at her with a gaze of great wisdom and
tenderness.

'I know what you mean. You've been very honest with

me—only—as you go on, this world may merge into another. That's what happens. I'll wait.'

'You know,' she said, half between laughter and tears, 'in old novels they always said: "But we can be friends, can't we?" I mean that I want a good friend very badly.'

He gave her his hand and pulled her to her feet.

'Friends always. There's nothing I won't do.'

They went out and down the stairs. At the end of the ballroom she found her uncle Larry. Beaminster left them together.

'Let's sit down here and watch everybody,' Larry said. 'He's been showing you the Tintoretto. I don't think it's genuine. Probably by a pupil. Lots of his big pictures are only partly by himself. He worked at such a pace. "Last Suppers," you know, for Venetian churches at extravagant prices. Old Beaminster's a good sort but an awful sentimentalist. Wonder why he's never married.'

Kitty liked her uncle but didn't, at that moment, wish him to throw his cynical regard on either Tintoretto or Robert Beaminster. She wanted him to talk, so that, under the protection of it, she might recover her own proper self-control. It had been her self-discovery, not Beaminster's proposal, that had excited her so strangely. She *was* moving into a new world. What *hadn't* life now to offer her? It was as though she were seeing things with a double vision—intensified realization and intensified imagination both together.

'Now—tell me things about people.'

The Three Witches were quite close to them: Mrs. Van Renn, Mrs. Bathorne, Lady Perivale-Hawder. They were sitting on a little gilt sofa, their heads close together as though they were muttering spells. The great room now, under a haze of soft light, magically formed the colours, the decorations of the men, the dark-light intermingling of rose and black, white and silver and malachite, into a ballet symmetry moving, it seemed, to some inevitable climax. Larry went on talking.

'It's perhaps the *last* great London ball. No, of course it *isn't,* but one has a kind of Brussels-before-Waterloo feeling, hasn't one? England's being so fine and noble. She doesn't want *anything* from *anybody.* Why *will* other countries be so selfish and grasping? Well, of course, she doesn't because she's *got* everything. For years and years she's had the world in her pocket. But the world's in her pocket no longer. Everyone thinks now they'll have a little bit of what England's got. How's she going to deal with it? Give up a bit here and a bit there or try to keep the lot? Don't you think the bright young things of the 'Twenties look a bit silly now we're in the 'Thirties? There's Bertie Colton still thinking he's a bright young thing. He gave a grand party last week in the country and everyone had to come as a vegetable. Nancy Eldon he's dancing with, went as a cauliflower and was a huge success. There's young Brinsley—he's run through twenty thousand in five years. Funny thing is he's a very nice chap. Who's that elderly elegant your mother's dancing with?'

'That's Sir Graham Pender,' Kitty said.

'Never heard of him.'

'No. He was a flame of mother's when they were young. He's been abroad all his life.'

'They've stopped. They are coming towards us. Who's the missionary female they're talking to?'

'That's Lady Pender, Sir Graham's wife.'

'Meg looks as though she's up to some mischief. I know that look.'

Some young man was approaching Kitty with a proprietary air. Larry got up.

'I must be moving. I've some business to do—to persuade Lucile Mounsey to sell those tapestries of hers.'

Kitty agreed to have the next dance with the elegant young man who, looking at her with appreciation, said:

'Thought I'd only look in for a moment. Never stay at a dance long, you know. Have something to drink and then move on. But this is a bit different, don't you think? Glamour and all that sort of thing.'

Kitty suddenly thought of Smoke Pullet. Why? She saw him as at the last time she had spoken to him—Smoke coming down the stairs of the Charles Street house.

'How are you, Smoke?' she had asked him gaily.

He had smiled, his charming, lonely, friendly smile.

'You know what, Kitty,' he had said. 'For the first time in my life I've got a job I like.'

She was delighted. 'Oh, I'm *so* glad, Smoke. That's grand.'

He had paused at the door.

'It's not a job anyone else would like much, though,' he had said and went out into the street. Next day he had killed himself.

But Smoke's death, after she had recovered from the first shock, hadn't saddened her. That was strange because she had been fond of him. Her own death—if she knew, for certain, that within three hours from now she would be dead—would neither sadden nor frighten her. She knew, as she moved off with the elegant young man, that she was too profoundly sure at this moment of her vitality for death to be anything but the ghost of an event. *Real* events had quite another shape and form.

'Quite a decent band, don't you think?' the young man said.

It would be absurd to pretend that Meg Delaney had not often in life acted foolishly. She knew very well her own danger-point. Her recklessness was roused always by something that her father's blood gave her. 'If I don't have this piece of fun now I may never have it.' Life was for her at times translated into a kind of fairy-tale, she was the fairy princess hitherto disguised as a beggar maid, and the fairy prince had just asked her to marry him. Would she not be an idiot indeed if she did not accept? So it had been when at the age of fifteen she had run away from Cannes and spent the night quite innocently with the young son of the Bishop of Dorlinton. So it had been when, aged twenty or so, after dinner at Madame de Florac's, she had gambled all her jewels, her dog Gisel and her maid Eva away to Mrs. La Tone. So it had been when, after Graham Pender had gone to China and she was feeling very lonely, she had engaged herself to an acrobat at the Tivoli music-hall, resisted his attempts on her virtue, and was only saved by his arrest on the Saturday evening for the attempted knifing of another acrobat.

To-night she quite suddenly threw all her bonnets over all the windmills. She said to Graham Pender, as they were finishing their dance:

'Yes, Graham, I will. . . . I will come for a weekend somewhere. It's wrong. It's wicked. We are both too old for it to be anything but ludicrous. And yet it isn't. . . . I shall tell Fred afterwards.'

She was looking lovely and incredibly young. It was her colour that was so perfect, the colour still of a girl, the darkness of her hair lit by the diamonds, her carriage superb.

He only said, 'I'm in luck to-night, Meg—the happiest of my life,' left her with a little bow, and they did not meet again that evening.

She had immediately afterwards the strangest conversation with Lady Pender, a conversation that should have shamed her dreadfully, but, as this is a truthful story, it has to be confessed that it did not. She had detested all her life to hurt or distress anybody. In all her escapades it had only been herself that she had ever harmed. She was now contemplating something cruel and unkind, but

her recklessness, caused partly by Smoke's death, partly
by a desperate sense that she was in for trouble anyhow,
partly by the force and maternal tenderness of her feeling for Graham, partly by the excitement of this night
and the sense that there was intrigue going on everywhere up and down, in and out of this Ball, and partly
by her old child-persisting complex of loving to climb a
dangerous tree because some other child had dared her
to do it, her recklessness made the world about her seem
iridescent, a little drunken, a little mad, a great deal
doomed: 'Who knows but the world may end to-night?'

And so, because she was intending to do Evelyn Pender
the greatest hurt in the world, Meg felt towards her a
kindness, beneficence, generosity, that was altogether a
new element in her relation to the Penders.

They sat down together and watched the scene. Really,
how queer a creature was Evelyn Pender! Was there no
one to tell her *anything* about clothes? What had induced
her to wear that queer green turban-like thing on her
head, that Venetian coral necklace? Too much make-up
was bad, but how powerfully a little rouge and powder
rightly applied would help that tight pale mouth and
those bony cheeks?

Meg said: 'It's a lovely ball, isn't it?'

Evelyn Pender looked straight in front of her, her
long, stiff, slightly freckled hands clasped together on her
lap.

'You know,' she unexpectedly said, 'it's you that ought
to have married Graham, not I. Why didn't you?'

'He went away and left me,' Meg said, laughing.

'Are you sorry now?'

'Lord, no! I wouldn't be married to anyone but Fred
in the world.'

'You love him very much?'

'I adore him.'

'Then,' Evelyn Pender said, turning round and fixing

her with her grey eyes, 'he doesn't mind your flirting with Graham?'

'Do *you* mind?' Meg asked her.

'I don't know. I can see that it's perfectly natural. Graham's terribly in love with you. I do hope you won't make him unhappy.'

Meg nodded her head. 'We mustn't be unhappy, any of us. We needn't be if we're sensible. I love my husband first, last and all the time. No one counts for me beside him. Graham knows that. Do you hate me, Evelyn? Am I making you unhappy?'

Lady Pender was a long time answering.

'No. As long as Graham is happy. He was never in love with me, but he has come to rely on me, to like to have me there—and I think that, plain and unattractive as I am, I'm lucky to have been given a man as attractive as Graham to feel like that about me. I've always thought that some other woman would turn up. No one has until now, and it may be it's as well that it's someone who *has* other ties as strong as yours are. I don't trust you, but somehow I'm not afraid of you. I rather like you. I can't help it. But don't make him unhappy. Don't go a long way with Graham and then drop him.'

'I don't trust myself,' Meg said. 'I never have. But I promise you that if things get difficult I'll come and ask your help and advice. And I won't hurt Graham—I promise that too.'

Then Evelyn Pender looked quite sentimental. But it wasn't Meg that caused it.

'There's only one thing I'd like to-night,' she said. 'And that is to look at Mr. Baldwin. I do admire him so. Do you think, if he's still here, we could . . . ?'

'We'll go and find him,' Meg said.

This night was a great stage in her development for Lizzie Coventry. It was, for one thing, by far the happiest moment of her life until now. For a brief while she threw off entirely her distrust of man, and when later, as was inevitable, she resumed it, it was not quite the same distrust. There was a rent in the nasty fabric. It was wonderful to her that these Delaneys had taken her to this great ball. They were not, then, ashamed of her! —for she bore always around with her, night and day, bore it with proud defiance, this sense of shame. There was no indecency, meanness, cruelty of which she was not aware, and it seemed to her that all the world must know that *she* knew! Moreover, with the exception of her aunt and the family in Westminster, Lizzie had never known anyone whose word she could believe, who would not desert her, betray her, instantly forget her. It seemed to her the rule of life. And now once more, in these Delaneys, she had encountered a family who seemed to mean well by her. They were quite different from her relations in Westminster—much more gay, adventurous, of altogether bolder colours, but now, by taking this trouble about her, by dressing her up to look older and then publicly before all the world presenting her at one of the most famous of London balls as their friend, they had done her honour. Her gratitude was warm, moving, stirring about her heart, although outwardly her small pale face, resolutely set, gave no sign of emotion.

But, most of all, she was grateful to Bullock. She was not sure, as she looked at his sturdy little body and round kindly face, whether her liking were not changing to something warmer. He reminded her of St. George in the Bellini picture (how awful had been that year in Venice when Mrs. Egret had made that shocking scene with her father in that old yellow-walled palace, accusing him of stealing her diamond bracelet, and how they had hurried afterwards in that gondola to the station, panting, perspiring on that dreadful August afternoon!), his fidelity and modesty and rock-of-Gibraltar reliability! And then he had talent: Lizzie was sure that soon he would write a very good book indeed.

But how strange the contrast! Lizzie as she danced with Bullock thought of that moment this evening in the rooms before she left, when her father, in his pyjamas (for he had been sleeping all day), smelling still of drink, his eyes half closed, had pinched her ear and said: 'Darling—any of your grand friends—handsome young men with fortunes—bring them along here—introduce them to your old dad. They'll be welcome.' And now, in this splendid room, the women so beautiful, the men so fine, the snarling rhythm of the band, the great portraits on the wall, above all the young Duchess who, although she had not known Lizzie in the least, had given her so sweet and, as it seemed, so personal a smile. Oh, this was another world, a world that she had never known before, but from which, it seemed, she was not absolutely excluded!

'Are you happy?' Bullock asked her, as they moved quite perfectly together. 'There's Winston Churchill.'

'And there,' said Lizzie, 'is that old man we met in the Museum.'

And so he was. When the music stopped they stayed quite close to him and he recognized them instantly. Old Lord Ragadoon looked quite as eccentric as he had done at the National Gallery, but it was to-night a kind of aristocratic eccentricity. Why he looked such a swell it would be hard to say. It was not the Orders that he wore nor the old shapeless evening clothes, nor the shaggy untidy beard; and he stood bending forward with no fine presence. It was his eyes, perhaps, which had the piercing fiery look of a proud, contemptuous but exulting eagle. Yes, it was his eyes, Lizzie concluded, and his bony hands and the iron-ribbed neck above the reluctant collar.

'So you're here, are you? Very pleasant. Dancing fun?'

'Yes, sir. Great fun,' said Bullock.

'I was a good dancer in my day and women were hand-some then. Something to put your arm round—not these scraggy leg-of-mutton creatures!'

Then abruptly, staring at Bullock under his shaggy brows, he said:

'Why don't you come to see me? I gave you my address, didn't I? Thirty Pelham Street—up three flight of stairs —no lift. Any afternoon after four.'

He patted Lizzie on the shoulder.

'You've grown up since I saw you. Suits you.'

Then he shuffled away.

'You see,' Bullock said to her. 'You've grown up. He said so.'

She put her hand through his arm and walked with him proudly. Yes, he was like the Bellini St. George. Or, perhaps, St. George's son. She was beginning to be, quite fiercely, proud of him.

There comes a moment in every function, great or small, when the question that has been asked all the eve-ning is answered: 'Is this thing a success?' It is just then that for the wife of the Vicar of Portcullis, or the Bishop of Polchester, or the Hon. Stephen Herries, M.P. for Rasselas, or His Grace the Duke of Wrexe, the evening's fate is settled—at the moment when the coffee comes in ('I told you that girl would make a hopeless servant'), when the Beethoven Sonata is ended. 'Everything went wrong from the first. Cook has always made that fish soufflé perfectly before.' But it wasn't so. The thing was still in the balance. One really funny story from the Vicar and all might have been well. '*In spite* of the fish it all went very well, I think.'

It was, at a certain moment, for Fred Delaney, as though fireworks had exploded through the great win-dows into the hearts of the dancers, changing them, with whirling colours of blue and crimson—stars and rockets and Catherine-wheels—into the Italian Harlequinade of Longhi, Pantaloon and Harlequin—or moving from that towards a huge Veronese canvas, a superb decoration without heart, the noble Duke in green splendour raising his arm while the Fool plays in his corner, the cat is under the table, and up the stairs climb the servants holding the golden goblets and the peacock on its lordly dish. So it was decoration now spread against the wall of the night sky, fronting the dark battlements of the sleeping city. The Ball was the success of the year. That bunch of idle young men, passing derisively from ball to ball, the terror of the indignant hostess, they had all stayed. Royalty itself had stayed to an astonishingly late hour, and there, in the little room papered with the old maps of the counties of England, Fred Delaney had held Alice Van Renn in his arms and at last, at last, had kissed her again and again, had heard her say:

'Yes. Why not? I'll come with you somewhere sometime.'

It was settled then. The conquest was made. When he had taken her back and left her to one of her admirers, he vanished (to be for a moment alone) up the stairs again and found himself, without intention, in the room with the Tintoretto painting. 'Damned fine painting,' he thought. (He was still breathing fiercely, the palms of his hands were hot, his heart was racing.) 'Wonder who it's by? What's its subject?' He bent (although his mind was so absolutely elsewhere) forward to see the name on the little gilt plate—'Tintoretto. Ah, yes, the "Bacchus and Ariadne" man.' Then he saw, lying almost at his feet, a woman's handkerchief. He picked it up. It made him think of Meg. Beloved, adorable Meg! And he was intending once again to be physically unfaithful to her! Perhaps for the last time. Physically only. He turned towards the door, stopped as though hit in the chest by the vision of the lovely Alice, so quiet, so well-disciplined, so sensuous. And he would not hurt Meg for the world. Oh, not for all the world and all the women in it! But this little pleasure he must have, and then—'who knows but the world may end to-night?'

The little handkerchief was crushed in his hand. Was it from that small square of lace there came to him the thought: And if Meg were unfaithful to you—only, you know, physically? A little joy for her before she settles, as you too are going to do, into a faithful domestic tranquillity? Would you mind? Would you care? Oh, but Meg—she *could* not! Meg unfaithful! But *why* not? She's still a fine woman with passions, desires, a longing, as all women have, for the unknown? No *real* infidelity, Fred Delaney. No more real than yours will be. Different for the woman . . . but in these wise tolerant days haven't we exploded that nonsense? Are not women doing everything that men can do? Why not this freedom as well? But then Meg is religious. She believes in God. Yes, but is she not gipsy as well, has she not her father's blood in her? Lightly he ran down the little staircase again. He stood at the corner of the passage whence, from a small balcony, he could see down on to the ball-room.

Oh, but he was happy! Life was fine! There was a doom hanging over them all. Smoke's shadow was at his elbow. The great ceiling of the ballroom split and the sky with a myriad of stars shone through. Under this brilliant fire the Town shrank, as the little handkerchief was shrunken in his hand, into a crumpled heap. The machines roared across the sky. Flame tore the cupped canopy and a great cry arose. Then there was silence and over the ruined plain the waters slowly climbed, reflecting the stars in their whirling torrent. He shook himself. The torrent was the band. A trumpet cried and the dance stopped.

His shoulder was touched and he found that Larry was at his side.

'I've been having a drink.'

Fred grinned. 'Come on. The night is young. I'm dancing this next one with my lovely daughter.'

Passing through the ante-room they saw in a gilt and velvet chair a little old man fast asleep.

'Who the devil's that?' Fred asked.

Larry looked.

'It's poor little Brun. You met him. He was dining with me at Corleone's. A little old Frenchman—rather a swell once—in his day.'

They went on into the ballroom.

PART III

The Green Park

CHAPTER I

We Meet Because We Must

As the light-years run at this present instant the river breaks through the Green Park and the blue-painted citizens are hunting the slimy eel-snake in its marshes, the countryfolk are chasing the wild boar in its woods, the citizens of Westminster are picnicking in its glades, and Claude Willoughby is taking the air and listening to the band and arranging in his head the disposal of his treasures after his death.

At this, our 1934 conviction of time, the Green Park is dusty, for it is the first week in September and we are blind to the marshes, the river, and the pleasant country dances. Behind Claude, out of his view, but present to his consciousness, are the Devonshire Gates, and early this morning the cheery, plump bachelor with the front windows of a 90 Piccadilly flat, awake and thirsty, has moved into the sitting-room, drawn back his curtains, and seen, under a trembling grey sky, the old man wrapped entirely in newspapers asleep under the gates, and on the bench three derelicts huddled together for comfort until the policeman arrives to move them on. The old boy, in his silk pyjamas, gives himself a whisky and soda, watches the light stir behind the thin skeleton of grey, salutes Westminster tower, the Victoria Memorial, glances down the sleepy nakedness of Piccadilly, and toddles back to his sheets. Five o'clock strikes from Westminster. For the Green Park is democratic if it is anything. The splendid avenue of trees from the Gates to the Memorial could be a Triumphal Way for armies, but in actual truth it is a pathway of liberations—liberations for clerks, shopkeepers, lovers, athletes, and, most especially, the dogs of Mayfair. These last pass, all day, across the dangerous rushing waters of Piccadilly traffic, straining at their leashes, cockers and airedales, dachshunds and fox-terriers, one purple-tongued chow who walks by himself, scornfully picking his way through the dangers, and one cat on a silken string, its mistress also cat-like. On the dusty surface of the grass the dogs break into ecstasy, the children throw balls and kites into the air, the weary cast themselves on to their backs and stomachs, the lovers press close together, and the grimy sheep play sulkily at a directed Arcadia.

All London presses in upon these trees and this grass. It is, if you like, the very centre of the world, and the spokes of the wheel radiate out to the green icy silences of the Poles, the dusty mysteries of Tibet, and Lenin mummified in Moscow. But this centre of the world is also the backyard of the universe. Nothing is real here but the trivialities of the meanest human, and out of these trivialities the great works of art must come—a lovers' quarrel, a worker's dream of idleness, a dog's realization of ecstatic joy, a child's wondering contemplation of a cloud sailing into a tree. When, with a bang rather than a whimper, the life of this star is ended, those cries, murmurs, petitions, ecstasies, slumbers, are not ended with it, but are immortal because everything created is immortal—even, it is to be feared, the Victoria Memorial.

So now Claude Willoughby, nodding his head to the school-girl lushness of *Madame Butterfly*, is immortal, and his present discontents are no more, in his unending

history, than the drifting of the dusty air into the band-
conductor's nostrils. *Butterfly* is completed. The band-
conductor blows his nose, and Claude thinks to himself:
'Very pleasant. Very pleasant indeed. I do like something
with a tune in it.'

He is looking pale and worn, for throughout a breathless August he has been under Brocket's eye, sleeping very
little, eating very little, the rumble of Time's chariot in
his ear ever more loudly.

It is better, however, in the summer in many ways.
You need not shiver over a sulky grumbling fire, you can
sit outside on Park benches, and watch the fountains play
in Trafalgar Square, and see the evening sun slant with
loving fingers across the faces of the Charles Street
houses.

For Claude has been very much in Charles Street of
late, walking up and down, looking up at the windows—
for who knows? At any moment he may see the pleasant
faces of that nice girl and that nice boy, and so life become
at that instant the safer. But, strangely enough, he never
has. Nevertheless Charles Street seems the safest place.
Almost everywhere else is dangerous and his own room
the most dangerous of all. He would have left it all long
ago, but now he is three weeks behind with the quarter's
rent—and doesn't Brocket know it? Brocket comes even
more often to his room. He never dreams of knocking
now. He stands there, his stomach heaving, the hairs
crawling on his arms, not saying anything until at last
quietly he murmurs:

'If you can't pay your rent soon you'll have to sell
those things of yours, you know.'

Those things! Sell those things! That would be indeed
the end of Claude's life. Not that *that* would matter
much, but it would be the end also of the Things! They
would be sold, would be broken and ill-treated and soiled.

Whereas at his death, if only he could satisfy his landlord first, there his Things would be on a table for his friends to choose, and each friend would come (Claude had long ago made out a list including, I fear, some *very* slender acquaintances), regard the Things tenderly, and, for years after, someone would be saying somewhere: 'Look out! Don't touch that cup and saucer. That belonged to poor old Willoughby.' It had indeed become an obsession with him, this dispersal of his things! He hugged his secret. He had told nobody save only, one day, little Best —wanting, I'm afraid, to impress him. And Best had guffawed and chattered and had been, after all, perhaps awed a bit.

'Not going to kick the bucket yet, old boy?' he had cried.

'Oh no,' said Claude feebly. 'Oh, dear me, no'—although at times he felt very like 'kicking the bucket'—very like indeed.

There was no harm in Best; nevertheless Claude wished that he had not told him. He had sworn Best to secrecy, of course, and Best had cried: 'Cross my heart, old boy—never tell a soul!'—and then Best had added: 'Those things—has anyone ever found them?'

'What things?' asked Claude.

'Why—the things that were stolen.'

'I've heard nothing about them.'

'No. Of course not. Of course not.'

But Brocket thought that Claude had taken them—the bath salts, the walking-stick, the library books. Brocket, standing in the doorway, would say one morning:

'See that in the paper? Feller got six months for stealing a cake of soap. Quite a gentleman too. Been at a public school, the paper said.'

And with every day Brocket seemed to come physically nearer. With every day the catastrophe hanging over the world, the catastrophe prophesied by that terrible little man at the evening party, seemed to come nearer. The ground did indeed now tremble under Claude's feet. He had no one to whom he could speak of it. Even the Pake ladies were now cut off from him, for Helen Pake was dying: at any moment now she might be gone. The fact was that Claude was starving. He no longer had breakfast in his room, for he had not money to pay for it. One meal a day at the little coffee-house in the Market. Old men of course do not need very much to eat, nor do they need much sleep. Nevertheless . . . nevertheless . . .

He had, however, an unconquerable cheerfulness, and this free, gay splendour of the band delighted him. Music was almost as good as a meal, and while he listened the ground seemed to steady itself and this green-golden hazy soil of the Park was firm beneath him. The people, too, seated in their chairs, standing when they could not afford the chairs, seemed happy and unafraid. He was reassured in their company. It was as though they whispered to him that no ill should come to him while he was in this company. He looked at them one by one, and—suddenly, miraculously—close, near to him was the lovely Miss Delaney with a large handsome woman, undoubtedly Mrs. Delaney herself.

Yes, it was truly Meg standing there, her hand lightly on Kitty's arm. They had come to take the air and keep up their spirits by listening to the band. For the Charles Street house was very silent: Patrick Munden's flat was empty, the Pullet flat was empty, Helen Pake was dying. Things were nearly as bad as they could be. The battle for the life of the house was in fact at its height, and only that morning Frank Frobisher, head pontiff of Gay and Tallent's, had been shut up with Fred for more than two hours offering him money so that the Charles Street house might be pulled down.

'You can't, my dear boy, stick to it,' Frobisher had been saying. 'You were lucky to have the place filled so long. It has after all been only a makeshift. Have you *seen* these modern flats? Every possible contrivance. Why, you haven't even central heating. And by the way no one else is going to offer you half the price we're suggesting. Even if you refuse you're safe only for a year or two. Look at the way the district's changing. The Market will be gone in another three years.'

Fred had come from that interview straight into Meg's arms. The two of them had clung together like a couple of babies.

'Of course,' Fred said, 'he's telling lies about Charles Street. Even if they do build a flat or two . . . But it's the money, Meg. Where are we to get the money?'

'Tenants!' Meg cried, as though she were Queen Elizabeth mustering her forces. 'Tenants! That's what we've got to find.'

Nevertheless she knew, and they all knew, that they must summon all their cheerfulness. It was for Fred's sake that they needed it, for between Fred and the house there was something deep and poignant. Take the house away and you take some of Fred's spirit with it. 'He'll never,' Meg thought, 'be quite the same again, and the Alice Van Renns of this world will multiply. . . . We must all save Fred. We must love him and cheer him and console him without his knowing that we are doing anything of the kind.'

So they came out to take the air and listen to the band. 'Tum-te-ta . . . tum-te-ta . . .' hummed Meg—and then she saw Claude. As her eyes rested on him so also did Kitty's.

'Why,' Kitty cried, 'that's my nice Shepherd Market man. I told you about him. His name is Claude something. I can only think of him as Claude . . . oh yes, Willoughby. Claude Willoughby. Bullock knows him. He

comes to see the Pakes. He's all by himself, Mother. Let's
speak to him.'

Kitty was happy. She didn't know why. The grass smelt
of gunpowder and a light haze like sprinkled barley-
sugar powdered the trees. She was happy. She didn't know
why. There was no reason at all except that the band
was now playing variations on the 'Londonderry Air,' the
most beautiful tune since the birds sang, unself-consciously,
in the Garden of Eden.

But Meg was looking at Claude Willoughby for quite
another reason. She had known instantly that this very
thin, shabbily dressed, wrinkled-browed old gentleman
would play an important part in one of her life's crises.
How did she know? What nonsense! Of course she didn't.
Not one of us knows anything at all. However, this wasn't
the first time that Meg had felt such things. When she
was quite a child a fruit-seller in Nice had sold her green
figs and afterwards picked up her purse with five pounds
in it. Hadn't she foretold something of the sort the moment she looked at him? Again, during the first week of
her honeymoon with Fred, in Venice, an attendant in the
Accademia had looked at her so strangely and the very
next day had thrown himself into the Grand Canal and
been drowned. They had told her when she went three
days later to see the Carpaccios again. And so now. This
old man would have something to do with her life. He
stood there like a prophecy while the band played the
'Londonderry Air' and Big Ben boomed like a beetle out
of the very heart of the sky.

They moved up to him.

'Mr. Willoughby, you don't remember me,' said Kitty.

His pleasure was a handsome thing to witness.

'This is my mother.'

'How do you do?' Claude's hand was shaking.

'He looks as though he doesn't have enough to eat,'
Meg thought, and at once her eagerness to help him

swallowed up every other possible notion or idea. The world was blotted out: only Claude Willoughby, pale and emaciated, existed for her.

'I come to your house quite often,' Claude explained, 'to see Millie and Helen Pake.' He looked anxious. His brow was dreadfully wrinkled and his nose longer than ever. 'I fear Helen——'

'Yes,' said Meg gently. 'But she is in no pain. Only lies there in a dream. The past has been her only reality for a long time.'

He straightened himself, looked dignified, symbolic, representing in his person a complete vanished society.

'When you are my age and Lady Helen's the past is all that you have. The present—oh, dear, I'm afraid I dislike the present very much indeed.'

'There you are!' Meg cried. 'I'm afraid I'm all for the present: I wouldn't want to live in any time but this one. And Kitty,' she went on, laughing, 'Kitty thinks only of the future. Don't you, Kitty? She doesn't know there *is* a present.'

'Oh, the future!' Claude said, shaking his head. 'I'm terrified of the future. We are all to be blown sky-high. However, I shan't be here. That's one comfort.'

He was cheering up immensely. It needed only that some pleasant person should be kind to him for Claude to take a very rosy view. It was as though nowadays he was only one skin thick. He felt any treatment of himself, even the mildest, as a blow or a caress. His whole heart went out to this Mrs. Delaney. Her splendid figure, her dress of rose and grey, her merriness and vigour and spirit of hospitality—these warmed him like a fire. But he was afraid that he would lose her. For weeks he had haunted Charles Street and the doors had been closed, but now Charles Street had come to him; here it was with this large merry lady and this lovely girl. Oh, he must keep them for a moment or two longer! And he

did. For the band played 'God Save the King' and everyone was on the move. They started, the three of them, to
walk back across the Park. What *is* it, thought Meg, that
makes this old man important to me? It isn't only that I
am sure that he is half-starved and lonely. It is rather
that he is going to do something for *me*. He is to be my
benefactor, not I his.

They talked about the Green Park.

'You know,' Meg said, 'if I were one of those men in
white hats and white trousers, always drinking whisky
in Africa and longing for home—you're always seeing
them in plays—it's the Green Park I'd be longing for.
I'd see the dry grass and the dirty sheep and the Victoria
Memorial and the heavy-leafed trees and the dogs running like mad, and I'd be so homesick I wouldn't know
what to do.'

Claude agreed, but thought it was cruel to keep dogs
in London.

'My son's got a dachshund,' Meg said. 'And I'm sure
he's very happy.'

'Just fancy!' Claude said, talking to Meg as though he
had known her the whole of his life. 'On this very spot,
or hereabouts, there was a very famous duel fought. I
forget the names, but I never can go past these trees
without thinking of them. One of them, I *know,* wore
mulberry breeches—I know he did. And the light was so
clear—very early morning—no smoke—and perhaps a
cart rumbling up Piccadilly——'

'Was it pistols or swords?'

'I don't know. Swords, I think. A great sensation.
People talked of it for weeks.'

He stopped for a moment. Was he going to faint?
What a horrible idea—now, in front of these new great
friends! But the trees were bowing before him, the path
rocking under his feet and a noise like the hissing of a
great kettle in his ear. He had had for luncheon two fish-

cakes in the Shepherd's Pie Café in the Market. Two
fish-cakes were perhaps not enough.

Meg had taken his arm. He saw, out of the rocking,
tree-filled mist, her eyes, large and full of kindness, comforting him.

'Now—let us sit on these chairs for a moment.'

'It's the excitement.' Claude, sitting down, closed his
eyes.

'The excitement?'

'Yes. You'll think me very foolish. But suddenly, unexpectedly, making new friends. I hope you don't think
me impertinent, but now, at my age—I don't see many
new people——'

He was talking, to beat down the nausea. To be sick
in front of these ladies. How terrible!

'It's natural enough. Why should people bother? But
I often think—if we weren't so frightened of strangers!
There must be so many lonely people in London. Not that
I'm lonely really, you know, but after seventy—of course
so many of one's friends are gone.'

Ah! that was better! Nature was pulling herself
straight again. The golden soil was steady and the dark
leaves did not fan the sky.

Meg's hand was on his.

'You must come and see us in Charles Street. I know
you've been there often, visiting Helen and Millie. But
you must come to see *us*. Any time you feel like it.'

Meg was thinking: 'He's starved. That's what the
trouble is. It's too late to ask him in to tea. And we're
all out to dinner.'

But Claude, now recovered, was his proud self again.

'Thank you,' he said with great stateliness. 'I shall like
very much to call if I may.'

Kitty said: 'And if you don't come, Mr. Willoughby,
I shall call and fetch *you*. We shan't let you off.'

But oh no, Claude thought, these charming ladies must

never see my room. It was bad enough Millie Pake coming in and looking round. But after all Millie is an old
friend and she's poor too.

'I shall come and call. Don't you fear,' he said gaily.
He must show them that he had engagements and friends
and everything he wanted. He despised himself for his
recent admission of loneliness. 'I must be getting back,'
he said, rising with dignity. 'I have an engagement.' They
walked along to the Gates. 'When I said that just now
about being lonely I was thinking of others rather than
myself. I am really very fortunate at my age—very fortunate indeed.'

His brow wrinkled more deeply. What if they should
expect to be invited for a cocktail, perhaps, or a glass of
sherry? They seemed to be determined to see him home.
Half Moon Street slept in the evening sun. Fleming's
Hotel was newly painted. Two young men in a silver
sports car stared at the two splendid ladies. Meg went
on:

'We'll just come with you into the Market, Mr. Willoughby. We must see where you live, you know. Before
long we may have to come and beg your hospitality. We
may have to sell the Charles Street house. Oh dear! I
hope not! But we've been looking round for a nice organ
to grind; haven't we, Kitty? Although you never see an
organ now, do you? I hope you'll be kind to us when we're
on the street. We shall need friends.'

It was strange to him to hear her talking of poverty
when she looked so fine and strong and rich. But she
conveyed to him in some mysterious way that she would
be happy whatever misfortunes occurred to her, and this
gave him a new courage and hope. While she was there
he was protected and secure. They passed beneath the
friendly sign of Miss Bonda.

The Market had surrendered to a golden quiescence.
On the front slab of the fish-shop the stout form of a

gentleman in a bowler hat and shirtsleeves was perched, his hat half tilted, while beside him was a notice, 'Fish kept fresh inside during hot weather.' A minute kitten outside the leather-shop played languidly with the wheel of a bicycle. Ladies in summer clothing hung out of windows, and a small boy with a minute crimson watering-can was pretending to spurt water at the black woolly dog lazing in front of the book-shop. A young policeman with the earnest gaze of a philosopher said to the seller of carnations, 'Now you know quite well, I won't have flowers sold on the pavement.' From behind the open door of the news-shop (in whose window are entrancing little china dogs) came the happy music of Henry Hall . . . the life of the whole world in miniature played itself lazily through the dusty gold of the evening light.

'That,' said Claude, rather nervously (for they might insist on an inspection), 'is where I live.' He pointed to a window. And then, as in a Goldoni comedy, the figures began to move, for there was Caesar, turning the corner with a young girl in a lilac-coloured dress, and there was Mrs. Rudge looking out of window. And for Claude there was Brocket, moving towards the girl and stopping. Caesar squaring his shoulders, old Mrs. Rudge staring, Caesar suddenly catching sight of Meg, the girl turning and slipping away, Brocket standing, his arms akimbo, the dance-music saluting them with a quick rush of sound, Meg exclaiming, 'Why, it's Caesar!'

'Yes, mum. I was only gone a minute to get some air,' and then, in a whisper of despair to Meg before he hurried back to Charles Street: 'Mother knows, mum, about my young lady. She's been carrying on something dreadful.' The man with the carnations, now that the policeman was gone, hoarsely whispering to Kitty: 'Beautiful flowers, lady—'alf a crown for the lot.'

Lastly Brocket, at Claude's elbow now, disregarding the ladies: 'Wait a minute, Mr. Willoughby. Something's happened at the house. Half an hour ago. Mr. Best's gone. Heart attack.' Brocket moved on.

'So that's where you live, Mr Willoughby,' Meg said cheerfully. (Poor Caesar! What a lucky thing that they were all out to-night! He would be so badly upset, poor boy.)

Claude was trembling. He wiped his forehead with his handkerchief.

'Unfortunate thing. . . . That's the man at our flats who spoke to me. Poor Best—one of the tenants—died half an hour ago of a heart attack.'

And without another word, with a funny, stiff little bow, he left them. He walked, his head up, as though leading an army. He was thinking: 'Poor Best! Poor fellow!' And once again the ground shook beneath his feet. Death, tall and very thin, with ears pricked like a listening hound, was waiting inside the house to touch him on the arm.

Word was passing round the Market that someone had just died.

CHAPTER II

Life of Fred Delaney

HEAT had gone from the Green Park. The trees were
turning and, once and again, a little amber mist of twirling leaves would trouble the grey sky. The Park lay
desolate, the little chairs unoccupied and the grand avenue
from Gates to Memorial occupied only by hurrying
figures too busy for a glance. Only for the dogs was it
the same unaltered Paradise. Now, as ever, they strained
the leash across the Piccadilly traffic, pausing at mid-way
safety, their tongues out, panting, wild-eyed, at last
within the Gates, looking upwards with frantic appeal
for release, then running, checking at a scent, running
again, recovering all the promises, suspicions, wild hopes,
present confirmations they had left behind them yesterday.

Above them the trees deepen in metallic gold, in paper-
thin russet, while above them again the clouds smoke and
tremble and shred into tatters of ragged grey.

Late in this September Helen Pake died. She was
buried in the country and Millie went to stay with her
brother.

The house, then, was empty save for the Delaneys.
Patrick Munden was in Paris and it was said that Dodie
Pullet was there with him. The house was empty and the
fantastic, outrageous thing was that the Delaneys were

delighted. Fantastic, outrageous, for very shortly the Delaneys must starve.

After the 1st of October there would be no more rents coming in and what would the Delaneys do then? Everywhere, all over England, for the last twenty years this same absurd catastrophe had been suddenly breaking into English family lives. The English middle and upper classes had for generations understood that starvation was for them a grotesque impossibility. Until the War of 1914 it had been so. There had always been land, a house with a garden, a bundle of relations, a fortunate marriage, a vacancy in a relation's business, a safe investment—and eternal, affectionate credit from the deserving but keep-him-in-his-place shopkeeper. Now, in 1934, there was no land, there were no ready-money relations, no jobs for young men, no obliging shop-keepers, no friendly overdraft bankers, and always dwindling diminishing investments. No one was safe, no one was secure, the pound was worth about thirteen shillings. Gentlemen like Signor Mussolini and Herr Hitler had apparently no money but got on splendidly without it; indeed the less they had the more they spent. This happy behaviour was, however, impossible for English ladies and gentlemen. 'But we *must* live!' cried the English ladies and gentlemen. No one but themselves, alas! saw the necessity for this. 'But we *cannot* starve!' they cried. No one, alas! saw why they should not. Every expedient was tried; friends were stayed with, bills were not paid, camp was continually moved, jobs constantly applied for, jobs once considered too humiliating for words. Lady Constance Belwether was a housemaid with a wealthy Newcastle family (she called herself Miss Allen). The Hon. Frederick Cochran was an assistant in Belfrage's great stores. 'Bunty' Milne was a chauffeur. And so, of course, all jobs were overcrowded, employers pestered with incompetents. The pedlars of toys by St. Paul's numbered in their ranks several members of the British aristocracy.

With every separate family the shock of surprise was equally staggering and incredible. 'There is not a penny in the bank, which refuses an overdraft. There is not one single friend or acquaintance who can help. I am fifty years of age and worth nothing to anyone. My two dear boys, so handsome, so athletic, so charming, have been to Harrow and Oxford and are not exceptional enough to be worth anyone's while. My beautiful daughters can cook, use a typewriter, know all about dogs and horses. They can do none of these things, however, as well as thousands of other young women.'

The Delaneys were happy, healthy, strong, altogether most excellent people, but not Fred nor Bullock nor Kitty had ever been trained to compete with the present incredibly efficient workers of the world. They simply were not worth anyone's pay anywhere. Such a crisis, so poignant and terrible, should have filled them with terror and despair. It did nothing of the sort. 'In actual fact,' a cold, cynical observer might have remarked, 'you are, of course, not worrying—for to-morrow you can sell the house and so assure yourselves against starving for the rest of your days.'

But the remarkable thing was that, as soon as the house was empty, the Delaney family loved it twice as much as before, and vowed that only over their dead bodies should anyone take it from them. Without a word spoken they banded together and faced the outside invader. They were constantly wandering up and down the stairs and in and out of the empty rooms. The house was theirs again and the house knew it. They made fantastic plans of how Bullock and Kitty would marry. Bullock should live in the Pake flat, Kitty in the Pullet. So all would be for ever under one roof. When children came they would manage somehow. They laughed and shouted and sang, played ridiculous games of hide-and-seek, and the house responded, not behaving, as most empty houses do, like a grumbling and dusty-faced ghost, but rather catching glints of sunlight and mantling corners and fireplaces with light and shadow, making friendly gestures with dusk and dawn and the reflections of the September evening city lights, catching clouds in the window-panes and letting the wind whisper merrily in the fireplaces.

Nevertheless the crisis was there and Fred knew it. He had all kinds of extravagant ideas about jobs. He spoke gaily to all his friends: 'Here's a poor fellow out of work. Can't you do something for him?' And everyone clapped him on the shoulder and promised and, behind his back, said: 'What's Delaney fussing for? He's only got to sell the house.'

Bullock had written nearly half of his novel but ran round suggesting himself to people. 'I'll do anything,' he said. 'Anything for a living wage.' He was a jolly little fellow and everyone liked him, but unfortunately he had no *technical* knowledge of anything. He was not a trained journalist; he knew nothing about mechanics except that he could drive a car. He was willing and eager and ignorant. All the same he didn't *really* worry, for he saw Lizzie every day and his novel was coming along nicely.

They were, in fact, all of them incapable of worrying. Somehow they would manage. They would camp in the house, live on apples and occasional eggs and bacon. They did not, as many of their contemporaries did, calculate the friends upon whom they could sponge. Both Bullock and Kitty knew numbers of young men and women whose lives were simply miraculous, the way that they invited themselves and stayed on and on, joined unsuspecting luncheon parties, left suddenly so that their drinks had to be paid for, vanished to the Riviera where they needed only two suits and a bathing dress, and then, when things were really bad, surrendered themselves, their souls and bodies, to anyone who thought them worth buying. The Delaneys were not of *that* world nor ever would be.

Fred Delaney had, however, hours of surprising foreboding and anxiety. He had, for one thing, never loved his family so much as now, and it was for them rather than for himself that he lay awake and sighed in his bath and shook his head over his newspaper. He did not lie awake nor sigh nor shake his head for very long. The sense of apprehension that had been with him now for several months could not conquer his natural happiness, his consciousness of his body and its many delightful activities, his love for his wife and children, for London and the house, his lusty desire to possess Alice Van Renn, and the daily excitements of seeing the shops, the changing trees in the Park, his many friends, and especially the constant procession of beautiful women.

His desire for Alice Van Renn seemed only to increase his love of Meg and of Kitty. Especially he was seeing his daughter just now in a fresh and wonderful light. She seemed to him radiant and lovely. Her sweetness, goodtemper, unselfishness, all sprang, it appeared to him, from her now mature virginity. She was something untouched, with a wonderful spiritual security, and the more he desired and intended to spend a week-end with Miss Van Renn, the more he loved Meg because she was his dear friend, companion and wife, the more he adored his daughter because she was pure and unassailed and above the vulgar clutch of men like himself.

And so, in the untidy sitting-room that somehow smelt of chocolate fudge and dried everlastings—the little Half Moon Street rooms—he told Alice Van Renn. He had been lucky enough to catch her alone on that last day of September. He was feeling reckless and so buoyantly conscious of his health, his sexual energy, his physical challenge to fate, that Alice herself responded to it.

He knelt beside her, his arms around her, and enjoyed

with her a kiss that was as long and as deep as Besnard's search for Atlantis.

'And now—which week-end is it going to be?'

'The last one in October.'

He had risen now to his feet, and looking up at him she stretched out her hands; he bent towards her, she touched his cheeks, then, sighing, she said:

'Mother has settled it all. . . . I am to marry Monsieur de Florac.'

'Old——' Fred paused. Little M. de Florac's nickname in the best male society was a very coarse one. 'But he has only——' He broke off.

'Yes,' Alice said. 'He is appalling, but it is a very, very old story. As you know, he is enormously rich, he makes no marital demands on me, he thinks I will look lovely at the head of his table at his beautiful château near Blois. He is right. I shall.'

Fred laughed.

'Strangely enough, although I have been in love with you so long, I don't know you very well. But I *do* know you well enough to be sure that you are not going to marry old——' He broke off again.

'No. I am not,' Alice answered. 'But mother thinks that I am. She is determined that I shall. It suits her exactly—plenty of money, she can be near me always. Moreover, she likes old de Florac. They murmur obscene jokes together. And because she is set on this she detests yourself and Bartlett. You are the two dangers. . . .'

'Myself? Why, I am married and adore my wife. Who could be safer?'

'Yes, but she's a wise old bird. She knows that you might give me just enough—what shall I call it?—well, enough anyway to make old de Florac impossible. She hasn't yet realized that he is impossible in any case.'

Fred knelt down again. The worn carpet was hard and dusty. He took her in his arms and then, after hear-

ing the bells of Atlantis once more, said: 'And Bartlett—
my God, what a fool!'

Alice Van Renn gently kissed his hair, then rose and,
looking out on to the one-legged street singer in Half
Moon Street, said:

'I am a fool too, remember. Monday morning, that
last Monday in October, as we get into the train, you
will be saying: "This woman is duller than an ox." I
shan't blame you. It will be true. I like Bartlett's stu-
pidity.' She swung round, looking at him with more intensity, a deeper and more genuine feeling than he had
ever seen in her. 'Of *you* I'm afraid, Fred Delaney. I
might become fond of you. Then, at the very moment
when you realize that flight is the only cure for such boredom, I might be longing for you to remain. That would
hurt, you know. And ever since mother beat me with a
hairbrush because I stole her sham-pearl necklace—I was
five and a bit—I have determined to avoid pain. Bartlett
and I suit one another exactly.'

She came close to him and put both her hands on his
shoulders.

'I am afraid of your high spirits, and although you are
kind you are restless. Your family is the only thing I can
imagine your being faithful to. Where you are concerned
I am *not* such a fool. Yes, perhaps the week-end will be
the greatest misfortune for me—will spoil hopelessly all
the wiser, safer things.'

Fred's behaviour then was very bad indeed. He was
the complete fool he could often be. Fortunately old Mrs.
Van Renn's wrinkled hand fumbled at the door-knob.
When she entered he was throwing some pennies down
to the one-legged street singer.

Her fury at having inadvertently assisted him to be
alone with Alice had its comic aspect, for when she was
angry she was speechless. She could only mutter like an
old monkey deprived of its banana-skin.

He was very charming and very gay and very kind. He was only at the top stair when he heard her voice, like the scream of a wounded bird, upbraiding Alice.

He went home through Half Moon Street, past the Christian Science Church and round the corner, humming a mixture of *Tosca* and *Butterfly,* for his physical being was now sure of its definite reward. This certainty made him cock of the walk and also at great ease with himself because one part of himself was entirely satisfied. This is where men have so marked an advantage over women, that they lodge their different selves so easily in quite separate apartments. Women never. Few women understand this. This non-comprehension makes marriage very difficult.

So, humming, thinking of those coming last days of October and of Alice in his arms, he entered his house loving Meg with a new kind of charity. Because he would be shortly unfaithful to her he longed to do her every possible kindness.

And there, having tea with Meg, were those tiresome Penders. He stopped on the threshold, loving, at the sight of Graham's long, brown, white-haired neck, Meg just a little less. What had bitten her over this tiresome pair? True that once, years ago, she had been engaged to Graham Pender, but now, with his white locks and museum expression, she surely could not be sentimental! And that, standing there in the doorway, he suddenly saw that she was, and, himself straight from his visits to Atlantis with Alice Van Renn, it roused in him an intolerable irritation. For he intercepted a look between Meg and Pender—on Pender's side a long dog-like gaze, a devoted please-take-me-for-a-walk-or-do-anything-you-like-with-me-only-love-me look, and on Meg's side a tenderness, a sweetness that really staggered him.

'Hullo, Pender . . . Lady Pender, how do you do?'

(But she, Meg, couldn't really be falling in love with this long-legged sad-eyed professor? Meg . . .)

'Yes . . . it's quite chilly. . . . Autumn is upon us, I'm afraid.'

'Here's your tea, Fred. You look quite flushed.'

'Yes. I've been walking all the way from Trafalgar Square. How are you, Lady Pender?' (What an appalling old scarecrow, and with that blue thistle sort of thing stuck in her hat!)

Lady Pender moistened her lips with her tongue.

'Not so very well, Mr. Delaney, I fear.'

'Oh, I *am* sorry. What's the trouble?' (There Pender was again, looking at Meg as though he would like to lay his head in her broad lap. And Lady Pender had seen it. Her eyes narrowed. She sipped at her tea, her gaze sharp as a hatpin over the rim of her cup, as she said:)

'Oh, I don't know. Anno Domini, I expect. We're neither of us as young as we were, are we, Graham?'

Pender laughed. 'I'm certainly not. One last little fling and I'm laid on the shelf.'

Fred stood over Meg for another cup of tea, swinging his broad body a little, straddling his legs as though to show Pender what a *real* body was like!

'Oh, surely not, Pender. You've years ahead of you. And what is the last little fling to be?'

'Oh, I don't know. . . . Egypt, perhaps. . . . Egypt suits my wife's health; doesn't it, dear?'

'You know we can't afford it, dear. And what does *my* health matter? Talking of which, you look so *very* well, Mr. Delaney.'

'Yes, I am. . . . Splendid. Ready for anything.'

'So's Graham really. Aren't you, dear? Men'—Lady Pender smiled like a coy death-mask—'never grow up.'

Meg smiled in return. 'I'm glad they don't. It's the only compensation women have—that they don't grow up, I mean.'

'Yes,' said Lady Pender. 'And it's fun sharing in their games. Women never know how to play together.'

Fred, who could think of several ladies of his acquaintance who knew very well, broke in with:

'Been to any of the new plays?'

'Well—it's rather a nuisance from Surbiton. It's so late getting back.'

'You must come with us one night.' (He was thinking: We shan't have a bean in the world unless we sell the house.)

'We should love to. Wouldn't we, Graham?'

'Delighted. I do enjoy a good play.'

They got up to go. Lady Pender said:

'Meg finds her way out to Surbiton quite often, but you've never been, Mr. Delaney. You're too busy, I expect.'

'Busy!' Fred threw his head back and laughed. 'I wish I were. I'm out of a job, Lady Pender. If you know of anyone who wants a chauffeur or someone to wait at table . . .'

There was much laughter. They were gone.

Back by the fireplace Meg said:

'Had a good afternoon, darling?'

'Delightful. Splendid walk.' He kissed her. Then, by an association of ideas, he said: 'By the way, last week-end in October I shall be away, going to shoot with a fellow in Norfolk.'

'That's lucky,' Meg answered. 'I shall be away myself that same week-end.'

Later on Fred Delaney walked with his beautiful daughter across the Green Park. He was dining with two friends at the Argonauts' Club, and at nine o'clock Bullock was picking him up there and they were going to pay a call on that funny old bastard, Lord Ragadoon. Fred, like everyone else, had known the old ruffian by sight for

years and years, but it had been an immense surprise to
him when he heard from Bullock of this queer friendship.

'But *however* did you get to know him?'

'We met in the National Gallery. He took a liking to
Lizzie.'

'The National Gallery! Of all places!'

'Yes, and he wants to meet you, Father. He wants you
to see his things.'

'Of course I'll see his things. I believe they're marvellous.'

So that was what, this evening, he was going to do.
Kitty was bound on some mysterious adventure of her
own. He recognized that something was happening to
her, and he was proud, both of her and himself, as he
realized his supreme confidence in her. She was a child in
actual experience, but her spirit was as strong and shining
as a sword-blade.

Poetry was alive in him as, Kitty's arm tucked in his,
they passed through the Gates and started down the
Avenue at whose other end there was a smoky bee-swarm
of orange light about the Memorial, while high in the air
above the black tree-tops hung the silver-illuminated
tower. There was a faint crackling spark of frost in the
air.

'Let's walk on the grass, darling. Look out for the
chairs. How the houses shine upon this mysterious place
—as though they were ringing it round with guardianship.
Stand still a moment. Big Ben's striking. You can almost
hear the river running under our feet, and the Piccadilly
traffic is like a man strumming on his guitar before he hits
the tune.'

They walked on, body close to body, very happy, very
tranquil-spirited.

'What are you up to, darling? Never mind. Don't tell
me. We're all up to something, your mother as well. . . .
What an amorous place this Park is! So many lives here

under the trees coming to one of their many crises. How can anyone say life is dull, or even frightening? Because after all it is over so quickly. When the crash comes, Kitty, when the planes overhead are raining down their bombs and everyone is cowering below ground, this Park will wait with silent contempt. Yes, contempt, because it has already seen so much and *will* see so much more. The trees will come crashing down. That illuminated tower will waver in the air, then crumble. Big Ben will cry its last hour. The river will rise and flow, the shops will submerge, the sky will be dark with light shifting smoke. And then, Kitty, there will be *such* a silence! Strange birds will fly over and hover on the ruins of the Ritz. Down Piccadilly will float the blurred soaking canvas of the "Bacchus and Ariadne" and over Westminster there will hang the stinking fiery pall from the smouldering Abbey. Round and round the Poets' Corner the ducks will go squawking. Only the Victoria Memorial will survive, immune, indestructible, virtuous, Imperial.'

Kitty laughed and pressed his arm.

'It's lovely to have a real poet in the family,' she said.

They paused near the bandstand and fancied for a moment, because the shadows beguiled them, that a ghostly orchestra was at play. Very faintly Cavaradossi with his absurdly unreal canvas and elegant painter's blouse rose before the marble pillars of the Roman church. It was a huddle of sheep, moving into the light from the near-by houses, drifting along like the ghosts of Caesar's murderers. A cry of some bird cut the beautiful stillness.

'Yes,' said Fred Delaney. 'It's a darling Park, a *darling* Park. My ghost will join all the other ghosts, and we'll go wandering, wandering, seeking our favourite little chairs and the young typist with the china-blue eyes against whose warm body we lay when the sun parched the grass, or looking perhaps up and down the paths for the cigar-ends and the cast-off sandwich and, who knows, a dropped enchanting sixpence!' He swung his umbrella round and round. 'I love to be alone with you, Kitty, just the two of us. You're a darling child, a *darling* child. . . . And now I suppose my time with you is short. Soon a man will take you away. I shall see you once and again and then I shall be a grandfather, and the day after that, who knows?—a great-grandfather, for I feel to-night as though I am going to live for ever, perched, like an old stork, on one leg, surveying the ruined world and hiding your babies under the shadow of my wing.'

'I don't suppose I shall ever marry,' Kitty said.

'Never marry? Why, of course you will! I thought you were engaging in a love affair at this very minute.'

'Oh no . . . I'm only perceiving a number of things quite for the first time.'

There occurred then one of those coincidences that God allows Himself once and again when He is too lazy to invent something more likely.

Out from the shadows there emerged upon the light circle of grass two persons. Bodies almost collided. There was a pause, a stare. Kitty gave a little cry. The young man, who was Alton Foster, raised his hat.

He stopped as though he would speak, but the stout lady hanging on his arm urged him forward. Kitty heard her say in a voice as odious and monotonous as a bath-water tap: 'People you know, darling?'

The woman was wearing red and green, was handsome in a kind of florid extravagance, very full-breasted. She was hanging on Alton's arm. She was years older. Alton had run from the thunderstorm across this Park crying: 'I'll prove myself . . . you'll see . . . you'll see . . .'

They were turning along the Mall, up the Duke of York's steps, and so immediately to Carlton House Terrace and the Argonauts. Fred, intent on his own flood of oratory, had not even noticed the pair.

'What a horrid vulgar woman!' Kitty said, five minutes after they had encountered them.

'Where, dear?'

'Oh, gone—long ago—nobody.' (Over the jewels in
Zanti's shop the young, pale, eager face hangs. 'I must
see you . . . I *must* . . . I must!')

Fred was happily talking.

'Don't think it fantastic, darling. Or you can if you
like. Life *is* fantastic. But I feel that if we let this house
go, everything goes. Everything for us, I mean. You see,
I think we're so happy because we have the luck to make
a perfect combination, the house and our four selves. It
happens sometimes. Once and again you meet absolutely
joyful people, *real* joy, independent of circumstances. And
it's always because they are fortunate enough to have
made a perfect union with something or someone. You
see it in married people, in friends, in brother and sister,
in two brothers, in an organization, in a saint. I believe
that's the point of life—to find the thing or person or persons that will prevent you living for yourself alone. And
there's a power—an evil power if you like—that will
upset that combination if it can. It's always at work, doing its best to destroy, to tear things and people apart.
I believe it's at work on us now, darling, trying to take
the house from us, to take us from one another. It's nonsense to say there isn't free will. Of *course* there is.
Plenty of it. We're all being tempted at this moment, all
four of us, and if we yield or lose the house we'll never
come together again—never, never. Never as we are now,
joyful and free. Joyful and free! Tum-te-tum-te-tum. The
Evil One is at our throats. The fight is on. United we
stand, divided we bloody well fall. We fall and are never
put together again. Lost for ever. We groan, scramble
in the dark, curse the Deity. But it isn't the Deity. It is
ourselves. We've yielded to our snorty, greedy, guzzling,

pig-troughing selves, and so we're lost, separated for ever. Our joy is over, our laughter silenced, our . . .'

'Hush, darling. You are making a terrible noise. Of course we won't let the house go.'

'No, we won't—but perhaps we will. Who can tell where the victory's going? What do you think your mother's up to?'

'Mother?'

'Yes. She's up to something. Didn't you know? Perhaps it's *she* who'll lose the battle for us. Or perhaps it is I— just for an ankle and the white curve of a shoulder. Ashes and worms. Worms and ashes. Or perhaps it's *you*. For we're all in it together. What is it *you're* up to, darling?'

'I?' Kitty pressed his arm and looked so lovely and so kind glancing up at him in the lamplight that he had lightly to kiss her forehead and so disturb a young straight-from-the-egg-Hendon policeman who blushed and looked passionately down the Mall. 'I'm up to nothing. Nothing whatever. If you'd noticed that vulgar woman in red and green you'd have known why.'

'Would I? How mysterious you are! Well, try and behave well in the next week or two. It's like the fairy stories. You're not to ask the Princess who she *really* is until the cock crows. . . . Lord, I'm weak. Weak as water. It's I who will ruin the lot of us, separate us and destroy us. God forgive me. God pardon me. Here we are. Up the steps. Into the decorous. Straight to the mausoleum of respectability. Good night, sweetheart. . . . Good night, good night.'

When Bullock, looking very babyish in a bowler hat cocked to one side of his head, called for him he had drunk enough to be quite sober and sensible. He stood for a moment, admiring his son's sturdy little frame. 'I have indeed two of the *sweetest* children in all the world,' and then, stamping on his sentimentality, scolded Bullock all the way up Lower Regent Street for wearing a bowler hat.

'They are altogether out of fashion. You look like a travelling salesman.'

'I wish I were,' Bullock said. 'Father, I *must* get a job somewhere. It's disgraceful. It seems I'm no good at anything.'

'Myself likewise,' said Fred.

'Yes, but you're of an age and I'm just beginning. Lizzie agrees with me that somehow I've got to save the family.'

'What about your novel? Won't that bring you a heap of money?'

'I don't know. For one thing, it isn't finished. For another, writing never seems as good the day after as it does the day before, if you understand what I mean.'

But Fred was worrying about the house again.

'Of course we could mortgage. But that would be just the same as selling it. I could *borrow* money on it, but that would be selling it again. No, we *must* find tenants or jobs. Jobs or tenants. You see, Bullock, I can't think of *anything* I can do. I'm too old and too heavy to be a gigolo, too fond of liquor to be a butler, too fond of your mother to be away from the house. I might help my brother sell things. I can be charming when I like. But I don't know the value of anything. I could cheat people, I suppose, in one way or another. There are all *sorts* of ways, I believe—but I'm not really bad enough. I don't like hurting people. Neither does your mother. That's one of our weaknesses in this hard, relentless world.'

'Never mind,' said Bullock consolingly. 'We'll live on eggs and cook them ourselves.'

'Yes, but you have to *buy* the eggs. And then there are rates and light and coal and clothes and soap.'

'Soap's *very* cheap.'

'Yes, but the water has to be hot and your mother and

Kitty have *got* to look handsome. You're beginning to look shabby already with that bowler hat.'

'Here we are,' said Bullock. 'Take care you don't stub your toes on the staircase.'

They had pushed a bell in the old dingy house and the door had silently opened. After three flights of stairs that smelt of mice and cheese there was old Ragadoon standing on the landing awaiting them. He had a tartan shawl over his shoulders, a shabby pair of blue trousers and large, soft grey slippers. He was smoking a pipe.

'This is my father,' Bullock said.

Ragadoon grunted, shook hands, motioned them into the room. There were three rooms, one a sitting-room, one a bedroom, and one a storeroom. There was also a little bathroom. There was a kettle on the fire. The room was infernally hot. In the course of the next hour and a half Fred saw many miraculous things. The walls were a dusty faded red, a saffron yellow, a dirty grey, and on these walls hung incredible masterpieces. Over the bed was a Giovanni Bellini, a landscape with a charming girl Madonna and a fat kicking Bambino. Over the wash-stand, hanging crooked on its wire, was a Rembrandt— 'Susanna and the Elders.' Over the mantelpiece was a Lorenzo di Credi—an Italian landscape with figures. Every inch of every wall was plastered with oils and drawings: drawings by Leonardo, Rembrandt, Titian, Tiepolo, Greco; there were Byzantine ikons, a triptych by Lorenzo Veneziano. There were cases packed with drawings and etchings. In the small and dirty bathroom were a number of Hogarths and Rowlandsons, coarse and vigorous and merry. They didn't talk very much. Ragadoon shuffled about, puffing at his pipe, muttering: 'Look at this. Fine, isn't it? What do you say to this? Here's a Degas worth looking at. Beautiful Longhis, aren't they? Genuine too. Only one Longhi in ten is to-day. Tell me when you've had enough.'

But Fred Delaney never had enough. He had no con-
noisseur's knowledge of painting, but he didn't pretend
to have. He did what any collector loves to have his visitor
do—showed, by the light in his eyes and the smile on his
lips, that he was heavenly-happy.

It was indeed the perfect end to a perfect day. Ragadoon and he liked one another.

'Have some tea,' said Ragadoon. 'The kettle's boil-
ing.'

'No, thanks,' said Fred. 'I've got to get back. Doesn't
anyone look after you here?'

'I have a man,' Ragadoon said grimly. 'I hate him so
much that he's now out somewhere getting drunk. A char
comes mornings.'

He patted Bullock on the shoulder.

'I like your boy. He's got a good girl too. Well, good-
day to ye, if you must go. Come again.'

In the street Fred Delaney said, 'Glory be to God!'

CHAPTER III

The Things

THE Park threw poor Claude out of its misty securities as
Big Ben struck five. He was so sharply sensitive now to
every kind of rebuff that he was well aware when the
Park had had enough of him.

It had been an afternoon of thin floating mist with a
smell of bacon and fried sausage in the air. That at least
was how Claude had felt it, for he was in a state of perpetual hunger. Also the sun had looked, through the mist,
like a large poached egg, and rather foolishly he had
stood on the damp grass watching it descend behind the
trees and fancying that it came swimming towards him,
and a gigantic footman handed it on a piece of toast made
out of a brown sun-edged cloud that was hanging over
the Memorial. 'Here you are, sir!' said the Celestial
Footman, and didn't Claude tuck in! Then—plop!—the
sun had gone and the Park turned distinctly nasty. The
trees flung their leaves at him, the mist came sweeping
like damp dishcloths flicking his face, and the houses
closed in. Very nasty the Green Park can be! You can
hear the underground stream running, and eyes, that may
be lamps or may not, look from between the trees, and
the long avenue is like the one Lady Dedlock once hurried

down to poor Mr. Tulkinghorn's ultimate disadvantage.

But no, the Green Park never has anything to do with the country, and especially in autumn and winter it is urban. Claude knows now, as he hurries through the Gates, that messages are pouring into the Park from little streets that smell of beer and strong tobacco, from rooms up three flights of stairs with unmade beds in them and tradesmen's calendars crooked on the wall and soot falling down the chimney, and dark corners with some property-for-sale notice and an iron urinal and a tobacco-shop with coarse postcards—and all the cheap cinemas and all the dart-boards in all the pubs, and all the area steps with all the cats, and all the broad thoroughfares with the motor-cars panting and the changing lights, and all the City churchyards with the mist groping over the forgotten graves, and all the 'meat with two veg. shops' with their cubicles and steaming hot cups of coffee, and all the pedlars in Holborn winding up their dancing bears and jumping niggers and little men turning some-saults, and all the old curiosity shops with netsukes and 'oil painting of Lady Hamilton' and chessmen of ivory, and bronze images of 'The Dying Gladiator,' and all the men and all the women and all the scarecrows and all the policemen and all the ladies of the Town—the Green Park is aware of them all and is busy collecting messages and sending them out again. For here is the very heart of London, and under the thin grass, if you put your ear to the ground, you can hear the heart beating.

One more flap of the dishcloth mist and Claude is gone, hastening, as though the assassin is at his heels, across Piccadilly, down Half Moon Street, under the arch into the Market, through the door and up the stairs, into his room where his Things are waiting for him, his only friends, his only comfort, his only security against the enemy.

He took off his coat, put on his dressing-gown, brushed

his hair, washed his hands. Then opened the glass doors
of the cabinet so that he could see the better. Then found
his faded old writing-case, opened it and drew from it
two sheets of paper. At the head of the first of these he
had written (the first letter of each word in red ink)—

GIFTS FOR MY FRIENDS

Under the title it was stated:

After my decease I wish the undermentioned persons to be
notified that, in gratitude for their good-will towards me, I would
wish them to have some little possession of mine in memory of me.
Therefore on a certain day to be named by those in charge of my
affairs they will, I hope, come and choose something as a gift
from me.

It had taken him much time and trouble to make this
statement. He had written it again and again, loving
indeed the labour that he had expended over it. Now,
reading it over, he disliked the ambiguity of 'they will,
I hope, come,' etc. Did not that mean that the persons
'in charge of his affairs' should come? That was not at all
what he intended. He was, in fact, very uncertain as to
the names of 'those in charge.' The natural thing would
be to appoint an executor, but that would surely be very
ridiculous in the case of someone whose 'leavings' were
so very slender. There might indeed be no 'leavings' at
all unless in some fashion he managed to pay Brocket his
rent. Plans for doing this now obsessed him night and
day. It was of this he had been thinking in the Park, and
it was there that it had suddenly come to him that he
would go to that delightful lady in Charles Street who
had been so very friendly to him, and explain to her the
whole affair. He would tell her that except for the things
named on this second sheet of paper everything must be
sold—his furniture, clothes, everything. This would not
amount to a great sale, but it would be sufficient, he

thought, to cover the rent. Then he would ask her, as a great favour, to see that his list of bequests was not interfered with. He would explain to her that this little scheme of his was now the only wish he had on earth. He would not tell her (what secretly he confessed to himself) that his great pride in it rose from its novelty. It was NEW. No one, he had by this time persuaded himself, had ever done it before; no one, in the wide world, had ever thought of it before himself. People would say: 'Well, he's gone. Not an ordinary man really. That was a charming thought of his,' and for years after they would remember him for his lovely little idea. This was not, of course, his *only* motive.

He had been always a sentimental, idealistic lover of his kind, longing for love in return. But, in that strange misty confusion of old age, solitude, poverty and hunger, his plan had grown beyond all its natural absolute bounds into a sort of fantastic poetic creation. Something *new* in the world like the *Odyssey* or the *Eroica*. . . .

He surveyed his list of friends. He had calculated that in all there were nineteen Things and he had put on to paper twenty-two friends. But of five of these he was not certain. They might be dead; he could not be sure. He had had some difficulty in summoning twenty-two friends, and, if the truth were known, they were not all very *great* friends. He did not, for example, know *Mr.* Delaney at all, but he thought that it would seem invidious indeed to include his wife and children and leave him out of it. One name troubled him considerably—Mr. Walter Cavendish. Walter Cavendish was a young man, son of his old friend Colonel Bertie Cavendish, some time deceased. He had known Walter only as a very small boy, quite a baby in fact, when in the enchanted days before the War he had gone to stay with Bertie at his place in Somerset. (Walter Cavendish must be now forty if a day, but Claude saw him still as a baby rolling under the table and crying because he had bumped his head against the table-leg.) Claude did know, however, that Walter was now gossip-writer for the *Daily Globe*. He detested gossip-writers, but when he could afford it purchased the *Daily Globe* just to see what his old friend's boy was saying. Now, quite frankly, he invited young Walter because he hoped that he might say a word or two in his column. This was disgraceful and pandering to all the vilest tendencies of this modern world. But he could not help himself. This one concession to vulgarity he must be allowed: and, after all, he had once given Walter Cavendish a rocking-horse.

His brow corrugated with the most serious attention, he went once more through the list of his friends. *Was* Charlie Knight alive? Hadn't 'Buzzard' Taylor gone to South Africa years ago? So, his pencil poised, looking about the room, he saw what he had failed to notice when he came in, two letters on his table. *Two* letters! Most unusual! The first was an ironic missive, an intimation from a fashionable tailor in Burlington Street that he had in his possession at this moment a most remarkable stock of suitings, etc. etc. He opened the other. It contained a card with black edges, and on the card he read that, Mr. Frederick Best having expressed, before his decease, a wish that he might show in some fashion his gratitude for the good-will that his friends had, for so many years, shown towards him, he had thought to manifest his thankfulness by arranging a collection of small possessions dear to him. This collection would be at the service of those same friends. These were invited, on October 5th instant, to attend at No. 23 White Horse Street, between the hours of 2.30 and 5 P.M., that they might choose some small thing for themselves and keep it as a memory of him.

Claude read this three times through. The third time he read it aloud as though the words were so incredible

that he must test their truth by sounding them. Then the
card dropped from his hands and he sat staring in front
of him.

His first violent emotion was of hatred and detestation
of Best. In his bewildered fancy it seemed to him that
Best was standing in front of him. Best, short, stumpy-
legged, red of face, blue of eye, wearing his Club tie and
canary-coloured waistcoat. Best was grinning at him
malevolently.

'You've betrayed me, basely, cruelly, wickedly!'

'Well, you silly old fool, what did you tell me for?
I thought it a damned good idea. I had as much right
to it as you.'

'You had not! You had not. It was *my* idea!'

'Pooh—*your* idea. Your little idea. It's nothing at all.
Why do you get so excited about it? You'd think you'd
discovered the North Pole.'

'It's all I had. It was my one comfort. You promised
you'd tell nobody.'

'How could I tell you'd take it so seriously? You
always were an old woman. Many a laugh Badget and
I've had . . .'

Yes, that was the way Best would talk were he alive.
But he was not. He was dead. When Claude had first
heard of Best's sudden death he had been most genu-
inely sorry. He had never liked Best and he was sure that
Best had suspected him of stealing those things, but there
was something infinitely pathetic in the sudden taking-off
of a man who had been so sure of his own health. He
could hear Best saying to Badget: 'In the pink of condition, old man. You should see me, stripped to the buff,
doing my morning exercises! Never dream I was fifty-
eight!' And there he was, gone in a moment! Poor old
Best! An awful bore, but he meant well, his heart was
kind!

Meant well? His heart was kind? He meant ill. His

heart was devilish, as were the hearts of all men in this foul, dangerous, malevolent world! With shaking hands Claude tore up the two sheets of paper. They lay in fragments about the table.

Then his ferocity changed to a dismal, miserable dejection. After all it had been his own fault. He had told Best and Best had thought it a good idea. Best with his light mind and gay loquacious character could not understand how much it would mean to Claude. And, after all, had it not been a kind of madness? Was not Claude perhaps going a little crazy in his loneliness? At this thought Claude began to tremble, his head to shake, his legs to quiver. For suppose they really did think him mad, and Brocket, with his malicious wickedness, complained to the authorities and they shut him up? This horrible thought made him cry out aloud and soon he was walking about his little room calling: 'No. No. They can't do that. They can't do that.'

Then, so doing, his eyes fell on the Things and he was filled with a sentimental pity for them. They must share in his own disappointment, for it would have been a glorious future for them, and now, when he was gone, they would have no future.

After all he could make a will and leave them, each by name, to a friend. But that would not be at all the same thing. They were too small, too unimportant to be left severally in a will. And how could he make a will when he had nothing to leave but these? He would not confess to himself that what he had wanted to do was to make a little show, to assert himself, even for a moment, before the callous, ungrateful world. And it had been not only his personal vanity, but also a desire for the glory of the Things themselves. He had seen them all set out on the table, and friends regarding them with loving admiration. . . . Oh, well, it had been a childish, senile notion, something that only an old man, very lonely, could

conceive. Best had taken it from him. He was welcome
to it.

But now there was nothing left. He sat down and
stared in front of him. There was nothing left at all,
except the unpaid rent, and Brocket was drawing closer
and closer. . . . He blew his nose. He went to the cabinet and closed the doors. The room now was growing
very dark.

He told himself that he would not go. Of course he
went. It was half-past three of a stormy, yellow-faced
afternoon. In Best's dining-room the electric light blazed
down upon a strange, struggling, noisy crowd.

At the door stood a sleepy-eyed housemaid who received the cards from the invited. At the far corner near
the sideboard on which drinks were arranged stood
Brocket in a shabby blue suit directing a fat boy with
his tie above his collar to serve everyone with cocktails
and sandwiches. The crowd seemed large because the
dining-room table on which the gifts were arranged took
up so much of the room; nevertheless Best's executors
had most certainly invited too *many* friends. It seemed
to Claude, as he stood just inside the door, that they
surged round the table like animals, talking, laughing,
pushing. Constantly someone made a stretch with an arm
towards the table. A lady—there were many ladies—
cried out: 'That's mine. Most certainly that's mine.'

When Claude, moving a little closer, saw the table and
its contents, any resentment against poor Best instantly
died. For they were extremely pathetic. Claude (for he
was tall) beheld a pencil, a ruler and an indiarubber, a
plate with the arms of Emmanuel College, Cambridge,
a volume of poems by Lindsay Gordon (shabby this),
a photograph of the donor in flannels holding a cricket-
bat, a green inkbottle in the shape of a negro's head, two
blue vases stamped with red flowers, a copy of *Decline*

and Fall by Evelyn Waugh, a copy of *Sorrell and Son*
by Warwick Deeping, a photograph in a gilt frame of
the Victoria Falls, a blotter of purple leather, a water-
colour of sea coming in under a large yellow and
inquisitive-looking moon, a cigar-case, a pair of silver
cuff-links . . . these things he saw. There were others.

He was aware of a curious trait in the human character. He felt it rising in himself. Nothing so far as he
could see on the table was of any value at all, and yet
so strong is the passion in the human breast for obtain-
ing something for nothing that the crowd around the
table was beginning to be very troublesome.

When he first came in it seemed that everyone was
politely social. Glasses were held in the air, sandwiches
nibbled, affairs of the day discussed. Oh, wasn't it splendid about Prince George and Princess Marina! Would
it be a really Royal Wedding, one of those *grand* affairs,
nothing hole-and-corner? Yes, and wasn't she truly lovely?
Yes, again and again, and wasn't poor Noel Coward's
misadventure in Corsica too unfortunate? He had lost
fourteen suits of clothes—and Ivor Novello—not very
good, *Murder in Mayfair,* do you think? But *The Shining
Hour.* You should see how naturally Raymond Massey
plays the piano when all the time his barn is burning over
his head! Dated! Dated! Even as the words rise and fall
in the air Time is passing. In another moment it will be
another play, another actor, another marriage, another
music . . . but *not* yet is there any period to that sudden cry (for the Ice Age Man cried it) 'It's mine! I saw
it first!'—and at that shrill voice social amenities are
forgotten, there is a surge towards the table. 'Doesn't
look bad, that razor-strop and blade,' a long thin man,
craning his neck beside Claude, murmured. 'If I could
only get to the table, blast it.'

A stout lady in bright blue, pushing with her arms
right and left, broke right through to the table. She

stretched her fat arm and secured a bronze copy of Hercules strangling a serpent. She held it aloft and cried: 'Fred always wanted me to have this. He said so again and again. It was always on his writing-table and he knew I admired it.'

'If you *don't* mind,' one furious gentleman said to another. 'If you'd kindly keep your arm out of my stomach . . .'

Then someone laughed and then everyone began to roar with laughter. It became, in a moment, the jolliest affair possible. Everyone shoved together. There were screams and cries and triumphant 'I've got it,' and 'Look out—that's mine!' but no hostility now; just a jolly friendly scramble.

And Claude joined in too. He found himself, with arms and legs and shoulders and chests and bosoms, struggling, pushing, until at last he was beside the table, had snatched at a hideous little ash-tray in beaten metal, had triumphantly, his tie hanging out over his waistcoat, secured it!

In the twinkling of Brocket's eye the whole table was cleared. Not a thing remained. Every face was flushed with pleasure, cocktails were demanded. . . .

Claude, in his room, opened his cabinet, took out the Things one after another, dusted each one with his handkerchief. . . .

The cabinet closed, he sat down and gazed at it. For the first time that day a gratified, benignant smile stole across his thin anxious countenance. His things were safe!

That was, however, a brief moment of respite. The wheezy asthmatical clock on the stairs had struck ninethirty. Claude's room was dark save for the reflection that always came from the lamp below in the Market. This reflection was like an old gentleman with a hooked nose. If the curtains were not drawn it settled itself, like one of the grotesques of Leonardo, on the faded wall-paper, and there it clung—an old gentleman with hooked nose and protruding chin and out of his left ear a banner of wavering light. . . .

Claude lay back in his chair, his mouth open, a thin whistling noise from between his lips, and on his fallen eyelids that damp sheen that seems to speak of infinite weariness. The old gentleman's head on the wall becked and nodded. Up from the Market came faintly the sound of someone blowing a horn.

Brocket stood there, watching. He was in an evil temper. The girl he had marked as his own resisted impertinently, said she was engaged to a boy who worked in Charles Street. A set of rooms was vacant and he did not know how long it might be before he found a tenant. And he had scooped in no profits from Mr. Best. That mangy sister of his, Mrs. Fotheringay, and his brother-in-law, Major Fotheringay, they had stood like gaolers over Mr. Best's effects. He'd give them gaolers!

And now he was looking at the sleeping Mr. Willoughby with absolute loathing and with a virtuous sadism too. Cruelty has its own foundation of morality. Brocket felt a very genuine disgust at this old sleep-whistling failure. And he felt his own virtuous power. One word from him, one lift of the finger, and the old man would leap from his slumber, his eyes would stare with half-awakened terror. He would stare like an old madman. Well, perhaps he was by now a madman—half out of his wits—ought to be put away by the authorities. That was a new idea.

'Mr. Willoughby! Mr. Willoughby!' he said softly. He stood with his belly jutting out from the wall, his head a little forward. 'Mr. Willoughby!'

Claude had been standing before the long windows of a glorious room, a room hung with tapestries with a painted ceiling of nymphs and cupids. Breakfast was just over. They were going for a ride. You could hear the horses now on the gravel. . . . 'Mr. Willoughby!' Claude opened his eyes and saw the shabby room veiled in a sort of smoky dusk, the reflection stirring like water on the wall, and then Brocket's belly and the dark form of his thick body in the half-light.

'Mr. Willoughby!'

'Well. . . . What is it?'

'I came to see if you were all right. I was on the stairs and you were crying out." (He was not, but that didn't matter.)

'I was asleep. . . .' Claude sat up. 'All right. What are you standing there for?'

'Are you quite well? You haven't been looking your-self.'

'Of course I'm quite well. What business is it of yours?'

'Oh, nothing.' Brocket came forward and bent a little as though he would see clearly into Claude's face. 'Bit peculiar you've been behaving. Don't know it yourself, I expect.'

Claude sat back in the chair. 'Don't come near me. You know I can't bear it.'

'No—and that's another peculiar thing. If you told someone about it they'd think it *very* peculiar.'

'What do you mean—told someone?'

'Oh, well—I have to see everything's right with my tenants, you know. The authorities trust me for that.'

'But of course I'm all right. There's nothing peculiar in not wanting to be touched by *you!*'

'Now that's rude, Mr. Willoughby, positively rude. But you *have* been talking wild lately. Several people have noticed it. Very wild at times. And the way you have of talking to yourself. . . . Well, well . . . good night. Good night.'

CHAPTER IV

Bullock and Kitty

THE Park has seen so many lovers in its time that it
cannot be expected to pay any very particular attention
to Bullock and Lizzie seated on two little chairs on a late
October afternoon. It is, however, a scientific fact, and
not merely a sentimental whimsy, that lovers are always
assured that clouds, grass, flashes of sunlight, sudden
storms and dust blowing in the eyes have their origin
in the emotions of the heart.

Little Bullock Delaney was never an idle sentimentalist, but he was convinced on this especial afternoon that
the thin October sun, the faint scent of chrysanthemums
from somewhere or other, the idle, twirling fall of an
orange-amber leaf or two—these things were beautifully
operating because he loved Lizzie Coventry so very
dearly.

No relation between any two human beings ever stands
still. Bullock and Lizzie were not where they had been
even a month ago. The great change had occurred during
a railway journey from London to Yarmouth. One fine
morning they suddenly thought that they would pay Yarmouth a visit. Lizzie, to whom Dickens was one of the
few delightful English novelists, wished to salute the
ghosts of the Peggottys. Bullock, monstrously extrava-

gant, bought first-class tickets, and they were, throughout the journey, alone in their compartment.

Bullock lay with his head in Lizzie's lap and her thin hand was on his breast. The morning was exquisite and beautifully silent. They talked very little. As is the way in life, there occurred for Bullock one of those moments of perfect experience when life seems to say: 'For this hour I have decided to deprive myself of all the irritations, disappointments, colds, malaises, bad tempers and incongruities with which it generally amuses me to cloud the scene. For once (and I may never be in the mood again) I allow you to look right through into the clarity of absolute experience. This is what I *really* am; it wouldn't be good for you to see me like this very often. Moreover it would be very dull for *me*.'

Lizzie said once, as though to herself: 'Yes—I know now that I love you, Bullock dear.'

Yarmouth, afterwards, was good enough and they had great fun; on the journey back Lizzie slept, her head on Bullock's shoulder. But it was the journey *thither* that had this great quality of perfection.

She trusted him now entirely and, in many ways, this made things more difficult for him. In years she was still a child, but she had, he now knew, a deep horror of all sexual experience. She might have this always. As a baby she had witnessed the naked wranglings, infidelities, cruelties of mature men and women. As a little child she had heard and seen terrible things. She had saved herself only by a savage and determined resolve to protect herself always from all physical experience. Two persons only in her life, her aunt Fanny and her cousin Edward, had won her trust. Now a third, Bullock, and possibly Bullock's mother.

Bullock knew well that at the slightest evidence on his part of any sexual feeling she would withdraw immediately, and while he had thought of her as a child in his care there had been no danger. But he loved her; she was very mature for her age; he must guard his every thought and action.

Intellectually their constant companionship had developed him with remarkable effect. He read as she suggested, argued, fought and now often won a battle. On this very afternoon they battled with energy over Gide's *Les Faux-Monnayeurs*.

'Well, of course,' Lizzie said, her small face tilted into patronage, 'you have to read a great deal of French fiction before you——'

'Nonsense,' Bullock said. 'I'm perfectly able to tell whether I like a novel in French or any other language. Gide in his dedication calls it his first *novel*. It isn't his first because it isn't a novel. It's simply another of his eternal autobiographies.'

'You're prejudiced against him because of his morals.'

'Certainly I'm not. Who cares nowadays anyway? But as a matter of fact in this case it *does* matter because it makes him lop-sided. Edouard is simply himself, and Edouard's ideas about the novel are so very old-fashioned, getting down to reality and all the rest of it. As though that isn't what everybody's been doing for years *ad nauseam*. Besides if you're a true creator you don't talk about your creation as he's always doing. You just go along and create.'

Lizzie smiled. She was very pale, and her clothes now had a worn, almost shabby look. The effect of them, if you did not see her face, was to make her seem a little old woman, beautifully neat and clean, but a little rusty. And then, when she turned and you saw her face, you saw that she was a child, delicate, anxious, proud. She refused to allow Bullock to do anything for her except pay for meals and transit, a cinema or a cheap seat in the theatre when they were together. Her father now never gave her anything at all. Sometimes she saw money

lying about and took some of it and told him. Then he
would be furious or humorous or indifferent. She hardly
ever saw him now alone. He seemed to be glad that
Bullock had taken her off his hands.

Once, in his own curious way, he had loved her. Now
his personal life was so desperate that he had no time
nor ease to think of her. On her side something remained
of the love that *she* had had, but she hated his surroundings and his companions so intensely that she could not
bear to be in that place.

Bullock knew that she was now in terror although she
would not confess to it. Catastrophe had been down the
street; now it was there down their chimney.

Bullock took her hand in his.

'Don't let's talk about silly books. We must go along
now because I want a word with your father.'

Her hand jumped in his.

'Oh no—why?'

'Because he's got to answer me certain questions.'

'What questions?' Her eyes devoured his face and
he was proud to see how truly now she trusted him.

'He's in an awful mess. It gets worse every day. You
know that. If anything happens what does he do about
you?'

'I go with him, I suppose,' she said simply. 'I always
have.'

'Oh no, you don't. Everything's different now. You
belong to me for ever and ever. You know that perfectly
well.'

'Yes, I suppose so. But you haven't any money either.'

'No, but somehow I shall always have enough to look
after you. And then there's your aunt in Westminster.
But the point is that if your father has to leave England
—well, in a hurry—I want to make it perfectly plain that
he can't just go and send for you whenever he pleases.
You don't belong to *him* any more.'

She sat there, looking in front of her, her small anxious face concentrated on a vision of the past. What a life it had been! What adventures and escapes and shabby intrigues! What lovely places and *lovely* people abandoned so often just when they were especially lovely! And what *vile* people and disgraceful words spoken and horrible things seen! And through it all, that handsome figure of her father, often so merry, kind, generous, loving her, she knew, when he cared for no one else in the world. And now that man was gone, gone for ever. There was no kindness, no generosity, no love. She knew, young as she was, that it had been by his own fault, and by no hardship or injustice of fate, that he had fallen. She drew no moral, made no accusation; only her hands closed tightly on her lap, and she bowed her head for a moment as she bade her father an eternal farewell.

Captain Nicholas Coventry was wearing dark-blue pyjamas and a dressing-gown of white and blue squares. His pyjama jacket was open and revealed his pink chest, and a line above the navel, where his belly began. He was running badly to fat. His ruddy chin wore a thin white stubble. On his feet were soiled red-leather slippers. He was broad, almost feminine, in the beam. His hair was too long above his ears.

But his eyes were wide open. He was not at all bleary-eyed; all his senses were alert. On the table were the dirty remains of a cold-ham-and-beer breakfast. He sat, his legs spread, holding on to the back of a chair, and he was quite clearly at bay, his ears cocked back for the slightest clink of a danger.

Although it was late in the afternoon Bullock could see, through the half-open door, that his bed was still unmade. It seemed from the appearance of the pillows that two persons had been sleeping in it, but there was no sign of anyone about the place. Lizzie had told him that the half-caste had disappeared some two or three days before. 'The first time he has left us for years. He was always *following* Father, but now I don't think he'll come back. He smells it's all over.'

Lizzie went into her little room to take off her hat.

'What do you want?' Captain Nicholas asked. He didn't draw his pyjama jacket together in regard for his daughter. He didn't recognize her in any way.

Then he said: 'Look here, have a drink. . . . I'm going to have a bath. I was up all night so I've been sleeping all day.'

'Did we wake you? Sorry,' Bullock said ironically. He had come to hate Captain Nicholas Coventry. 'No, I don't want a drink.'

'You can talk to me in my bath,' Captain Nicholas said, hitching up his pyjama trousers.

'No I can't,' Bullock said firmly, 'because Lizzie has to be here. Come here, Lizzie.'

'What the hell do you want Lizzie for?'

'Because she must hear what I have to say.'

She stood near him. He put out his arm and drew her close to him.

'Lizzie is still a child in years, but she isn't a child all the same. You know I love her and she loves me.'

'Well?' said Captain Nicholas. 'Get on. I want my bath.'

'What a beast you are!' Bullock said, his round face flushing, his hand trembling ever so slightly on Lizzie's shoulder. 'Here's your only child who's stood every kind of horror and unkindness from you, and you don't give a hang what happens to her.'

Captain Nicholas scratched his left breast. 'My dear boy, I don't care, just now, what happens to anyone but myself. I'm in the hell of a mess if you want to know, and Lizzie will shortly have to look out for herself.' He looked at Bullock, and for a fleeting moment there came into his face the old humorous charm that had once been so persuasive. 'You're writing a novel, aren't you? My daughter tells me so.'

'I am,' Bullock said briefly.

'It'll be a damned bad one. I can tell you that. You're much too penny-plain twopence-coloured about human nature. You think people are either good or bad. You're the hero and I'm the villain. I assure you it isn't so. I'm *weak* if you like. Deliberately so. I think it more amusing to yield to every temptation that comes along. But I'm ever so much better a fellow than you are. Now you don't do anything at all except try to write a novel. I keep ever so many people employed and occupied, including, it seems, the London police. I make young men, who would otherwise be lazy, want to earn money that they may play cards with me. Then I'm infinitely more amusing than you are, know more about life than you will ever know, and make all kinds of women believe that they are handsome and witty.'

'Never mind paying yourself compliments,' Bullock said. 'What I've come here to find out is, if you have to leave the country suddenly, what do you intend to do about Lizzie?'

'Oh, I leave her to you, dear boy, I leave her to you.'

'Yes. That's what I wanted to know. When you go I shall take her to her aunt's in Westminster. In two years' time from now I shall marry her.'

'She's a lucky girl,' said Captain Nicholas, grinning. 'Aren't you, Liz?'

Lizzie said: 'If you want me, Father, I'll come with you.'

'No. I don't want you. It's got beyond that. It's come to a time when it's all I can do to look after myself.' He moved into the little bathroom. Behind the door he was turning on the water, which made a tremendous noise. He appeared through the door, stripped to the

waist, red and grinning. 'But we're safe for a day or two, I think. Be happy, my children.'
Then he shut the door.

'And so he's still unhappy—and wants to see me. Although it's weeks now. . . .'
Kitty looked at the brief letter which said: 'I have been inexcusable. I am in despair. Please give me a quarter of an hour. I can be in the Park by the bandstand to-morrow, Wednesday, about five. I shall be there in any case. Alton.'
They made assignations in the commonest way—although why not? They were not lovers. She had not seen the boy since she had met him with the florid woman in the Park on the last day of September.

Kitty had, however, paid four visits to Alton's father. She liked him. She was not in the least afraid of him. He was like his paintings on the wall in his room—bad taste, strength and honesty and, behind them, real and authentic beauty. He was the strangest man she had ever known, but through contact with him she was awaking to a kinship with reality that would give life an additional dimension. But Alton? He was weak, hysterical, foolish, but she felt for him a great tenderness. He was the first person who had ever roused in her the feelings that she might have for her own child.

She went to the Park. There was thin, slightly aromatic mist as though she were in a windy lighted hall slightly dimmed with cigarette smoke. He was waiting there, the collar of his overcoat turned up, his hands jammed in its pockets.
'I wonder you've come. . . . You must hate me.'
'Hate you! No. Of course not. Let's walk a little. It's chilly.'
'I didn't think you'd see me again.'
'But why on earth not?'

'I've let you down so horribly. And when you passed me the other night . . .'

She said gently: 'I'm only sorry we haven't seen more of one another.'

Words poured from him. 'I wasn't going to see you again. I'm no good, no good at all. I'm still just as I was when I first saw you. Just the same. But it's all no good. I can't write. My play's hopeless and you knew it from the first. But you gave me a sort of hope. There are millions like me who think they have talent, who, when they read a thing, say: "I can do better than that." But they can't really. And then they hear a woman like you and who seems to be interested in them say: "Well, why not? What does class matter these days? We're all the same now." But we're not. There's a great gulf fixed between men like me and women like you. When I kissed you that day of the storm I thought I'd be a new man, different, wonderful. The world would recognize me as a genius and then I could claim you. But of course I'm not a genius, and just because you've been kind to me and visited us it only makes the gulf seem wider.'

'Of course there's no gulf,' Kitty said. 'I told you I'd be your friend and I will be always.'

'How can you be my friend? You can't take me into your world—only if I were a wonderful artist or if you loved me so passionately that you didn't care what happened or what people said.'

'I don't care what people say.'

'No, I don't believe you do. But all the same I haven't the kind of character to make it worth your while. And you're not in love with me.' He paused.

'I'm not in love with anybody,' she said.

'No. It was a new experience for you and you were sorry for me. And then soon you saw how ordinary I was. Why, my father is more interesting to you than I am!'

He paused again.

'He is, isn't he?'

'I like your father. I think he's a very unusual man.'

'I hate my father. He's a beast.'

'Alton!'

'No. What do you know about it? You haven't lived with him for years and years as I have—he pretending he's crippled so that he can be lazy and get us to slave for him, and he do his horrible paintings.' He looked up at her beseechingly. 'I don't know what I'm saying. It isn't true that there's nothing the matter with him. He did have a fall and hurt his spine. But he's been getting better and better. Ever since you first came. Did you know he's sitting up now and he can walk round the room? Well, never mind. What does it matter? I only wanted to tell you that I'm grateful to you for being kind and I mustn't see you again. There's another lady. She's not like you. There couldn't be anyone more different. But she's what I'm meant for. She's my sort.'

'Are you going to be married?' Kitty asked.

'No. Of course not. She's older, years older. Don't ask me about her. Not a word. She's nothing to do with us. I'm no good. I had a dream. I've woken up.'

She put her hand on his arm.

'Now, Alton, listen to me for a minute. I don't think you know much about life yet and I don't either. We're both alike in that. But what I said before is true. I'm your friend now and always. What you do with your life isn't my affair, but at any time—years from now if you like—I'll be your friend just the same, help you if I can, perhaps ask you to help *me*——'

She broke off. She wanted so dreadfully to help him and she hadn't the least idea how to do it. Standing there under the misted trees she realized that she knew nothing about men, nothing about life, nothing about Alton. She had everything, absolutely everything, to learn.

He stood and held out his hand.

'Well, good-bye. You'll be always a kind of miracle to me. A moment's miracle.'

He touched her hand and went.

Kitty Delaney felt anything but a 'miracle' as she walked through the thickening mist homewards. She was very unhappy. In the first place, she was a really nice girl and, like most of the young women of her generation, hated that anyone should be miserable. They are reputed, her generation, to be hard and fast and selfish. On the contrary they are practical, tender-hearted, and think less about sex than the general state of the world. This last thing they find rotten and they have, for the most part, learnt how in this way or that to ameliorate it a little. But this Foster affair was actually Kitty's very first effort at ameliorating something, and she had done, it seemed, nothing but harm to the Fosters.

She had heard, from time to time, the epithet applied to the Delaneys, generally in scorn—the 'joyful' Delaneys—and had always resented it. Now she saw the reason for that resentment. Their family happiness had kept them all from knowing anything about real life. They were all playboys, and to be that at this terrible time of world crisis was dreadful indeed.

They had been happy because they had been living in a kind of fairy-tale, but *now*, Kitty reflected more cheerfully, everything was about to change. Soon, very soon, they would either be penniless or have sold the house. Either event would plunge them beyond question into reality and would surely check their good spirits. But would it be so? She and her father and mother had, during the last week or two, suffered intolerable hardships. That is—there had been, in answer to advertisements in *The Times* and the *Daily Telegraph*, a constant succession of ladies and gentlemen wondering whether

they would take 'a flat.' Old gentlemen, young gentlemen, ladies who were so ancient that they had to be carried from room to room, young women brisk, practical,
full of sex, without any sex at all. The would-be tenants
had apparently only one thing in common—they wanted
something for nothing. When they heard what the rent
was they all exclaimed alike; and yet Fred Delaney had
thought the rent moderate. They said the flats were not
modern enough. The water-closets were especially unsatisfactory, although Fred could not discover why. And,
of course, there was no central heating. It came to this:
that for those who had the money the flats were not good
enough, and those for whom the flats *were* good enough
had no money. The *rudeness* of those who had the money!
Their patronage, conceit, laziness! And those who had
not the money, how friendly they were, how obsequious,
how anxious to move in *at once!*

One lady, carrying a Pekinese dog, smoking a cigarette from a holder as long as her pedigree (she gave
Fred reels and reels of this), with a little squashed face
creased with powder, irregular eyebrows and lips so
bloodily red that it was like reading a murder case in
the paper to look at them, wanted, in a high shrill baby
voice (the sound that comes from a poke-me-in-the-
stomach doll), to move in at once, at once! 'Why should
I wait?' she screamed. 'Why should Po-Ko and I wait?
They suit me perfectly. I can send for my things. All that
I really need is a saucer of milk for Po-Ko!' It was
quickly discovered, alas! that Mrs. Lane Fosby Feather-
stone had not a bean in the world and owed mountains
and mountains of beans to unfortunate, trusting shop-
keepers. Then one slim lady, suddenly flashing her eye
like a lighthouse beam on to Meg's innocent countenance,
said: 'A young man committed suicide in these rooms,
did he not?' After that, everyone seemed to know it,
always enquired ghoulishly to behold exactly the spot

where the deed had been committed, and then, after a thrilled and exhaustive examination, declared that it wouldn't be possible to live in a house where there had been a suicide.

'Statistics,' Fred Delaney said cheerfully, 'show that there has been, at one time or another, a suicide in every house in London.'

'But this is so recent.'

'That means that there won't be another here for at least a century. The average is—one a century.'

Beastly of them, Kitty thought, to behave thus about poor Smoke; but then they hadn't known him. It did make such a difference if you knew somebody!

Very shortly a decision must be come to—sale, mortgage, or tenants. Kitty loved both her parents, but especially, perhaps, her father, and she did realize that leaving the house would be appalling for them and would separate all the family for the first time in their lives.

Bullock would *have* to get a job somewhere and would marry one day, she supposed, that funny pale silent child of his. And she—would she marry Colonel Beaminster?

Oh no, no, no! Never, never! At that she realized, standing now in Charles Street, just outside the beloved house, why it was that she was happy in spite of her dreadful failure with Alton Foster, and Colonel Beaminster's ardent desire for her. It was because she was free! Alton's father had in some mysterious, coarse, but vital fashion, given her a sense of the positive *experience* of life—hurting, wounding, scorning, maiming, slaughtering, but *life!* She was free, she was alive, she was in love with no one. But she would be, she would be! She was on the verge! She was about to plunge into a miraculous, tossing, spuming, thundering sea!

All very well. But what she found when she entered the firelit, friendly, gaily-coloured room was little Millie

Pake looking so old, so wan and so fragile that it was heartbreaking to behold.

'Millie! You darling! At last! We thought we were never going to see you again!'

Millie was greatly touched by her love and sympathy; indeed for a moment Kitty thought that Millie was going to cry. She was made of sterner stuff. She sat down in her rather faded black dress and talked.

'But where's Mother? Does she know you're here?'

'Oh yes, dear. We were having a nice talk when someone arrived to see the flats.'

'Poor Mother. . . . But tell me—where are you living and why haven't you been to see us before?'

'I've been in the country with my brother. I didn't want to come and see you until I was settled.'

'And where *are* you settled?'

'In Bloomsbury, dear. A very nice room quite close to the Ivanhoe Hotel.'

'Why,' Kitty thought, 'I don't believe she's having enough to eat. I'm sure she isn't.'

'Bloomsbury—but do you like it there?'

'Not so much as here, dear, of course. But one must go where one can afford.'

'Oh dear—how I wish you could come back here! But I'm afraid we shall have to sell the house.'

'So your mother's been telling me. It seems *such* a pity, such a terrible pity.'

'Of course it is. I don't know what poor Father will do. But it's money. Everything's money nowadays.'

Meg came in. 'Thank heaven *they're* gone! . . . Oh, there you are, dear. Now, Millie darling, we'll have some tea.'

'There's something up with Mother,' Kitty thought. 'She's in a very odd state of excitement.'

Caesar brought in the tea and there seemed something strange about him too.

'What's the matter with Caesar?' Kitty asked.

'He's having a dreadful time with his old mother. She's found out he's got a girl and he won't give her up.'

'I should think not indeed.'

Millie got up to go. There was a slight fog and the bus would be slow. Kitty felt a sense of acute discomfort at the thought of the dreary lonely room to which she must be returning.

'Look here, dear. Mother and I will come and take you out to lunch to-morrow.'

'Very soon, dear, we will,' Meg said, kissing Millie.

'I'm afraid I can't to-morrow. I'm going away for the week-end.'

Kitty turned on her.

'You are? First I've heard of it. Why, wherever to?'

'To some friends, dear.'

'What—you and Father?'

'No. Father *is* going away, I believe—but somewhere else. To some shooting, I think.'

'Well—what do you think of that!' Kitty cried.

'Very nice,' Millie Pake said at the door. 'Going away for the week-ends. I used to think it the greatest fun.'

'I'll come and take you out to lunch by myself, then. What's the address?'

'I think we'd better meet somewhere,' Millie said.

'All right, then. Let's meet at Oxford Circus outside the Tube. One o'clock. Good-bye, darling. Look after yourself.'

Back in the room again Kitty looked at her mother.

'Where on earth are you off to to-morrow?'

'I'm going to stay with friends.'

'And that's all I'm to know?'

'That's all you're to know.'

Kitty kissed her.

'Oh, well, you deserve a bit of fun.'

'Yes,' said Meg. 'I think I do.'

CHAPTER V

Meg

'CROSSING the Park is like crossing the Rubicon,' Fred
Delaney had once said. Meg was not quite sure of anything about the Rubicon except that it was a river, but
she did wake very early in the morning from a strange
dream in which a schoolmistress in a gown and mortar-
board had cried out: 'Now, Meg Delaney, if you can't
jump the Park you've failed. It ought to be quite easy
after all the exercise you've been taking.'

She looked at the Park and it was a broad brown piece
of soil with trees on the other side. The trees were
crowded with birds, all squawking at once. She jumped
—and woke to the thin grey light behind the curtains
and Fred's stout body in the next bed huddled and sleep-
soaked, his gentle comfortable breathing speaking its
usual reassurance and safety.

Safety! That was all very well. *This* was the day! She
did not sleep another wink.

At about a quarter to twelve Fred Delaney, looking
very smart and debonair, kissed her and patted her on
the shoulder.

'Well, old dear, I'm off.'

'What time's your train?'

'Oh, somewhere round one. I shall look in at the Club.' She kissed him.

'Good-bye, darling. Sure you've packed everything?'

'I think so.'

'Look after yourself. Mind you shoot well. Don't disgrace the family.'

There was a little pause at that.

'And you look after *yourself.*'

'Oh, of course. What time will you be back on Monday?'

'Oh, I don't know. Some time in the morning.'

'I'll expect you for lunch, then.'

Fred was gone. And then there was Bullock.

'I say, darling—it's such a lovely day. Why don't you come to Kew this afternoon with Lizzie and me?'

Meg sat down in a corner of the sofa with her book.

'Didn't you know, dear? I'm going away for the week-end.'

Bullock stared.

'Oh, are you? Wherever to?'

'Just to some friends. People you don't know, dear.'

'Oh, Lord! . . . and Father's going away too, isn't he?'

'Yes, dear. . . . He's gone.'

'How extremely rum! Who's going to look after the prospective tenants?'

'Oh, Caesar will show them round if you and Kitty are out. They don't come much at week-ends.'

'No. I suppose they don't.'

Bullock stared at his mother speculatively for a moment, kissed her on the forehead.

'So long, darling. I hope you have a lovely time. Back Monday morning?'

'I expect so.'

'Right-ho.' Bullock went out, whistling.

Meg sat there with the very clever novel on her knee. She was holding it upside-down. The house was silent about her, the sun pouring joyfully into the room.

She was to meet Graham Pender at Paddington Station at four o'clock. Caesar would bring her in a little something to eat on a tray. Her face was hot, as though someone had slapped her. She was in a state of thrilling anticipation, dismay, self-disapproval, self-glorification, vanity and tenderness. She felt as though she were sitting in the middle of the sofa, one arm round Fred, the other round Graham. No—*not* round Fred, for he had gone to spend a week-end of sin with Alice Van Renn. She hated Alice Van Renn! Oh, how she hated her!—and this week-end of hers that was to be spent near Oxford was in a way a slap in the face of Alice Van Renn. Not that Alice would care. But Fred would and did.

He had come out of his dressing-room that morning and said, as she sat at the looking-glass brushing her beautiful hair:

'Where are you going, Meg? This week-end, I mean?'

'I'll tell you,' she had answered, 'if you'll tell me where *you're* going.'

'I think we're a pair of bloody fools,' he had answered.

And so perhaps they were. Meg had, of course, never been unfaithful to him before. She did not *know* that she was going to be unfaithful to him now. She was hoping to give poor Graham a little happiness for an hour or two, so that, as he said, he 'would have something to remember.' She was doing, she said to herself over and over again, 'no one any sort of harm.' She was sure, by this time, that that strange woman, Evelyn Pender, knew all about it and was quite agreeable to Graham's 'having a little adventure.' She was as sure of Graham as Meg was of Fred. Or was she? Was anyone ever sure of anyone? Well, then, suppose no one was. This was a definitely *wicked* thing that Meg was going to do—and Meg didn't care! It was her last, her very last fling! And how many middle-aged, happily married women there were who would adore to have a last fling and would be all the better for it if they did! How many virtuous married women there were, who saw old age stealthily approaching and *did* have a last fling—if only the whole truth were known!

But it was no use at all to think of other women! Other women might commit their sins their own way. Everyone's history was his or her own history.

She remembered a dear old priest to whom she had listened once as he talked on the wireless about Chastity. It was clear that he had a most charming personality; it was also clear that he knew nothing whatever about the perils and sins and urgencies of the flesh. Here was Meg Delaney, middle-aged and handsome, happily married, who yet had the devil in her and longed before she died that some man, not her husband, should tell her that he loved her, should say the pretty things and look at her as though she were the queen of the earth and tell her that she was still beautiful. Only this once before she died! And why was it so evil? She was married to a man who loved her, but who yet had been physically unfaithful to her and would be again. He did not love her the less for that infidelity, and she, through long training, had learnt not to be inquisitive and not to be jealous. The fires in him were already dying down. Already he almost never left her side. Had she been the other sort of wife, tiresome, nagging, resentful, reminding, would he not have fled from her long ago? From her babyhood almost she had learnt that men must be patiently borne with by women. Even the best of them would stray at times. No. *Not* the best of them! There *were* men whose fidelity, self-sacrifice, chastity, made them miracles. She had met one or two. But then she had always noticed that their chaste marital fidelity gave them a kind of thin, unhumorous, greedy air. They sat over their wives as a hen sits brooding on an egg!

Ah! it was a difficult, difficult world, and women who loved life and knew that soon—ah! so soon! so soon! —they would wither and decay—poor women—God be merciful to them!

And—at that moment's thought of the God in Whom she believed—she pushed her mind away and turned her novel right side up and walked about the room and sat down again and said: 'Ah, Caesar, here's the lunch —that's good!' because she knew that it was a wicked thing that she was about to do and that the less she thought about God (until the thing was over) the better.

Caesar was looking extremely lugubrious. There were heavy lines about his eyes as though he had not been sleeping.

'Here are the soup and the fish. I'll bring in the cutlet presently.'

'You don't look very well, Caesar. What's the matter?'

He stood before her, in his black suit, a mere unhappy child.

'It's my mother, Mrs. Delaney. She's been carrying on something dreadful.'

'I shouldn't live with her, then.'

'I can't very well help it. She'd be all alone by herself.'

'It's ridiculous. No mother can stop her son marrying. It's right and fair he should.'

'What's all wrong, Mrs. Delaney, is that she won't see the girl. She's ever so nice and sweet. If Mother saw her she'd *have* to like her.'

'I shouldn't count on that,' said Meg.

'No, perhaps you're right, Mrs. Delaney. And there's something else. There's this man in the Market won't leave her alone.' Caesar's brow darkened. He looked really formidable. 'I'm a bit of a boxer,' Caesar said.

'And if I catch him at his games there'll be murder done. My girl hates him and slapped his face night before last.'

'Who is the man?'

'His name's Brocket. He's a beast, that's what he is.'

'Don't you worry, Caesar. It'll all come right.' She sighed. 'The only sad thing is that it really looks as though we shall have to sell the house. We *can't* get any-one to take the rooms.'

'No. I know,' said Caesar, looking even more lugubri-ous. 'Aren't they awful? The people that come, I mean. They don't know *what* they want.'

'They know only too well what they want. They don't want to live here—that's all. However, you'll soon get another place. And better than this!'

'Oh, Mrs. Delaney, I don't want to leave you—I don't indeed. And my girl and me's been thinking. If you've got to go to a smaller place—well—she cooks beautiful. She's an artist. She really is. And we were thinking——' Then embarrassment suddenly took him, and muttering something about 'cutlets' he retired.

It was half-past two. She need not leave for the station until half-past three. In her state of agitation she could not remain still. She would walk a little.

She walked slowly and as she walked she thought: 'I'll have to go now anyway. It would be too awful to have the long Sunday in London knowing all the time where Fred is. Suppose Evelyn Pender is planning some horrible trick, suddenly turns up or sets spies on us or something! Suppose she divorces Graham! Oh, but she *never* would! . . . I feel ridiculous—exactly as I used to in Nice when I had fifty francs unexpectedly to spend, and as I did when I hurt Mademoiselle's feelings by say-ing something rude and personal. I feel *now* as though already I had done some incalculable wrong to someone. . . . How ridiculous! There are, I suppose, hundreds of women—and not so young either—going off this week-

end with men they're not married to. The curious thing
is that I'm terribly excited but *not* very happy. Not my
usual happiness. But when I see Graham waiting there at
Paddington I shall forget everything else in seeing *his*
happiness! But there must be no more of these meetings
—not after this one. I must make that clear to him. There
must never be another. Oh dear! Here I am in Shepherd
Market. . . .'

It was strange, she thought, that as soon as you passed
under Miss Bonda's archway your standards of excitement, beauty, sensation, seemed to alter. There was,
for example, nothing exceptional about 'Ye Grapes' at
the corner of Market Street, and yet it would not at
all surprise you to see Shakespeare and Ben Jonson
walking out of it arm in arm, wiping their beards. Nor
was there anything out of the ordinary handsome about
the fish-shop, and yet it positively *reeked* of the sea as
though you were enjoying a holiday at Mevagissey, Pen-
berth Cove, Bedruthan Steps and Bude all at the same
time.

Meg had a curious sensation as though, when she
stepped into Market Street, something whispered to
her: 'You've altered your life by walking in here. Everyone who walks in here at certain changes of the moon
does.'

She looked at her wrist-watch. It was ten minutes to
three. She would have started back to Charles Street,
but a curious, cracked, rather 'horsy' voice detained her.
She was standing, without knowing it, outside the book-
shop that had the shelf of 'sixpenny' and 'twopenny'
volumes; and very good value most of them were!

At her side was a middle-aged lady, short and square-
shouldered, wearing a black straw hat with a pin through
it such as they wore in the nineteen hundreds. She was
searching rather short-sightedly along the row of 'six-
pennies.'

'If you see,' she said, without even looking at Meg, *Red Pottage* anywhere, do let me know.'

'*Red Pottage?*' asked Meg.

'Yes. By Mary Cholmondeley. It's got a red cover and was published by Edward Arnold. It turns up in every six-penny lot, as fresh as a strawberry. It was a best seller in its day—like *The Heavenly Twins* and *The School for Saints*. They turn up too all the time, poor things. Not the three-volume *Heavenly Twins.* That's rather rare, of course. But *The School for Saints.* I'm sure there's one somewhere. Yes, there it is. You can't mistake it. There must have been *thousands* of it. Poor Pearl Craigie. I knew her very well. Such a clever woman, but too sensitive. Took herself too seriously. All women novelists do. But it's *Red Pottage* I'm after. Such an exciting book! The clergyman burns Hester's manuscript in the fire because he thinks it immoral. *What* a lot of manuscripts he'd have to burn nowadays, wouldn't he? I'm sure they *must* have *Red Pottage* somewhere.' Then she looked up at Meg and smiled. She was one of those plain dowdy Englishwomen who, because they are so plain and so dowdy, are so obviously ladies.

Meg would have been delighted to stop and talk to her, but she said, looking at her watch again: 'No, I've never read *Red Pottage,* I'm afraid.' She smiled in her friendly easy way that had led her so frequently into quick intimacy with the completest strangers. 'I must be getting on. I've got to catch a train.'

'Ah, going into the country for the week-end,' said the other lady, nodding her head. 'Very pleasant in fine weather like this. I've got to go to a meeting of the Down-at-Heels Committee. Such a bore.'

So they parted in the friendliest manner and Meg turned once again to the Market exit. But now she was stopped by a cat. Cats, of course, abound in the Market, but they are mostly of the secret-purpose I've-no-time-to-

waste-on-humans variety. This cat was a large yellow one
and he came deliberately and rubbed himself against
Meg's dress. This was more than Meg could resist and
she bent down and stroked him. This enchanted the cat,
who purred like a giant tea-kettle, arched his back,
walked a little like a bandmaster in a royal procession,
and looked up at Meg with large green eyes full of love.
Meg was delighted. The cat seemed in some way to reassure her. She walked a little way, the cat following
her. Then, as though the cat had directed her, she looked
upwards. There was White Horse Street, in no way
remarkable or beautiful. A window on the top floor of
one of the buildings was open. As Meg gazed, in it appeared the terrified, agonized face of Claude Willoughby.

The face stared at her without seeing her. Yes, it was
terrified and agonized—an old, worn, seamed countenance, of an old, old man crazy with fright. Meg thought
that he would call out but he did not. He was there and
was gone.

Without a moment's hesitation Meg crossed to the
building whose window it was. As she arrived, a tall,
very complacent elegant gentleman came out. He looked
seriously in front of him as though he were recognizing
that God had truly been made in his image and should
be grateful for His good fortune. This, although Meg
did not know it, was Colonel Badget going for his afternoon walk. Letting Badget out let Meg in. Inside the
dark and fusty hall was the traditional serving-maid of
the music-hall, grimy, sniffing, and looking surreptitiously
through the 'gentlemen's letters' just arrived by post. On
to her Meg seized.

'Tell me, please, which is Mr. Willoughby's room.'

The girl, startled, dropped the letters, looked down
at them stupidly, then said as though speaking in her
sleep: 'Upstairs. Top floor.'

And up the stairs Meg went. The sunlight struck the

top landing, illuminating a rickety hatstand, a mildewed print of Frith's 'Railway Station,' and a pail with a dirty cloth. There was also a door, and on this Meg knocked.

There was no answer, so she turned the handle and went in. She will never forget every small detail of this afternoon. Especially not Claude's room—the shabby table with the worn silver brushes, the cabinet with the Things, the grate with a fan of red paper, the bed with the tear in the counterpane, the open window in whose air the sun played like a water-misted firework. She saw these things later. For the moment her attention was caught fixedly by the actors in the little drama played here.

Claude Willoughby was stretched in the sunlight against the torn wallpaper, almost as though he were crucified. But his thin arms were bent forward as though he were protecting himself against something. Almost touching him was a man, his shirt-sleeves rolled up, a dirty apron round his belly, his shabby back distended towards the door. This man's horrid nose was but the breadth of a hair from Claude's nose. His eyes stared into Claude's eyes. One dirty hand at the end of the naked hairy arm moved like an animal in space. Neither heard the door open. The man was saying: 'It's come to this, then. You're not safe to be left. You do what I tell you, see, or I'll be handing you over to the authorities. It's no sort of good your trying to throw yourself out of window. That won't help you. Anyhow, you haven't the pluck. What *you* 'ave to do, Mr. Claude Willoughby, from now on is to do as I tell you, see? When I says "Go" you go, and when I says "Come" you bloody well come. I says "Stand up" and you stand up. Otherwise they'll be taking you away, and do you know where they'll be taking you?'

'No,' whispered Claude.

'They'll be taking you to a lonely house, miles from

anywhere, and the windows will all have bars in front of
them, and there you'll be, shut up in a little room with
padded walls, and all you'll hear, night *and* day, will be
the screams of the other loonies—see?'

'Oh no, no,' whispered Claude.

It seemed to Meg time to break in upon this mono-
logue, so she said:

'I wish to speak to Mr. Willoughby.'

The man sprang round as though a hornet had stung
him. He stared at Meg Delaney as though she had
spectre-thickened straight out of the dirty carpet. He was,
she thought, as nasty-looking a man as she had ever set
eyes on.

'And what the hell . . .' he began. Then his voice
changed. As I have said elsewhere, Brocket had been
trained to recognize a lady when he saw one. Meg must
have been a handsome sight, very smart in her dark-blue
travelling costume, wrath and indignation in her splendid
eyes, as tall and noble and commanding as Juno herself.
Brocket knew nothing about Juno, but he began: 'I beg
your pardon, madam. You have mistaken, I think——'

However, he was interrupted by a little sigh—the
sort of sigh that a child gives when it turns over in its
sleep, and he swerved to find Claude Willoughby in an
unconscious heap upon the floor.

Meg went at once and, picking him up, carried him
like a baby to the bed, upon which she laid him.

'Don't stand there gaping, you fool. Get some water.'

Brocket went to the jug and basin and poured out some
water. He handed her the basin and the towel. She bent
over Claude, bathing his forehead, undoing his collar,
chafing his hands and murmuring: 'There! There . . .
there's nothing to be frightened of. No one shall hurt
you. It's all right. You're quite safe.'

Once she turned fiercely on Brocket. 'He looks half
starved. What have you been doing to him?'

Brocket murmured: 'It's none of my business. He's old.
He wants looking after.'

She turned back to the bed. She had taken off her hat,
and her glorious hair was revealed to the unworthy
Brocket. As she bent forward he could not help thinking,
in spite of the discomfort that he was feeling, that she
was as fine a woman as he'd ever seen.

Claude stirred. He opened his eyes, saw Meg, smiled
faintly and closed them again.

'Soon,' Meg said, 'when he's recovered a little we must
get him to bed.'

'Yes, ma'am,' said Brocket. He had recovered his assurance. After all, this commanding woman had overheard, in all probability, little of what he had been saying. He was, however, instantly undeceived.

She was sitting now on the bed's edge, rubbing Claude's
wrists and moistening his forehead. He seemed to her,
with his even-drawn lips, sunken cheeks, dark heavy eyelids, like half a ghost already. She turned to Brocket, who
for her unpleasantly scented the air.

'What have you been doing to let him get into this
state?'

'It's none of my business. He's only my tenant.'

'Of course it's your business.' Meg's eyes seemed to
swallow him into their angry dark depths and he turned
his head away. 'In any case what were you saying to him
when I came in?'

'I was saying nothing, ma'am.'

'Oh yes, you were. I was standing there several minutes
before you knew it. You were threatening him with an
asylum.'

'Not threatening, ma'am. Only saying that he oughtn't
to be left alone by himself.'

Meg broke in furiously. She lost her temper at times
with royal abandon.

'I've had enough of your lying. One's only got to look

at you to see what lies you tell. You've been bullying Mr. Willoughby for ever so long. I can see you're the sort of person that loves to bully.'

Brocket's body gave a sort of squirm.

'You'd better be careful,' he said. 'That's libellous.'

'What the hell do I care for libel?' Meg got up and stood over him like an avenging demon. She gave her hair a tug as she always did when she was in a fury. Her long crystal ear-rings swung backwards and forwards as though they were greatly enjoying the scene.

'Do you think I've lived so long and been thrown about anyhow ever since I was born to worry myself at being threatened by a fat worm like you? You talk to me again like that and I'll go straight to the window and call the police. There's plenty you don't want *them* to be interfering with, I'll be bound. Here's this poor man, starving to death in this cold bare room, and instead of kindness you've been trying to drive him into madness. Oh yes! I heard every word you said. Another piece of impertinence from you and straight to gaol you go. And that's the bloody truth. And if you don't think that ladylike, you can just take it that "bloody" is the only word that applies to men like you. Do you hear?'

'Yes, ma'am,' said Brocket, frightened, of course, but thinking that she'd be a grand piece to make love to if she'd been in another walk of life.

Claude opened his eyes again. He said very feebly: 'Don't let him touch me.'

'No, of course he shan't,' Meg said. 'Nor myself either if I can help it.' She turned back again. 'Here you. What's your name?'

'Brocket, ma'am.'

'Tell them to get a hot-water bottle ready. And to prepare some good strong soup. Is there a telephone anywhere?'

'In the passage there's a tube you blow down.'

'Go and blow down it, then.'

Brocket went. Claude seemed to be sleeping. He was breathing now quietly and gently. It was then that she suddenly thought of the time. She looked at her watch. It was a quarter past three. Good God! She could just do it now if she started at once back to the house! Of all inconceivable things she had entirely forgotten Graham! She stood up and in her agitation began to speak aloud.

'This is frightful. I must go. How *could* I forget?'

Brocket re-entered.

'The bottle and the soup are both ordered, ma'am.'

She had just time if she was very swift to get Claude into bed and see him comfortable.

'Hurry now. Help me. Where are his pyjamas? We must get him to bed.'

Brocket felt beneath the pillow without disturbing Claude and produced some worn-threadbare pyjamas in white and brown stripes.

'Now I'll lift him. Get his boots off.' She put her broad arm round Claude and his head rested on her comfortable bosom. He opened his eyes again and said once more: 'Don't let him touch me.' He stared into her face and was quite unaware, happily, of Brocket's movements.

'He doesn't seem exactly in love with you,' Meg said grimly.

'These old gentlemen get funny ideas.'

'Yes, I daresay. This will want looking into.'

Brocket, not ungently, had pulled off his boots and socks. They stripped him and put the pyjamas on. What a skeleton he was! How white with that deadly whiteness of the starved and dying! Meg kissed his forehead, then, picking him up in her arms, holding him for a moment against her breast, while Brocket turned back the clothes and patted the pillows as though he had loved dear Mr. Willoughby all his life long, they tucked the old man in.

'Now—keep away. He'll have a fit if you touch him. What have you done to make him so frightened of you?'

'I haven't done anything. In fact I've been good to him, letting him off his rent and one thing and another.'

'I *bet* you've been good to him. Anyone can see that. Where's that hot-water bottle? Go and blow down that thing again!'

Brocket went.

She stroked Claude's forehead. He seemed to be in a deep slumber. Now she must really go.

But Claude had turned and laid his thin blue-veined hand on hers. He was speaking and she bent towards him that she might hear him better.

'You won't go, will you? Not for a minute. That was foolish of me—fainting like that. That man frightens me. Silly—very silly.'

'I'm afraid I must go,' she said gently. 'I have a train to catch.'

His hand tightened on hers. 'No, don't go. Don't go,' he whispered.

She stared at the door. Where *was* that oaf? Had he gone himself to fetch that water-bottle? She looked again at her watch. What was she to do? Now, even if there was a taxi in Curzon Street and she rushed straight to the house and on to the station, it would be a very near thing.

She saw very clearly a vivid picture of poor Graham pacing the station. There he was with his dear friendly face puckered and anxious, staring at the entrance, gazing at the station clock, knowing the crowding-in of all those fears that he must for days and nights have confronted, that, after all, at the last moment she would be frightened and not come.

'Yes,' he would be saying. 'I might have known it. But she should have warned me. She should have telephoned. It's cruel, it's cruel. . . .'

'I must go,' she cried, springing up. 'It's all right. I'll see that someone comes to look after you. I'll make it all right. I'll make it all right.'

It was twenty to four. In another five minutes it would be too late unless she went straight to the station without luggage, clothes, anything. . . .

Brocket entered, carrying the hot-water bottle. 'The soup's coming up and this is Colonel Badget's bottle. I don't know what he——'

She snatched it from him.

'Give it me!' She put it into the bed, bent down and kissed Claude's forehead once more. 'There. I must go. Indeed I must. But now a nice sleep——'

Claude caught her arm with a hand astonishingly firm. He agonizedly whispered: 'Don't leave me. Please don't leave me. He's here. When you've gone he'll send for them and they'll take me to the asylum. He said so. He——'

'Nonsense.' She tried to release her arm. 'He won't do anything. I've talked to him. He won't do a thing.'

Then she looked and in Claude's face was such burning naked terror that she knew that she could not go.

'Very well, then,' she said, laying her hand on his forehead. 'Don't be frightened. I'll stay.'

'Here's the soup, ma'am—and a little chicken. I thought it could do no harm.'

'Harm! I should think not.'

She sat by the bed, taking the soup, leaving the chicken on the table. She spoke to Brocket:

'You needn't stay. My name is Mrs. Delaney. Here is my card with my address. You'd better be careful what you're up to. I shall come and see Mr. Willoughby every day. I will leave a list of things I want you to get before to-morrow. Who's his doctor?'

'His doctor, ma'am. Why, he hasn't got one.'

'Who's the best general doctor round here?'

'Doctor Thompson in Half Moon Street. *He's* a good doctor.'

'I shall telephone to him in the morning. If Mr. Willoughby is worse in any way, you're at once to ring up Doctor Thompson and ask him to come. Do you understand?'

'Yes, ma'am.'

'Look in here later in the evening and see if he wants anything. But don't stay. He can't abide you. Neither can I.'

'No, ma'am.'

'If I find you've been disagreeable to him in any way whatever I'll have you instantly arrested.'

'Yes, ma'am.' Then with a sudden unexpected sense of humour Brocket added, grinning a dirty grin: 'You *would* look foolish, ma'am!'

'Never mind what I'd look. Now clear out. I shall stay for a short while until I see Mr. Willoughby is properly asleep.'

'Yes, ma'am.' Brocket withdrew, his slippers flapping behind him. He threw her one last surreptitious look. He had really never seen a finer, better built-up woman!

Claude took the soup and then the chicken. He never said a word, only smiled once and again. When she had given him everything he turned over, like a baby, and went to sleep.

Meg sat down in the old chair and looked at the red paper in the grate. The sun now did not shine directly into the room. Everything was alive with a dancing light. She got up and closed the open window. Now all was very still.

She sat there staring in front of her, and then, quite unexpectedly to herself, began to cry—softly lest she should disturb Claude.

She could see and feel nothing now but Graham Pender's disappointment. There he was walking up and down the station! There he was and there was the entrance, figures hurrying in and out! He would think that she might have mistaken the platform. He would enquire again its number. He would have, under his arm, a bundle of illustrated papers that he had bought for her. He would watch the clock now, in a kind of agony, for the thin greedy fingers were eating up the minutes. Something had delayed her. She would arrive, breathless, full of apologies. Ah! that was she! At last! At last! He would move eagerly forward. No. . . . No. . . . Five minutes to four. He would speak to the porter. 'Take my things out of the carriage. My friend may not be coming.' Ah, now! Surely there she was, the porter behind her carrying her bags. No. . . . No. . . . They were closing the doors. He stood on the platform, his two bags at his feet. The whistle blew. The train moved out.

Oh, poor Graham, poor, poor Graham! Her tears stained her cheeks. Furtively she blew her nose. Poor, poor Graham! For it would not happen again. She knew that with a sudden sure certainty, and after that, came with a clarity as though someone had spoken to her—she was glad that it had not happened!

Glad? Yes: there was about her, around her, permeating the room, a strong deep conviction of relief.

It was as though the air, which had clouded her senses for months, was now unexpectedly clear. It came, in a fashion that she could not then explain, from the bare shabby room in which she was sitting, from the old tired man asleep in the bed. It had some resemblance to the intense relief and happiness that one has when, after a long meaningless quarrel with someone whom one loves, there is a joyful reconciliation.

With whom was she reconciled? With herself?

There was an element of roughness and violence in her that came, perhaps, from her muddled and messy childhood. How very vulgar she had been, for instance, when she lost her temper with that man just now! And that same violence had played its part in her flirtation with Graham.

She saw now quite clearly that it would never have done, that however right and natural it might be, in these enlightened days, for other married women to have affairs with men not their husbands, it was not right and natural for her.

Her vision and comprehension moved swiftly forward. It was as though, in this stillness and removed from her own surroundings, she saw twice as clearly as she had ever seen before. Everyone must judge his or her own individual case. One must never judge anyone else. But for oneself there were rules and circumstances, and if one did not follow them, decline and fall ensued.

She saw, with amazing sharpness, the relationship between herself and Fred. In their eagerness to give one another freedom and liberty everything had been conceded. 'We love one another,' they had said. '*Nothing* can touch that ever. So we may have complete liberty.' But something, she saw, *could* touch it! Had she gone for that week-end with Graham, her relation to Fred would not afterwards have been the same. Nor her relation to Graham. Nor her relation to Evelyn Pender. Nor her relation to her children. The events of that week-end might be slight indeed. Everyone declared that the old morality was dead and that women especially in these days must have the same freedom as men. But never mind about women! *This* was the adventure of one woman, Margaret Delaney, and for one woman such an act would be damaging, destructive, and would undermine all the security of her married life.

There were laws and rules for herself which now she saw had to be obeyed if the things that were important to her were to be safe. Fred had said to her: 'I ask no questions. I love you too much.' But Fred himself did not know, although he had lived with her so long, what were *her* laws.

She was careless, excitable, passionate, impulsive: but beneath all that she was something more. She had something good in her possession, and, almost, that good in her had been tarnished.

This was her link with God. He had not said a word. He had not stirred a finger. There had not been a whisper of His voice. But He had not forgotten her.

She bent forward and, with closed eyes, prayed.

Claude was deeply asleep. She stole away. She let herself into the house and gave a little shiver as she saw the room, the fire out, the clever novel on the chair, silence and emptiness.

She took off her hat and sat down. The week-end would be terrible. During every minute of it she would be aware of what Fred was doing. Well, she must face it and must greet him on Monday morning as though all was well. Was she perhaps allowing *him* too much freedom? Were his gay adventures beginning to interfere with their happy security? When they left this house, as undoubtedly they must, would they slip apart and lose one another? She sighed. How difficult life was! How cold and lonely was this room!

Then something moved. It was Endless, who had been sleeping under the chair. He came and rubbed his cold nose against her hand with that ironical attitude of friendly indifference especially his. She stroked his sleek coat, and her cheerfulness began to return. She could never, God help her, be depressed for very long!

She would steel herself to Fred's absence. She would spend a gay Sunday with Kitty and Bullock and a friend or two. She would not think of Fred—and of the detestable Alice: of Fred, of Fred—nor hear his laugh, nor see his eyes, nor feel against her lips the rough manliness of his cheek. She got up. She would bathe her face, brush her hair, telephone to somebody.

She moved. She stood still—for she could hear, through the half-open door, the turn of a key in the lock. Ah, thank heaven, Bullock or Kitty was already back!

The door was pushed open, and there, staring in surprise, stood Fred Delaney.

CHAPTER VI

Fred

FRED DELANEY threw a glance across at the Green Park while he waited at the corner of Half Moon Street, hailing a taxi from the rank opposite.

He had walked that far, carrying his bag, the sort of imbecile thing that he was for ever doing. He had simply gone straight out of the house, his bag like a feather in his strength, virility, happiness at the events in front of him. Easily he could walk thus all the way to Victoria. The elegant page-boy, coming out of the flats at No. 90 to run across the street and post a letter, stopped for an instant and stared.

That brought Fred to his senses. He must not, to-day, make himself too conspicuous! In any case he was not going to Victoria Station—yet! He engaged a cab and told it to drive to the Moonstone in Apple Tree Yard. The Moonstone was a small Bohemian club of which he had been, for many years, a member. He would lunch there, a cosy place where he would be unlikely to meet anyone save a casual acquaintance.

The first person he *did* meet was Patrick Munden. He was delighted and in his delight most genuine. He had always been fond of Munden, had missed him badly during these last months, and had felt perhaps a certain guilt and responsibility with regard to him. If he had spoken earlier Smoke might have been saved. But would it have been better if Smoke *had* been saved?

Munden was arrogantly and amicably cheerful. 'You must come and lunch with *us,* Fred. Two writing fellows. Rose and Pargiter. You've heard of Rose, of course—an absolute ass and writes the most awful tripe naturally, but Dodie likes him. . . . Oh yes, Dodie and I are living together in Paris. Get on very well. May marry. I don't know. . . . Work? Well, I *am* on a poem—a long one. Title? I think of calling it "Nails and Rust." I'm not sure. Come on. You'll like Pargiter.'

Fred didn't in fact like Pargiter very much; nevertheless it was an agreeable luncheon. As with all the heroes of history from Hector to Landru, Fred felt the uncrushed grapes of conquered love anticipated on his palate. He had all the genial happiness and tolerance of a male triumphant at the end of a long and difficult chase. He drank the very poor Burgundy Munden had ordered, secretly toasting the lady to whom he hoped to give, that evening, the best wine a certain resort provided. So he found Rose, who had all the anxious amiability of a popular traditional novelist fallen among young highbrows, a pleasant, if rather talkative, fellow, and although he couldn't say that he *liked* Pargiter he listened to him with considerable sympathy. For it seemed that Pargiter, who was thin, pale, with a large faintly yellow nose and untidy corn-coloured hair, was quite obsessed with his own injustices. Delaney noticed that he never, from beginning to end of the meal, paid the slightest attention to Rose, behaved as though he were not there at all, and that stout rubicund benevolence was clearly distressed by his rudeness. But perhaps it was not *really* rudeness! Pargiter was too bitterly absorbed to notice irrelevancies.

'But it's damnable!' he cried. 'They say I'm the best

short-story writer in England—they all do—but then they compare me to Tchekov. "Finer than Tchekov." Bunyan himself says it in the *Literary Observer* only this week. Well and good. I *am* finer in many respects. But can't they see they're destroying *all* my sales by that comparison? Simply ruining me! After all I've got three children even though I do live in the country. But who wants to read Tchekov? The moment they mention him in connection with myself I'm dead. I'm done. No one will buy me. And, after all, what comparison is there? My English prose is as good, I fancy, without undue conceit, as any there's been. Where's a better? But I'm English. My scene is English. My characters are English. *Where* is the Tchekov comparison? Nowhere. But it stops my books selling.'

Rose beamed upon them all.

'Of course short stories *don't* sell. In book form I mean. Now my last book of stories as compared with my last novel . . .'

But Pargiter behaved to him even as Betsy Trotwood to Miss Murdstone. He disregarded him completely. He even addressed himself to Fred in preference.

'You see,' he said very earnestly—'I'm afraid I didn't catch your name.'

'Delaney,' Fred murmured.

'Mr. Delaney. I write novels too, as you probably know, but they are another question altogether. Tchekov *couldn't* write novels and so the comparison doesn't apply. But doesn't it seem to you monstrous that someone in my position should have to review rotten commercial fiction and read for publishers and all the rest of it simply because people *will* compare me with Tchekov?'

'I think it's *monstrous*,' Fred said cheerfully. Then he turned to Munden. 'When are you coming to see us, Patrick, old boy?'

'I'm returning to Paris to-morrow. Dodie has come into a bit of money, you know. Yes, from an old aunt. Hard luck, isn't it, on poor Smoke? If this had happened earlier *everything* might have been different. However, I expect it was all for the best. Dodie thinks so.'

'If you're coming to see us you'd better come soon,' Fred said. 'We'll have to sell the house, I'm afraid.'

'Will you?' said Munden quite indifferently. 'What rotten luck!'

But Fred did not mind his selfishness. Quite natural! Everyone was selfish, except a few divine women like Meg.

But he was truly in that transcendental and disconnected state of happiness that was a deeper drunkenness, in which there was a spiritual as well as a physical element.

Munden's bad wine had not affected him at all, nor was he in any actual truth of the word drunk: he was like a bird in a golden cage, soaked in sun, and the golden cage was Alice Van Renn. . . .

So, exactly as though he *were* drunk, he heard himself talking.

He knew nothing about literature but said a lot. 'Hope I haven't hurt any feelings——'

'Oh, not at all,' said Pargiter, smiling in rather a sickly fashion. 'I must be getting on, Munden, I'm afraid——'

And Rose didn't make things any better by saying in a very hearty way:

'I assure you, Mr. Delaney, Pargiter's stories are grand stuff. Simply grand. As good as any we have.'

But Fred didn't care. After a brandy or two by himself in the smoking-room he hailed a taxi again and started off for Victoria.

He had reached a condition now when he was soaked in nothing but his Alice. He had forgotten altogether his wife, his children, his house, his non-existent tenants, the terrible state of the world—everything alive or dead. Soon he would be in the train alone with Alice. Because he was so sure that in a short while he would have her beautifully in his strong arms he need not now do anything but look at her, seated opposite to her, enjoying to the very last fragment of physical enjoyment her loveliness. How he would feel on Monday morning, or even on Sunday morning, did not now concern him at all. Nor any rules of equity or honour. On the other hand, although he was not at this moment ethical he *was* extraordinarily benevolent. There was nothing he would not give away (if he had it) to anybody (except, of course, Alice). 'He loved every dog and wished that every dog should love him.' He sat back, one knee over the other, his hat tilted to one side, humming a tune.

The taxi-man, looking at him through his little glass, reckoned on a handsome tip, and his reckoning was not disappointed.

Arrived at Victoria he saw that he was a trifle early. He knew just where it was that Alice was to meet him— by the bookstall on the Dover platform. He looked at the bookstall and wondered, as he had often wondered before, why it was that bookstalls never had anything that anyone wanted to read.

He looked at the people around him and felt for them a loving and tolerant benevolence. A porter offered to carry his bag. He told him that he did not need him yet. Why had he not hired a magnificent Daimler and carried Alice away with him in that? It was Alice's suggestion that they should travel by train. She said that it seemed to her more romantic. He had thought, when she said that, that she had looked at him a little quizzically. But then she *was* an ironic woman—an ironic modern woman of the world who knew just what she was about. If she hadn't known he would have felt a good deal of a cad.

He beamed upon the world. The holiday season was

well and truly laid, but there were many anxious women and hustled men and one or two casual indifferent beauties. There was also one family that made him, against all his will and intention, feel uncomfortable.

A stout father, a stout mother, two small boys, a smaller girl. They were going on to the Continent and were crazily excited about it. The stout father produced at the barrier his packet of tickets, and while the collector looked at them he marshalled his two small boys and his smaller daughter as a hen its chickens. They passed through the barrier, and at once, as though that barrier had been a desperate danger before which they had had to summon all their courage, now they broke into movements and noises of joy and freedom. The stout father, his daughter's hand tightly held, moved along, his hat a little on the back of his head, as though France would be irretrievably gone did he not hasten. Fred wished he hadn't seen them. Oh, well . . . both mother and father were well past the romantic age!

Then he saw Alice. She was standing, a little beyond the bookstall, looking at him. For a moment he stared back at her, lost in wonder at her beauty. She was dressed in dove-grey like a bride. He had expected that she would be in good serviceable tweeds. He went up to her and held out his hand.

'Hullo, Alice,' he said, grinning all over his face.

'Hullo, Fred,' she said.

'I was afraid you might be late. . . . But of course I knew you wouldn't be really.'

She cleared her throat.

'No. I'm a very punctual person.'

'I must get the tickets. I won't be a minute. Where are your things? I'll find a porter.'

He was so deliriously excited that he wasn't sure of his words. So insane was he that he had almost said 'Pargiter' instead of 'Porter.'

She put her hand on his arm.

'No, Fred. Wait a minute.'

He knew at once that something had happened. He looked at her.

'What's the matter?'

'I'm not coming.'

He was furious. The blood pounded into his face.

'By God, you are.'

'No, I'm not, Fred. I can't.'

'What do you mean—you can't?' He snorted and resembled, had he but known it, an indignant and frustrated calf.

She didn't, for a moment, answer.

'Is your old mother ill?'

'No. My old mother is *not* ill.'

'Are you ill yourself, then?'

'No—I'm not ill either. I'm simply not coming.'

'But you are—even though I have to carry you.' His voice was suddenly soft, bewildered and touching. 'Listen. You *must* come, Alice. You promised most faithfully. You swore that you wouldn't go back on it. I know you're not that sort—the sort that plays with a man. We've been friends for so long——'

She looked at him as though she really loved him. Her beautiful eyes brimmed with tears. She shook, gently, remorsefully, her head.

'I can't come with you, Fred. I was married this morning.'

He stood staring, his tongue passing over his lips. He took off for a moment his hat and then put it on again.

'Good joke you've played on me,' he said at last.

'No, I haven't.' She looked at him more kindly than she had ever done. 'It certainly isn't a joke. Come in here a minute.' She pointed to the Third Class Refreshment Room. 'If you'll let me explain.'

'Who's the happy husband?' he said at last. He was glaring at her and his fingers were moving as though he would really delight to wring her neck. This way murders are committed, but not by people like Fred Delaney and Alice Van Renn in Victoria Station. At any rate not to-day.

'Harry Bartlett,' Alice said.

'Good God . . . Bartlett! I might have guessed.'

'It's not as bad as you think,' she suggested.

'As bad as *I* think? All I know is you've tricked and teased and made a blasted fool of me.' He looked at her with a true schoolboy savagery. 'I'll pay you out for this.' Then he added (and she saw that he was really not far from angry, frustrated, passionate, shamefaced tears): 'No, I won't. Of course not. Men are always being fooled by women. It's no new thing. Only I never thought that *you* would—I thought that you were fond of me—in a sort of way.'

'I *am* fond of you,' she said. 'That's why I've done this.'

People were pushing past. Some looked at them inquisitively. It was not a good place for so tender an interview.

'Come in here. Please, Fred. I can explain better.'

'Where's Bartlett?' Fred asked.

'Waiting—in the Jermyn Street flat.'

'Afraid to meet me, I suppose.'

'Not in the least. He wanted to come. I told him I'd manage better without him.'

She led the way into the refreshment room. Young men, one very ancient clergyman and two elderly spidery women were standing at the counter as though performing some ancient sacrificial rite, and indeed the tea-urns and the glass pyramids guarding the sandwiches looked like important Druidical survivals.

They sat down at a little table and ordered coffee for decency's sake.

He was taking it more severely than she had expected. She had known him always gay, full of humour, buoyant. He was now a man she had never seen before. His pride was desperately hurt, and whereas a woman in such a situation would be thinking more of revenge than of self-humiliation, Fred could see nothing but that he'd been 'made a complete ass of.'

'You needn't have done it just to-day,' he said. 'You might have let us have our week-end.'

'So I meant to. Then, a few weeks ago, I found that I was falling in love with you. First time in my rotten life. And what are *you* to fall in love with, Fred? Stout, middle-aged, a man who has loved dozens of women before and will love dozens again. But none of that would have mattered perhaps, because I was beginning to feel pretty reckless, if it hadn't been that you love your wife. Love her! I've never known a husband love a wife as you love Meg. You're for ever talking about her, for ever thinking of her. That you want to sleep with other women means nothing. So do all healthy normal men. Of course they *want* to! Lots of them don't do it because they are afraid of their wives or their neighbours or their careers or something. But they don't love their wives as you love Meg. So what chance is there for *me?* One week-end with you and where might I not have been? Would I lead that hellish life of waiting for letters that don't come, listening to telephones that don't ring, hearing a step that isn't there? Not I. Right up to a week ago I thought I'd risk it. I wobbled this way and that. Mother was after me to marry, of course—neither of us has a penny-farthing. But she hates Bartlett and loves you, so she couldn't bear me to have anything to do with either of you. Harry has money, of course, but he *detests* Mama—simply loathes her. So I knew that if I went off with you for a night or two it might lead to personal suffering, and I've suffered enough in my young life already. If I married Harry it would mean that I should have, more or less, to desert Mother—on the other hand, she'd have enough to live on for the rest of her days. There were *other* suitors. One old boy with money who unfortunately revolts me. Two or three young ones with nothing but debts. Harry was really the only solution.'

'But you don't love him,' Fred said. He was recovering ever so slightly. She had flattered him. What she had said about Meg was true.

'Not in the least. But he's got his points. He's long-suffering, which he needs to be with a girl like me. He'll never change and, what is best of all, he's incapable of suffering. I don't *mean* to treat him badly, but I'm really so rotten through and through that you never can tell. And it's a great comfort to me to know that he's too stupid ever to be hurt.'

She looked at him. She held out her hand.

'Forgive me. I'm not worth your troubling about. And I think you're the luckiest man alive.'

'Lucky?'

'Yes, because you and your wife love one another as you do. I think she's swell—a lot sweller than you are—but *you're* not so bad.'

('Meg *is* swell,' he thought, and began to his own surprise to resent the thought of her week-end.)

'I'm forgiven,' Alice said. 'That's good. And now you've got to do something for me. You're to go straight to Mama and tell her that I'm married to Harry, and am not coming back.'

He stared at her. All he wanted now was to get away. It would be horrible this week-end without Meg, but somehow it would have to be endured. He felt flat and tired and quite desperately Puritanical. However, he would certainly *not* see old Mrs. Van Renn.

'See your mother! I should think not!'

'Oh, please! . . . You're the only person in the whole world who possibly can. She's always been secretly in love with you. You're exactly her ideal of what a real man should be.'

'She hates me. Anyway, she's always very rude to me.'

'That's to hide her feelings,' Alice went on. 'Listen, Fred: if you will do this it will be the first thing any man's ever done for me. Not that *I'm* anything, but I'll say to myself: "Fred Delaney has so magnificently played the game that it's the least I can do to be decent to Harry." Because it *will* be difficult sometimes, you know.'

'What do you want me to do?' Fred growled. He liked the idea of his own nobility. After all, what was a quarter of an hour with that old woman compared with his own new sense of heroism? It was certainly many years since he had felt so virtuous.

'I want you to go straight to her now in Half Moon Street and to tell her that I'm married to Harry. I've brought a letter you can give her. It will make the whole difference if *you* tell her.'

'Yes. She'll feel that we've *both* been damnably treated.'

'Exactly.'

'And so we have.'

'Well—*you* have. Mother's much better off really. Harry will make her a decent allowance and she won't have me always coming in and out. When you tell her you can pretend to be absolutely furious.'

'And so I *am* furious!'

'Oh no, you're not. Already you're relieved. You're thinking of Meg.'

They both got up.

'Pay for the coffee. And here's the letter.'

As she got into the taxi-cab she turned round and said in a very low sweet voice :

'All to-night I'll be thinking of you.'

He made his taxi drive about for a considerable time before he went to see Mrs. Van Renn.

He sat there, seeing nothing and thinking of nothing. He was miserable, ashamed, forlorn, humiliated. And somewhere, beneath all this, a feeling of intense relief was stirring.

Mrs. Van Renn looked as usual like a sick monkey. Her old fingers were stained with nicotine.

'What do you want?' she said. 'Why are you here? Alice is away for the week-end.'

'She's not,' he said. 'She has asked me to give you this letter.'

The old woman took it and, huddled in her chair, read it. Then she looked up at him with a face of almost piteous dismay.

'Why didn't you stop her?'

'Stop her! I hadn't the least idea of it.'

'Where did she give you this?'

'She asked me to meet her. It was at Victoria Station, as a matter of fact.'

Mrs. Van Renn gave him a sharp look.

'Oh, was it?'

Then he thought she was going to cry. Her wrinkled lips moved and twisted. She threw up her head derisively, tried to speak and could not.

'So that's over,' she said at last, and tore the letter into fragments which fluttered to the floor.

'Well, can't you say something? It's rather rough on *you,* isn't it?' Then she muttered: 'That idiot!'

'She asked me to tell you,' Fred began, 'that she was sure it was the best thing. She's fond of Bartlett. The sort of life you were both leading wasn't good enough. You'll be free and independent. She hopes you'll come and stay with them. She's coming to see you very soon.'

'She could have told me all this herself.'

'She thinks you'd have both lost your tempers.'

Mrs. Van Renn got up.

'All right. . . . It can't have been pleasant for you either. I won't. . . . It doesn't. . . .' She turned on him quite furiously. 'Can't you see I don't want anybody to . . .? Don't look at me like that. To marry such a fool . . . Good-bye. Good-bye. Come again some time—although Alice won't be here now.'

He said something and went.

He walked in the Park. He couldn't for the moment face the empty house. The week-end when he knew where Meg was. . . . Why had he been so tolerant, so lazy—about her, about himself? He had never before loved Meg so dearly as now when he walked under the bare trees, kicking the leaves with his foot.

At last he walked slowly home, with a sigh let himself into the house. It was as still as a morgue. He could feel all the rooms above him pressing on his head with their undeserved emptiness. He would have a *ghastly* week-end! He pushed the door back, then stood staring.

Then, his face grinning with happiness, he rushed forward.

'Meg! Meg, darling! . . . By all that's marvellous!'

CHAPTER VII

This Dark November Day . . .

And now, early on this November afternoon, the little
Park is really forgotten, unseen, for the yellow fog has
almost obscured it. Almost, not quite. You can still walk
with comparative safety if you keep your eye on the railings which are visible like stakes in a marsh. The Piccadilly lights are shining, and quite suddenly, outside Hatchett's and all the way to Burlington Arcade, the fog van-
ishes, revealing a space of blue sunlit sky, some rakish
chimneys and the cakes and buns behind the windows at
the end of Old Bond Street. Then, as though angry at its
carelessness, the fog sweeps down and is like wads of
yellow flannel underclothing. The road is coated with a
thin filmy mud and the cars stagger and hoot, hoot and
stagger. An old gentleman's pocket is picked just outside
Burlington House. . . .

Kitty Delaney is giving Millie Pake luncheon in Hatchett's restaurant and is feeling very dejected indeed. Her
reasons for dejection are—this fog, her father at breakfast has announced, finally, definitely, that the house is to
be sold, Millie Pake looks shabby and hungry, and—last
of all—she, Kitty, is this very afternoon going to say
farewell to the whole of the Foster episode. She feels, in
fact, very lonely.

Hatchett's, which is a kindly and human restaurant, has all its lights on, but you cannot forget, all the same, that Piccadilly is in the process of being villainously strangled by the fog just above your head.

'When we were girls, Helen and I,' Millie said, 'I can remember very well that a real London fog seemed the most exciting and adventurous thing in the world. Of course we were never allowed out alone, but even to run for two minutes into the Square was dreadfully exciting. Dear, you won't think me disgraceful, will you, but I'm afraid I simply can't eat any more of this delicious veal.'

'No, dear, of course not.'

Kitty was finding, once again, that it is very difficult to help people who are proud. She had also learnt by this time that it is only too easy to help people who are not quite proud enough.

Millie Pake's rings were gone. They had been such beautiful ones. Millie's hands were beautiful but dreadfully thin.

'Millie, where are your rings?'

Millie, her old head trembling a little as it did sometimes, looked Kitty full in the eye.

'I've pawned them. I won't lie to you, and I won't take a penny from you, dear. Not a penny. After all if things became really bad I could always ask my brother, although I must admit he doesn't like being asked very much. There's no need to ask anybody. There's some money coming in next week and really I ought to be very happy in my bed-sitting-room. It's very cosy indeed with my pictures and a plant or two. But the fact is, Kitty dear, I've been spoilt by the Charles Street house. No place will ever be to me what that was, partly because I was there with Helen I suppose. No, I can't pretend I'm happy where I am. In Charles Street I seemed to be protected. I don't mean by God. Of course He is *always* looking after me— but where I am now I seem to meet so many old ladies who are in the same circumstances as myself or worse. And I'll admit to you, Kitty, that it *is* depressing. What *is* depressing is that for most of them no one cares in the least whether they live or die. That is really dreadful to me. When one is old and poor one's a nuisance. There's no doubt of it. And I don't think the old ladies would mind their poverty and aches and pains one little bit if there was only someone who didn't think them a nuisance. Of course no one has any time, what with the state the world's in and so on. In Charles Street, Helen and I were always perfectly happy because of you dear people and I'm afraid we didn't think of anyone else much. I think it was that day that I found poor Smoke—that was the day I realized how wrong Helen and I had been not thinking of others more. And there was poor Claude of course. Do tell me more about Claude.'

'There isn't much more to tell. Mother has been to see him every day and he's quite well now. I don't think that horrid man of his will touch him again. He's terrified of Mother. But poor Claude's so dreadfully frightened all the same. He only seems to feel safe when he's with us.'

Millie nodded her head. 'I know how it is. That Charles Street house is a kind of refuge.'

Kitty had said nothing to Millie about its sale. That would be too dreadful. She looked now at the odd little figure in the funny hat and old green cape and vowed that something *should* be done. But what? They, the Delaneys, would themselves be soon on the street!

Millie, however, was immensely cheered up by the luncheon. Kitty took her back to her bed-sitting-room in a taxi. She left her warm and cosy, reading *Middlemarch* and laughing a great deal at the jokes in the *Punch* that Kitty had given her. Her eyes were as bright as stars, and her little round, but now lined, aristocratic countenance had that look of sweetness, irony and half-impertinence that was especially hers.

'Good-bye, Kitty darling. I've had a most lovely time!'
But, still, something *had* to be done!

She had written a line to the elder Foster saying that
she would come 'to say good-bye.' She named a choice
of days and received a strange reply. In a dreadfully common handwriting was a quotation from one of the poems
of Ella Wheeler Wilcox to the effect that the sun rises
in the morning, sets at night, and that all the birds and
flowers rejoice thereat. Underneath was written: 'Thurs-
day 3.30 O.K. by me.'

Lucy Foster admitted her and she noticed at once
several things. First, that all the vulgar oil-paintings had
vanished from the walls. The faint colours of the two
young men were now beautifully clear. Secondly, that the
couch and screen were gone and the room seemed larger.
Thirdly, that instead of the horribly impressive tea of
her first visit there were now on the table only a teapot,
one teacup, milk and sugar and a plate of buttered toast.

Then she saw that Foster was standing leaning on a
stick and grinning at her. This was the first time that she
had seen him from head to toe. He was very impressive
with his white hair, red face, broad shoulders, strong
stomach, heavy thighs. He was wearing a buttonhole and
a country-looking suit of black and grey stripes. He
looked cheerful, clean, healthy, vulgar.

Lucy Foster at once said, rather primly: 'You'll excuse
me, Miss Delaney, I'm sure. I've a visit to make if you'll
excuse me.' Then she went out. He shook hands with
Kitty but didn't ask her to sit down.

'Where's Alton?' she asked.

'Oh, didn't you know?' His eyes never left her face.
'He's been gone a fortnight.'

'Gone?'

'Yes. He's on the French Riviera now with Mrs. Bet-
tison Stuart, a lady twenty years older than himself, a

widow, rich, who fell in love with him at Zanti's. He's her secretary.'

'Oh dear, oh dear,' said Kitty.

'Yes—oh dear, oh dear. It's unromantic, isn't it?' He went on: 'You'll have noticed several things, I expect. My paintings have gone from the wall. You'll be glad of that. No more painting for me. I've better things to do. Also there's only one cup on the table—that's symbolic.'

'Why?' she asked, smiling.

'I'm not asking you to tea. You're to stay five—at most ten—minutes.'

'Good-bye then,' she said, holding out her hand and laughing.

'Oh, not so quick as that,' he said, pushing a chair towards her with one hand. 'We'll never meet again. We may as well have our five minutes.'

'Why will we never meet again?' Kitty asked, sitting down.

'Because I'm nearly well. A bit stiff after lying down so long. That's all. You cured me. Oh, I *had* my accident all right. My back was bad for a long time—but after that when I really *was* better there didn't seem any reason for my getting up. Alton earned enough to feed and shelter me. Lucy looked after me, I was amused with my painting, I had a visitor or two—no trouble. A grand life. But then *you* came in and the moment I saw you I cried to myself: "Why, there's women in the world, thousands, millions of them, moving about, laughing, waiting to be made love to, old though I am—and I wasting my time!" And that's why *you* mustn't stay—because I'll be making love to you. And it won't do. You like me a bit. You know you do. In spite of my white hair. And you know nothing about men. Nothing at all. So it's good-bye once and for ever—and thank you very much.'

'But I'm not frightened of you in the least,' she said, smiling at him. 'And it's quite true I *do* like you.'

He looked at her very fixedly. Then he shook his head. 'You *would* be frightened of me. If there was another cup on that table—about an hour from now you wouldn't like me at all. No. Get along, Miss Delaney. You've brought me to life again. That's a good deed, I suppose.'

He held out his hand. She took it. They stood very close to one another.

'It's funny,' he said. 'All these years I've loathed those paintings on the wall. You've made me like them. Another thing that's funny. You're in the grand world, have thousands of swell friends. It has needed the obscure Fosters in this obscure room to start you on life. And now you're started don't think life's anything but coarse and strong and vulgar and a bit savage, because that's what it is. It doesn't care a damn about you, life doesn't, but you can get from it some perfectly swell moments—and by God, I'm going to have a few more before I go. Look after yourself. Give me a kiss for Alton's sake if not for mine.'

She kissed him and he held her tightly, kissing her eyes, her mouth, her throat.

He murmured: 'It's grand to be on my feet again.'

Then he took her by the hand and led her to the door. Before she took her hand from his she said:

'You know, if you're ever ill again or anything——'

He broke out: 'Oh, for God's sake! I don't want you as a *nurse*. . . . You can send me a photograph sometime if you like.'

Meanwhile Bullock was having *his* adventures. In fact the climax of his life, as he wrote in his Journal, jumped up at him in the very middle of this twisting, turning, poke-saltpetre-up-your-nostrils fog. The climax of his life! That shows how very young he still is, but for anyone as quiet and humorous as Bullock was and is, it means something. At the very moment when Kitty Delaney was embracing Alton Foster's father, Bullock Delaney was falling, his head in a stranger's stomach—but this is how it happened.

First, on that foggy day Bullock went and had luncheon with—but that, too, had better be kept as a surprise for later. In any case this luncheon was to make all the difference to the Delaney family.

Then, about half-past three he climbed into a taxi and told the man to go to Borden Street. This wasn't so easy, and they bumped and blundered and stopped and hooted while the lamps looked at them like the eyes of wild beasts out of a yellow jungle, a bell sounded somewhere like a foghorn, and you could almost hear the waves of the fog swish, swish against the flimsy barriers of the thread-paper houses.

At last they were there, though, and Bullock ran up the narrow smelly stairs eager to take his young beloved out to tea, although they mustn't venture in this weather further than Shaftesbury Avenue, that mingling of theatres, cheap shirts and collars, and the Trocadero. He found the door locked. He banged the old knocker that was in the shape of the west door of Canterbury Cathedral. He knocked furiously. The fog crept up the stairs and fingered in a stealing, inquisitive way the peeling wallpaper. At last Coventry's voice could be heard quite clearly from the other side of the door:

'Who is it?'

'Delaney—Stephen Delaney.'

The door was opened cautiously and Captain Nicholas looked out.

'Come in then. I was wanting to see you.'

Bullock entered and found the room in shapeless disorder—empty whisky bottles, empty syphons, shirts and underclothes on the floor, Lizzie kneeling packing, one of the sporting prints, its glass shattered, on the carpet near the bathroom. Another sporting print crooked on its string, bedroom door open, and there in complete disarray, most astonishing of all, tilting on a chair near the window, a stout streaky-faced gentleman, his waistcoat unbuttoned, bald-headed save for a few wet black hairs, his round red loose mouth open. He was apparently protesting at something. Nicholas was standing in his shirt-sleeves, in one hand a half-empty glass, in the other a roll of soiled-looking collars. Lizzie gave one look upwards and when she saw who it was went on with her packing again. Captain Nicholas was a little drunk, but not very. He went quickly to the door and locked it.

'Leaving?' asked Bullock.

'Leaving is right. It's a bit of luck your coming in. Lizzie said you might. I would have telephoned only you don't know who's listening.'

'What's the matter?' asked Bullock, feeling that the room was extraordinarily small. He supposed that it was the stout gentleman in the window that made it seem so thoroughly overcrowded.

'The matter?' asked Captain Nicholas gaily. He seemed to be in excellent spirits. 'The matter is that I shall be in gaol to-night if I don't get a move on.'

The stout gentleman began to shout, 'You don't leave this room until you pay . . .' and so on.

'Oh, I forgot,' said Nicholas. 'I ought to introduce you. But why should I? Shut up, you son of a bitch, or I'll——'

The stout man rose and stood, swaying a little on both legs. He stared at Nicholas as though fascinated.

'You're not taking Lizzie?'

'No. I'm *not* taking Lizzie. This is where we bid one another an eternal farewell. Here. Get up, Liz. I mustn't wait another second. This fog is God's own gift to His erring son. There. Close that bag. That's as much as I want.'

'If you don't pay me every farthing——' shouted the stout man.

'Every farthing! That's good!' cried Captain Nicholas. 'When I've just enough to get me across the Channel.'

'I'll inform——'

'You can jolly well inform whom you like,' said Nicholas cheerfully.

The stout man advanced and caught Bullock by the arm.

'I charge you, sir, whoever you may be, to assist me in calling the police.'

'The devil you do!' cried Nicholas.

After that things happened swiftly. Nicholas turned and caught the stout man a splendid blow straight on the jaw. The stout man tumbled forward, embraced Bullock, and they both fell together, catching the tablecloth as they fell. On to the floor went the stout man, Bullock, bottles and glasses.

When Bullock had disentangled himself from the stout man's waistcoat and was on his feet again he saw that Captain Nicholas, his coat on, was standing there very calmly, bidding a long farewell to his daughter. His hands were on her shoulders.

'There. Leave him. He's all right. And now, Liz, my darling, good-bye. Not au revoir. Really good-bye. You don't like me any more, but you did once, and I may truly say that you're the only human I've ever loved or ever will love. I hand you over to this young man, who's so good that he ought to be in a fairy story. You can trust him. He has no imagination whatever. Put me right out of your mind. We've had some good times together and seen the world. I don't regret a damned thing.'

And with that, snatching his bag, he was away into the fog, never to be seen again by his once loving daughter.

She, Bullock saw, was now kneeling by the stout gentleman and bathing his forehead with her handkerchief and water that dripped from the tablecloth. The gentleman opened his eyes and said: 'Another one, miss, please. Just like the last.' A furious disgust for this filthy room and everything in it seized Bullock. He caught Lizzie quite fiercely by the arm and dragged her to her feet.

'Come. Put on your hat and coat. It's beastly here. Disgusting. He's all right. . . . Leave him, leave him!'

In his impatience he shook her, and like someone in a dream she obeyed him. She went into her room, came out dressed for the street.

The stout man was now in a chair; he was feeling his jaw while his head swayed. About him was all the débris of a ruined adventurer. His round eyes watched them. He said not a word as they left the room. In the street the fog had miraculously cleared, as though indeed Captain Nicholas had collected it all in his hand and carried it off with him.

And, as often happens in London, instead of the fog there was a dim sea-green mist. London had suddenly, as it were, gone under water. Borden Street is no beauty as streets go, but she was a beauty for a moment now. The sweet-shop with the heavy pile of chocolates, of coconut icing, of white and pink sugar, the door of the 'Stag' public-house, the three houses in a row with white steps and faint pink window curtains, the railings in front of the old, packed, grey and green churchyard that might have sheltered the broom and tatters of Poor Jo himself, the London mingling of stale beer and evening papers and sliding gratings and stealing cats—all swam now in this green under-sea mystery with some gay orange wisps of cloud caught in the crooked chimneys and a man's voice singing from inside the 'Stag.'

In Shaftesbury Avenue they found a cab and Bullock told it to drive to Westminster. Inside the cab he sat with his arm round her. She shivered once or twice but said nothing.

'You knew it was coming,' he said. 'We both did. Don't worry about him. You couldn't be with him any more. He knew that.'

At last she said: 'I'd have gone if he'd wanted me.'

'I'll be so good to you. Did you hear what he said to you—that I've no imagination? Well, if that's true—and I don't think it is—I can be faithful and love you for ever.'

'No one loves for ever,' Lizzie said.

'Oh yes, they do. And they love one another more and more because of all the things they've done together.'

'No one loves for ever,' she repeated.

He held her closer, she leaned her cheek against his, then turned and kissed him.

At the Westminster house of Fanny Carlisle he rang the bell. They stood together on the steps hand in hand. The woman who opened the door was the woman Bullock had seen before.

'Miss Lizzie! Oh, Miss Lizzie!' she cried.

'I've come back, Janet,' Lizzie said, then turned and kissed Bullock and walked into the house.

'Just tell Mrs. Carlisle,' Bullock said, 'that I've done what I said I'd do.'

Then he walked away.

The fog came back about six o'clock, having, we may suppose, seen Captain Nicholas safe across the Channel. With its wet slimy tentacles writhing up and down, in and out, it settled down upon London. Outside the Charles Street house, about ten o'clock, it was like a wall of thick, stifling grey-black ectoplasm. Inside the Charles Street house the Delaney family sat in no very gay frame of mind.

Bullock, his little body curled up like a ball at the end of the sofa, was reading *The Hillyars and the Burtons*.

Kitty, her long legs stretched out in front of her, was looking into the fire. Meg, with Endless asleep against her shoe, was reading *Time and Tide*. Fred, looking rather too stout and choleric, had his chair tilted forward and he was staring in front of him. The William and Mary clock was ticking, Endless was snoring with that snore so peculiarly human that it makes you stare at your dog with discomfort and doubt the survival of personality after death, the coals were tit-titting in the fire.

'Remember Snails and Oysters,' Fred Delaney said suddenly, and then, as they all looked up, he remarked, yawning: 'I only wanted to attract your different attentions. I would remark that this is one of the few evenings we've all been gathered together in one room for months —and I'd like to say I'm wondering whether you're aware that to-morrow morning as ever is I sign the agreement for the final and absolute slaughter, destruction, murder of this house. And that, once it is gone, we will be the Joyful Delaneys no longer, but wanderers on the face of the earth. And that not only is the house going, but London too—very, very shortly—and after that the British Empire and after that the Planet, and after that —well, the First Cause will have to start planning all over again.' He stopped. He loved, he had to admit it, the sound of his own voice, for he was at heart a poet and all poets love the sound of their own voices even when they are very squeaky ones.

Fred Delaney had been pulling himself away from his dream, the dream that he had in the Club that afternoon seated in one of those big armchairs in front of the fire. An extraordinary dream because of the vividness of its detail. He had been at some party and with him had been his old friend Reeves, and Reeves had been drunk. This in itself was absurd because Reeves had never been drunk in his life. He had walked into the street with

Reeves. It was one of the most horrid of London days, a wild freakish wind blowing, gusts of rain, and the road slimy with mud. The traffic, as it does sometimes on a windy day, seemed to be moving at a furious, almost insane rate. Well, Reeves had said good-bye and started to walk down the street. Then, quite unexpectedly, he had fallen flat on his face all amongst a group of playing children, and Fred had seen how his mousy-grey-white mackintosh had been caught by the wind and blown in little fantastic gusts above his recumbent body. The children were jumping about him and beating him with little spades. Fred was about to start out to help him, but suddenly Reeves got up and began to run again. Fred could see him as he reached the corner of the street where there was a great deal of traffic. Suddenly Reeves stepped right into the middle of the road and fell flat on to his face again, and there he lay while the traffic roared past him, missing his body by a shadow's breadth, and especially a bicyclist, a boy bending forward on his machine and looking ahead with furious intensity, who flew round the corner and made Reeves' mackintosh rise as though in protest. It would never do to let Reeves lie there—he would be killed at any moment—so Fred ran madly down the street, crying out 'Snails and Oysters!' 'Snails and Oysters!' which words seem to contain some most fearful warning. But when he got to the corner of the street there was no sign of Reeves anywhere, the wind caught Fred so abominably that, filled with fear, he clung on to the wall close behind him. Then he woke up.

A silly, meaningless dream, but it had greatly oppressed him, so he talked to forget it.

'So you see, this is really our last night in this house —the last night anyway that it belongs to us.'

Bullock began to speak. 'All the same, Father——'

But Fred Delaney cut him short.

'I don't want any arguments. The thing's done and settled. There's nothing more to be said.'

'I saw Marjorie Blandin to-day,' Meg began rather dreamily, 'and she said why don't *I* start taking people from the country and introducing them to Duchesses? She says of course it's boring but really *is* paying, and with all the people Larry knows and my own fine and handsome presence . . .' She was thinking: 'I can see quite clearly from his last letter that he will never forgive me for keeping him waiting at the station like that. *Never.* It was exactly the thing that in the old days he never could stand. So perhaps it's all for the best. Because it's clear that he doesn't believe my reasons either. He thinks all that about poor Claude made up, and if he doesn't believe me what hope would there ever have been?'

Aloud she said:

'The people really weighing on my mind are Claude Willoughby and Millie Pake. If only we could do something for *them,* get them out of the awful places where they are! If only we could afford to have them here! Oh, but I forgot. There won't be any *here* after to-morrow morning. What *are* we going to do, Fred?'

'Of course we'll have enough to live on—in Surbiton or somewhere like that.'

'Surbiton!' Meg cried before she could prevent herself.

Fred gave her a malicious grin.

'It needn't be *actually* Surbiton, of course, but that sort of place. Kitty will marry. Bullock will write for a living and not merely for pleasure as he is doing at present. The point is we shall be a joyful family no longer. We shall all be broken up.'

Bullock began: 'Wait a minute, Father. I've got something——'

Fred trampled upon him ruthlessly.

'Yes, I know what you're going to say. Your blessed

novel—it's just about finished. I don't want to hear about it until it's sold and you've got the money. That will be time enough.'

'But I wasn't——' Bullock began.

'Oh yes, you were. Now what I *mean* is that what this house has given us we ought to keep. It has looked after us for hundreds of years and bound us all together. We must keep that bond. We must be a family still. I want—I want——'

And then an awful thing happened. They all saw with horror that Fred's lip was trembling, that he couldn't speak, that he was on the edge of tears. He got up and went to the mantelpiece and laid his forehead against it just under the William and Mary clock.

He saw with fearful distinctness Reeves' body lying in the road and the young bicyclist flying round the corner with insane determination in his eyes.

Then he felt Meg's hand against his cheek.

'Don't take on so, darling. We'll stick together, we four, of course we will—more than ever now, I think.'

He turned round, laughing, although his eyes were bright with tears.

'Listen!' he cried. 'Here and now we'll make our procession up and down the house, saying our farewell to it. We'll light the Georgian candlesticks and carry them to light our way. We'll go into every corner, every nook and cranny, saying good-bye to everything. We'll tell it we couldn't help ourselves, that a mortgage or borrowing money on it would have been just as bad. It will understand. They say you can't get fond of a house in London, that one's only a bird of passage, that everything changes so constantly. But that's not true. This house has all the love and fidelity and tenderness of all the finest people who have lived in it and loved it. And now to-morrow I'm going to murder it. With my own hand and my fountain-pen I——'

'But, Father——' said Bullock.

'No, my boy. I know what you're going to say. It's no good. We must face facts.' He lit the silver Georgian candlesticks, and then in a little procession, Endless leading them, they marched out.

They started up the stairs. It was as though the house was listening to their footsteps, was waiting for them. . . .

The street-door bell rang. They all turned on the steps and stared down into the hall.

'Who *can* that be at this hour?'

'In this fog too,' said Meg.

The bell rang again, insistently, in a bad temper.

'I think I know who——' said Bullock.

'Caesar has gone home.'

'I'll open it.' Bullock was down the stairs, the door swung open, letting in thin gusts of fog as though a demon cow were breathing outside in the street.

But it was not a demon cow. It was old Lord Ragadoon.

He had on his head a cap with a peak and a button to it, over his shoulders a striped plaid. His bright old eyes peered from his hairy old face like a robin's from a winter thicket.

He bowed very punctiliously.

'Excuse me,' he said in his rumbling, drumming emphasis. 'May I have five minutes' business with you?'

The door was closed, they all shook hands.

'This is my wife,' said Fred, 'and this my daughter Kitty.'

They all trooped back into the drawing-room. Fred still carried the candles.

'Where's your young woman?' Ragadoon said to Bullock.

'In bed, I hope.'

'Yes, yes—of course. She's only a child.'

Inside the room he looked about him. 'Nice clock you have.' He bent down and stroked Endless. 'Like dogs.' Then he straightened himself. 'It's a bit of business,' he said.

'Won't you sit down?' said Meg, showing him a chair.

'Thank ye. Thank ye.' He sat down and, leaning forward, holding his cap in his hand, addressed them.

'I know it's late. You must forgive that. I'm an old man and have my own habits. Besides, there's a fog. How I hate fogs! Yes, ma'am. Fogs would be enough, if there weren't anything else, to prove that the Deity doesn't know His job. And they ruin pictures. Let fog get into a decent water-colour drawing . . . Well, as I was saying, this is business. Your boy Bullock' (he jerked his thick stumpy finger towards him) 'was taking luncheon with me to-day, and I expect he's told you although I asked him not to——'

'No, I haven't told them,' Bullock interrupted. 'I've been trying to hint, but Father wouldn't listen.'

'Just as well. Just as well,' said the old man. 'Mr. Delaney, I want to rent the whole of this house excepting, of course, your own quarters.'

'You want—what?'

'I want to pay you the rent for this house you require —all the flats in it except your own. I want to move in immediately with all my goods and chattels. And when I say my goods and chattels I say *something*. I shall live, of course, in my own flat myself. I propose that you should let the other two flats to any two friends you may have who are decent, respectable, trustworthy bodies, but too hard-up, maybe, to pay the rent themselves. Your boy here told me at luncheon to-day that you might have such friends. The only proviso I make is that I shall be wanting to hang my pictures and drawings in every part of the house except, of course, your own quarters, and that therefore your friends who live in the other flats must not object to having such pictures on their walls, must to some extent indeed be guardians over them and must be willing at certain times for visitors to be shown them.' He looked round upon them all, and then, as they appeared to be speechless, went on: 'I have it in my mind that my collection of pictures may be left here, under my will, in perpetuity, as a gift to the nation. That would ensure, of course, the permanence of this building. But of that we can speak later.'

He stopped. He twirled his cap round.

Fred at last said: 'Well, I'm damned!'

'You like the idea, Mr. Delaney?' Ragadoon enquired politely.

'Like it! Like it! It's a dream, a miracle, a phantasmagoria, a Cinderella Ball, an Elephant and Castle melodrama with the heroine saved in the nick of time.'

The old man grinned, a peculiar phenomenon, Endless must have thought, for without warning he barked twice.

'Call it what you like, Mr. Delaney. You must thank your son and his young woman for this. I'm living in a pigsty and quite rightly he told me so. I like your son and could teach him something useful about pictures if he'd learn. . . . And now, Mrs. Delaney, ma'am, with your very kind permission I'll bid you farewell. Details can be settled later. But I'm an impatient man and I'll be moving in by the end of the week.'

He got up, went across to Bullock and laid his hand on his shoulder.

'See me to the door, young man, and find me a cab.'

CHAPTER VIII

The Happy Moment

THE Park, on this last day of the year, dripped water from the bare trees, oozed water from the sodden soil and veiled its shabby disgraces with trails of sulky mist.

But the fact that the Park was sulky had nothing to do with the spirit of Shepherd Market. Although they are always in close touch with one another, these two, and realize a great deal more about what is going on in the one or the other than matter-of-fact people know. (And it's sad, if you think of it, how very little of what is really going on people who call themselves matter-of-fact *do* know.)

There's nothing more unpleasant than the truly whimsical or I-spy-you're-a-fairy kind of writing, but it is not to be denied by anybody who has watched life with any closeness that there are moments, both with places and people, when everything goes very odd indeed, as it does, for instance, at the end of the second act of the *Meistersinger*, in the middle of the *Flegeljahre*, at the Eatanswill Election, at that party in Barchester when the Signora behaved so badly, or at that other grand private party in Illyria when Malvolio was unable to stop the ballad-singing.

Some madness of this kind overtook the citizens of

Shepherd Market on that afternoon of the last day of the year of grace 1934. Time passes so swiftly that there are in all probability few people alive to-day, only four years later, who remember the ludicrous and whimsical and eccentric scenes of that brief half-hour. They occurred nevertheless.

It was not an afternoon to encourage end-of-the-year eccentricities, warm and muggy and dark enough to have lights in the shops quite early in the afternoon. It was also a Monday, and everyone knows what a poor day of the week that one is!

Nevertheless here was another year all but dead and gone, and who knows what glorious things the next year is going to do?

Quite early in the afternoon people were moving about, having no business apparently to bother with, and the sense of *community*, always very strong in the Market, grew with every minute. Someone's cat had had kittens, a lady had had twins, a gentleman had won a surprising amount arranging the winners of football matches, and somebody's daughter in the Manchester Pantomime had sent word home to say she had engaged herself to a Manchester business gentleman.

In the dusky lamp-lit afternoon the year seems a little unreal as it fades towards its close, and men and women stand about as though they are expecting something. If, at the end of Market Street, two angels suddenly appeared blowing triumphant trumpets of gold and crying in ringing voices that the end of the world had arrived, no one in the Market would be very greatly surprised. There have been so *many* strange things happening lately!

Caesar had come over from Charles Street to help Mr. Willoughby move his things. There was very little to move, for the furniture had gone over to Charles Street in the morning, the bed, the armchair, the pictures, the christening mug, the miniature of his mother, the

Jacobean dagger, the ancient Toby jug and the rest. He
himself in his bowler hat and overcoat stood in the empty
shabby room and bade it a sentimental farewell. He was
exceedingly happy; he could not yet believe his good fortune, but at the same time he could not but realize all the
years that he had spent here, the thoughts, hopes, dreams.
Yes, that *was* sentimental, for the truth was that he had
been exceedingly unhappy here and gone almost crazy
with loneliness, insufficient food, and terror.

He was already great friends with Caesar. It was
wonderful that someone should treat him with politeness
again just as in the old days.

'I think we've got everything now, sir,' said Caesar,
looking like a bright, intelligent child masquerading as
a mature man.

'Yes, I think we really have. Dear me! Do you think
I ought to say good-bye to anybody?'

'I shouldn't trouble, sir, if I were you. Mrs. Delaney
is expecting you to take tea with her, I think, sir.'

'Oh, is she indeed? Very charming of her. Well, that
settles it, doesn't it? We'll be moving, shall we?'

What he was really frightened of was a last meeting
with Brocket. He had paid him his rent—all relationship
between them was over—but he couldn't believe, even
now, that the shadow of that grey-fleshed, corpulent body
was to hang over his waking and sleeping moments never
again! However, he was to see Brocket once more and in
dramatic circumstances. He had walked with Caesar as
far as the middle of Market Street when he saw him—
and Caesar saw him too!

Brocket was there and standing in front of a girl, pushing his face into hers, preventing her passing.

Caesar said: 'Excuse me, sir, will you?' and a moment
later had caught Brocket by the arm, crying, 'Leave
her alone, you dirty bully!'

At that shrill cry all the Market seemed to stir into

action, windows opened, people turned and gazed, shop-doors filled, voices were raised. For Brocket had struck out at Caesar, and Caesar had struck out at Brocket.

The girl cried, 'Don't, don't, Caesar! He'll kill you!' a woman ran into a doorway and screamed, 'Mrs. Rudge! Mrs. Rudge! They're murdering your son,' and Caesar and Brocket were instantly an indistinguishable con-fusion.

It was not a very handsome fight. Caesar was a diminu-tive beside his enemy, but he had been a boxer in his time. The trouble was that he found himself involved so des-perately in the stuffings and swellings and soft places of Brocket's ill-conditioned body that he could never get himself clear to strike an honourable blow. Brocket, who was altogether out of condition, believed in nothing so tame as fair play. He kicked, he bit, he tore at Caesar's collar, coat, hair, or anything else in his way, and did achieve one big scratch with his dirty finger-nails all down Caesar's left cheek. That was, however, his solitary success.

After losing his breath in Brocket's beastly belly and wriggling within his indecent bear-like hug, Caesar suc-ceeded in ducking his head, breaking away, and, in one instant of glorious freedom and vision, managed to de-liver so successful a blow on Brocket's nose that that undoubted villain of Claude's and Caesar's story fell backwards, flung his arms in the air, shrieked aloud and lay, a writhing monstrosity, on the Market Street pave-ment.

By this time the whole of the Market was calling aloud, singing, shouting and, on the part of a number of small boys, skipping and dancing. It was a glorious end to the year. There should have been a policeman, but there wasn't one, and for a brief ecstatic moment, in the lights and the mist and the flowers and leather and fish and newspapers and antiques and cuts off the joint and rooms for single gentlemen, the Market knew once again, as it had known often enough in its historic past, what it was to assert its common spirit and sense of fun and general light-heartedness.

The moment was quickly ended. Caesar straightened himself. He was breathing hard, his cheek was bleeding, his collar was torn, his trousers covered with mud. He showed nevertheless a fine and simple dignity.

'That'll teach him a lesson he won't soon forget.'

He attended then to his mother, who now that the fight was over was remembering that she had once been lodge-keeper at Wintersmoon and was at present surrounded by a crowd of common vulgar populace. And there, the origin of all the trouble, was that horrid nasty girl.

'Now, Mother,' said Caesar, 'you go along home. I'll be visiting you later. And this,' he had his hand on the girl's arm, 'is Miss Margaret Dundee, to whom I am engaged and hope shortly to marry. Now let's have no more words.'

This he said in front of the assembled Market.

Mrs. Rudge gave him one look, then recognizing for the first time since she bore him that he was her master, without a word went meekly to her home.

'Now, sir,' said Caesar, 'I'm ready if you please. And you won't mind, I hope, sir, if Miss Dundee, my fiancée, comes as far as Charles Street in our company.'

It was half an hour to midnight. They had turned off the wireless because of the noise that it was making. They would turn it on again just before Big Ben struck.

Very little was said. It was clear enough that everyone was happy. Fred Delaney looked at the three old people and was glad that he was their host—Millie Pake, Claude Willoughby, old Ragadoon. They sat near to one another, all very straight-backed, for they were of the generation

that had been taught to sit up straight even though you
were tumbriling guillotine-wards. The happiest of the
three, perhaps, was Claude Willoughby. He sat there, a
glass of something in his hand, staring in front of him,
not speaking, unable to believe his luck. When, that
afternoon, a tattered and torn Caesar had led him into
the house, and dear, kind Mrs. Delaney had taken him
up to his flat, he had with trembling lips said: 'Thank
you! Oh, thank you very much!' and, after that, had lost
all power of speech for the rest of the year. The good
things are quite as true as the bad things, and this was
one of the good things. His bed, his table, his chair were
there. His Things had been laid out on the table for
him to arrange. The Jacobean dagger glittered at him,
the Toby jug grinned, his christening mug, always protective, was greatly relieved to see him again. But when
he saw the fresh cream-coloured walls, and on the walls
some of the pictures from the great collection of Lord
Ragadoon—in the bedroom drawings—a Turner, a Cotman, a Caracci, an Ostade—and in the sitting-room an
oil sketch of an old man drinking by Frans Hals, a still
life by Manet of some roses in a silver dish, a small oil
by Constable, and the lovely head of a lovely lady by
Alfred Stevens—when he saw these things and understood that he was appointed as guardian of them—then
he sat down and his thin chest heaved and his hands rose
and fell again, and he knew the happiest moment of all
his life.

He understood, too, that Lord Ragadoon, weary of his
many years' 'piggery,' had brought servants to Charles
Street with him, and that one of these (an elderly kind-
faced woman whose name was Mrs. Mumble) would
look after his wants, that the only expenses he would
have would be to pay for his food, that he had his own
bathroom and need dread no longer any Major Pierson.
Then, for the first time for many, many years, his heart

changed from its odd, leaping, frightened beat to a
steady, normal, friendly monotony.

So now he sat in the Delaney drawing-room waiting
for the New Year.

Millie Pake was placidly looking into the fire and thinking of the past. She was very happy, of course, to be back
in the old room, and Helen seemed to be there with her. It
was true that the Bloomsbury room had been horrid, but
she was worried a little about all the other old gentle-
women who hadn't encountered her good-fortune, who
were still wondering where the next meal would come
from, who were still eking out a miserable scuttle of slack
shrivelled coal, and, worst of all, had no one, at this end
of another dreary year, to give them a thought or care
whether they were alive or no. 'I shall speak to Meg
about them,' she thought. 'She's sure to have an idea.'
She was thinking also of her Aunt Sybella, who had lost
all her hair in a fire and been racked with pain and
had yet never lost her cheerfulness. 'I'm afraid I lost
mine once or twice. There's no doubt I might have behaved better.'

She was pleased that Lord Ragadoon trusted her to
look after his pictures, but in her heart she would have
preferred to have a few of her own—a nice water-colour
or two and some photographs.

Of what old Ragadoon was thinking—he was quite
smart to-night, his beard combed, wearing a black velvet
jacket and silver buckles on his old-fashioned evening
shoes—no one ever knew. He appeared, however, to be
in excellent spirits.

Bullock and Lizzie were sitting together on the sofa,
and *their* happy moment seemed to be extending itself
indefinitely.

Kitty was sitting in a chair near the fire. Whether she
were happy or not she did not know. Happiness did not
seem exactly the point with her. Perhaps it would never

be. Rather her spirit was charged with the sense of expectation. The Braque picture, Zanti's shop, her friendship with dear Sarah Grafton, the adventure with the Foster family, these things had, all of them together, opened a door for her, promising her a life not of happiness but of active developing experience. Foster Senior had been right (how could she ever have thought of him as Mr. Turveydrop?) when he had said that life was rough and brutal and meant to be, and that from it you extracted if you were truly alive great moments of experience, and that, feeding on these, you must grow. Painful, cruel moments fed your growth perhaps more truly than happy ones. He was right, too, when he said that she knew nothing as yet about men and women. To-morrow, with the New Year, she would begin to learn. Her capacity for love—her greatest gift although she did not know it—spread over all her friends—poor Alton, Sarah Grafton, Foster whom she would like to see again but would never, Robert Beaminster who would, she hoped, soon marry someone very nice indeed—and then about everyone in this room and especially her own beloved family—her father, her mother, Bullock. She shaded her eyes with her hand from the firelight. . . . Whom else would the New Year bring? All her real experience had yet to begin.

Fred Delaney noticed that Meg was not there. He went quietly into the bedroom and found her brushing her hair.

'I want to be tidy for the New Year,' she said.

'It's ten minutes to.'

She leaned back against the chair and looked up at him. He came over to her and kissed her.

'You know,' she said, 'we've never discussed it. Not a word. That day, I mean, when we didn't go away.'

He grinned. 'There wasn't anything to say. We both made fools of ourselves.'

'I just didn't. I don't know what happened to you. I don't want to know.' She took a look at the glass. 'There! I'm as right as I shall ever be. I only want to say this, Fred. You need never worry about me again. *That* will never——'

'Here,' he said, interrupting, 'I don't want any discussion. Haven't we always agreed that we trusted one another?'

'Perhaps we trusted one another too much. What we agreed to really was a kind of act of collusion—and now that seems to me somehow horrible.

'I don't really know what possessed me. The funny thing was that I saw him so little—Graham Pender, I mean—and almost always with his wife. It was the sight of my long-lost youth recovered so unexpectedly that led me on, I think. Affection for him—and then something wild in me. It will always be there—but it won't go *that* way again.'

'All right, old girl,' Fred said.

'And I'll tell you why. Not religion and not morality. They've got a lot to say, but oddly enough they were neither of them as important as something else. Am I being very solemn, Fred darling?'

'You are rather.'

'For once I want to be. It was our relationship that would have suffered. If I'd gone with Graham for that week-end our relationship—yours and mine—would never have been the same again. You mayn't believe that, but it's true. We've always believed in giving one another absolute liberty, haven't we?'

'We have and do.'

'I see now that we ought to have fixed our eyes on something else. Through years and years, trouble and fun and anxiety and relief—through a million little things —we've built up a wonderful relationship—a sort we can neither of us ever have again with any human being.

And all the time something in life tries to pull it down, to destroy it. It's attacked ceaselessly. Every action of ours damages or improves it. It's the same, I think, with every friendship, passion, marriage, parents and children. And so, when it's the best thing you have, the grandest and greatest, what an idiot you are if you do anything, say anything, think anything that doesn't strengthen it.' She stopped.

He was greatly moved and amused too. He put his arms on her shoulders.

'And I, Meg—what about *my* damaging it?'

'That's for *you* to decide,' she said.

They stayed in a close embrace.

'Come,' he said. 'It's three minutes.'

As she turned back to her dressing-table again for a moment he said:

'Is it right for us to be so happy?'

'I think so—as long as we are not fools nor too selfish.'

'This crazy world——'

'We're part of it.' She went toward the door, turned for a moment. 'Not now, not in our lifetime, Fred, dear, will the last word be said. Men are not mad for ever. It's a long, long story.' She sighed, looked towards him with an absolute devotion. 'Meanwhile let's love one another—and not be more afraid than we can help.'

He stood there for a moment after she had gone. The house was secure, for a while at least. It had been a dangerous year, but at the end of it they were all together.

He saw his beloved town, danger, destruction hanging over it, but it seemed to him indestructible. He remembered his conversation with Patrick a year ago. Aye Bourne and the stream running through Marylebone across Oxford Street and May Fair . . . the meadowlands of May Fair, the milkmaids' song where the Ritz is. Old Q with his muff, Robert Baker the tailor. . . . And now it was on tiptoe to welcome the New Year, the dance bands playing, the lights shining, the wind blowing through the Park trees, the barges lying dark on the river, the men and women kneeling in the churches, so many stairs and rooms and roofs and chimneys—the spirit indestructible, the soul eternal.

He went into the other room. The wireless had been turned on again. The three old people were sitting straight in their chairs, Lizzie and Bullock hand in hand, Meg and Kitty standing side by side.

Big Ben began to strike.

'Come on,' he cried. 'Join hands. For Auld Lang Syne.'